DRAGONS

OF THE

DAWN BRINGER

THE GODDESS PROPHECIES

BOOK  FIVE

ARAYA EVERMORE

StarFire
Published by Starfire Epic Fantasy

Paperback First Edition
ISBN-13: 978-99957-917-3-5

Also by Araya Evermore:

The Goddess Prophecies:
Night Goddess
The Fall of Celene
Storm Holt
Demon Spear
Dragons of the Dawn Bringer
War of the Raven

Acknowledgements

Thank you to Jon for his unending support and patience. Thanks to Ian for all his help, ideas and encouragement. Thank you to Jill for her excellent editorial work.

A special thank you to all my Beta Readers who made this work that much more epic. Thank you to my precious Reader Team who make this work especially fun.

Thanks to Milo and the Deranged Doctor Design team for their wonderful cover art. Thanks to the Cosmos for making this work possible. I would also like to thank you, the reader, for continuing the adventure.

For Love

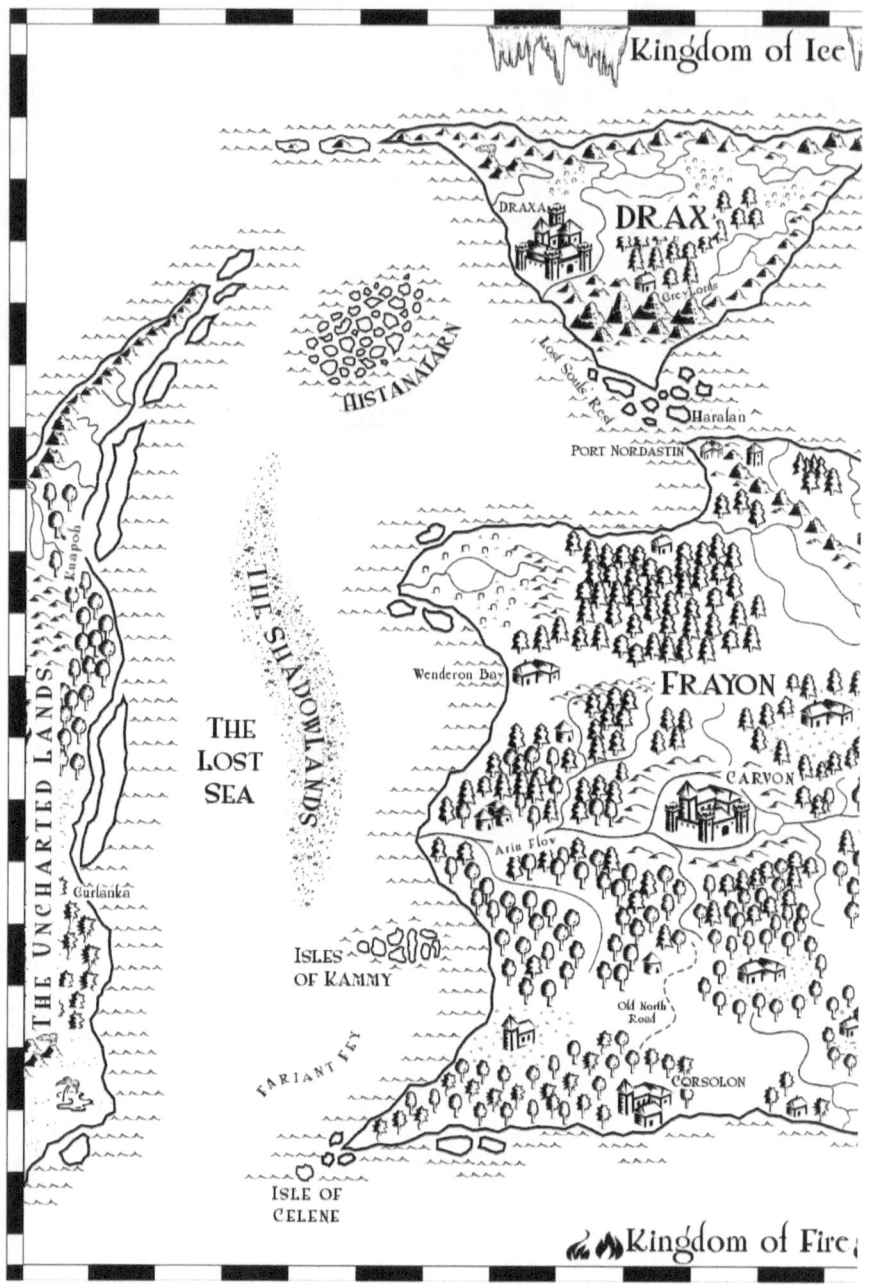

Kingdom of Ice

Kingdom of Fire

DRAX

DRAXA

Greylords

Lost Souls Road

Haralan

PORT NORDASTIN

MISTANATARN

THE SHADOWLANDS

Wenderon Bay

FRAYON

CARVON

Aria Flow

THE LOST SEA

Knapoli

Gurlanka

THE UNCHARTED LANDS

ISLES
OF KAMMY

Old North
Road

CORSOLON

FARIANT FEY

ISLE OF
CELENE

MAIORIA
THE KNOWN WORLD

MUNLAND

LANS HIMAY

TERAMIDES

INTOLANA

MAPHRAX

Mountians of Maphrax

ISLES OF TIRRY

Myrn

Escerthic Mountains

DAVONO

REDBEN

VENOSIA

TARVALASTONE

OSTASIA

HALLANSTARYA

JUNOS

ATALANPH

Ocean Kingdom

CHAPTER 1

Eye of Betrayal

THE great cry of a dragon awoke Morhork.

He felt a terrible wrenching then the shutting off of something valuable, the loss of something precious.

Faelsun, he thought, lifting his head as a chill swept through his body. In the Recollection, a thousand dragon souls cried out in pain and mourning, and then fell silent.

Faelsun was gone. That knowledge was as real as the ground beneath his feet. The wrenching away of his brother's soul made him tremble. How could it be? What had happened?

He'd spent millennia hating his brother and thinking up ways to kill him—to feel his death now left him shaken, his feelings in turmoil. His brother—the one who had sided with the humans and fought against him, the one who had ripped the wings from his back, and thus his power, strength and birthright as a dragon. His brother who had been nurtured by the same mother and had shared the same nest thousands of years ago.

Gone forever.

But what about the Dragon Dream? He swept his mind through the Recollection and closed his eyes, overcome with powerful, confusing emotions.

Gone and lost forever. If the Guardian of the Dragon Dream dies, then so too, the dream. The shared dream of dragons—their glorious realm and safe haven—did not exist without the dreamer. The world had changed and would never be the same again.

Out there in the wilderness, Morhork felt the dragons stir, their minds lifting a little from their nightmares. Even in the dream state, they would never be able to enter the Dragon Dream again. Should he return to the world and try to help in some way? Perhaps he could awaken them fully and bring them back to Maioria.

No. The last time he, a dragon, got involved with the world of men it had cost him his wings. He wanted no part in it, not even now.

'Not yet, my brethren and sistren. The world of man still rules. Our time is not now,' he said, sending his thoughts to them to soothe them. The dragon minds settled then slipped back to sleep.

Morhork decided to do the same, forcing the immense sorrow and anger away. Such emotions confused him. There was no point being a dragon in this world ruled by humans. His human form was already far more effective, even if he used it only to keep a check on what was happening.

He lay back down in the cold darkness of the cave and shifted his great bulk amongst the dust and bones. This cave in the cliffs above a thick ice flow was deep, and at its end were the ancient bones of two dragons.

Not all dragons who went into hibernation survived. But it was not a bad way to go. The bones crumbled under his feet, reminding him how old they were. He curled up on top of them, sighed, and sought a deep and long sleep away from this world ruled by men.

A world now with one less dragon in it.

The stoic, gleaming towers of Castle Carvon shone through the black smoke billowing far below.

Apart from a blackened crumbling section to the west, the city and its walls were unblemished, strong and whole amidst the destruction.

'Look, the city still stands!' Issa cried above the rushing wind, her heart leaping for joy as she gripped Asaph's golden claw, the wind whipping her hair about her shoulders.

'They tried but failed to take Carvon. The heart of the Free Peoples still beats strong,' Asaph rumbled, angling his wings to slow their pace. The smoke came not from a razed city, as they had feared, but from the forest beyond.

Asaph dropped lower towards the ballooning smoke concealing the ground and any enemies that might be there. She felt his muscles tensing for attack and gripped the pommel of her sword. They'd only had a few hours' rest and a meagre amount of food before returning to the city at war and her muscles were still sore.

'They've pushed the enemy back. Now the people are trying to put out the forest fires,' Asaph said, his far superior dragon vision picking out through the stinging smog what she couldn't see.

The smoke cleared briefly allowing her to glimpse beneath it. Around the lake where she had first called the boatman was utter devastation. Great swathes of trees were snapped and flattened, the forest floor was blackened and the lake was grey with ash.

A thousand-strong city folk were frantically filling buckets, pots and pans with the dirty lake water and passing it between them to hurl upon the flames. As Asaph swooped low, many dropped their buckets and froze, trembling in dragon fear. Some at the forest edge ran away screaming.

Ignoring the people, Asaph hovered above the flames and beat his wings furiously. People flattened themselves against the ground to avoid being blown away and the trees bent over with the force of his gusts. Under his onslaught, the flames were driven down to the ground and extinguished, leaving a smouldering, charred forest.

Struggling onto their knees, the people burst into cheers and raised their hands. Issa laughed and waved down at them. Asaph lifted into the air.

'Where's the front line?' she asked, straining to see where Carvon's soldiers might be. 'And where are the Dread Dragons?'

'Maybe they've pushed them back,' said Asaph and turned to the west.

After a fast mile Issa spotted something. 'There!' she shouted and pointed into the faded distance where more smoke billowed above the trees. Black shapes flew in the sky.

Asaph slowed, his heart beating faster. 'Dromoorai. But they're retreating,' he said, flying cautiously forwards.

'Let's go after them and hunt them down,' Issa growled.

After a moment, Asaph said, 'As much as I want to, we should regroup with the others for a conjoined attack. There are too many.'

He was right. No matter how much she wanted to chase them across Frayon and into the sea, her revenge would have to wait.

'Look. The others have stopped too,' she said, spying the glinting armour of hundreds of tiny figures in the distance.

Asaph picked up the pace, covering the miles fast.

At the edge of the tree line where the forest gave way to grassland and craggy fields, the king's army massed. Pikes bristled and pennants thrust proudly into the sky. Many were covered in dirt and stained in blood.

The halted army stood apprehensively before a strange purple haze that billowed over the ground some fifty yards in front of them, weapons drawn and at the ready. No one dared enter it.

Feeling the soft buzz of magic, Issa searched for the source. There, on a high point behind the frontline and surrounded by soldiers, stood several wizards in their purple robes holding their staves aloft.

'Freydel! Thank the goddess,' she breathed, spotting him amongst the others.

Even from this distance he looked aged and hunched with exhaustion. His new crystal staff shone blue in the light and it pulsed with magic. It was alluring, transfixing her gaze, and she wondered where he had got it from, having never seen such a thing of beauty in his study.

Beside him stood all other members of the Wizards' Circle and the Flow pooled thickly around them as the wizards drew upon it to work their magic. As Asaph neared, she could feel the crackle of their magic in the air.

Finding a clearing a short distance behind the army, Asaph landed, set her down, and changed from his dragon form into a man swiftly in an effort to avoid spreading dragon fear.

They made their way through the forest, clambering over fallen trees, brambles and ferns until they found the main track. All along the path wounded soldiers lay. Physicians and healers tended them wrapping bandages around wounds and setting splints to broken bones. Some soldiers lay permanently still and white sheets covered them completely.

Issa's heart became heavy.

'Look, there's King Navarr,' said Asaph, touching her arm.

Through the crowds of milling soldiers, she saw the king of Frayon. He was encased in chainmail and shining plate armour; even his cowl was made of chainmail held in place by a simple gold circlet.

As they neared, the king walked towards them, a determined smile on his soot-streaked, blood-smeared face. There were also smears of blood and dirt on his tabard. He was not a king afraid to fight with his men. His soldiers parted to let him through and bowed slightly as he passed.

'They've retreated—for now,' King Navarr said, his hard grin deepening. He gripped Issa's shoulder and slapped Asaph on the back, which Issa noted surprised Asaph as colour touched his cheeks. 'We've sent several units and a routing party to chase them back as far as they can. Led by Sir Marakon, of course.'

'Thank the goddess he's all right,' said Issa.

'It's been a long, vicious fight and I don't think it's over yet, but the enemy haven't managed to set up bases close, so eventually they'll have to retreat back to the coast with us harrying them all the way.

'As always, they knew exactly where to strike and when we were least prepared for it. With those bastard Dromoorai, they're able to hit hard and fast whilst we watch shaking in our boots. I did not expect to see Carvon still standing, but then I refused to imagine it falling, too.

'Scouts report that the north-west coast is lost, but we'll do all we can to drive them from our shores.' King Navarr's jaw clenched.

With a caw, Ehka swooped low and landed at Issa's feet. Laughing, she crouched down and stroked her raven guardian. 'I knew you'd be all right,' she said, but still she worried for his safety whenever there was a battle that drove him from her side.

The big black messenger bird of Zanufey crowed softly, clearly glad to be with her again where he could protect her.

Issa glanced up at Asaph. 'What do you reckon? Should we help Marakon?'

He shrugged and looked to the west, hand resting on his sword pommel. 'I guess there's no point hiding anymore. Everyone and Baelthrom now know there's a Dragon Lord still alive.'

They were back in the air within the half hour and following Ehka.

After five miles or so, the raven squawked and dropped down into the trees. Asaph flew lower and Issa glimpsed soldiers running through the forest with their familiar gold shield on red Feylint Halanoi tabards. Ahead, a mob of Maphraxies fled. Their guttural grunts and clanging black iron armour sent shivers down her spine.

Asaph ploughed into the unsuspecting Maphraxies as they emerged from the trees and blasted them with flames. Inhuman, gargled howls filled the air and an acrid smell assaulted Issa's nostrils. They did not burn easily and it took all Asaph's blue fire and another pass to incinerate them.

Those not incinerated scattered, their flesh smouldering. Asaph struck a claw down through the trees, catching one. It gave a sickening squeal as he clenched. He dropped the crushed body and lifted up. Issa heard the Feylint Halanoi cheering below.

'Look, there are more.' Issa pointed to another horde of black shapes running through the trees; Maphraxies, foltoy and death hounds. 'They're retreating, but if we let them go now, we'll only face them again in the future.'

'This enemy knows no mercy,' rumbled Asaph. 'But we don't want to follow them into a trap.'

'Then let's stay close to the soldiers,' said Issa. 'We're stronger together.'

The ground below turned rocky and a ravine loomed ahead making it difficult to get close enough to flame the rest whilst flying.

Asaph made a tight landing on a huge, jutting rock surrounded by tall evergreens ahead of the advancing soldiers. Setting her down on the flatter section, he changed form in a sparkle of air. Issa watched in awe as the light surrounded him and then a man stood there in the place of an enormous dragon. Her change into a raven seemed far less glamorous, she thought.

Together they ran through the trees to meet the routing party. They found the soldiers paused at the entrance to the ravine.

'We're friends,' Asaph called out as they emerged from the forest holding up their hands.

A hundred weary, blood and grime-smeared faces stared back at them and lowered their weapons. They'd been fighting all night, Issa realised.

The soldiers relaxed and took to settling on the grass and patches of bare rock. She searched for Marakon amongst them and finally found him with Bokaard surveying the ravine.

The big Atalanphian slapped her back and Marakon squeezed her shoulder. The half-elf commander had lost the eyepatch he usually wore to cover his old wound. Instead, he had wrapped a piece of cloth around his head to hide his white eye as he'd not had time to find or make another. Marakon shook Asaph's hand and gave a slight bow of respect.

'It's good to finally meet the last Dragon Lord,' he said, eyeing Asaph.

Bokaard nodded, deep respect in his eyes as he looked at the Draxian.

'Issa's told me a lot about you,' said Asaph. 'That you were once a great king and beloved leader. In this life, you are the best the Feylint Halanoi has to offer and I'd be honoured to join your knights.' Asaph returned the bow.

'The honour would be all mine, Sir Dragon Lord. But perhaps we can wait until after the battle?' Marakon grinned and slapped his shoulder.

'Are you going after the Maphraxies?' asked Issa, peering over the edge into the darkness of the ravine.

'No. Here we rest. We're all too tired and now spread too thinly. There is only this entrance to the ravine which we can guard easily enough. We'll rest here and set up camp when the supply team catches up. We need at least two more fresh units to harry the enemy further.

'They took a lucky strike at our heart to shake us up and let us know they could. It worked. Whether we can push them off Frayon's north-west coast remains to be seen. Do not relax your guard. This fight is not over yet.'

Issa helped tend and heal the injured while Asaph cleaned and sharpened weapons as the army prepared the camp. Apart from a foltoy hurtling into their midst and being felled in a hail of blades, nothing else attacked them.

At dusk, the supply units finally caught up with them, bringing much-needed food, water, bandages and blades. Soon, tents, campfires, and the delicious smell of cooking filled the forest.

Being on the early bed schedule for night watch, Issa found herself restless and sleep far away. From the rustling sounds beyond the fabric of her tent, so was the rest of the unit she camped amongst. It wasn't easy getting to sleep knowing your enemy was near and could strike at any time.

Asaph seemed to be doing all right, however. His chest rose and fell steadily as he slept on a rough blanket next to hers. They were fully clothed and armoured in leather as ordered. Not that she minded; it was too cold to sleep with any less on.

Shifting a dozing Ehka beside her, she got out of bed, picked up her sword, and tiptoed out of the tent, heading towards the latrine.

Marakon sat beside the campfire and looked as if he, too, was having trouble sleeping. He glanced up at her and nodded. She nodded back, but the gaze of his unbound white eye made her shiver and something about it made her want to get away as fast as possible. He must have sensed this for he dropped his gaze.

Issa turned away, feeling confused. She had nothing but the deepest respect and awe for Marakon but his eye filled her with dread.

It was dark and still in the forest. Only the light of the campfires behind barely lit her way. The air was cool and the moonless night sky filled with stars. She walked along the freshly cut path to the river winding between clusters of beech trees. The water was dark and slow moving and very deep.

She bent down between the ferns and splashed cold water on her face, wishing she could have a long hot bath. At least the water was cool and refreshing so she took several gulps to invigorate herself.

As she drank, a cold, dark feeling crept over her skin and the hairs on her neck rose. She froze, her ears pricked for the slightest sound.

There came no noise, just a fleeting dark shadow as a wire noose slipped over her head, tightened around her neck, and dragged her backwards. Issa slammed hard against the huge, metal chest of a Dromoorai, the sickly sweet stench of the undead filling her nostrils and making her gag. How had she not smelled the Sirin Derenax before now? How had she not heard anything?

She tried to scream—for Asaph, Ehka or anyone—but the noose lifted her off her feet and tightened until she couldn't breathe. She squinted through watering eyes into the darkness. Ehka was on the ground, unmoving in the grass.

Grimacing against the pain, she kicked backwards, smashing her soft boots into hard metal shins and hurting her heels. Her hands grappled for the wire around her throat, trying desperately to loosen it. She struggled uselessly as an impossibly strong hand bent her arms back, one after the other, and tied them.

The Dromoorai made no sound except for its heavy rhythmic breathing as though each inhale and exhale were made through a tube. She quickly felt faint and her struggles lost their strength. Her head started to pound and her heart thundered madly.

Between the trees towards the camp, a figure appeared and paused, swaying. The Dromoorai turned to face it. *Marakon?* Issa thought. Blinking through the tears, she choked, trying to scream to catch his attention but failing. Why wasn't he running to fight? Surely he could see the Dromoorai? Tears streamed down her cheeks. She gritted her teeth, feeling her consciousness slipping away.

Marakon's white eye blazed into light and he fell against the tree trunk groaning as if he struggled against something within himself. Had a Life Seeker taken him? Marakon gasped and clutched at his head as if possessed by a demon, then he stood straight and came stalking towards her, his face set in a fury.

'Now I have you,' he said in a voice that wasn't his, but Baelthrom's.

Issa's legs gave way and she sagged. Terror turned her heart into a hammer. Blackness seeped around her—or maybe she was passing out. The cord loosened and she gasped in a breath, wincing in pain as it scoured her bruised windpipe. The Dromoorai still held the noose in one hand and crushed her against his chest with the other so she couldn't get away. Not that she could if she tried, her body was as weak as a child's.

'Marakon, please help me,' she rasped, tears streaming down her cheeks. Marakon had to be in there somewhere, if she could only reach him.

Slow, impossibly heavy footsteps shook the ground. There came a loud snort from behind and the rotting odour of sulphur assaulting her nose told her a Dread Dragon was near. Her insides wobbled but she was already too terrified to succumb much further to dragon fear.

The Dromoorai grabbed her hair and pulled her head up, forcing her to stare into Marakon's blazing white eye. Marakon's face contorted in pain as his eye slowly turned red—red like Baelthrom's.

'Marakon is gone. I control him now,' said Baelthrom. 'Bring her back to me.'

The Dromoorai lifted her. Issa struggled to find the Flow but there was only the thick, cloying blackness of the Under Flow. Without a word, the Dromoorai turned and slung her over the Dread Dragon's saddle. She wriggled furiously and tried to kick at the Dromoorai. It grabbed her legs and wrapped wire around them, yanking it so tight she gasped. A mouldy piece of cloth was rammed into her mouth making her retch.

The Dromoorai pulled itself into the saddle beside her and gripped the huge clanking reins made of chains as the dragon stood up. Breathing hard against the gag, Issa stared down at Marakon. Why wasn't he fighting? How could he let this happen? Dear goddess, what had happened to Ehka? Where were the soldiers? Why couldn't anyone see what was happening?

'Marakon,' she tried to scream past the gag but only a muffled noise came out.

Something in the trees growled, then a beastly roar ripped through the forest. The Dread Dragon paused and whipped its head around.

The roar was echoed by two more. Ferns and bushes shook violently between the trees as something huge bounded towards them.

'Marakon!' a female voice howled.

Issa strained to see through her sweaty strands of hair plastered to her face. A strange sight appeared at the edge of the trees partially hidden by foliage. A brown-skinned, blindfolded woman with very short hair rode atop a giant, roaring bear. The woman was dressed in sackcloth and holding aloft a glowing staff. She was flanked by two other riderless bears.

'Get away!' Marakon screamed at the woman in his own voice. He thrashed and fell onto his knees, clawing at his face.

'Go, now!' Baelthrom roared at the Dromoorai as Marakon writhed.

The Dromoorai yanked on the reins and the Dread Dragon lifted its head and beat its wings.

The blindfolded woman screamed. Light pulsed from her staff, blasting into Marakon and flooring him. The riderless bears roared and bounded towards the Dread Dragon. One leaped, gaining a shocking height for its size, and landed on the dragon's tail. Lumbering up the dragon's horny spine, its thick claws ripped into scales. The other bear attacked the haunches of the dragon with its teeth.

The Dromoorai pulled out its claymore but the bear was already upon it. A huge paw knocked the sword away with such force that the surprised Dromoorai lost its grip on it. Issa watched the black metal blade glinting as it spun down to the grass below. The bear reared and hurled itself at the Dromoorai, knocking it from its saddle. Bear and Dromoorai rolled down the dragon's side and hit the ground with a thud.

Wriggling madly, Issa started to slide off the Dread Dragon but caught her bindings on a spiny horn. Dangling by her feet, she managed to dislodge the gag with her tongue and spat it out.

'Bring her!' Baelthrom roared through Marakon.

Obeying the command, the dragon kicked the bear attacking its haunches and sent it rolling through the grass. Temporarily free of its harasser, the undead beast flapped its wings again and lifted into the air. Issa screamed as loud as she could. Surely the whole army would have heard her and all the commotion by now but why weren't they here?

The ground fell away with shocking speed. The dragon turned in a sickening arc as she dangled by only her feet. She would fall to her death if the Dread Dragon didn't kill her first.

A blaze of fire torched the night sky in an arc of light. Issa hunted for the source but could see nothing from this angle. The Dread Dragon howled as it was suddenly shunted violently sideways. Issa's bindings slipped off its spine and she fell, screaming.

Between the tumbling trees and stars, a golden dragon hurtled towards her; blue eyes flaring, ears held flat against his sleek head and huge teeth bared. The Dread Dragon was on his tail.

A tree tip slashed her face just as Asaph's claw wrapped around her. The rushing air stopped, leaving her body trembling in stunned shock. With barely a pause, Asaph landed, laid her on the grass, and turned and leaped back into the air to meet the attacking Dread Dragon.

Issa rolled onto her side. To her left, the Dromoorai fought three bears and the woman. Marakon writhed on the grass, clutching his head and screaming. A cold black shadow slithered beside her, then tiny cold hands grappled with the wire around her throat. She blinked into the barely materialised, ugly face of Maggot. Barely two feet tall, the tiny Shadow Demon's big yellow eyes were wide and his red tongue hung out.

'Maggot?' Her voice was ragged. Had he really just appeared from the demon world or was she seeing things?

'I knew you were in trouble,' he said as the wire came loose in his small hands.

Issa lay there gasping, finally able to breathe properly and deciding her unlikely friend from the Murk was indeed real. Maggot undid the bindings on her wrists and she shook them off, reaching down to free her ankles.

Jumping up, she ran to Ehka with Maggot following on furiously beating stubby wings. Gently she turned the bird onto his back. His eyelids fluttered and his claws moved a little. She couldn't see any wound or blood on him. Perhaps magic had stunned him.

Grabbing her talisman, she held it over him. With a command, indigo light blanketed the bird. He twitched and gave a slight croak. One eye opened. Thank the goddess he was still alive.

Issa glanced ahead. One bear lay unmoving on the ground, with badly ripped ears and dark blood soaking its fur. The other two fought on against the Dromoorai.

She gripped her sword and was about to run and join them when the Dromoorai fell, watery black blood spraying from its throat. It shuddered violently then was still. The blindfolded woman dropped Marakon's blade. Issa stared, wondering how the woman could see to kill the beast.

The two bears sniffed the fallen corpse and flinched away. One went to the other fallen bear and hung its head. Issa swallowed a lump. There was no saving the bear lying still.

Marakon groaned, got onto his knees then collapsed back again, blood trickling out of his nose, ears and eyes. Issa pulled the Flow through the talisman, now finding the Under Flow weakened. She took a deep, steadying breath and focused on the man. Was Baelthrom still in him?

Sheathing her sword—she wouldn't be needing it—she took out the orb. Holding talisman and orb high, she pulled harder on the Flow and stepped slowly and deliberately towards Marakon. Maggot followed behind her heels. Baelthrom still fought for control of the man's body— she could feel his unholy presence thickening around her as she neared. Sweat beaded her forehead. She forced down the fear. Marakon's life was at stake.

'Get out of him,' she snarled.

It had been Marakon all along. The realisation made her pause and stare at the possessed man. Somehow, he had led the Dromoorai here. Had he been working with Baelthrom since the beginning? Betraying them all? Fury exploded within her, blotting out all reason. The man had betrayed them. He must be destroyed.

'You traitor!' she screamed. The words seemed too stupid to express the hurt and betrayal she felt inside. 'We trusted you with our lives!'

The man howled and writhed on the ground. The veins in his neck stood up and he clawed at his face, making deep welts in his skin.

'Marakon!' the bear-riding woman shouted. She limped towards them, swinging and tapping her staff in front of her like a blind person.

'Shield,' Issa commanded the orb. A shimmering blue dome flared around her and Marakon, forcing the blindfolded woman back and blocking anything that might attack or disturb them.

'Get away,' Issa hissed at the woman. 'This man is a traitor. A spy!' Her words made her even more furious. She would kill Marakon herself.

'He doesn't know what he is, what he carries,' the blindfolded woman pleaded frantically, pressing herself against the blue dome that was as solid as glass. She slapped her hands against it. 'I've come here to tell him. Please don't hurt him. I can help.'

Issa barely heard the woman as she turned back to the commander groaning at her feet. He jerked and convulsed, then his white eye opened and glared at her.

'Come to me,' Baelthrom's voice commanded through Marakon's lips. His voice moved around her, cold and draining like the Under Flow.

Maggot squeaked and clung to the back of her leg. She had forgotten the demon was there. A heavy, woozy feeling came upon her. Her hand holding the orb trembled and her grip became sweaty and weak. She swallowed hard, her pulse throbbing in her ears. It took great effort to slip the orb out of sight into the sack tied at her belt.

Ignoring the voice and focusing on her actions, slowly and deliberately she pulled out her sword. The tremble in her hand became violent tremors that shook her whole arm. Her sword began to burn in her grasp and she fought to hold onto it.

'Come to me,' Baelthrom's voice echoed around her louder, even inside her own head.

She raised her sword but it burst into fire and she screamed, dropping it. Marakon howled, clamping his hands to his temples. His eyes turned entirely black and his hands whipped out and clawed the air as if trying to reach her. The Under Flow seeped from his palms. Black magic spewed into the dome, easily and swiftly overcoming the Flow. Issa's protective shield became her prison, plunging her into choking icy blackness.

The talisman burned in her grasp and the orb pulsed at her side. Protect the orb! She had to protect the orb! Her body stepped forward through no will of her own. She gritted her teeth, fighting for control of herself and the Flow. Marakon's eyes blazed in the dark, the only light she could see. She tried to look away.

'Use the talisman, Issy,' Maggot squealed from somewhere far away.

It seemed to take an age for her arm to lift the throbbing talisman in front of her.

'Come to me,' Baelthrom's voice boomed all around her.

Marakon raised a hand out of the blackness and her body betrayed her as she reached for it. He gripped her wrist in an iron clamp. She screamed as deathly cold filled her body and mind. He began dragging her down to him. She had to fight the cold. She tried to jerk away but his strength was absolute.

She strained to lift the talisman to her chest. With a scream, she slammed it against her torso and fell onto Marakon. The raven mark burned, pushing back the cold. Indigo light flared from the talisman, fighting back the blackness of the Under Flow.

'A'farion. A'farion. A'farion!' She screamed at the rushing din as the battle blazed between black and indigo magic. But her words came out so slowly it seemed time was stopping.

The world trembled and lurched. She felt herself being torn in two as the spell tried to take her to the realm of the dead and Baelthrom battled to hold onto her.

Marakon was screaming beneath her, his chest heaving, but she clung to him with the raven talisman pressed between them as the world wrenched between two opposing forces.

CHAPTER 2

Lifting Curses

THE blackness bulged and rolled away.

Issa fell into silver light still clutching Marakon. They thudded onto hard ground, Marakon's scream catching up with them.

She let go of him and staggered onto her knees, her raven mark burning. His white eye bulged horribly and his eyelids were peeled back as if he couldn't blink. He choked and quietened, his face ashen. As his screams died, he became stricken, as if paralysed.

Panting, she whipped up her sword and held the raven talisman high, half expecting Baelthrom to appear before her. When he didn't, she looked around. A grey, deathly silent place assaulted her ears as the din of before echoed away.

Maggot was a shadow to her right, Ehka a few paces to her left. The raven was awake but listing on his side, his wings splayed to steady himself.

Issa dropped her gaze back to Marakon. His eye glared at her and her breath caught in her throat. She was looking directly at Baelthrom.

Through the burning hot pain in his eye and the madness in his mind, Marakon blinked in darkness up at the woman. *Not a woman, a goddess.* She was swathed in midnight blue and covered in stars. Only her perfect chin and lips were visible from within her hood.

Zanufey.

The wind moved her cloak and she said nothing, though he could feel her eyes upon him. Something very wrong was happening to him. He fought for control of his body as something utterly evil and dark tried to fill it, shoving him aside. Pain radiated through him as if his body was tearing itself apart from within.

Even as the pain ripped through him a contrasting serenity began to seep in. Soon, waves of calm flowed over him. In Zanufey's divine presence, the evil began to scatter and the pain receded. He groaned in relief as his senses returned. Blinking, he looked around. He was on his back and couldn't move. A desert plain stretched out all around and into the far distance. A star-filled sky wheeled above.

'Blessed Zanufey, where am I?' he asked, alarmed when his voice came out a croak.

Pain exploded in his eye again and he screamed. Baelthrom's helmeted face surrounded by raging red fire filled his vision. The Immortal Lord held out a huge hand and slowly clenched his fist. Marakon's heart squeezed as he did so. He gasped and writhed, sweat beading then trickling down his face.

Zanufey filled his mind again, cool and dark, driving away the pain and chaos. Then Baelthrom returned bringing raging fire and agony. Marakon howled, his eye burning in unseen flames. Zanufey returned and between her and Baelthrom, between agony and madness, and soothing calm, his reality flipped.

'Help me!' he screamed. What was happening to him?

'Marakon.' In a moment of calm, a voice he recognised called from far away. His heart lurched at it. He longed to be with that voice.

'Jarlain?' he rasped. What was she doing here? Had he gone completely mad?

The pain receded, the crushing fist around his heart relaxed, and the images of Baelthrom and Zanufey went.

He opened his eyes. A grey, lifeless world appeared. He lay upon the cold hard mud of a battlefield in the aftermath of war. Everyone had been slaughtered; bodies were strewn everywhere, pale and unmoving. Bloodied faces, eyes wide in horror, stared unseeing from within crushed helmets. Armour, swords, spears and axes all covered in gore lay strewn amongst the dead. Horses lay with flies already swarming their corpses. Some still carried their mounts, soldiers half-crushed beneath them. Nothing moved except the torn pennants in a frail wind. The stench of death reeked everywhere.

He tried to sit up but could not. He tried to raise a hand but found he couldn't even move a finger. Panic spread through him. Was his body broken? Had he died? Great Goddess, what was happening to him?

A raven cawed. He saw it circling above him. It cawed again and again then descended towards him, its black eyes gleaming. Marakon tried to move, afraid of the glare in its eyes, its sharp talons and flashing beak.

I'm a Knight of the Raven. I should not be afraid of it!

But he was afraid. Its cawing grated his ears and his white eye began to water and throb. He blinked the streaming tears from his eyes. Black wings filled his vision. The raven landed on his head, sharp claws scratching his cheeks and tearing at his hair as it tried to balanced itself. He tried to shake it off but his head wouldn't even move. He began to pant in terror.

The raven bent its head low, its dark eyes looking into his. He saw not himself, but the hideous form of Baelthrom reflected in them. Marakon opened and closed his mouth but couldn't draw breath.

I am not Baelthrom! What trickery is this?

'He's mine,' Baelthrom's voice howled around him. The Immortal Lord's eyes blazed red. Cold flooded Marakon's body and his breath came in short, ragged gasps. Madness filled his mind, scattering his thoughts.

The raven tilted back its head, opened its beak wide and cawed raucously, the noise deafening so close to his ears. Then it angled its head closer, its long, sharp beak gleaming in the light. Fear trickled down Marakon's spine.

The raven lunged at his white eye. Searing pain exploded in his head. He screamed as it stabbed again. He couldn't even move to shake it off. Blood and tears streamed down Marakon's face as he felt it stab deep into his skull.

The agony of its relentless, hateful, stabbing beak filled his mind and body, sending him mad with pain. He felt on the verge of passing out, and prayed that he would as there came a great pull—as if his entire brain was being yanked out of his eye socket—then the most terrible tearing pain. A blast of searing heat ripped through his body, and only then came blessed release.

Something hot, heavy and wet slid down his face.

Marakon passed out.

Issa couldn't keep Marakon in the realm of the dead for more than a few moments. Just long enough to break Baelthrom's hold on him. As the man writhed before her, the shadow world jerked and faded. Baelthrom's voice boomed and darkness engulfed her. Marakon screamed horribly, then the shadow world began to withdraw.

Grappling with the Flow she tried to push back the darkness and remain in the realm of the dead where Baelthrom couldn't reach her. She failed. The greener forests of Frayon materialised. There was blood on the grass at her feet, blood all over Marakon's hands that covered his face. He was groaning and more blood trickled through his fingers.

Ehka had something round, white and bloody in his beak. Issa fought not to vomit. The raven spat out Marakon's eye and hopped back, keen to get away from it. The bloody white eye lying in the grass suddenly burst into red light. Issa yelled, lifted her boot and stamped on it. The hateful eye made a sickening squishing sound and a blast of black magic flared beneath her boot. The Under Flow fled away, and with it Baelthrom's presence.

Unable to control it this time, Issa leant over and vomited. She slumped to her knees, gasping, dropping the protective shield around them. Ehka wiped his beak on the grass and nestled beside her leg. Utterly spent, she watched the blindfolded woman run to Marakon and drop down to hug him. He bled heavily from his eye socket and she did her best to stem the flow. The half-elf commander wasn't conscious.

Issa tried to reach the Flow to help in some manner but the magic was wild and erratic and she was too exhausted to form any control over it. Besides, she didn't pity him or any spy of Baelthrom. The man had betrayed them—how many times? How many lives had been lost because of him? She didn't want to know. She'd placed her utmost respect and trust in him, and he'd been a spy of Baelthrom all along. She blamed herself for not guessing sooner.

'How could you do this? You could have killed him,' the blindfolded woman shouted at her. Her bear was by the river, drinking. The second bear had disappeared, and the third still lay unmoving beside the dead Dromoorai.

'We could all have been killed,' Issa said tonelessly. 'It had to be done. By Baelthrom spying through him, countless lives have been lost.'

The other woman pursed her lips.

The shadows drew together besides Issa's knees and Maggot's ugly face peered up at her. His cold, little hands rested on her thigh and his big eyes darted fearfully to the other humans then back to her.

'How did you know to come, Maggot?' She smiled at the little demon despite the heaviness in her heart.

'Ever since you helped us in the Murk, I can feel when you're in danger. The Great Carmedrak has done something to me. He says I must help you when I feel that.'

Issa didn't know why their Lord Carmedrak would be interested in her, but she was grateful.

'Then you must thank him for me. You saved my life. If you had come a moment later I would have been captured or even killed.'

Asaph stumbled out of the woods several yards away, sheathing his sword. He was dishevelled, his shirt ripped and left shoulder bloody, but he walked strong and upright. A wave of relief washed over her. On unsteady legs, she stood and embraced him, burying her face against his good shoulder. Maggot slipped behind her ankles.

'Are you hurt?' said Asaph, drawing back to look her over.

'No, not really. Just shaken and drained,' she said, looking up at him.

Soldiers came bursting through the trees, their swords raised. Maggot melted into the shadows. Why hadn't they come sooner? Dark magic had been at play, that was a given.

The soldiers halted and did a double take on the strange group assembled, their eyes coming to rest on the body of the Dromoorai. Those closest to the bear raised their swords fearfully but the bear yawned and lay down placidly next to the blindfolded woman.

'It's all right, there was a Dromoorai.' Asaph raised his eyebrows and laughed at his own words. 'We took them out. There was only one. The Dread Dragon is impaled on the tree over there.' He pointed.

'Just one is enough,' said a soldier, wide-eyed. The other soldiers nodded and gripped their weapons nervously.

'Baelthrom could see through Marakon's eye,' Issa said, turning to Asaph.

Asaph stared at the prone man, a look of horror spreading on his face. 'How much?'

Issa shrugged and kept her voice low, not wanting to alarm everyone. 'Maybe everything. I think that's how they've always known what we are doing, where we are and how to attack us so precisely. So devastatingly—'

'And how they found you,' Asaph cut in with the words she didn't dare utter.

She gave a faint nod. 'More might come this very night.'

When Jarlain first heard Marakon call her name from beyond the darkness of her blindfold, a great weight lifted from her heart. In her red vision, he had appeared through the trees as a white beacon of light leading her on. Despite her blindness, her heart had won and led her to Marakon. The terrifying, giant flying lizard in her vision could not have stopped her running to his side.

Cradling his head in her lap, she stemmed the blood that flowed down his face with a ripped piece of her sackcloth clothing. Taking a deep breath, she closed her eyes. She had found him at last. All the long days of suffering and the cold nights alone in an alien world had finally come to an end. The weariness in her body and soul lessened.

The cloth she held to his bleeding head was soon soaked wet with blood, but despite the horror of his missing eye, that unmistakable uneasy feeling she had around him was gone. As much as she hated what the woman with the raven had done, the darkness surrounding him had disappeared. She murmured healing words and felt her hands grow warm, then laid them on his body bringing him back around.

'Where am I?' he said, his voice weak. 'I feel so strange. Like I'm free, but my head hurts and I can't see properly.'

'Shh, you're safe. You need a healer but you'll be all right,' she whispered.

'Jarlain?' His voice was filled with wonder. She felt his hand stroke her cheek then fumble with her blindfold.

'Why? Are you hurt? Have you been blinded too?' he asked.

Without saying anything she bent to kiss him, tears soaking her blindfold. He kissed her tenderly and she stroked the stubble of his cheek. He reached behind her head and, as easily as tearing paper, the blindfold fell away.

With a soft gasp, she lifted her head and squinted into the painful light of the soldiers' torches. Her eyes streamed with the pain of sudden light after so long. It was a pain she welcomed. She peered down at Marakon's terrible, pale and bloodied face.

'I was cursed, like you, but now you're with me that curse is lifted,' she whispered in wonder. 'And I'm certain your curse has been removed for good. It is better to lose an eye than carry that evil within you.'

'How are you here? I can barely believe it,' he said. 'So many strange things have happened.'

'Shh, rest.' She bent down to hug him close. 'Now is not the time to talk. I've done what I can but you need a physician. You won't believe it, so let me just say this: when I first met you and you lifted your eyepatch, I saw in your damaged eye my people destroyed and us together. And now both those things have come to pass.'

CHAPTER 3

Swords and Armour

ISSA walked the subdued streets of Carvon.

After harrying the enemy as far as they dared, she'd returned to the city with Asaph and several units of exhausted soldiers. They were all glad to rest in proper beds and eat rich food whilst seated at tables.

In the city, there wasn't the usual laughter of children, the chatter of women or the bellows of hawkers. People went about their business in silence or speaking in hushed voices. Most worked on a section of the city wall that had been destroyed by Dread Dragons, or on clearing the debris of fallen roofs and broken glass covering the streets.

The taverns were mostly empty too. Today, people needed sobriety and clear thinking. The enemy had reached them and they knew they could be attacked at any time. Now, everyone understood that the days of the Free Peoples were numbered unless they fought with everything they had.

But despite the sombre, weary faces she saw everywhere, Issa noted there was a firm set to their chins, a hard look in their eyes. They were determined and resolute. The enemy could come but they sure as hell would fight back.

But would it be enough? Issa doubted it. To defeat the enemy, they had to come up with a different plan. They had to counter-attack; take the offensive and start trying to regain lost lands.

Lost in her thoughts, she found herself at Edarna's door without knowing exactly how she'd got there. She rapped the heavy, rusty door knocker. There came the subtlest shimmer of earth-based magic and the door swung open.

Issa grinned and went inside. The old wooden stairs creaked loudly under her feet. At the top, she paused at the open door.

'Hello?'

She walked into a small room that was stuffed full with two beds. Rammed up against the window was a cooker with two hobs.

'There she is!' squealed Edarna. The plump, old witch emerged from what looked like a closet.

Mr Dubbins meowed loudly and sprung into Issa's arms. She laughed and cuddled the blue cat, then set him down.

'Hmm, I think you need a bigger place,' said Issa.

'Indeed. I need a whole shop! I've been thinking on names. "Higglesworth Enterprises" or "City Witches" or "Coven Accessories".'

Issa suppressed a giggle at the dreamy wonder on Edarna's face.

'Yes.' The witch nodded, her green eyes bright as she clapped her hands together. 'It's all on the up. Oh, imagine all the witches coming together again. Hah!

'Now then, Dearie.' She looked over her half-moon spectacles at Issa with a serious expression. 'No matter what wizards, seers or even witches might teach you, you still need to wear physical protection in your line of work. Whatever people might like to believe about the Raven Queen, the prophecies clearly state she was a warrior, probably with a sword, armour and other *stuff*. So, I've been busy. Here's an extra special gift for you— you'll find nothing else like it in all Maioria.'

The witch passed Issa a large parcel wrapped in brown packing paper.

Issa wondered what on earth was Edarna giving her as she took the heavy bundle. She hoped it wasn't any more of her foul-tasting potions. She squeezed it gently. Thankfully the package felt soft and not hard as if filled with vials. Intrigue replaced her concern and she set it down on the bed and undid the ties.

Inside was the strangest, black metallic material she had ever seen. There were two pieces; leggings and a long-sleeved jerkin both made of leathery scales sewn expertly together and lined with soft fabric. The surface was like snake skin in texture, but tougher and more flexible. The scales varied in size, from being as small as one of her fingernails, to bigger than her head, and each one was perfectly woven on to the next.

'You made this? It's exquisite. And the craftsmanship...stunning!' Issa stroked the smooth surface. It glimmered with many dark colours; green, purple and black, like oil.

Edarna grinned.

Issa traced one of the larger scales with a fingertip. She stopped when recognition of what she stroked dawned on her. 'I know this material. It's...it's...*Dread Dragon.*' She almost dropped the jerkin, feeling suddenly faint.

'Now don't you go worrying about where it came from.' The witch shook a finger at her. 'This material is fire resistant, incredibly strong, and if torn it will mend itself and you along with it. These days you gotta fight fire with fire resistance! It can't harm you, you know, so why not use it to protect yourself?'

'Yes but, it's the skin of my enemy!' Issa said, still horrified.

She looked back at the tunic, slowly realising that the material she held had strength in more ways than one. Strong, flexible, fire-resistant armour. The first of its kind. 'I guess it *is* the perfect protection. But where did you get the scales from?'

'Well, you don't come across a perfectly fine dragon corpse very often now, do you? Dread Dragon scales are priceless to a witch. You wait and see; in a few months, I'll be the richest witch that ever lived. Now go on, go on; try it on.'

Issa stared at her, dreading the thought. But she couldn't turn away such a gift so she reluctantly undid her royal blue velvet cloak—another gift given to her by King Navarr—then slipped out of her leggings and tunic dress and put on the dragon scale clothing. It was strong enough to have to be tugged firmly over her hips and shoulders, but as soon as she had done up the last of the buttons and zips, the material pulled around her snugly, moulding perfectly to her form like a second skin. No other clothing had ever fitted her better.

'Perfect,' Edarna grinned. 'Just like I thought. The scales know exactly what to do.' The witch yanked hard on the tough material, checking her own stitching and nodding approvingly.

The armour was cool. Issa had been expecting it to be hot and constrictive but it was the exact opposite. She felt very strange, wearing the skin of her most hated enemy, but for all the grisliness, perhaps the witch was right. It would protect her, she was a warrior, and these were evil times. She stroked the material, mesmerised by the oil-slick sheen.

'And here are your boots,' Edarna said proudly, passing her a pair of calf-length boots of the same material. 'The cobbler only just finished 'em the other day. And no, I don't need payment. Like I said, soon I'll be far richer than you anyway. Consider this a gift to protect you from our enemy. Just make sure you destroy those bastards wherever you find 'em.

'Now, where is that mirror.' Edarna disappeared off into the closet room.

Issa slipped on the boots. Again the fit was uncanny as they moulded to her feet and calves. They were the most comfortable footwear she had ever worn.

Edarna reappeared from the closet and, wearing a beaming smile, held up a long mirror.

'Now then, look at you. Just as I thought you'd look…'

Edarna's voice faded into the background as Issa stared disbelievingly at her reflection. She stroked the black scales and took a hesitant step towards the mirror.

'Maion'artheria,' a voice whispered faintly.

Tears filled her eyes. She was *her,* the warrior woman in the sacred mound; the Raven Queen. Could it really be? The armour was exactly as she had seen it, black and shimmering and clasped in the same places.

She gripped the mirror. Was she afraid? *No, I'm terrified.* There was no going back, there never had been since she'd first decided to follow the raven through the doorway into the sacred mound.

'A fearless heart can conquer all,' a voice whispered in her mind.

Issa blinked back the tears.

'What's the matter? Don't you like it?' Edarna sounded worried.

Issa shook her head, lost for words, remembering the first time she had met the Night Goddess on the desert plains of Aralansia.

'I have become that which I saw in the mirror, saw in my dreams. I have become the Raven Queen.'

Edarna dropped her gaze. 'That is as destiny must be. I do not envy you. But we will give you all the help we can. I saw you in that armour long before I even knew who you were. Why do you think I knew I had to make it?'

Edarna took the mirror from Issa's hands and set it against the wall. With a sigh, she sank onto the bed. She appeared really tired, perhaps from making the armour or, most likely, from the recent attacks. It angered Issa that an old woman should suffer from such violence. It reminded her of Fraya, her mother in all but blood, who died when the Dread Dragons came. They couldn't even leave a bed-ridden woman to die peacefully. Thoughts of home came flooding back.

'I'm sorry you lost your home like I lost mine. It's as they say, they will come for us all in the end. Every day I struggle with it, with who I must be,' Issa said. 'Sometimes I wish for all the world that I could return to Little Kammy and how it used to be. Other times I'm so angry, so vengeful, I can barely contain the rage. I wish I felt the fearless certainty of the warrior I'm supposed to be. I feel so helpless most of the time. I've done nothing but fight skirmishes when what the world needs is a hero.'

'That, my dear, is surely what all warriors feel,' said Edarna. 'Can you have compassion whilst still wielding a sword? The time of the bard and the poet is over, now is the time of the warrior.

'We do not live in happy, fanciful times, my dear, and the world will ask us—demand us—to fight for that which we love or it will be taken away. In these dark days, we're asked to stand up for that which matters. Do we care for freedom? Would we die for it? For die for it, it seems we must—or lose those things we value most.'

'Your words inspire me,' Issa smiled, even as her eyes misted up. 'I hope I can be that brave. Marakon has asked me to lead the Knights of the Raven, although now he might want to kill me after Ehka plucked out his eye.'

'A blessing,' Edarna shivered and held up her hands. Clearly not wanting to hear any more details of the story than she already knew. 'Who knows what damage that man has wrought with his evil eye. But may he find peace now. Despite his curse, he has suffered much and has become a great warrior. You will learn a lot from him.

'My oh my, I never imagined the Immortals would reach Carvon in my lifetime. If only I were younger, I'd have more energy, more power. I cannot bear to watch my beautiful Maioria fall.'

Issa touched the witch's shoulder. 'We'll defeat them, I promise... Especially in this new armour,' she grinned.

Edarna laughed. 'I hope so, my dear. I hope so.'

In his room in Castle Carvon, Asaph held Coronos' sword on his lap. He stroked the leather-wrapped hilt and the cold metal of the polished pommel. Simple, powerful, beautiful. He gripped the hilt, imagining how many times his father might have done the same all those years ago.

'You were more a man back then than I am now. Why did you leave me? How did I not save you? I need you.' He clenched his jaw and blinked back the tears.

There came a knock at the door followed by King Navarr's familiar voice. Asaph straightened. Despite what he had feared, the king had not thrown him out of the castle for jeopardising his son's life when the foltoy had attacked their camp.

After the siege of Carvon, and Asaph's fearless battle in dragon form, everybody was in awe of him. Even Prince Petar turned pale and dropped his gaze whenever he was near. Not that Asaph cared any more for his respect or even his friendship. He'd lost his desire for friendship and fear of pretty much anything since Coronos had been murdered.

The King, however, always commanded his utmost respect. Asaph jumped up and wiped his face, noticing his unshaven chin as he opened the door.

'I hope I'm not disturbing you,' Navarr said, his voice tinged with concern and his gaze penetrating.

'No, I was just...' Asaph couldn't think of what to say, so he shrugged.

The king nodded. 'Good. Well, I have some of Coronos' belongings that you should know about and have—other than those that remain in his room. Of course, you are welcome to keep them here, since you have no fixed abode. Come.'

Asaph followed the king past richly detailed tapestries, down many winding staircases and below ground where it was cold and the stone walls thick and unadorned.

They came to a stop beside a room adjacent to the wine cellars. The smell of wine stained oak hung thick in the air. Taking out a huge iron key, Navarr unlocked the heavy door. They stepped inside and the King slotted his brazier into the sconce, the flames filling the room with light and warmth.

The solid-stone room was filled with chests of varying sizes and designs all stacked neatly on top of each other, with the largest at the bottom and the smallest on top, and no more than three high around the room. A wooden table and four chairs stood in the centre.

King Navarr walked along inspecting the top row of smaller chests, then pulled one down. He placed it on the table. It was made of dark wood and decorated with iron metal studs. Was that all that remained of his father's legacy? Asaph swallowed.

'Don't be fooled by size,' Navarr said, seeing his expression. Clearly, the King already knew what was inside.

'It's not that... I...' Asaph's voice was unsteady. 'He knew so much. Everything that was Drax was contained within his mind and the orb. Now...so much has been lost.' As he spoke he realised the unfathomable wealth of information that really had disappeared.

'The future lies before us, not behind,' Navarr said firmly, his voice gruff as he looked into the middle distance. 'Now we must focus on surviving. The battle has reached us and we are plunged into the fight for the entire world.'

Asaph considered this, then took a deep, silent breath. The King's priorities were right; the past didn't matter when your own life was at risk.

'Nothing can bring Coronos back, but we can make sure he didn't die for nothing,' said Navarr. 'The orb still exists, we just have to take it back.'

It sounded so simple, yet impossible to do. The king passed him a brass coated iron key. Asaph could feel Navarr watching him.

As he opened the chest, beautiful white light burst out from it, filling the room. Asaph's eyes widened as he stared at three fist-sized, oval-shaped crystals that nestled in the box. They were perfectly smooth and sparkled with all the colours of the rainbow. Now released from their prison of darkness, their light shone out making Asaph catch his breath at their beauty.

'I've never seen anything so wonderful. What are they?'

'Infinity stones,' said Navarr. 'Ten times more valuable than gold and their uses are said to be infinite. Every wizard, alchemist, witch, healer, machinist, miner and countless other crafts have a hundred uses for these stones. They can be found only at a river's source. Coronos personally searched for, and found, all three of these. He was a bit of collector at heart, a bit of a geologist. And he knew how to travel light and travel clever to complete such long, difficult and dangerous journeys. You can build an entire kingdom from the riches of just one of these stones.'

Asaph touched one. It was warm. He gently held the crystal up to inspect it and it sparkled even more in his hand.

'They're beautiful,' said Asaph. 'Coronos told me he liked to travel and explore as a young man. But I had no idea he was interested in collecting rocks. Although, now I say that, I remember he'd often study the sea cliffs and boulders at home in the Uncharted Lands.'

He looked back in the box and his eyes widened. Beneath the stones were at least one hundred gold pieces that gleamed in the light. The coins looked as if they had been freshly minted. His eyes moved on to another object that instantly made him forget about the stones and gold. Nestled in the corner and partially concealed by coins was a key, its base heart-shaped and instantly familiar. With his other hand he hesitantly pushed the coins aside and lifted it up, finding it attached to two other, identical keys via a chain.

The Recollection opened in his mind and he saw his mother holding the same keys before her, a half-smile on her handsome face. The Sword of Binding flared behind her, calling to him stronger than ever before. Coronos' voice echoed in his mind.

"She also passed to me three enchanted keys and whispered so no other would hear. "The keys to the chamber of the Sword of Binding," she told me. Only one key would work. The Holder of the Keys would know which one, and no other. The other keys were certain death. I tried to protest, but her will was sacrosanct. I still have the keys, but only the goddess knows how to reach the sword."

'Asaph?' Navarr's voice filtered down to him.

He blinked as the Recollection closed and he looked at the concerned king.

'Are you all right?' Navarr repeated.

'Sorry...Yes. The keys are special. They lead to a sword; the great Sword of Binding. It's somewhere in Draxa and it calls to me.'

The King laid a hand on his shoulder. 'A sense of destiny makes us strong, it makes us fearless. Those without it lack purpose. Find what it is you have to do, and do it.'

'You sound like my Father,' Asaph smiled. He looked at the keys, then at the contents of the box. Taking only two gold coins, he put them in his pocket along with the three keys, then he closed the lid.

'When Drax belongs to us once more, I'll use the infinity stones to rebuild it.' Asaph stood tall.

'Spoken like a true king, King Asaph,' Navarr patted him on the back. 'I'll be there to help you when we get through this. You'll have many allies.'

'Thank you,' said Asaph. 'I will need them. On another note, Issa and I plan to leave for Myrn. We don't want to leave you, but this is important. The seers have requested that she go, and I don't want her going alone. I also think I'll learn something there myself.'

'I don't want you to go, either,' said Navarr. 'We could do with a Dragon Lord defending this castle and assisting my soldiers, but I can see that you must. The seers protect ancient wisdom; you'll undoubtedly learn a lot. I just hope it will be something to end this infernal war and free Maioria for good.' The King's eyes were fiery.

Asaph smiled. 'I would like that more than anything in the world. But don't worry, should things get really bad here, we'll return. Fast. It's my deepest hope that I can find the Sword of Binding and with it awaken the dragons I know to be sleeping far in the north. With them on our side we have a greater chance of defeating the enemy.'

'It almost sounds too good to be true.' Navarr laughed. 'If you believe there are still dragons out there, I'll believe it too. Come now. Fancy sharing some wine or dwarven spirits with my dukes and I? I have the night free and could do with a drink after that bloody battle.'

'Sure, I'd be honoured.' Asaph nodded, pleased to be invited. 'Looking forward to it.'

CHAPTER 4

Council of War

ISSA returned from Edarna's via Duskar's stable in Castle Carvon's grounds, her dragon armour packed neatly in her shoulder pack.

She didn't fancy wearing it just yet and scaring everybody with her change of appearance. The black horse poked his head out, ears pricked forward, and whinnied at her over a mouthful of hay.

'There you are.' She stroked his nose and checked him over, relieved to see he was all right and unscathed.

'He bolted, Lady Issa. During the attack,' said the stable boy hurrying over to her from another horse's stall. He had freckles scattered over his nose and an eager look about him. 'Clever horse unbolted the door and ran to the forest, almost trampling down the guards. We think he was looking for you. Anyways, he returned of his own accord at dawn.'

'Clever horse,' Issa nodded. 'Well, at least he's safe now. Thank you for looking after him. He certainly deserves an extra bucket of oats.'

She passed the boy a copper coin and his eyes lit up.

'Absolutely, Lady Issa, thank you.' The boy hurried away to find the oats.

Back in Castle Carvon, she opened the door to her room to find a strange sight. Sitting on her bed and facing each other were Maggot and Ehka. The demon and the raven both turned to look at her, as if they had been deep in conversation and she had disturbed them. Ehka cocked his head at her and Maggot tugged an ear under his chin then let it flick back up on his head.

Issa raised an eyebrow. 'I thought you didn't like this awful bright world or any of the living things in it,' she said to the demon.

Maggot stuck out a red tongue and looked at his toes. 'It *is* awfully bright but it's not as bad as it used to be. And King says I must come often, to protect you.'

'I don't need protection,' she said, 'and I certainly don't want you getting in harm's way. Wherever I go, harm follows. I'll never forgive myself if you get hurt, Maggot.'

She scratched his bald head. Initially he flinched, then, as though making the decision to enjoy it, he closed his eyes and grinned. Issa laughed when his tongue rolled out.

'How are things at Carmedrak Rock?' she asked, taking a brush to her hair and sitting before her dresser as her thoughts turned to Gedrock.

'We have our home back.' Maggot's expression was awe-filled. 'And the Grazen and Shadow Demons are united after hundreds of years at war. But I still miss my secret place overlooking the greeb forest and the Bone Mountains. Carmedrak Rock is full of tunnels, though. I could explore it forever and never know it all. And it isn't as scary as when I had that awful spear.'

'That was a brave thing you did, Maggot. Great Carmedrak, Zorock and King are well pleased with you.'

The little demon gave a grin that spread from ear to ear.

Issa paused her brushing. 'Hmm, I've been meaning to for a while now; I think it's time to pay your king a visit,' she murmured.

Not wanting to return to the Murk, she'd been putting it off. Now her bargain with the Shadow Demons was complete, she didn't hear them in her mind or dreams anymore. But she still had to keep them close; one day soon she would need their help against the Maphraxies.

She stood and changed into her dragon armour, a smile spreading across her face. She wanted to look the part if she was going to meet the King of demons. For added effect, she buckled on her sword then took her knife from the dresser. Dipping her finger in a jug of water she drew the symbol of the Murk—two crescent moons back to back with a straight line crossing the two—on the wooden floor, then nicked her thumb with the knife.

Understanding what she was doing, Maggot slipped off the bed and clung to her leg. Ehka flew to her shoulder. She watched two drops of her bright blood fall and splatter on the symbol. The crescent moons flashed green and then hissed green smoke, which swiftly engulfed them.

First appeared the familiar, green crystal shard, and then a whole cavern of green crystals materialised. Issa stood upon a smooth, dark emerald floor. Uncut quartz crusted what could only be described as an enormous cave. The rough gem ceiling stretched for several yards above her. Lit braziers made the rocks gleam and flash. It was stunning and she found herself gawking as Gedrock spoke.

'I had a feeling you were coming,' the King's deep, demonic voice rumbled, sending shivers down her spine. 'You are the first human to ever see this place. Welcome.'

Gedrock's huge face materialised out of the shadows, followed by his muscular body. His yellow eyes and narrowing black-slitted pupils made her take an involuntary step back. Even though the demon was a friend, of sorts, and she had fought beside him, she couldn't keep her heart rate from rising. She ran a hand through her hair and let out an apprehensive breath.

'I've been meaning to come to see how you're doing but we have had trouble with our enemies. I am honoured to be here in this stunning place.'

As she spoke, Maggot sat on the crystal floor and stared at his reflection.

Gedrock nodded. 'This is the heart of our kingdom. You look like the Raven Queen I saw so long ago in the vision that raven gave me.' He indicated to Ehka still perched on her shoulder.

She assumed he meant her dragon armour and gave him a wry smile. 'I guess not all destinies are bad. However, I'm concerned for Maggot's safety. Why do you send him? I cannot guarantee his protection. Wherever I go, danger and death follow.'

'Maggot has been told to look out for you as a gift from us and a reminder of the agreement we had. We are vulnerable as we rebuild ourselves. We need your alliance and can ill afford to have humans invading and warring with us.'

'That will never happen whilst I'm alive, I promise you,' Issa resolved.

'Maggot can look after himself, and he also comes of his own free will,' Gedrock said.

Issa blinked in surprise and looked down at the little demon. Maggot glared at the floor, ears twitching. She almost laughed aloud at his attempt to appear nonchalant.

'Ever since he reached you beyond the Abyss, he's felt a connection to you,' said Gedrock. 'Great Zorock has put it there.'

Issa was surprised. Would Zorock really have done that? Not knowing what to say, she mumbled, 'I'm honoured.'

'Why do you really come here, Raven Queen?' Gedrock asked, ever in his hard, direct manner.

Issa suppressed a smile at his keen observation. There *was* another reason she was here and Gedrock was always able to sense intention. There was no point being other than direct with him.

'Our homeland was attacked; the very heart of our stronghold. We fought them off but are badly shaken. We'll be attacked again, and by greater numbers. I am considering what needs to be done in retaliation. We cannot always be on the defensive. If Baelthrom and his Maphraxies defeat the Free Peoples of Maioria, the Murk will fall to him too. This you know. So I've come here to be sure that I have your allegiance when the time comes.'

'What is it you require exactly?' Gedrock asked, his unreadable eyes reflecting the green crystals glittering around them.

'I need your demon soldiers, as many as you can spare, to fight upon Maioria's soil when the last battle comes, as surely it must. Just as we fought against the greater demons on the earth of the Murk. I cannot say when these battles will be, but they will be soon and I need you to be ready.'

'Your enemy is unknown to us,' Gedrock said. His voice was thoughtful rather than dismissive. He turned to Maggot.

'Maggot,' said the King.

The little demon tried to stand up tall and looked anywhere else but at his King.

'You will spend as much time with the Raven Queen as you can, particularly when she engages her enemies. Learn about them and report back to us everything you see.'

Maggot nodded curtly, his tail flicking nervously.

Gedrock looked at Issa. 'When I have chosen them, I will send a handful of demon warriors to assist you when you engage the enemy. That way we can faster learn this enemies' way.'

'Thank you, King Gedrock. Again, I am honoured,' Issa bowed deeply and smiled.

'Why are you smiling?' Asaph asked over dinner, his fork filled with delicious pie pausing on its journey to his mouth.

He'd been much brighter of late, Issa thought. Especially since their long discussions on everything that had happened regarding Cirosa. Perhaps it was knowing that she didn't hate him for falling for the evil seductions of the twisted High Priestess. Just thinking about the woman made her angry and vengeful. Imagining them being intimate with each other made her shiver with cold. But Asaph had been enchanted by her evil magic given to her by Baelthrom. Issa couldn't blame him for that, she just hoped he was free of her for good.

The smile on his face now pushed away all thoughts of Cirosa and her own grin broadened even more as she thought about the demons.

'Hah! I just can't believe we have the demons on our side. I thought they might renege on our deal once they had won back their homeland, but they haven't.'

'Hmph,' Asaph frowned. 'I'll believe that when I see it. I still can't bring myself to trust them. I wish I had been with you and Marakon, there in the Murk.'

'I told you not to worry about it. The battle belonged to Marakon and his knights, I merely assisted him. I'll be honest, I didn't want to. After all, why should we help demons when Maioria is burning? Well, now it's obvious. If we hadn't helped the demons, we would never have made this powerful allegiance. Having demons fighting alongside us could, oddly, be the one thing that wins back Maioria.'

Asaph stayed silent and mopped up the gravy on his plate with a piece of bread.

He'd warm to the thought, she was sure. She carried on. 'What we desperately need is a council of war. It just seems the Feylint Halanoi are functioning alone with only King Navarr truly supporting them. It's not enough. We need a much bigger order of the Knights of the Raven formed from exceptional soldiers within the Feylint Halanoi—an elite band of the most skilled warriors. We need stronger allegiances between all countries and all races. And the Wizards' Circle needs to pull together all their students in magic.'

'What are you planning?' asked Asaph. He had that familiar suspicious look in his eye he always got whenever he thought she was putting her life in danger.

'I don't know, I'm not a war leader or even a commander, but I think we need to attack, and we need to do it soon and attack hard. I'm sick of being on the defensive all the time. All it says to the enemy is that we are weak.' She sipped her wine.

'You heard what Marakon said, we've been attacking them in the north for years and lost countless soldiers,' Asaph sighed.

'Not the north,' Issa shook her head. 'We just need to hold them off Frayon with a solid wall of defence. There's no point attacking where they are strong and where their attention is fully focused.'

Asaph looked at her expectantly. She let go of her breath.

'I've been thinking about it a lot and, though I'm not sure, I think we should attack enemy-held lands in the south-east.'

Asaph's eyes widened.

'Think about it,' she said, setting down her wine. 'Remember, the Karalanths are massing in the mountains of Davono and gathering their clans. They want to take back what was once Karalanthia. If we can convince Davono to join them, and the dwarves, and maybe even the Atalanphs, we could invade west Venosia—don't look at me like that, I'm not crazy. Ambitious, yes. Baelthrom will never suspect it.'

'And how do you propose we even get there?' Asaph's voice was sceptical. 'You would still need the expertise of the Feylint Halanoi. How would you march them across the whole continent?'

Issa grinned at him. 'Velistor.'

'What?'

'Velistor. With it, we can find and open Maioria's Transplaneal Gates, as Freydel calls them. If that fails, we'll try the more numerous demon tunnels. Something has to work.'

Asaph sighed and rubbed his eyes. 'I only half believe in those gates and I sure as hell don't like the sound of demon tunnels. It sounds crazy.'

'I know, but we have to try; we have to do something. We only ever defend and look where that has got us. They're now on Frayon soil and the Uncharted Lands have likely already fallen. We can't go on like this.

'I've already asked the Wizards' Circle to start searching for the ancient gates. Any texts or folklores they might come across. Yes, it's a long shot, but I'm tired of fleeing, of living in fear, of losing.'

'Me too,' Asaph agreed. 'I want to attack and win as well. If only I could awaken the dragons, I think I could lead them.' Pain passed across his features and she touched his hand.

'I know you grieve for Faelsun and the Dragon Dream,' said Issa, noting the second flicker of pain. She dared not admit even to herself how powerful Baelthrom had become since he'd gained the dragon orb. 'I'm sorry, I wish it hadn't happened. But that is why we must start counter-attacking. One of their key spies has been removed now, poor Marakon, and we can attack with stealth and surprise. I can think of no other way. We're all afraid of war but war is upon us. I want revenge, and as poisonous as vengeance might be, I cling to it because it keeps me strong and my resolve firm.'

Asaph picked up his wine and sat back, his blue eyes beholding her. 'How and when do we do this?'

'I think we should have a meeting with everyone; the wizards, the seers, Navarr, Marakon, Bokaard, Edarna, the Feylint Halanoi... Everyone. We must form a council of war and propose this plan at the earliest convenience.

'I've been thinking about something else too,' she added. 'I've decided to go to Myrn, probably straight after the council. I'd like it if you came too.'

'Of course!' He beamed, took her hand and brought it to his lips. 'I need a holiday, especially with you.'

With King Navarr's royal ability to send couriers scurrying in every direction at a moment's notice, the war council was arranged for the very next morning. The importance of such a meeting was not lost on the king who had so recently seen his kingdom attacked.

It was with a certain amount of nerves that Issa walked the long, wood-panelled corridor towards the massive, ornately carved doors of the meeting room, her new Dread Dragon boots echoing loudly in the hallway. Her armour and Grast'anth's sword at her side gave her the confidence she felt she needed to conduct this war meeting.

Two guards stood to attention before the doors. They were dressed in thick white tights, navy blue tunics and small hats with a single white feather. The polished short swords that were strapped to their waists gleamed, as did their shining black-patent shoes.

They looked harmless, maybe even silly, but Issa knew they were highly trained soldiers—the king's own personal guard—and thus his very best. They knew how to use their swords most expertly, the king had proudly informed her, and had at least five other weapons hidden about their bodies.

Issa took a breath, hoping she was ready for the meeting and knowing she never would be. She had spent hours last night fleshing out her ideas and plans on paper with Asaph, only to rip them up again. She was not a great speaker, nor steeped in the art of warfare. She wasn't a battle-seasoned commander and couldn't rally anyone to her call. All she had was a vision and a vague plan of how to get there; attack the enemy, invade their lands. She just couldn't seem to formulate the right words or find the correct terminology. After a final fit of frustration, she'd given up planning anything and decided to simply speak her thoughts.

She slowed as she neared the doors. She was late, deliberately so, to make sure everyone had some time to chat amongst themselves before she arrived. The guards bowed slightly and opened the doors. She stepped into the room.

Sweeping her eyes left and right, she never failed to be awed by the grandeur of Castle Carvon. The rectangular boardroom was larger than her entire house on Little Kammy. Dark wood covered the floors, and the high, white ceiling was decorated with flowers and leaves made cleverly out of plaster. They filled the coving and spiralled inwards to the unlit crystal chandelier that held a hundred candles.

Decorating the far wall was an impressive blue marble-fronted fireplace. Within it, a small fire crackled, taking away the morning chill. To her right, sunlight streamed into the room from windows which reached from the floor all the way up to the ceiling. The heavy, grey velvet curtains were pulled far back to let in as much light as possible.

Garnet red wallpaper reached to waist height, after which the walls were painted white. Unusually, there was only one picture and one tapestry in the room. The tapestry hung on the wall opposite the fire and as she entered she glanced over her shoulder at it, sparing a moment to marvel at the intricate needlework. It was filled with people, animals and trees, and too complexly detailed to decipher what it depicted with merely a glance.

The lone picture hung above the fireplace. Gold-painted scrolls framed a life-sized portrait of a man and a woman who looked to be in their fifties. The man was striking with sharp cheekbones and a short white beard flecked with black. He held an intense look that dared anyone to utter a lie in his presence. A firm but just man, Issa judged.

The woman's expression was softer, but her blue eyes were equally penetrating. The previous King and Queen of Carvon, she realised, recognising them from the other paintings in the castle. She could see the likeness to King Navarr. The painted couple carefully surveyed those gathered at the meeting.

She turned her attention to those seated around the long mahogany table dominating the room. They were mostly men, chatting. The wizards Freydel, Drumblodd, Averen, Haelgon, Luren and Domenon were on the left with the king's chair in the centre, empty. Asaph sat beside the king's chair and looked rather uncomfortable about it. Marakon sat next to him, followed by Bokaard.

She caught Marakon's gaze and suddenly felt terrible for what had happened. Since the night Ehka had pecked out his white eye they had barely talked—mostly because Marakon was too sick and in pain. He gave a half-smile as if sensing her worry and forgiving her just a little.

He looked stronger now, though his face was pale and his features drawn. *Ravaged by guilt and betrayal, no doubt.* She had Jarlain to thank for allaying her anger at the man who had betrayed them. The woman who rode the bear had told her how he suffered, and her devotion to Marakon had moved Issa deeply. Whatever the man had done unwittingly through being tricked, all his life he had faithfully served his country and the Free Peoples of Maioria. For that Issa could forgive him. He'd had dark magic woven around him, just like Asaph, and both had suffered terribly.

She returned his smile then wondered where Jarlain was. She had not returned to Carvon with Marakon. Perhaps she preferred to stay with her beast in the forest. It was unlikely Navarr would host such an animal in his home. Though rumours of a bear rider had spread, Issa doubted that the people of Carvon were ready to let the huge beast wander their streets.

Beside Bokaard sat two older men in grey military uniform with the Feylint Halanoi tabard over the top. She didn't know them. Maybe they were Marakon's superiors. She couldn't imagine the half-elf having anyone more senior than he was.

Next to them sat the only other woman in the room; Edarna. The witch's face was positively mischievous and she winked at Issa. A meow came from somewhere, letting her know Mr Dubbins was present.

Opposite the king's chair was an empty seat, to which she walked, feeling everyone's gaze heavy upon her.

'Greetings, ladies and gentlemen,' she nodded to them politely and sat down. As soon as she had, the king's chamberlain entered the room from a side door and all eyes turned to him.

'The King arrives. Please stand.' The chamberlain bowed stiffly.

Everyone dutifully stood as King Navarr stalked into the room, a frown of determination on his face.

'Greetings all. Sit, please sit,' Navarr wafted his hand as if to do away with the aplomb and get on with business.

His fur-trimmed, red velvet cloak flowed out behind him as he walked. Underneath he wore a cream-coloured suit with medals of honour decorating the left lapel.

The chamberlain rushed to keep ahead of him and pulled out his chair, only just managing to push it in in time as the king sat down. The chamberlain passed a hand over his forehead.

'Thank you, Sir Kenon. Now then,' said Navarr, his eyes passing over everyone, instantly forgetting the dismissed chamberlain who silently stepped away. A big grin spread across the King's face, 'Let's talk war.'

Issa nodded, appreciating the direct manner and coughed to clear her throat. The last thing she wanted was a long, boring meeting where nothing got decided. War was upon them, there was no time to waste. She jumped straight to the point.

'Gentlemen and lady,' Issa sat straight in her chair as she addressed the assembled party. 'It is my proposal that we combine armies to create a powerful force and attack West Venosia now while the enemy is least expecting it.'

Ignoring the murmurs spreading around the table, she pressed on. 'We must attack hard, fast and as soon as we can. Too long have we spent on defence, allowing the enemy to think we are weak. Even we think we're weak. But I tell you we are not. We are strong. I see it in the eyes of the ordinary people walking the streets. The heart of our free land has been attacked, and we sure as hell must attack back.'

'Ridiculous. Where will we get the numbers from?' asked the Feylint Halanoi officer with the monocle. The monocle made one of his eyes twice as big as the other.

Issa held his gaze steady but Haelgon spoke before she could. 'I can have a thousand soldiers ready to sail from Atalanph within a week. A thousand more in two weeks. If we all agree to this, of course.'

The officer took off his monocle and squinted at the wizard.

'I can start moving our soldiers immediately, they are already waiting to join the Feylint Halanoi,' Drumblodd nodded, emboldened by Haelgon. 'A couple of hundred at least. More if I don't send another unit west to join King Navarr's army.'

Issa smiled. Already there were two armies waiting to go.

'What about Queen Thora?' Issa rested her eyes on Domenon.

The wizard leant forwards. 'The Queen does not like war being brought near her shores, nor will she enjoy her land filling with foreign armies, but I will speak to her and try to convince her.'

'Thank you,' Issa nodded. She had expected more resistance from him. The recent attacks really had shaken everyone to the core.

'But how will this ever work?' asked the other officer, smoothing his thick black moustache between finger and thumb. 'Nobody knows the terrain nor what horrors might be there. Maybe Baelthrom's war factories are stationed there. Maybe the Dark Dwarves have their empire lurking beneath the surface. Everything is an unknown and that is ripe for a slaughtering. Attacks like these take months of careful planning.'

Issa began to realise why the Feylint Halanoi were slow and largely ineffectual. Already her proposal had met with the most resistance from these officers. The resigned look on Marakon's face told her he felt the same and had attended these meetings more times than he cared to. She felt sorry for him, it certainly was frustrating. Perhaps they had been too long at war and were too tired, their motivation low.

'We don't have months, we don't even have weeks,' said Issa. 'We could all be slaughtered anywhere, any day. Baelthrom is too powerful now. We have to act and we have to act fast—'

'To act *this* fast is surely suicide,' growled the officer with the monocle, shoving it deeper into his fleshy face and squinting at the sheets of paper before him.

'To *not* act is suicide,' Issa said quietly.

She glanced at Marakon. He had not said anything yet and she sorely needed his thoughts on the matter. He leant back on his chair and folded his arms behind his head, waiting for her to say more. Was he trying to get her to be the leader? She clasped her hands on top of the table and looked at them.

'We have an army of Karalanths amassing at Davono's borders—'

'Karalanths,' scoffed Luren.

Freydel shot him a warning look and the young wizard smoothed his face.

'Karalanths,' Issa repeated, giving the young wizard a hard look. He turned away, colouring. 'They know the land like no other and they can lead us.'

'They *knew* the land,' said Bokaard.

'Yes, but still, there is no one better,' said Issa. 'You forget I have those who can help; ravens. If I ask them they will scout the lands unseen looking for places where we can land ships and attack. Regardless, gentlemen, if we ever want to regain the lands we have lost, we must attack. Push them back from Frayon and invade their bases. Let them know that we are strong.'

Nobody seemed as enthused as she was about the idea. They turned to each other and talked quickly amongst themselves. The wizards looked amicable, the soldiers sceptical. Asaph looked worried. Edarna smiled and nodded at her. Only she seemed impressed and, wearing a big grin, she dunked her biscuit into her teacup. Everyone else had largely ignored their tea.

Marakon leant forwards on the table.

'She's right.' His voice stilled everyone to silence and all eyes looked at the half-elf. 'Always we defend. Now we must attack. Nothing has worked, what have we to lose?'

'Everything we have left?' said the officer with the monocle.

'Those are the words of a soldier who is afraid,' said Marakon. 'One who fears to lose. Mark my words, ladies and gentlemen; he who dares, wins.'

Bokaard grinned and smiles spread across many of the wizards' faces. Issa nodded her thanks to Marakon and he winked.

'It's a very daring, dangerous, terrifying plan. I think we should do it.' Marakon's eye gleamed.

'There is one thing I need,' said Issa, holding Marakon's gaze. 'I need Marakon and all his knights and best soldiers at my side.'

'Done,' said Marakon slapping the table.

'How on Maioria do you propose to get thousands of soldiers from the north-west coast of Frayon to the south-east coast of Davono?' said the officer with the moustache. 'And how can we protect the north, the west, *and* Carvon?'

'We'll only take those soldiers we can spare,' said Navarr. 'We will not leave ourselves exposed.'

'We can't spare *any*,' said the officer smacking his fist on the table.

'We can spare what we must,' said the King, his chin firm.

'But what about the journey? It could take them months,' said Haelgon. 'Months of travelling slowly across Frayon whilst our borders are attacked.'

Everyone nodded and looked at her. Issa glanced at Marakon. A knowing grin spread across his face that mirrored her own.

'Velistor,' they said in unison.

'Oh no,' Asaph shook his head and slumped his shoulders. Freydel covered his eyes. Everyone else frowned and glanced at each other, confused.

'When the time comes, you won't need to spare Marakon until the very last moment. We'll either use the Transplaneal Gates or the ancient demon tunnels to get there,' said Issa, triumphantly.

Looks of horror spread across the faces of those before her.

CHAPTER 5

Meeting the Trinity

THE swirling magic cleared.

Issa wondered how she must look to the seers as she and Asaph materialised within the amethyst circle on Myrn, dressed in her Dread Dragon armour with Ehka perched on her shoulder. Now she wore dragon scale, his claws no longer dug into her shoulder quite so much.

She had one hand on Duskar's back and the other gripping Asaph's hand. He held the reins of Ironclad. The wooziness descended, making her sag. Duskar's flanks quivered and Asaph groaned.

'Freydel said the translocation sickness won't last long,' said Issa, gritting her teeth and trying not to vomit. But she could fight it no longer and sank down onto the grass. Asaph did the same and hung his head.

Naksu's familiar voice cut through the woozy fog. 'Welcome to the Western Isle of Tirry. Here, drink this. Edarna told me her recipe for the sickness.'

Issa took the small vial Naksu passed to her and, after a moment's hesitation remembering Edarna's potions, quickly downed the foul liquid.

'Ugh, that's definitely Edarna's recipe,' Issa grimaced. She glanced at Asaph as he drank his, and the disgust on his face soon matched her own.

Naksu chuckled.

'It's working though.' Issa nodded, already feeling the sickness recede. A little relieved, she looked around.

They were on a grass-covered hilltop surrounded by beautiful amethyst crystals, and chestnut and oak trees beyond them. Strong magic emanated from the amethysts and she was certain a faint hum came from them. It was lush and warm, the skies were blue, and the leaves of the trees only just beginning to turn brown with the oncoming autumn. The wooziness had almost gone, and she took a deep breath, enjoying the serenity of the Western Isle. Asaph stood and held out a hand to help her up.

Three other women were walking up the hill and they came to stand beside Naksu. All were seers dressed in pastel blue robes and holding white staves, and all were much older than Naksu. One seer was grey-haired and very old and stooped, but had a kindly face. Another was a middle-aged brunette with unruly greying hair, and the last was tall with white hair and sharp, clear eyes. They wore their hair long and unbound, and they all studied Issa intently. They gave the impression of being very wise. Issa felt more nervous under their gaze than she had when she'd first met the Wizards' Circle and been scrutinised by all those men. Maybe they sensed this for, as one, they smiled at her and Asaph.

'Welcome to the Isles of Tirry, Issalena Kammy and Asaph Dragon Lord,' said the tall, white-haired woman.

Asaph shuffled awkwardly at his title.

'We are the Trinity and I am Iyena.'

'I am Dar,' said the greying brunette making a small bow.

'And I am Suli,' said the oldest women, nodding her head.

'We have been looking forward to your coming here for a long time,' said Iyena. 'Naksu has told us all about you and we have seen many things in our sacred pools. Don't worry,' she held up her hands when Issa opened her mouth to speak, 'all things we have seen will be revealed to you. We do not hide the knowledge that has been gifted to us from those who seek it.

'Come, let us eat and talk and rest. You both look weary and we know you have seen the evil of war not a week past.'

Issa and Asaph followed the seers across the lush grassland and through a thick grove of orange trees laden with rich orange fruits. They were too taken up with the beauty of these mysterious isles to talk. The seers felt little need to speak as they walked, and so the short journey was spent in tranquil silence.

The sea between the isles was calm as they walked the jetty towards a white wood boat. Two men waited patiently to row them across. They took their seats and Issa watched with some excitement as the bigger island of Myrn approached. Its main port was small as ports went, but very busy with all manner of boats and ships coming and going. It was dominated by a huge Atalanph merchant ship filling the harbour. Its crew was busy loading and unloading crates and barrels, and the bellows of the captain could be heard.

Had her mother travelled these waters when she'd left Myrn carrying her? Issa liked to think that she had, it made her seem closer. Could her mother be here somewhere? Someone had to know who she was and where she had gone – surely they had records? Fraya had said she was kind yet strong, that she was tall with eyes like her own. Maybe someone would recognise her mother's face in her, but then, the older seers had not said anything yet.

The boat docked at a white-painted jetty and they walked the smooth paved streets into Oray, the tiny capital of the Isles of Tirry. There were no tall buildings, rickety steeples, smoking chimneys or grey slated roofs. Instead, pristine, round, white-domed houses lined the freshly swept streets. Each house was surrounded by a neat garden filled with herbs and flowers. Butterflies and bees danced cheerily among them.

Further into the centre, the houses became larger domed buildings that turned out to be shops. Their wide open doors were filled with wares; bread, fruit and vegetables, or clothing, or tools. Seers of all ages, mostly women and a handful of men, smiled at them as they passed. The city 'square' was not a square at all but a circle surrounded by shops. At its centre was a beautiful fountain shaped out of leaves and flowers.

'The fountain is also the main well,' Iyena explained.

Two giggling children filled up their flagons and splashed water at each other. Issa noticed that the streets were also set in circles; with the pretty, white domed houses spiralling out from the centre and back into the trees. The city was more like a town in size, and beautiful in its simplicity and cleanliness.

They came to a larger house and passed under an archway covered in purple clematis and entered a courtyard. On the patio stood a wrought iron table and chairs shaded by manicured grape vines. A young girl emerged from an outhouse and came to take their horses.

'We have a stable and a small paddock behind the house,' said Iyena. 'The horses won't be far and they'll be well looked after.'

Issa nodded and patted Duskar. She was surprised when he didn't make a fuss and followed the girl with his ears pricked forwards. Maybe the serenity of Myrn was calming him too.

'Why don't we take a seat and have some food? It's nearly dinnertime as it is and we have lots to discuss.' Iyena motioned to the chairs.

'I can always eat,' said Asaph, making her laugh.

Issa sat down on the cushioned chair beside him. The seers disappeared through a glass door leading into the house and soon emerged with other, younger, seers carrying plates of food, steaming bowls, fresh bread, water and wine. They set them out on the table and Issa inspected them, her stomach rumbling. Some of the dishes were deliciously pungent with spices she had never smelled before. She took a plate and spooned yellow rice onto it. It was rich, sweet and tasty.

'Those dishes are from Atalanph,' said Dar, pointing to the steaming dishes filled with some kind of lentils or pulses in thick, vivid red or orange sauces, 'and all the fruit and vegetables you see are grown on these isles.'

Issa nodded and eagerly began piling up her plate. As they ate, she caught Suli's eye and wondered if the woman had been watching her the whole time. The old seer smiled and her face creased into a thousand wrinkles.

'I may have come late to the Sisterhood, Iyena, but I recognise Tusarzan blood when I see it,' said Suli. 'My grandma was Tusarzan after all.'

'I wondered when you'd say something, Suli,' Iyena smiled.

Issa felt her cheeks colour as everyone looked at her. She set down her spoon. 'You know where I'm from? Do you know of my parents?'

'Hah, yes to the first,' Suli nodded. 'Tall and dark, graceful as an elf. Often gifted in magic, and we all know you are Daluni.

'But no to the second; I do not know your parents. As I said, I was late to join the seers, filled as my life was with family and hardships. Only I remain of a family of ten. The rest were taken by Baelthrom. It is my rage that keeps me strong and living long, but it gets in the way of my spiritual growth.' The old woman laughed and winked.

Issa wasn't quite sure how to respond to her comments and said, 'I'm sorry to hear that.'

Iyena laid a hand on hers. 'We have spoken at length on it but none of us are sure who your parents are. It is a little strange, but then, over the decades, many have come to Myrn and left in these turbulent times. We can assume that they are not with us now, though we have no idea where they might have gone. There is, however, a sacred place we can go to where you might find the answers. When the goddess wills it, all things are revealed to us as we have need.'

Issa nodded, masking her deep disappointment. 'I had hoped, with all my heart, that you would know.' Her parents now seemed more distant than ever.

Asaph squeezed her hand and Naksu gave a sympathetic smile.

'Moonlight.' Suli nodded knowingly. Seeing Issa frown, she said, 'Your name in Tusarzan. It means "moonlight".'

Issa tingled all over.

'And I'm the Dawn Bringer,' Asaph grinned at her.

Issa laughed at him.

'With a name like that, it's obvious your mother knew your destiny,' said Iyena looking up into the sky. 'Zanufey's Chosen…Perhaps that's why she whisked you away—to save you and us. We've been trying to piece together what we know of this story ever since Naksu first told us about you. Baelthrom's Dromoorai attacked us over twenty years ago. We almost lost our shield. Luckily we were able to react fast and hid ourselves deeper.

'But if your mother was here with you, surely she would have left then. I would, if I thought my child was being hunted by Baelthrom. If that is true, then she did it to protect Myrn.'

Issa swallowed, wondering what to think. Even her mother had had to flee because of her, the whole of Myrn had been jeopardised. She forced down another mouthful of spiced rice. It was delicious but she had lost her appetite.

'You cannot blame yourself for your mother's actions. There's great honour in such acts of heroism,' said Naksu quietly, reading Issa's emotions perfectly. 'Tonight, why don't we see if we can find out more about your mother?'

The thought lifted Issa's mood and she smiled. 'I'd like that very much. It's hard not knowing where you're from or who your parents are.'

She caught Asaph's gaze and saw her own pain reflected there. He forced a smile.

'Well, now you know you have Tusarzan heritage, so find honour and strength in that,' said Suli, giving her a warm smile.

Issa nodded, feeling better. The old seer was like the grandmother she'd never had. The lost and forgotten land of Tusarza now became filled with mystery and intrigue in her mind.

'It's a pity you were not raised a seer from a young age,' said Iyena. 'You would have had the chance to answer all your internal questions and quell the turmoil. And you would have a strong sense of self and placement in the world.'

'Is it too late? I know there's much I have to learn but...' Issa paused, wondering how to say what she was feeling without being rude. Becoming a seer just didn't feel necessary. Sure, their knowledge and wisdom were invaluable and she hungered for it; she wanted to learn everything they could teach her, but becoming a *seer* was as unnecessary as becoming a wizard or a witch, or anything else for that matter.

The seers all looked at her.

Issa sighed. 'I'm sorry, I don't know how to say it without seeming rude... But it just doesn't seem necessary that I become a seer—or, rather, that it's not so important. The world is changing fast and things that went before won't be important in the time to come. I apologise, I'm not explaining this very well.' She shrugged.

'No, on the contrary, please go on. What you say has meaning,' said Iyena, frowning in concentration.

'Well, as we know, the magic of the world remains divided ever since the Ancients orchestrated its division. But, over time, divisions have arisen with the people also. It's as Freydel taught me, things that occur in the macrocosm, appear also in the microcosm.' said Issa. 'The elves have left and the Ancients have been destroyed...In the past, wizards and seers were one. When the orbs were whole the magic was pure. It's such a long time ago now but I dream of a future where the people are united. The wisdom of seers and wizards would be far stronger if they worked together.'

Issa expected to see frowns, but she saw smiles instead.

' "When the world is in pieces and entering the void, there will come one in whom all things are made whole",' said Dar, shaking her mane of hair. 'That is the ancient prophecy written by a seer called Yoo. Could the Raven Queen be this great unifier?'

Issa's eyes went wide. 'I don't know how it will be done, I only know that it *should* be done. It's obvious. Even without Baelthrom, it will take a long time to get from here to there. Baelthrom is a master of war and we are all divided in so many ways. I'm almost beginning to see how he has turned us against each other, by luck and by design. I still can't decide if the Ancients should have ever split the orbs.'

'The time for divisions has certainly run its course,' Iyena said, looking weary. 'Perhaps talks with the Wizards' Circle should begin again, though I wish it were they who'd come to us. Always it looks like we are begging…'

Issa wanted to know more about what hung between the wizards and the seers, but the frowns of the seers stilled her tongue. With a rediscovered appetite, she filled up her plate, noticing Asaph was already finishing his second; the conversation had certainly done nothing to mar his appetite.

'Asaph Dragon Lord,' said Iyena, cupping her teacup in her hands. They had finished eating and Issa was full to bursting. The young seers returned from the house and began clearing away the plates. Asaph smiled at the seer, looking nervous as she spoke.

'We mustn't forget that the last Dragon Lord upon Maioria sits before us. We are honoured. I cannot even remember when a Dragon Lord last came to Myrn. Certainly not in my lifetime.

'There are many things concerning recent events that we would like to know, if you would both honour us by sharing your knowledge?'

Issa nodded, then dropped her gaze. She didn't want to recount what had happened in the Storm Holt. She trusted the seers, but she didn't know them well and talking about her pact with demons always made her uncomfortable. Demon-speakers were executed, and that was enough to make her want to keep her mouth shut.

'We have also seen terrible things concerning the Dragon Dream,' Iyena continued. 'One of our seers has seen darkness and destruction, a world with two suns turning black. We knew then what had befallen the Dragon Dream. Such a terrible thing…After, she saw dragons rising from snow.'

Issa glanced at Asaph. His face was pale.

Asaph looked at his hands. 'The Dragon Dream is no more. Losing the Orb of Air, the dragon orb, weakened it and made Baelthrom strong.'

With a start, Issa remembered the orb she had left in her pack on Duskar's back. 'Oh, our saddlebags!' she said, sitting up.

'It's all right, they'll be quite safe,' said Iyena. 'The stable girls will have taken them off the horses. If there is something you need, we can go and get them.'

Issa nodded and got to her feet. She trusted their things would be perfectly fine on Myrn, but she wanted them near, nevertheless.

Whilst Naksu, Suli and Dar engaged Asaph in conversation about the Dragon Dream, Issa followed the leader of the seers along the cobbled path through the grass towards a row of stables.

'Naksu told me everything about your time in the Storm Holt,' said Iyena, an understanding smile on her face.

'Demon speakers are executed,' said Issa, looking at the ground.

'There are few demon speakers these days, and those who are involved in the black arts. You, clearly, aren't,' said Iyena. 'And I suspect your relationship to the Underworld will have great importance in the turbulent times to come. In the history of Maioria, you are the first to form a positive relationship with the demons of the Murk.'

Issa blushed under Iyena's gaze. 'I didn't do it by choice. I only hope they will do as they say and help us fight in our coming battles. I know very well that demons cannot be trusted.'

'You are wise to have caution,' Iyena nodded.

They paused beside Duskar's stable. He stuck his nose out and nudged Issa. She scratched behind his ears. Ehka perched on his stable door, dozing. A stable girl stuck her head round the corner and Iyena motioned to her.

'Yes, Seer Iyena?' the girl said.

'Please collect their saddlebags and give them to Asaph, the young man seated beside Dar.'

'Yes, Seer Iyena,' the girl curtsied and ran off.

'So, you saw the Demon Lord Zorock?' There was bright intrigue in Iyena's eyes.

'Yes, he saved my life. But as grateful as I am, I don't care to see him again ... He's rather terrifying,' Issa added under her breath.

Iyena chuckled. 'There is more to how you got the spear, Velistor, isn't there? Someone tells me you have made a loyal friend.'

Issa frowned, wondering what the seer knew. 'You mean Maggot? Yes, well, he's a small shadow demon, and without him, I doubt I would have retrieved the spear at all.'

Issa felt the Flow move—move in a way as if it were parting, like curtains. Something pressed against her leg, but when she looked down there was nothing there. As she stared she saw her boot indenting as if something was indeed pressing upon her.

'What the...' she began.

With a small chuckle, Iyena raised her hand. 'It's all right. You can come through, little one.'

Issa frowned. Then she felt the Flow smooth and relax. A shadow bulged next to her leg, then Maggot's face materialised, his thick red tongue darting out to lick his protruding tooth. His yellow eyes were wide and they fearfully flicked from her to the seer and back again.

'Maggot, what on Maioria are you doing here? It's all right, she won't hurt you,' said Issa.

One clawed hand materialised and scratched his head. 'You called me.' His tiny shoulders shrugged.

'I could feel pressure on our shield the moment you spoke his name,' Iyena explained. 'The Trinity are keyed to the shield that covers and protects out isles. I relaxed the shield to let him through. The bond between you must be strong for him to find you here.'

'Perhaps, but even so, how can he come here from the demon world?' said Issa, reaching down to scratch the top part of his head that he was struggling to reach with his short arms. He let out a sigh and grinned. He was always scratching when he came to Maioria, the very air seemed to irritate his skin. Duskar reached his head down to sniff the demon and Ehka opened one eye to look at him.

'Humans themselves are walking portals to other places,' explained

Iyena. 'Everything is energy, remember?'

Issa nodded, but she didn't fully understand.

'When you go to a place, you share energy with that place—you make an imprint on each other. In the same manner, people make imprints on all those they meet. It seems that you and Maggot are linked in some way. Just like the ring you wear forms a link to Asaph which is visible in the Flow.'

'Maybe through the power of Zorock,' Issa said, half to herself as she fiddled with her flame ring.

'It could be.' Iyena grinned. 'Having a friend on call can only be a good thing. Now then, Maggot, I've heard all about you.' The seer bent down but Maggot slipped behind Issa's legs and peered between them at the seer.

'How do you know?' Issa asked. 'I thought I only told Freydel and Asaph about him.'

Iyena looked at her with a knowing smile and stood up. She reached into her robe and pulled out a beautiful round vial. Etched into the thick, clear glass, were flowers and leaves. She gently rubbed it and the contents began to glow bright green.

'Urgh,' said Maggot, wrinkling up his nose. 'A swamp fairy!'

Iyena unstoppered the glass bottle and spoke soothingly. 'Come on. Come out and say hello. You can sleep after.'

The light in the bottle wiggled then shot out with a loud buzz. It whizzed around in circles, as if glad to be out of the bottle, then buzzed in Issa's face like a fly. She wafted it back.

'They're so annoying. And they stink.' Maggot huffed and folded his arms. The green spark circled down gracefully and settled on the top of his head. He lifted a hand as if to squash it then sighed and dropped his arm.

'Miss me?' a high-pitched voice squeaked.

'No,' Maggot growled.

'Liar!' squealed the fairy.

'Hmph,' said Maggot, and clawed the ground with a toe. 'Maybe a bit.'

'It was you!' Issa said, staring at Iyena.

The seer laughed. 'Me what?'

'You sent the swamp fairy. To help. To find the spear?'

Iyena nodded. 'You can't leave everything to chance, can you? After all, the goddess helps those who help themselves.'

'You really sent the fairy to help me? How? Where did you find her?'

Maggot had told her how the swamp fairy had come out of the green crystal just to annoy him and thwart his mission from god. In the end, he'd conceded, without the fairy's help, neither of them would have been able to steal the spear from the Demon Wizard Karhlusus.

'Swamp fairies are one of the few creatures who exist halfway between Maioria and the Murk. Which is why I sent her to help you,' said Iyena.

The fairy giggled. Iyena smiled down at the green spark. 'Thiashar and I have a friendship that began many years ago when her home and family were destroyed. Now she prefers to stay inside her bottle never far from my side.

'I feed and house her, and she runs errands for me and finds out all sorts of information. So, in that way, we help each other.'

'I'm a princess, you know,' squeaked the green spark.

'I lost my home and family too, so I know how you feel,' said Issa, still stunned at how everything had come to pass.

The fairy buzzed but remained on top of Maggot's head. He didn't shake her off and instead sat down scowling as if to make himself seem her fierce protector.

The fairy rolled around the bald surface of his head then slid down his arm to the floor. In a flash of glittering light, a green being crouched beside Maggot. She was fine-boned, very slender, and probably less than two feet tall if she stood up. Her skin was emerald green and her face was small and delicate with a pointed nose and chin, long ears and dark green eyes.

Strange wispy rags adorned the creature and long thin wings like a mayfly's lay folded on her back. She crouched on the ground staring up at Issa, an uncertain grin forming on her face. She wasn't pretty, not like other fairies, but she wasn't ugly like Maggot either. With a giggle, she became a spark of green light again and jumped onto Maggot's head.

'She told me all about Maggot and you,' said Iyena. 'It's a handy way to keep me informed as to what is going on in the Murk.' The seer winked.

'You mean a spy?' Issa grinned wickedly.

'Hah, well, you could call her that.' Iyena tapped her nose. 'I prefer to call her my Informer.'

Issa laughed. 'Well, thank you for looking out for me. I'm very glad you sent her to help, otherwise we really wouldn't have retrieved the spear.'

'Come, Thiashar, you can rest now,' Iyena held out the vial. With a sound like a yawn the fairy slowly rose into the air and disappeared inside the bottle. Maggot lifted his hand as if to wave. Iyena stoppered the vial and tucked it inside her robes. The little demon's shoulders slumped as if he were sad the fairy had gone.

'Don't dislike them as much as before?' Issa raised an eyebrow at the demon. He sniffed and shrugged then looked away, making her laugh. She bent down and patted his head, making him grin again.

'There is something special I would like to do tonight at one of our sacred springs,' said Iyena. 'But for now, let's return to the others, rest, and meet again later. We'll come to you an hour before midnight.'

The seer smiled enigmatically, making Issa wonder. Would she meet another strange creature, learn a new secret or finally find out about her parents? She suddenly couldn't wait for tonight to come.

CHAPTER 6

Fire and Water

THE young seer curtsied, turned and shut the front door, leaving Asaph and Issa standing alone in the small, domed house at the edge of Oray.

A beautiful, pink crystal mosaic covered the floor and emanated a faint light. The house was round and the central main room was filled with reclining cushions. Against one wall stood a wooden table and four chairs. Four rooms with partially drawn, plain curtains surrounded the central room and two of them contained beds.

'Finally, our own home,' Issa smiled. Asaph grinned.

Ehka nestled down on one of the colourful cushions and shut his eyes. The sun was setting and its rays burst full through the window, casting the white walls ablaze in orange. There came a knock at the door and a different young seer carrying a bundle of towels and clothes stepped inside.

'Iyena sent me to tell you that the water is hot if you would like a bath.'

Seeing them frown, the girl walked over to a room and pulled back a pair of curtains to reveal a small wet room complete with a ceramic bath. A half-pipe stuck out of the wall, and when the girl turned the nozzle above it, hot, steaming water gushed out into the bath.

'Wow!' Asaph began inspecting the pipe and where it led.

The girl smiled. 'The spring here is hot, like many on the Isles. There's wine and cake in one of the cupboards,' she added, then left them to explore.

Excited by hot, running water, Issa barely heard her shut the door. 'My own bath,' she sighed and swirled her hand in the water. 'I'm going in first,' she said firmly.

'Oh really?' said Asaph, coming close and stroking her arm. 'Who says I'm not joining you?'

He pulled her to him, making her stomach flutter as he bent to kiss her. She hesitated then found her passion awakening.

'Perhaps this isn't prudent,' she said when they paused for breath, her face pressed against his chest where his shirt was partially unbuttoned. She was all too aware of the firmness of his muscles and the smoothness of his tanned skin. 'I mean, this is a seer's house and not our own.'

Asaph laughed and ran his hands down her back. 'I don't think they would know or even care. And besides, you look so ravishing in your new armour.'

'I thought it was less revealing,' said Issa, shocked.

'Well, it hugs here,' he passed a hand over her hips, 'and here,' his hands trailed across her abdomen making her catch her breath, 'and especially here…' His hands wrapped around her back and squeezed her bottom, making her yelp in feigned shock as he pulled her firmly against him again.

He kissed her and Issa's head span dizzily. She began to feel as if she were in a carriage that was moving faster and faster and she couldn't slow it down. She wanted to see more of him and found herself reaching up to unbutton his shirt fully. Her hands trembled a little and her heart beat faster.

She pushed the shirt off his shoulders and trailed her hands over his chest, liking it when his nipples hardened. For the first time, she could look clearly at the flame scar on his chest. She touched it lightly and heard his sharp intake of breath. Had she hurt him? She looked up but his eyes were closed and he made no move to stop her. Her fingers tingled when she touched it again, and then her raven mark tingled as well.

Asaph undid the fastenings on her armour and pushed the leather jerkin off her shoulders. She let it fall to the floor and closed her eyes, enjoying his touch on her thighs as he slipped off her leggings. He held her against him and kissed her hungrily, his hands hot on her underclothes. His whole body was hot against hers and when the firmness of his groin pressed against her belly, a huge tidal wave of desire, or fear, or both, carried her away.

She always clammed up when he touched her. She'd thought it was because she was afraid of getting close to him and losing him like Tarry and Rance, or her mother and Ely, and everyone else she knew. It was that but, she realised, she was also afraid of losing herself, of drowning in her own desire.

This time she rode the wave, allowing the ecstasy to carry her as he caressed her firmly, his hands moving everywhere; around her shoulders, down her back, over her belly then cupping her bottom.

She looked up into his eyes, seeing fire within them and a golden dragon in the flames. For the first time, she was fascinated by, rather than afraid of, this Dragon Lord. His caresses became tender as he pushed the straps of her slip from her shoulders and the silken material glided over her underpants to the floor. His hands moved so slowly and gently over her bare breasts that she found herself trembling. She was losing herself.

He was kissing her again, his tongue dancing between her lips, sending sparks of lightning through her body. He groaned as she pressed her breasts against his chest and felt the thunder of his heart overpowering her own.

Desire made her moan a little and she pressed harder against him. Her raven mark touched his flame mark and the Flow exploded into her vision. Above them, a sea of swirling indigo, orange and yellow flames raged.

The magic surged around her, pulling her into it. She let it take her, unable to resist it if she tried. She fell then rose, completely at the whim of the energy moving through and within her. Her mind spun and she closed her eyes, unable to comprehend or master the forces.

She could feel Asaph's strong arms around her physical body but he was lost in the Flow with her. Was he calling to her or groaning with pleasure? It could be either. Was he experiencing and seeing what she was? He must be.

She blinked, but all she could see were the waves of energy endlessly rolling around and through her. The flames surged closer, warm but not burning. The indigo sea lifted her, cool and calming. In an abstract manner, she understood the flames were Asaph and she was the indigo water.

'Don't let me go,' she said. Or had she simply thought it? She was utterly lost and out of control, was that why she'd said that? Only he could hold onto her and stop her losing herself.

Those strong arms pulled her closer. Again their marks touched and the energy intensified until she felt as though she was rising out of her body completely.

The flames became more ordered, joining together to create a great fireball. *A sun.* The indigo light separated from the flames and also became a dense spinning orb. *The dark moon.* They turned on their axis and orbited around her; she, the centre of the galaxy.

She reached her hands out to them and they moved closer. She whirled her arms and the planets increased their speed. She turned around and they followed where she desired. Issa laughed with pure joy at the power to move planets.

'I love you,' she said, whether to Asaph or the planets or the magic, she wasn't sure. Her voice came from somewhere far below. She *was* complete love.

The flaming sun responded, returning her love in feelings rather than words—the warmth and complete harmony of love, the playful freedom of pure joy, the safe contentment of protection. The sun and moon began to change and became fields of fire and water again. The flames drew her down into them. Under she went and the energies became gentle flows that calmed and caressed her.

To Issa, aeons passed in this gentle bliss. Eventually, she took a long, deep breath and opened her eyes. Asaph was looking down at her, his reddish-blonde hair dishevelled and framing his face. He looked frightened, excited and worried all at the same time. They were on the floor, both naked except for their underpants, and he was leaning over her, his belly still deliciously touching hers.

'What happened,' she breathed, closing her eyes and wishing the wave of ecstasy was still there. She trembled all over.

'I don't know,' Asaph ran a hand through his hair. 'We were kissing and...and then our marks touched and...this intense energy moved. The Flow, I guess. And we were rising, or you were rising and lifting me up. I could barely hang on! I was so excited I...I can't explain it. Then we were back and you were gone. I laid you down, you were barely breathing.

Then you came back!'

He stroked the hair from her face and passed the back of his hand over her breasts that glistened with perspiration.

'You look so beautiful,' he sighed.

She blushed and looked away, her cheek splashing in the pool of warm water in which they were both laying..

'Oh goodness, that's why it's wet!' She burst out laughing and pointed to the overflowing bath. Warm water seeped over the rim and all around them.

'Oh no!' Asaph jumped up and grappled with the lever. He managed to stop the flow and stared at the flooded wet room in dismay. He looked at her then laughed. She felt heat rising in her cheeks and covered her breasts with her hair.

'Well, I guess we may as well share the bath now,' he grinned wolfishly.

'Only if I get in it first.' She stuck out her tongue. 'And you're not allowed to look at or touch anything. I can't do that again tonight, whatever it was.'

They bathed in relative modesty, and to her surprise, Asaph didn't try to touch her again, at least not in that way. Perhaps he was also scared or confused as to what had happened. She needed a long time to think about it. The premonition that strange things would happen on Myrn had already turned out to be correct.

Hot after her bath, Issa hesitated as she picked up her dragon skin armour, wondering whether to wear it or the soft seer's robes they had both been given. The more she thought about it, the more her sense of dilemma deepened. She was here, as the Raven Queen, the warrior woman she was prophesized to be, and yet she was not at war right now. She was here as a guest and under the tutelage of the Trinity. *Who am I supposed to be?*

Asaph, already dressed in his robes, massaged her shoulders. He looked clean and handsome with his hair drying around his shoulders. Issa pulled on the seer's robes. She didn't want to stand out tonight.

There came a knock at the door. Asaph opened it wide to find Naksu standing there.

'A seers' attire suits you both,' Naksu nodded at them.

They followed her out into the cool, moonless night. Stars crowded the sky and the Blaze of Eight shone perfectly above them.

'There will only be us and the Trinity,' said Naksu.

'Where are we going?' Issa asked.

'Well, that's sort of up to you tonight. There's an especially sacred place here on Myrn but you can only find it if you are ready to. You'll be alone. The Trinity wishes to speak with Asaph whilst the world is quiet and sleeping. You will both go on a journey, but in different ways.'

Issa was intrigued and a little dubious. What if she wasn't ready for this mysterious journey?

Heading away from the city and into the trees, Naksu led them along a path lit only by the dim glow of orange crystals set along its edge. Issa hadn't noticed them in the daytime and thought how pretty and useful they were. She realised they glowed brighter when they neared and then dimmed after they had passed.

'How clever,' she said in delight. Asaph stared at them too and gave a surprised murmur.

As they left the city, the trees crowded close, and it became darker even with the glowing crystals to light their way. Naksu tapped her staff on the cobbles and it gave off a soft light. They wound their way up a gentle hill through old chestnut trees and the sound of tinkling water could be heard somewhere close.

Before long, they came to a small waterfall that stood some fifteen feet high and trickled gracefully over water-smoothed rocks. The waterfall was made even more beautiful by yellow crystals that glowed softly around it, creating a serene mood. There was even a crystal submerged in the pool at its base that lit up the clear water. Around the pool, stood the Trinity. Hearing their approach, the women turned and smiled at them.

Issa stared into the strangely glowing pool. Was that gold lining the rocks? The sheen of yellow reflected the crystal's light, making it look even more sacred and otherworldly.

'There is gold here?' Issa asked, her eyes hunting the waterfall for hidden ingots.

Asaph bent down to inspect the pool so closely he was forced to grab the bank to stop himself falling in.

'Yes,' Iyena nodded. 'Seers a long time ago collected it and used it to cover the rocks and thus purify the water here. You'll know from Freydel that gold is a universal purifier. Rather than taking from our beloved Maioria, our predecessors used what nature gave them to beautify and embellish their surroundings. Not all the waterfalls or river sources here have gold, some have silver, and some, other metals or precious stones.

'Now then, young Issa, there is a sacred place Naksu says you have visited many times from afar but now you might be able to visit it in person, if you're ready.' Iyena gestured around her. 'No one can you lead you there, only you can find it. There are many paths in this ancient wood. When you are ready, follow your heart and explore them.'

'Now? In the dark?' said Issa. She didn't fancy walking around a forest alone in the dark.

'You will have all the light you need. Some things require the stillness of the night, when the world is quiet of human minds, to be found,' said the seer.

'Prince Asaph, last of the Dragon Lords.' Iyena turned to him. 'If you wish, we would be honoured if you could join us while we look into this sacred pool of Feygriene.'

'Of course,' said Asaph, bowing. Issa detected a hint of nervousness in his voice.

The Trinity motioned for him to come beside them and they all looked in the pool, quickly forgetting she was there. Feeling rather left out, Issa surveyed the dark forest, wondering which of the two paths to take. One led up the hill and into the darkness of the trees, and the other led down towards the city where it was brighter.

She decided to take the darker path. It would be nice to gain a clearer look at the stars. The voices of Asaph and the seers soon faded behind her and, now alone, she wished she'd worn her armour, brought her raven talisman, orb and sword. Even Ehka had disappeared after she had let him out of the window earlier.

She halted her steps. Would the orb be all right left in the house? *If it isn't safe on Myrn, then it isn't safe anywhere.* She took a deep breath and carried on. There was nothing dangerous here, surely.

There were no crystals to light the way this deep into the woods but her eyes adjusted to the dark just enough to allow her to see the path ahead—a pale outline winding upwards between the trees.

A faint mist rose above the ground here and the air was so still it just hung there swirling around her feet. She relaxed and trod quietly like the Karalanths had taught her, not wanting to be the one disturbing the peace. It was so still, there weren't even any owls hooting or bats squeaking, and the voices of the others had long since faded away.

The trees were mostly oak and chestnut now, and the further she walked, the bigger and more ancient the trees became. Some were so huge, a horse and cart could easily pass through their trunks. Their extreme age was almost intimidating.

The Isles of Tirry had managed to survive the ravages of Baelthrom and his many wars by hiding themselves. But how long had the seers been here? When had the sisterhood begun? It was certainly older than when the schism between male and female magic wielders had occurred. She made a mental note to ask Naksu.

Leaves crunched underfoot. Issa turned around, looking for the path she had evidently strayed from. She must have lost it in the mist. She peered through the ferns and bushes but couldn't see it. Even looking back at the mist-shrouded trees, there didn't seem to be an obvious gap in them through which she had come. The mist was thickening too, rising up to her waist now.

She walked forwards and came to a glade. She jolted to a stop, her breath catching in her throat. Ahead, two great standing stones loomed above the mist, silent, dark and intimidating. They gave off a faint blue glow, spread further by the mist clinging to them. They demanded reverence.

Her raven mark throbbed, growing hot. She loosened her shirt to let the cool breeze blow against it and saw that the mark glowed indigo blue. Was it this place making it do that? What was this place exactly? She stepped slowly forwards. The mist parted before her and in the clearing, two more stones appeared beyond the first.

She walked, spellbound, to the first stone. There were ancient markings upon it. She touched its rough surface. Energy moved, flowing between her and the stone like some kind of communication was taking place, perhaps an exchange of information. Her raven mark pulsed and the writing on the stone burst into indigo light.

Issa dropped her hand with a gasp. The intricate swirls and scrolls of the ancient writing…she *knew* it. She shut her eyes, ancient memory—memory from before this life—pressing upon her. The stones told a story—why they were put there, where they came from and what they did—only she couldn't recall the details, she couldn't remember enough of the language to actually read it.

She carried on forwards between the stones and the mist thinned along the passageway. Her feet slowed to a stop and her mouth opened. Ahead, the sacred mound appeared; a high, perfectly round dome of grass-covered earth with a pitch-black entrance framed by a lintel and two monoliths. Smaller, whiter stones that looked almost like quartz surrounded it. She gazed up at the Blaze of Eight star cluster above, assuring her she was still upon Maioria. Tears filled her eyes as she looked back at the mound.

'I knew you were real. I knew you weren't just some old forgotten place in my mind.'

Was it the same place she had visited on Little Kammy or another? Could there be many such sacred mounds scattered everywhere and hidden like Fairy Pockets? She sidled closer. The horizontal entrance stone was collapsing on the left, just like it had been when she'd first visited it on Little Kammy. It was the same.

A black bird landed before the entrance.

'Ehka!'

She ran to the raven, scooped him up and hugged him. He squawked in surprise.

'It was you who first brought me here and saved my life. I always knew it was real,' she said, kissing his head then setting him down. She walked around the mound and laughed, feeling like a little girl discovering a beautiful secret garden.

'It's real, Ehka!' She smiled and traced the words on the entrance stones. They flared indigo blue.

'Star Portal,' she barely whispered the words, afraid that she understood them. Underneath them was a name written in the Frayonesse alphabet.

'Aralansia.'

The other words written beneath in that strange yet beautiful scrolling language found on the previous stones she didn't understand. She stepped back and stared at the entrance itself—a black, liquid film as it always had been. Raising a hand, she touched it and watched as her reflection now rippled before her. All the stones glowed blue now, even the smaller, whiter quartz ones surrounding the mound itself, as if touching the entrance had activated them all.

'Well,' she said to Ehka, 'I guess my answers will be found inside, as usual.'

Now she was here, entering the mound seemed more terrifying than ever before. What would she find in there? Would she be able to return?

'I suppose it's obvious where it leads, since it's written on the door. Aralansia.'

Aralansia, the same place she'd gone all those times before with the blue desert and Zanufey waiting for her. But when she entered the mound it didn't always go to the same time on Aralansia. Sometimes she'd seen the crystal pyramids, other times, the Storm Holt. She chewed her lip.

'I can't *not* go in. I hope you're coming,' she said to Ehka.

With a squawk he flew into the entrance and disappeared, creating ripples across the strange liquid surface. Clenching her eyes shut and wishing she had her sword and talisman, she held her breath and stepped into the freezing cold.

CHAPTER 7

Feygriene's Pool

ASAPH stood knee-deep in the shining, gold-mirrored waters of Feygriene's pool.

The seers were right, the water and the rocks beneath his feet were still very warm having been heated earlier by the sun. He turned to scan the trees but Issa had already disappeared along the path. Here, of all places, he prayed she would be safe.

'You may pass us your robe if you prefer,' said Iyena.

'What am I supposed to do?' Asaph asked, feeling clueless as he slipped off his robe. He rubbed his arms self-consciously standing in only his underwear before four women.

The Trinity linked hands and surrounded the small pool, each looking down into it.

'You do whatever you feel guided to do,' said Iyena. 'This is a place where you may commune with Feygriene, Mother of Dragons, and where you may hear your soul more clearly. Water is an advanced substance. It holds memory, and it shares those memories with all the water covering the planet.

'Look into the pool, what do you see?'

Asaph looked down into the water, enjoying how the gold rocks glinted in the light. He stepped deeper into the pool swirling his hand across the surface. The gold beneath reminded him of something and he bent lower to peer into the depths.

There, in the deepest part of the pool, he was certain he saw a structure, a temple. He walked towards it, the water reaching up to his chest, but it wasn't close enough. He took a deep breath and submerged. The water was so pure that when he blinked it didn't sting his eyes. Though his vision was blurred, the pool was much larger than he had first thought. It stretched miles down.

There was definitely something down there, he just needed to get closer. He laughed a bout of bubbles and swam down towards the golden structure, his dragon vision clearing as he did so.

He paused, hanging suspended. There, nestled between the rocks, was a stunning golden temple with a dome and gleaming walls. It was built in exactly the same manner as the temple by the frozen lake, only on a far grander scale. But it wasn't just a temple—beyond it stretched a huge golden castle almost as big as Castle Carvon. Grand turrets and spires rose high above the golden keep and walls. Who would build such a massive structure down here in Feygriene's pool?

Needing air, he tore his gaze away and swam back to the surface, gasping for breath as he emerged from the water.

Gone were the expectant seers and Feygriene's pool. Instead, he was paddling in a lake and blinking up at huge mountains that surrounded it. Disturbed by his sudden appearance, white birds with long necks and legs skittered across the surface, flapping their large wings and squawking.

Where in the world was he?

He shivered. The lake was freezing compared to the warm pool. He swam to its edge and dragged himself out onto the grassy bank. At least the sun was warm and the sky clear and a beautiful deep blue.

Hugging himself, he stared at his surroundings. He'd been here before. The mountains were the same as those he had stood upon in the north beside the temple, only they weren't covered in ice and snow but in evergreen trees, just the tips of which had a dusting of snow upon them.

In the distance, on the opposite side of the lake, he glimpsed gold glinting in the sunlight. *The golden temple I laid Coronos before, it has to be.* Ducks and the same long-necked white birds swam on the lake and the air was cool but not cold.

He looked to his right. Hugging the eastern shore, an incredible gold-gilded castle and adjoining temple shone in the sunlight, the same as he'd seen in the bottom of Feygriene's Pool. The architecture was incredible;

they were the most beautiful buildings he had ever seen.

He squinted. There were people walking the road before it. There, striding purposefully along the road beside the lake with her red cape flapping behind her, was a tall, slender woman who had short blonde hair. *Ralan Afisius, the Master Wizard. I'd recognise her anywhere.*

He immediately felt a dragon mind near and looked to where she was headed. The great mass of the dragon Ark sat serenely at the base of the mountain to the right of the castle and temple.

The dragon was impressive not just from his great size. His scales were the deepest red and so dark that they sometimes appeared black. His eyes were great glowing amber orbs and his horns shone like black onyx. He was polished and preened and sat so regally he seemed as royalty.

Asaph could hear the dragon's thoughts in his head. Distrust, respect, cautiousness and intrigue tumbled through the Arc's mind as he watched the human wizard approach.

'Ralan and Ark brought together the First Code.' A deep female voice reverberated around Asaph.

He turned and the world became filled with yellow light as if the sun were shining directly upon him.

'Who is there? Who are you? What is this place?' asked Asaph. 'I've seen it before in the Recollection with Morhork and Faelsun.'

He looked for the owner of the voice but saw only light. An immense emotion rolled over him. Joy, awe and reverence shook him to the core.

He blinked back tears and whispered, 'Feygriene.'

The voice spoke again, soft and low. 'Don't let the First Code be broken. With the destruction of the Dragon Dream, the dragons are rousing from their slumber. If they fall back to sleep now, they will die in their lairs never to awaken again. They will only rise and remember the First Code when you find and take that which belongs to you.'

'The sword,' Asaph said in wonder. 'But it's so far away and within enemy lands. How can I hope to reach it?' He breathed deeply as the voice of Feygriene echoed around him, filling him with purpose.

'You must find a way, Asaph Dawn Bringer, last of the Dragon Lords. For in you the First Code is made flesh and blood. The Dragon Dream may have shattered, and your heart is heavy with the loss of those you love, but all is not hopeless. You can bring back the Dragon Lords and a new dawn to Maioria. It is your destiny to take back the sword and awaken the dragons.'

'I will do everything in my power to make this come to pass, my goddess,' he said.

The golden sunlight faded and he found himself on a grassy plain before different mountains. These were made of dark grey granite with sheer sides and dominating jagged tips striking high into the sky. *The Grey Lords.* The sun was warm but the air cold as it picked up his hair and threw it about his shoulders.

The roar of a dragon called overhead. Asaph looked up and saw a bright red dragon circling. It was joined by two more, one red, one green, then others flecked the sky, coming from all around. He trembled with the excitement of seeing them. Somewhere to the west beyond these mountains, lay his lost city, Draxa, and the dragons had come to help him reclaim it.

A great cheer exploded behind him, making him jump and turn, sword in hand. A thick line of a hundred or more soldiers—mostly tall, reddish-blond Draxians—with determined looks on their faces cheered at him. Had the exiles returned? Some wore Knights of the Raven tabards; a raven flying across a blue moon, others, the familiar gold shield on a red background of the Feylint Halanoi.

Asaph raised his arm and saw he held the Great Sword of Binding. The blood red pommel glowed and the sun gleamed off the blade filling him with warmth and need. With a cry, he let the dragon within take control, and his cry became a roar.

Asaph blinked, struggling for his footing in the warm water as the here and now held sway. Wiping water from his eyes and face, he looked up at Iyena who smiled kindly at him.

'That was so strange,' he said after a moment, staring back into the water. The gold covered rock looked normal now and there was no sunken temple in the deeper parts. It wasn't miles deep as he had thought, either.

'What you saw is for you alone,' she said, passing him his robe.

'But you may tell us if you wish,' Dar raised an eyebrow and grinned.

'At first I saw a place I have been to before, far to the north, only it was warmer and greener,' said Asaph, recalling everything in great detail. 'There, Ark the dragon and the Master Wizard, Ralan Afisius, formed the First Code, Feygriene's Accord.'

'Wait, wait,' said Dar. She rummaged in a bag at her feet and pulled out parchment and a pencil. 'I must write this down for our records, if you don't mind.'

'Dar is our scribe,' said Iyena with a smile.

'Sure,' Asaph shrugged, and continued explaining what he had seen. He hesitated as he recounted the last part, still trying to believe it himself. 'It is my destiny to find the sword and awaken the dragons. Only then is there a chance of taking back Drax.'

Iyena nodded, an approving yet mystical smile on her face. 'Feygriene has spoken. We are blessed. May her light guide you, King Asaph.'

Asaph swallowed and dropped his gaze, the weight of responsibility and destiny heavy upon him.

CHAPTER 8

Portal to the Stars

THE freezing cold receded and a small stone room took shape.

The air was cool and fresh, not musty or damp. In opposite corners, two small, pale blue crystals let off diffuse light.

The doorway ahead filled with light and three beings stepped through into the room. They were tall and slender, dressed simply in flowing white cloth that shone. They appeared to be half made of light and half solid, and exuded that familiar feeling of ancient wisdom and deep serenity.

'Guardians of the Portals,' Issa breathed.

As one, they smiled and nodded, although the shimmering light from their faces made it hard for her to determine their expressions. She looked closer at them, trying to see the outlines of their faces, their eyes, noses and cheeks but she couldn't even tell if they were male or female. Their features were not solid either. Sometimes they were human and then they would melt into something more… *Aralan*. Their longer skulls and larger eyes were instantly recognisable.

'Are you Aralans?' asked Issa. The sudden thought excited her.

'Once we were,' the trio said in unison, their combined voices creating a rich and harmonious sound. 'When we were forced to leave our physical forms during the destruction of Aralansia, our spirits chose to remain to guard the portals between Aralansia and other places rather than return to the light.'

Issa was shocked. 'You've chosen to remain here, after Aralansia was destroyed, to keep the gateways open? Why? How long have you been here?'

'Without us, there would be no portals, no link between Aralansia and other worlds, and no ability to help those afflicted by the darkness of the black rift. Time has little meaning beyond the realms of matter when the spirit is no longer bound by the physical. But for us, in Maiorian years, we have been here, waiting for the time that is now, for many thousands of years.'

They must have seen her frown for they added, 'It is hard to imagine such things when your spirit is bound in a physical body and tied to the very construct of time itself. Your spirit understands these things deeply, but your mind cannot.

'As spirit, we form the bridge across time and dimensions between Aralansia and Maioria—two light filled planets of similar encryption. We are, in essence, the portals themselves, the energy of transference between two points. We can see it is very hard for you to grasp this, but just as you know in the realm of the Flow, all things are energy; energy and intention.

'Through us, the last living Aralans were able to make the passage to Maioria and escape the utter annihilation of our race. Some Aralan souls have guarded other portals to other places for trillions of years. Waiting for a time of their release.'

Issa dropped her gaze and caught her breath, unable to comprehend such a number or that a civilisation far more advanced than her own could exist—and fall—so long ago.

'But…it's such a long time, to wait here in this…place. Don't you long to return home?' she whispered, blinking back unbidden tears. Had these beings really devoted their souls to protect the portals and help others? For so long they had remained here, waiting. The thought was humbling – she knew she could not have done it.

'We yearn for the One Light with all of our being, it is what keeps us strong and devoted to our purpose. Our time here is coming to an end.' Looks of adoration made their faces even brighter, touching Issa deeply.

'What is the end?' Issa barely dared to ask. If these beings had been waiting for her, waiting for the prophecies, she did not want to know about it.

'Greater cycles move in the heavens than you bear witness to upon Maioria, though Maioria and her lifeforms are inextricably bound to them. Either the darkness will consume her or she will overcome it. The sickness has spread far and deep, it will not be easy to overthrow.

'It will be done,' said Issa between clenched teeth. 'It *must* be done.'

She tried to still the anger in her heart in the presence of these holy beings. It wasn't easy when her planet was dying and her people murdered and enslaved. The desire to utterly destroy Baelthrom and annihilate the Dark Rift became almost overpowering, drowning out sense and reason.

The guardians held the same smile on their serene, radiant faces. 'There is always hope. Through the power of the One Source, the impossible is made possible.'

Issa swallowed and changed the subject, hoping they couldn't see the violent thoughts in her mind. 'The standing stones at the entrance, they glowed blue.' She motioned behind her.

'The stones know you. They are from Aralansia' said the guardians.

One stepped forward and spoke separately from her kind, her voice deep, yet female-sounding. 'They recognise those who carry the encryption of Aralansia in their souls. For the soul lives on and takes other material forms, but it remembers all that went before.'

Issa found herself nodding slowly, it kind of made sense now; why the stones glowed when she touched them, why she recognised the language written on them, but Aralansia seemed so far away. She didn't want to remember her life then, didn't want to remember seeing her planet destroyed and her body dying—just as she didn't want to witness Maioria's destruction. *Another life, another time. I can barely manage myself in this one life, let alone think of others.*

'What did Aralansia look like before it fell?' Issa asked.

Light spread from the guardians and a beautiful image engulfed her, replacing the room and the beings. Great trees, bigger than those on Maioria, towered above her. Birds of all sizes and colours flittered through the branches or glided high above. Some had heavy, long orange beaks, others were enormous and had luminous pink plumes on their heads. Bird-song filled the forest with life. Tall, golden-furred animals moved amongst bushes that were covered in red flowers, their big doe-like eyes watched her serenely and their long, tufted ears flicked back and forth.

Everywhere her gaze fell, there were flowers in full bloom. Yellow bells the size of her fist dripped from the trees. Six-foot high orange lilies bowed in the breeze. Her bare feet stood upon soft grass and the air was warm. The sun was beginning to set across the forest; a sun that was larger and whiter than Maioria's. As it set, it shaded the sky with a beautiful indigo hue.

Extremely tall people appeared, walking in a graceful flowing motion. Their skin was golden or silver, their eyes large and slanted, and their long heads were hairless. Aralans. They exuded intelligence and power; she could almost see the magic moving around them without even entering the Flow.

The world around her began to change fast, reminding her that she witnessed merely an image and she sadly wasn't really in paradise. Hundreds of Aralans gathered in a small clearing facing the great forest. They began to chant the same phrase again and again, although it was more like singing as their voices rose and fell in harmony. Animals and birds gathered close to watch, ears and tails flicking back and forth, wings ruffling.

Then the trees began to move. Their canopies swayed and their trunks shook. Issa's jaw dropped as they lifted their great roots out of the earth and began to amble backwards, a whole section of forest moving away to create a bigger clearing. When they stopped they pushed their roots back into the earth. Issa was certain she could hear them sighing as they settled down.

The scene moved fast again and she watched in awe as a grand city was built before her eyes, all to the sound of the beautiful singing of the Aralans. Great blocks of stone and crystal a hundred people could not lift, floated easily into the air without ropes or pulleys or hard labour of any kind. There was just the sound of singing. Now she focused on it, Issa could hear a low thrumming note played from an instrument she could not see.

Issa watched spellbound as they created beautiful crystal and stone houses without chisels and hammers. Stunning turrets and spires, walls and gardens, pathways and courtyards appeared before her eyes. She remembered the Ancients had been able to create such dwellings out of rock and crystal, too. The city was the most beautiful she had ever seen, more beautiful even than the Elven city in the Land of Mists. Crystal houses glinted in the white sun and birds circled the pointed roofs.

Animals, some horse-like and others dog-like, walked the pristine streets placidly besides the tall beings. They wore no collars or halters and didn't seem as pets or used for labour. The animals were simply companions, or passers-by, come to look at the latest great creation of the Aralans.

Other, human-like beings began to visit the Aralans—from where they came, Issa did not know. They arrived in the small, raised stone and crystal enclaves clustered between the city and the forest. Light collected within each enclave and then a being would arrive, much like how a translocation spell operated, she assumed. Perhaps the enclaves operated like the amethyst circle on Myrn? The Aralans gathered around, excited to meet the strange visitors.

The new arrivals were slender but shorter than the Aralans, their eyes were disturbingly all black, although their faces were pretty. They had smooth, pale-pink to white skin, and most were bald, though some had black hair tied back. Their movements were quick and agile to the point of edgy—the opposite of the calm and relaxed demeanour of the Aralans.

Issa felt a sense of deep unease towards these new beings. Something about them was untrustworthy, their smiles didn't reach their eyes and looked false. They did not look well and they acted nervously. An Aralan spoke with them at length. He was taller and broader than the others and she could feel power move around him. Could he be the one Freydel had shown her in the orb? Could he be Ayeth? She strained to see an amulet but could find none upon him, and as he wore pale clothes like the others, she couldn't be sure.

The scenes flowed on, but often she glimpsed the same tall Aralan communing with the black-eyed visitors. More arrived and, under their direction and agreement of the Aralans, the new beings began to erect other structures around the city; giant pyramids from vast blocks of crystal. The forest was pushed further and further back, though from their facial expressions, the Aralans appeared reluctant to do this. Dense energy exuded from the pyramids, not bad but potent and heavy. Issa felt tired just being within sight of them.

A small, pretty, black-eyed female passed a gift to the tall Aralan. With a look of wonder, he lifted the shimmering, dark blue material and wrapped it around his shoulders. It conveyed the impression of liquid, the way it rippled and fell around him. Issa stepped back. He was familiar now.

'Ayeth,' she said.

Issa stared into the face of the beautiful being with burnished gold skin and large, dark blue eyes that matched the colour of the robe he wore. His eyes drew her into them. They were vast and deep and she sensed he knew about a great many things she could barely dream of.

He smiled at the female and Issa felt his compassion as a tangible thing.

'Chosen by Zanufey,' Issa said with a shiver.

More visitors came and more crystal pyramids were built, pushing back the forest further and further until they stretched to the horizon. They were beautiful, expertly crafted with their shining white tips reaching up into the sky, but they were also dominating and stark and filled Issa with unease. They were powerful, yes, but either the power was unnatural, or the intention behind its use was impure, she couldn't put her finger on which.

'He became tainted with the darkness of the Yurgha by becoming one with them.' The guardians' voices echoed through the image.

'When two beings share themselves, each take on a part of the other. He did nothing wrong, for sharing himself with the Yurgha was what he had planned. Such couplings are often how beings who are sick can become well again, by melding their energies with those who are healthy.

'We understand now that the Yurgha pretended to want help when they really only wanted to take over Aralansia and subjugate the Aralans to their dominion—such was the completeness of their affliction. Though Ayeth had willingly taken their sickness into himself, he was not able to withstand it. In the end, our desire to help others caused our downfall. We were an advanced and noble race but utterly naive and innocent in the face of evil.'

'How can we ever help others if this happens?' Issa frowned. Should she not help anyone for fear of failing?

The guardians spoke softly, without judgement. 'By better knowing and understanding those whom you help, and by judging a being by its own values, not by your own. The One Source values all beings equally, but not all beings are the same.

'In the worlds of matter, there are many things a being may choose to experience, of the darkness or of the light. All choices are honoured, but those who choose the light must remember that here, in this system, they also exist amongst those who choose the darkness.

'Deception is a tactic used by beings of darkness. What we Aralans as a race needed to learn was that beings of the dark would deceive us.'

'But I don't understand why they did it. What did the Yurgha want? Why would they hurt those trying to help them?' said Issa. It just didn't make logical sense.

'It is the light of the One Source that nourishes all things eternally. All beings who choose darkness cut themselves off from this light and desire dominion over all others. To survive they must feed off something else—the light of others.

'Lona fed off the light of Ayeth, just as Baelthrom now feeds off the beings of Maioria. When that light is gone, the fallen must move on to find another food source or die themselves.

'They can be seen as sick with a disease that makes them finite. A finite mind believes the cosmos is limited and scarce. Scarcity creates competition. Competition creates conflict. But the cosmos is not scarce, it is by nature infinitely abundant. But only an infinite, healthy mind that has remained attached to the light of Source can know this.

'The Yurgha weren't always sick, were they?' asked Issa. As wonderful as the thought of the infinite was, she didn't like the other implications of this conversation. It struck to the core of her deepest fears; that something could fall from the light by simply trying to help others.

'No, the Yurgha were a pure and beautiful race. Advanced, like we, the Aralans, but in a different manner. It was the Rorsken and Anukon races who invaded their planet, bringing the sickness with them. Like a plague, it spreads through the cosmos consuming and destroying all.

'The Yurgha were deliberately attacked because their planet Yurgharon was once a gateway to a higher dimension. The fallen ones were trying to break into the higher realms and consume the greater light, for it would sustain them for vast amounts of time. And so the darkness spreads,' said the guardians opening their hands of light.

Issa turned back to the image and stared at Ayeth standing before a crowd of Aralans. He became angry, lifting his hands high and raising his voice, gesticulating in fast, hard movements just like the Yurgha did. The compassion was gone from his eyes, and in its place she saw resentment and deep inner conflict.

Lona was never far from his side standing still and emotionless, her face impassive and her dark eyes missing nothing. A chill crept down Issa's back as she looked at the female.

The image changed and she stood once more upon the crystal courtyard. Above her, the planets, great orbs of lights, were aligning once more. Awesome power burst from the pyramid tips and white beams of light surged towards the closest star, just as she had witnessed before.

This time she looked to a part of the sky that was further away and noticed another beam of light coming out of the star to meet it. The beams of light exploded where they hit. Power flooded into the planet through the beam of light connecting it to the other star. The ground shook and rumbled, and though it was only an image she felt huge waves of energy rolling through her as before.

Tears spilled down her cheeks and she closed her eyes. 'I don't want to see anymore,' she whispered, and felt the image, and the energy, fade. She did not want to witness the beautiful Aralans screaming and running in terror. She did not want to see Aralansia destroyed again.

'How many survived?' she asked, wiping her eyes.

'At most, a thousand,' said the female guardian, her voice sounding lonely without the others. 'Only those who suspected the peril Ayeth had placed them in and were closest to the portals got out. Ayeth never realised Lona had betrayed him and had taught him, unknowingly, how to use the pyramids so they would flood the life energy out of Aralansia.

'When the alignments of the planets occurred, he activated the pyramids with his great knowledge. Yurgharon, in return, sucked the life force out of Aralansia, shutting down its crystal seed and ending the planet's life.

'Ayeth firmly believed his own people had tricked him and not Lona. In a desperate attempt to reach her he tried to go to Yurgharon but ended up shattering his quantum in the process.'

Keeping her eyes closed, Issa imagined Ayeth desperately trying to leave the quaking planet via the stone enclaves.

'When Aralansia pole-shifted, the sudden backflow of energy hit the sun, causing it to undergo immediate and devastating changes. Great solar forces ripped through the planets, destroying everything on Yurgharon as well. What had been a small rift in the cosmos first doubled, then tripled in size. It is what your species call the Dark Rift, and it attracts all the darkness in the cosmos to it, ever growing in size.'

Behind closed lids, Issa could see the light of the image flaring. When she opened her eyes, the great black tear in the galaxy hung before her, beautiful stars glinting around the black nothingness. What was in the blackness? *Things that should not be, things I don't ever want to see.* She swallowed.

'The Aralans who escaped, where did they go?' Issa asked.

'It would not be helpful to you at this point to explain the immense technical details of the cosmos for it takes a young being a long time to understand its divine structure. But, simply, they went to several places and a hundred or so managed to make it, with our assistance, to your planet, Maioria.'

Issa nodded and smiled. 'I thought you might say that. Through the portals, which are you?'

'Yes.' The guardians smiled, speaking as one again. 'Maioria's guardians—whom you call Doon and Woetala—agreed to allow these orphaned Aralans onto her soil. But to survive the new, denser and more primitive planet, they had to adapt their forms. They understood that their race would die eventually so they secretively and selectively shared themselves, and thus their blood, with certain members of your races, most notably the elves, some humans and wykiry. Their hybrid descendants are the beings you call the Ancients.

'They knew that, without their planet to sustain their physical forms, their future was doomed.' The guardians became quiet. Their deep, silent mourning affected Issa and she gave up trying to hold back the tears.

The guardians continued. 'They knew that the darkness would forever hunt them and, one day, find them.

'Out of the Dark Rift Baelthrom came—formed from the twisted, scattered essence that was Ayeth—following the trail of his kin and wanting to destroy them utterly as he believed they had destroyed him, his home and Lona. He never once blamed himself for all that had happened. For this is the curse of the Fallen Ones, blame. The fallen blame others for all that is wrong in their lives, unable to take responsibility for their own choices and creations.

'Ayeth became unrecognisable as Baelthrom. He succeeded in

destroying all but two of the descendants of the Aralans. But still, some beings on Maioria today carry minute amounts of their blood in their veins, such as the wykiry, the elves and the Tusarzans. It's small wonder that these are the races most persecuted by Baelthrom.'

Issa's mouth hung open, a barrage of questions filling her mind. 'I can't believe Baelthrom—Ayeth—was chosen by Zanufey to save people and then he fell. Is that what will happen to me if I fail? How can I be sure not to fail? Is that why I'm terrified of "sharing" myself with anyone, as you put it? Well, I'm damn well more terrified now! I don't even have half the power Ayeth has and even less of his drive and compassion. What hope is there?'

Issa felt sick to her core and very angry. She stared at the floor as the image of the Dark Rift faded completely, leaving the room empty.

'You have witnessed what is so, and no more,' said the guardians, their gentle smiles soothing her anger and fear.

Issa sighed and swallowed her emotions. 'I did ask, I suppose. Can he be reasoned with to stop him destroying everything?'

'For him to stop feeding off others means he will die, and so will the Dark Rift. He has grown so powerful now, the Dark Rift itself feeds off planets through him.'

'Then he must be killed,' said Issa, pursing her lips.

'No being of the light, whether guardian, goddess or the Great Source of All, will agree to the destruction of another and neither will they tell you what to do,' said the guardian. 'That is, and always will be, up to every being alone. But if you ask for wisdom and guidance, it will always be given to you. Before you incarnated on Maioria, you knew very well the things you have witnessed and of which we have spoken. Your soul guides you to fulfil the purpose for which you came.'

'To destroy Baelthrom,' Issa said, her face hard and her vengeance growing.

'It was vengeance that destroyed Ayeth in the beginning.'

Issa dropped her eyes from the wise gazes of the guardians, feeling her cheeks colour. 'I'm not as advanced or as clever as you. I have simple human feelings, thoughts, emotions—which is why this is hopeless.'

'Do you think you came to destroy or to restore?' the guardians said.

Issa caught her breath, wondering if everything she had believed was wrong. No, not wrong; incomplete in some way.

The guardians continued. 'All the things you've seen and learned today, and all the times you have visited Zanufey, the guardian of Aralansia, you have been given the truth. This is a great gift given only to those who are strong enough to handle it—perhaps the greatest gift. More than any other on your planet, you now know the truth of many things. Write it down, share that truth with others, with your Wise Ones; the seers and wizards.'

Issa nodded though she didn't feel like she deserved this gift or even wanted it. Truth cut deep and painful. She shivered and a potent need filled her. 'I wish I were with Zanufey.'

The guardians smiled and raised their hands. Issa blinked as they and the chamber began to fade and a warm wind blew.

Issa looked across the blue sand at the impressive, sparkling stone trilithon rising up out of the desert. It was always night here and the sky was filled with stars.

Now she knew why.

There was no sun and no atmosphere. This place—all that was left of Aralansia—was a barren rock, orphaned and abandoned in the great emptiness between the stars. And there weren't any clouds because the planet and its atmosphere were dead.

She walked towards the trilithon and touched the dark, glittering stone, noting how identical it was to her raven talisman. The stone hummed so low she could barely hear it. She dropped her hand and the humming stopped.

'All that remains of one of the Star Portals,' Zanufey said quietly from behind her.

Issa turned to face the goddess. Her perfect chin and lips were set in a faint, compassionate smile and Ehka perched upon her shoulder.

'The energy and function of the portal remains because of the guardians who nurture it, but its beautiful structure is gone,' said Zanufey.

'It hurts to see the destruction of Aralansia and the hope and the loss of her people,' said Issa, suddenly overcome with sorrow, her eyes glancing over the black hole swirling on Zanufey's robe. 'It all seems so hopeless. I don't understand oblivion or evil or how beings can destroy each other and themselves. How can I win against that which I don't understand?'

She tried to imagine turning to the darkness and wanting to cut herself off from the light. Wanting to hurt and destroy things and use them for her own pleasure. In this place, her thoughts were more powerful. Darkness entered her heart and mind, the light paled and the stars above looked weak and distant. Zanufey faded into a dark hooded figure that was swallowed by the night. A cold wind tore across the barren desert making her shiver.

Why did the goddess leave her now?

Anger filled her heart. Why did she make her do these stupid things she couldn't do? It was hopeless. She wished they'd all just left her alone. So what if she'd died a nobody on Little Kammy? Her mother didn't want her anyway and Asaph had betrayed her by going with her most hated enemy.

Hatred for Cirosa burned in her mind. She would kill her next time. Issa smiled, thinking of murderous revenge. Surely by now she, the Raven Queen, had enough followers and power to destroy Baelthrom and his horde. The people would do whatever she said, she would make them.

The wind howled and it was very dark. Would Zanufey come back? Who cared anyway? She was alone and always would be. She hugged her shoulders.

'Maion'artheria.' The voice whispered across the desert, easing the hatred in her heart.

A breeze carrying the barest warmth touched her skin and she closed her eyes blinking back tears. She was not alone and never had been. Light fell across her lids and she opened her eyes. The heavy anger and hatred lifted and she felt lighter, her mind clear. She let go a deep sigh of relief wanting never to feel the dark loneliness again.

Zanufey stood before her once more with Ehka on her shoulder and her robes settling in the calming wind.

'That is what the darkness creates; anger, hatred, resentment, fear, emptiness, purposelessness,' said Zanufey. 'When a being falls so far from the One Source, it can no longer be reached, it can no longer find its way home. But in the eyes of the One Source, that being is never lost or forgotten, and when the Source takes a great in-breath, that being will be returned into the Light. Nothing is ever forgotten or lost, for everything in existence is all a part of the body of the One Source. How could it ever lose a part of itself? Remember these things in your darkest hour.'

'I know so little…my mind is so small,' sighed Issa. 'Why can't you just tell me what to do? I'll do it, I promise.'

Zanufey smiled. 'No being, whether great or small, can be anything other than your guide. Your soul is your closest friend. You have a gift you'll one day understand; that in you, all things are made whole.'

Issa wondered what she meant. 'At least I have finally found the sacred mound on Maioria.' She smiled. 'I always knew it to be a real place somewhere. But now I'm here, I don't know how to return.'

'It is easy. Just step through the stones,' said Zanufey.

Issa blinked, looking at the trilithon that led nowhere. Ehka flew over Issa's head and disappeared into it. She started forwards then looked back, but Zanufey was gone. Wearing a determined smile, Issa stepped through.

CHAPTER 9

Seer Training

'ASAPH told me what he saw in Feygriene's pool.

I'm pleased he's found his purpose but sad because my destiny does not lie with him in Draxa,' Issa said, turning the flame ring around her finger. She stood by the open window where Ehka perched enjoying the late morning sun. The Trinity and Naksu were sitting before her around a simple, pale wood table. They were in a large domed house with white walls and arched windows, and a colourful mosaic spread across the floor. Dar scribbled on parchment as Issa told them of her experience within the sacred mound—or star portal as the guardians had called it.

'Destiny is not a simple thing that ends when one thing is achieved,' said Iyena. 'It goes on and on with achievements all along the way. Our bodies may die but our spirits are eternal, and so, naturally, destiny is eternal. What we have seen in our sacred pools is the Raven Queen and Dawn Bringer together. Do not fear that destiny or death will drive you apart.'

Issa took heart in her words. 'Perhaps you're right but I worry. I think that, when the time comes, there'll be a great battle and we might not survive it.'

'We all fear the coming battles. That's why your destiny is to reach out to all who'll stand against the darkness.' Suli squinted over her glasses at her. 'Already you have won over the Karalanths, the wizards, witches and us seers. Even the wykiry come to your aid. With Asaph's help, you may well have the dragons returning. And, dare I say it, you have the demons of the Murk. You must realise what a vast army you have already.'

Issa looked at the old seer. She was surprised when the seers hadn't balked at her in-depth account of her Wizard's Reckoning. She'd been talking non-stop about that and her experience in the star portal for hours and now her voice was hoarse.

'I didn't want to make friends with demons.' Issa rubbed her eyes.

'But you have, and no one else has ever done that,' said Dar, not looking up from her scribblings. 'Also, you found the *star portal.*'

'Edarna said it first came to Issa,' Naksu spoke to Dar. The albino woman had been silent all the time Issa had been there. 'And I saw in a vision everything coming into motion when the Chosen One entered the sacred mound. That was when Zanufey's disciple was consecrated and the prophecies set in motion.'

Issa cast her mind back to the first time she'd entered the mound, that feeling of something monumental initiating that could not be stopped. 'If I'd known then what I know now, I'd probably never have done it,' she said, wishing for a moment that she was back at home and bored on Little Kammy again.

The seers laughed.

'And we will be eternally grateful that you did,' murmured Iyena, nodding her head slowly. 'At least now there is hope.'

'Still, the star portal is sacred,' said Dar. 'And it can be found only when it wants to be—in the divine right order and timing of things. Only a few ever find it, and usually in the later days of their lives.'

'So, it becomes clear to us now why you are Zanufey's chosen,' said Iyena. 'That you carry the ancient knowledge—the encryption—of Aralansia in your blood, the planet of whom Zanufey is guardian. We had some understanding of the guardians of Maioria—our great Doon and blessed Woetala, the loving light of Feygriene and the night guardian Zanufey—but the knowledge you bring to us is priceless.'

Iyena stood up, awe in her eyes as she looked into the middle distance. 'Indeed. We will write down and make copies and protect all that you have told us, Issa. Everything you have said supports and greatly expands our teachings. Thankfully, nothing contradicts.'

She turned to Issa and smiled. 'As the prophecies have foretold, already the Raven Queen is teaching us and not the other way round. Still, there are things we can teach you while you are with us, for it is clear you will not stay here for long before your destiny calls to you. We have decided, if you would like, to teach you what all our initiates learn.

Also, there are some basic fundamentals about energy that one should understand. It will help you master the Flow very effectively.'

Issa nodded her head vigorously. What there was to learn about magic seemed infinite and she longed to know more.

Iyena continued. 'After lunch, I will ride with you around Myrn and show you the island. Whilst we ride, I'll tell you of many things. Lessons amongst nature, under the sun and in the wind, instil a greater, deeper knowledge. Asaph may join us if he wishes.

In the evening, after dark, Naksu will teach you more about magic. Tomorrow, we'll start early at dawn, and the same the next day until it is time for you to leave.'

'I would like that very much. Thank you.' Issa bowed slightly, keen to start learning whatever they could teach her this very minute.

Duskar pranced and tossed his head as they cantered along a track. The forest rushed past on their left, and on the right was a meadow filled with long grasses and blue flowers. Issa had to gallop him ahead of Iyena and Asaph then bring him back just to use up his joyful energy. The afternoon sun was warm but every now and then blew a chill breeze that swirled the fallen leaves into the air.

She cantered Duskar back to the others for the third time, laughing.

'Maybe it's Myrn,' said Issa, breathlessly. 'He's so happy and full of life. Look, he doesn't even mind the other horses.'

Sure enough, Duskar stood close to Ironclad and Iyena's white horse, Bree, even lifting his nose to sniff them a little.

'The crystals that create the protective shield around our islands also keep out the negative energies of the Under Flow and anything else,' said Iyena. 'It makes you wonder, if we didn't have those negative energies at all, the whole planet might be more joyful.'

Duskar settled down beside the others but still held his head high and ears pricked forwards as they travelled along the coastal path that circled the island. It was warmer here than Little Kammy, but not as hot as

Celene, and it was quite beautiful.

They trotted through deciduous forests clustering at the edges of white cliffs and over rich grasslands where the path passed so close to the edge she could see the deep blue sea swirling against the rocks below. The track frequently wound down into turquoise bays and coves where villages of white-domed houses nestled. The people there smiled and waved at them and many wore simple attire rather than seers' robes.

'People come here for healing and respite,' Iyena explained. 'Some have settled. Though, unless they wish to become seers, we urge them to return to their homes and share what wisdom they have learned on Myrn with others. Look, here is the eastern most point of the island.'

Iyena slowed Bree to a stop. A couple of hours of easy riding and they had covered the first half of the island. Issa stared over the sea to the horizon, straining to see land.

'You won't see Maphrax—it's too far away, thankfully,' said Iyena.

'I would have liked to have seen Tusarza,' said Issa. 'It's sad to think the land of my ancestors is gone.'

Iyena nodded. 'You can look to the past and see and feel all the things lost and forgotten—even I do—but it helps to realise that our time is now and our hope is for the future. Good things are lost, but they can be created again, bigger and better than before.'

'All things will be ours again. Drax will be free, one day,' said Asaph, his eyes shining. 'I think I'd like a gold painted castle like the one where Ralan and Ark met.'

'And I hope you'll be inviting seers to your golden castle when you do,' Iyena laughed.

'Of course,' Asaph nodded as they continued north along the path. Issa grinned, imagining again the great wizard and dragon he had told her about. He'd promised to show her the golden temple someday if she could bear going somewhere so frigidly cold.

They stopped the horses beside a spring where a stone basin had been carved in the rock to collect the water. Letting the horses drink, Issa and Asaph filled up their water canisters whilst Iyena poured elderflower cordial into the ceramic cups she had brought in her saddlebag. She also took out jams, Davonian cheese and oat biscuits to snack on.

Taking a bite of a biscuit, Issa realised the seer hadn't taught them anything yet. She'd been too busy riding Duskar and enjoying the beauty of Myrn to notice. She studied the older woman. Her white hair was loosely tied back with a blue cord and her slender hands were busy spreading jam on a biscuit.

'What are you going to teach us?' Issa asked.

'You've already been learning the lessons for today. That joy and freedom are the greatest gifts to the spirit. When the soul plays, the universe sings.'

Issa glanced at Asaph, who mirrored her befuddled expression, then she laughed. 'I wish all my lessons at school had been like that.'

Iyena smiled. 'A long time ago, in the good old days before we all forgot who we are, all we did was play and learn about ourselves and the world, and create. We understood that the universe loved us, that the world was naturally abundant, and that there was enough of everything for everyone.'

Issa tried to imagine such a time. The beauty of such a world filled her with wonder. Could it really have been that way? She wished she lived in such mythical times. It seemed so different to how things were now; a world filled with death and pain and struggle—a world of endless wars… But it had been different on Aralansia too before the darkness came. A world of light and happiness, and wise, joy-filled beings. That world, too, had changed, had fallen, just like Maioria was falling.

She remembered her religious lessons at school. Lessons about the darkness and the light and there always needing to be a balance between the two. Those lessons had always scared and fascinated her, for how could there ever be too much light and good in the world? What happened when the darkness needed to grow and balance itself?

'But it can't always be like that, can it? There has to be darkness, for how can the light exist without it? We need the darkness to balance the light,' said Issa, feeling bad for marring the mood.

'That is a lie spread by the evil ones who seek to dominate others,' said Iyena, her voice light despite her words, sorrowful even. 'We've discovered that such twisted teachings have now made their way into the teachings of the Temple and have spread even into Maioria's schools. Such evil is infectious, spreading like a disease.'

Issa stared at her. How could the seer deny everything everyone was taught at school and knew as truth?'

'How so?' Issa raised her eyebrows.

'You do not need the darkness to balance the light because the light requires no balance. It is, in itself, perfect harmony. The darkness spread the lie of balance to justify its own evil existence and deceive the light workers. If there weren't any evil beings, the good beings wouldn't have to go around healing and fixing everything they had broken.'

'How can you be sure?' Asaph was equally sceptical. 'I mean, how do we know the reasons for creation?'

'We all know the reasons, the first cause, because it's within us,' said Iyena. 'It's just been buried very deep and overlaid with the confused teachings of the dark. Only a loving Creator would desire to create and then keep that creation in existence.'

'It sounds awful, but what if the creator wanted to create a place where bad things happened?' Issa stared glumly down into the depths of her cup.

'Then it would already be destroyed and nothing would exist,' said Iyena. 'Evil does not last long when there is only evil present. It turns inwards and destroys itself quickly. Words are very limited to explain these concepts, but if you think of love as perfect harmony then it immediately follows that it is perfectly balanced. It is the darkness itself that destroys the natural balance and harmony of the cosmos. Disharmony must occur for evil to exist.

'Be careful and ever watchful for the tricks and lies spread by those who are evil. There is an old saying, "Evil is live, spelt backwards." That is, evil is the opposite of life, it is life reversed. Do you remember the old myths and legends that spoke of a time when people lived forever?'

Issa nodded.

'Yes,' said Asaph. 'Coronos spoke of many legends, but I thought they were just fairy tales.'

'Well, there is much truth in them,' said Iyena. 'They are not stories but old historical accounts. The accounts may have grown and been embellished with time, but there is truth in all of them.'

Issa blinked. 'I remember now. True life is eternal. Zanufey told me this a long time ago. Imagine that? Living forever. Hah.'

'Well, our souls are eternal, but in the past, people lived forever until they had grown enough and were ready to leave this dimensions and move on to the next,' Iyena smiled.

'Then we are trapped here,' Issa said, reaching over and washing her empty cup in the spring. 'I wonder if, when Baelthrom is gone and the Dark Rift closed, we will be able to live forever again.'

'It seems like a dream, doesn't it?' said Iyena, her face childlike as she smiled at them both. She gazed across the ocean. 'Still, I was ever one to think big. Maybe that time will come, although I'm not sure if I want this body to live forever. I'd much prefer a younger one.'

Issa grinned.

'Let's walk for a bit and stretch our legs,' Iyena said, packing away their cups then taking Bree's reins off the tree stump.

As they walked she spoke. Issa listened with absolute fascination.

'All things have a soul that exists in the next dimension. The soul is a very real thing. The soul also has a soul—an over-soul if you will—that connects again to the next dimension. The over-soul also has a soul and so on right until you connect right back into the fields of inner creation.

'As we emerge from the great Source of All, we individuate ourselves. That is, as we move further away from our point of creation we leave parts of ourselves at specific points along the way and we get smaller and smaller as our quantum stretches and reduces. Yes, you can look at me strangely, but even the priestesses of the Temple taught this at some point.

'Our journey out into external creation and into individuation is supposed to be a joyful one, and so is the journey back to the One Source. Everything in existence once came out of the Source, and to it we all eventually return—we are never apart from the One Source and our soul is always with us.

'Now, the problems start when beings choose to explore paths that are in opposition to divine creation—which is allowed because we have free will. I guess they're not really *problems* but complex explorations and intense experiences. Anyway, these beings deliberately cut themselves off from the One Light, even though you can never really be outside of it. They forget their connection to the divine and so begin a painful journey of woe, separateness and loneliness.

'A true Wise One knows that all things are connected, and through all things the divine force flows. The beings of the dark have forgotten this and the divine does not flow through them. They no longer feel the Great Source of All, they no longer feel part of creation. This forgetting allows them to do terrible things that they would not otherwise be able to do. It is only the beings of the light who are able to help them—although many are so sick they seldom want help and often turn upon those trying to assist them.'

'Like Lona and Ayeth,' Issa breathed. 'Ayeth tried to help her and the Yurgha, but they tricked him because they didn't really want to heal.'

'Indeed,' Iyena nodded. 'Lying and deceit—these are the hallmarks of evil; the actions indulged in by those who are falling from the One Light. But it does not make them happy. Disharmony breeds sickness and death, so ultimately those beings falling from the light suffer the most. The ancient texts used to call it, "The Path of Sorrow," for all the suffering choosing such a path brought.'

'So "evil" is like a sickness, isn't it?' said Issa.

'Yes, you could say that.'

'Can they recover? Is it possible to help the fallen ones? Ayeth, with all his power, failed, and now look at him.'

'I wish I knew, but that sounds like a question for a goddess,' said Iyena, throwing Issa a half smile.

The seer said no more and they walked silently along the north of the island through groves of apple trees. Issa pondered deeply on the notion of the soul and how it emerged from the One Light. Asaph asked Iyena all about the animals, birds and trees of Myrn and her sister islands, but Issa found herself only half-listening.

Would Myrn be her new home? It was certainly beautiful and peaceful. But what if she lived forever? She could have many homes in many places. Could she imagine living forever and never dying? A small smile curled her lips.

Yes, she could.

Issa watched Naksu as she placed a pebble-sized, polished amethyst on the stone pedestal. They were alone in a small, gracefully carved, stone outhouse whose slender pillars formed pretty arches above them. There were no windows or doors and it was open to the elements. A tiny brook tinkled nearby and it was dark, save for the amethyst and Naksu's softly glowing staff. The night was cool and Issa hugged her cloak closer over her robes.

'Focus your attention on the crystal,' said Naksu, her eyes fixated on the amethyst which cast her pale skin in a purple glow. 'Try and *feel* it rather than see it.'

Issa reached out with her mind and imagined what it would be like to be the crystal, how it would feel.

'Crystals hold very special energy,' said Naksu. 'They are one of the only elements that retain their form when you take them to the higher dimensions. If you took a crystal into the Astral Planes, it would stay the same material. Very few objects do.

'Do you know what else retains its form? Well, we do. So, crystals and humans share similar energetic properties. You could say we have a natural affinity with them which makes it possible for us to communicate with them.

'Most elements change their form as they move between dimensions—which is why alchemists are always trying clever ways to turn lead into gold, for example.

'Now, once you have established this rapport with the crystal, ask it to glow. I say "ask" because telling is commanding, which is dominating. Asking is co-creating together.'

Issa nodded and, as best as she could with a silent, inanimate object, mentally asked the crystal to glow.

Nothing visibly happened but she felt something shift, as if the crystal may have been awakened by her touch.

'Like this,' said Naksu, staring intently at the rock. The crystal began to glow purple, subtle at first, then brighter and brighter.

The seer smiled and looked at Issa. 'It's actually exactly the same method you use to access and command your orb and raven talisman, only you do it naturally and without thinking about it.'

Issa raised her eyebrows. 'Now that I am thinking about it, I've no idea how I do that.' She focused again on the now dimmed crystal. It seemed more responsive—almost alive. Again, she asked it to glow. After a moment, the faintest aura surrounded it.

'Ha-ha!' Issa laughed.

'Well done,' Naksu clapped her hands. 'The crystal needs to get to know you. So you see, all things, even rocks, have a life force and thus an aura—albeit a much smaller, slower moving one. Crystals are powerful because of their purity. Like magic, they can be made to do good or evil, depending on the will of the person commanding them. Power isn't evil in and of itself, it just depends on how it's used.

'Crystal Command is one of the first lessons we train all seers in. Some of them feel a natural affinity with crystals and they take it to grand levels—such as using them to help create the protective force fields around the Isles of Tirry.

'Now, there are four other commands; water, air, fire and elemental—with Crystal Command being what most others call Earth. Seers may train in any and all of these, according to their desires. We already know, from what we have seen of you in our sacred pools, and heard from Asaph,'—Issa raised her eyebrows—'that you are naturally affiliated with Elemental Command, though you might not know the technical word for it. You have used fire, water, air and earth in all your magical spells, have you not?'

Issa thought about it, then nodded. 'Yes, I used whatever was necessary at the time and in response to whatever my enemy was doing.'

'Ah, now there's a thing to be aware of,' said Naksu. 'You don't just use the Flow to destroy and fight. You have used it for healing too, yes? It's obvious. Now, most wizards use only one of those elements. They can use all elements but they find they excel in only one. Have you found which you excel in?'

Issa began to shake her head, then paused. 'Well, since I have the Orb of Water, I find it comes more easily.'

'Yes, naturally. But, orb aside, because you command each element with equal ease, you have Elemental Command. This is the command that commands all the elements—it is pre-element, if you will. It's no surprise because Zanufey, of the night and dark waters, is considered to be of the pre-creative force. Does this sound familiar?'

Issa nodded vigorously. 'Yes, that's what the guardians of the portals and Zanufey alluded to.'

'Well, obviously, this is quite a power to have,' said Naksu. 'No wonder the wizards are keen to have you on the Circle.' She smiled, but Issa felt heavy and turned away.

'What is it?' asked Naksu.

'I don't know,' Issa sighed. 'Well, it's not right, this separation between everything. The orbs, elves and humans, seers and wizards. Divided. Everything is weak. The more I think about it, the more I feel— no, the more I know—we should try to combine the orbs and heal the divisions between us all. The old arguments have to be forgotten for us to move forward. That's why I don't want to sit upon the Wizards' Circle or be a witch or maybe even a seer.'

'The world is changing, it *has* to change if we are to survive,' Naksu nodded, her face serious. 'I imagine a time in which seers do not exist, and it scares me. But now…what you say, it's true. We have been divided in many ways for too long.'

'You manage to put into simple words the confusion I'm feeling,' said Issa, twirling a strand of hair around her finger.

'Well, you are right,' said Naksu. 'Men and women belong together, their powers balanced and complimenting each other. It's not just a nice concept but it makes sense energetically too. You have your physical body, but extending out around you are your energy fields. You may see one of these as your aura. You don't just have *an* aura, you have many energy fields and they can extend several feet around your body. You won't be able to see these fields in this dimension but you can in the Flow.

'We all have physical bodies, but ultimately our true form is light and sound. That is why we speak of the One Source as the One Light or the Word or sometimes the Divine Voice. We forget that there is sound too. First there came sound, and then there came light. But before any of those, there was Intention. These are our sacred teachings that we hold in our hearts and minds and will never let Baelthrom destroy.

'The One Source held the Intention, spoke the Word and the Light burst forth. External creation was created and everything began. When you're as far out in external creation as we are, these are hard concepts to grasp and even harder to articulate. Know that the part of you that remained with the One Source understands this fully. It's like trying to imagine time not existing when you are bound in the world of time—it's not really possible.

'In the furthest realm of external creation, the male and the female are quite pronounced. In energy terms, there's electrical and there is magnetic. Male and female hold both types, but male energy is mostly electrical. It drives out from Source. Female energy is more magnetic. It pulls back to the One Source.

'When these energies are in perfect balance, there is perfect harmony and the flow of energy from the One Source can circulate. This harmonious energy is called love and within it, all things flourish. Those things not able to feel this love, to receive it and to give it, wither and die. Anyway, I can see you are tired.'

'On the contrary, these teachings are deeply stirring to me,' said Issa, stifling her yawn. 'My mind just wishes it could hold more.'

'This information is heavy and it's just the tip of that knowledge, said Naksu. 'I said to Iyena that I would touch upon a few things and see where our conversations took us.'

'I would love to know everything, but I see now there is not enough time, at least tonight, to learn it all.' Issa gave a rueful smile. 'You know the guardians of the portals? Well, it occurred to me that, if we all came from Source and left a piece of ourselves at each dimension then, somewhere, perhaps we are guardians too.'

Naksu smiled. 'You have just explained simply a very difficult concept. Perhaps you should be the one teaching us.'

Issa coloured. 'It just seems like a good idea, I suppose.'

'Don't be embarrassed, let the soul speak,' said Naksu. 'Our unlimited, higher selves instinctively know far more than we do here, bound as we are within the constraints of time and matter.'

Issa was about to say more but caught herself, suddenly unnerved by her own question. If Zanufey was a guardian, a goddess with the power to create beings, did she have a part of herself down in the realms of matter? If Issa herself had a soul and a part of herself at the level of Zanufey, was she also a guardian somewhere? She instinctively felt the answer to be yes, though the feeling unsettled her.

Naksu turned back to the crystal. 'Now, matter and energy are really the same thing, just one's particulates are moving faster than the other. Rocks have very slow moving particulates.'

Naksu spoke at length on the nature of energy and matter. Though the information was fascinating and Issa wanted to learn, she began to yawn with increasing frequency.

'So you see, elements themselves are beings in their own right,' Naksu concluded. 'Therefore, the most powerful and effective way to command them is through rapport, through co-creation, by asking them if they would *like* to create with you. I've never had an element say no.'

Issa began to see the Flow and her interaction with it in a completely different light. The Flow itself was alive, with a consciousness of its own.

'I should have known all of this at school,' said Issa.

'We used to instinctively know all this at birth,' said Naksu. 'But we have devolved a long way from what we once were. Come, let us talk as we walk home. I think I need my bed, too.'

'Do you think we'll get it back? What we once were?' asked Issa, following Naksu outside.

'I don't see why not. But we'll need to become strong, courageous and fearless again. Millennia of war have weakened us, body, mind and spirit. Perhaps making whole what is divided is the first step.'

Asaph was already in bed and breathing deeply by the time Issa tiptoed in through the front door. She slipped out of her clothes and into her own bed. She thought she'd lie awake thinking about what she'd learned, but sleep came fast. Her dreams were relaxing at first, but they turned dark just before dawn.

In them, people screamed in terror, their howls echoing around her but she couldn't see them through the thick cloying smoke that stung her eyes and made them stream. Between the billows of black, great tongues of fire licked. Heat scorched her face. Smoke clogged her nostrils and the Under Flow surged around her making her feel woozy and sick.

A voice shouted, one she recognised, but took a while to place.

'Averen?' she cried, wafting at the smoke and choking. 'Where are you?'

She could feel him in the Flow, the familiar glow of his aura was somewhere ahead, but she couldn't see him.

'Our sacred land is falling!' He shouted, then screamed.

The High Wizard's magic surged, a wave of light in the Flow that was swiftly swallowed up in the black maw of the Under Flow. Everything felt like it was falling, as if she stood on the roof of a house that was collapsing beneath her. The smoke and the Under Flow dragged her down with them in a tide she couldn't fight.

Naksu smiled as she walked the empty path to her house in the centre of Oray. It was very quiet and everyone was in bed. Issa would be a great seer, more than a seer; a wizard and a witch as well. She would bring great changes.

Naksu had never thought wizards and seers might become one again, nor dared to believe the orbs and the magic of the world would be reunited—but now, she did. And it opened up a whole world of possibilities, of realities, if they just dared to take a leap of faith.

She stopped beside a stone water basin cut into the rock to catch the spring, and scooped the fresh water to her mouth. Like all the spring water on Myrn, it was deliciously pure, and this one had been cooled by being run through rocks.

A red glimmer in the depths caught her eye and she reached a hand down to it, thinking someone had dropped something.

Flames spread across the water as the vision engulfed her. Fire raged all around, burning great ancient trees whose outstretched limbs became a canopy of tormented yellow and orange above. A wall of intense heat hit her. The trees screamed in agony. Naksu covered her ears and wailed.

People's voices joined the tree's screams of pain. Flame covered figures ran and staggered between the trees, many collapsing as the fires consumed them. She glimpsed faces, elven faces, filled with agony and terror. They ran everywhere but there was nowhere to go that wasn't on fire.

The Under Flow seeped forwards, a black carpet in the Flow, smothering any magic they might have been able to cast. Naksu gasped in the heat, the smoke and the black magic, each breath becoming harder and hotter. Her throat burned.

A terrible voice boomed, shuddering her organs and the ground beneath her feet. She tried to scream but only a rasp came out. The Under Flow covered all, turning everything to black.

Naksu sank to the ground beside the water basin, gasping and clawing at her still burning throat. Her whole body shaking, she dragged herself up and staggered to Iyena's house.

CHAPTER 10

Elven Fall

A thousand elven voices wailed in pain, wrenching Averen from restful dreams.

He fought to awaken. The Under Flow was all around him trying to drag him under, and his lungs were filled with choking smoke and the horrible smell of burning flesh.

A voice of terror boomed in his mind, the heavy, airy, scouring words of Baelthrom were too distorted to make out. Fear slithered through every fibre in his body. Shouting an Elven spell-breaking command, he tore himself out of the dream and threw himself from his bed. Crouching on the floorboards on all fours, he remained there panting and gasping.

It felt like an eternity before the Under Flow receded. Finally, the smoke in his chest cleared and the clamouring of thousands of terrified voices dimmed.

'The Land of Mists is in perilous danger,' he breathed, dragging himself up.

His hands shaking so much he could barely dress; he went over the words of the translocation spell to Myrn in his mind. Hopefully, the seers would not mind his abrupt arrival. Scrawling a note to Harrodan, he hoped the man would not be offended by his sudden leave from his plain but extensive manor house in western Lans Himay.

Averen set the quill down and took hold of his staff. With it, he drew the rings of earth, water, fire and air, forming the swirling vortex around him, and reached out to Iyena or any member of the Trinity that might be open to his call. Having no time for greetings or such niceties, he plunged himself recklessly into the translocation.

The spell was violently fast, executed hastily, and he vomited as he materialised on the Northern Isle of Tirry. Sinking onto the grass on legs that were unable to hold him, Averen wiped the perspiration from his brow. It was dark, save for the glowing amber crystals arranged in a large circle around him. The crystals flashed once brightly as he arrived and then dimmed. He smoothed his hair back, his hands still shaking, the terror of his people still wrenching his heart.

He glanced down the hill over the tops of apple trees and made out the dark blue flatness of the ocean. Upon it was a tiny boat with a lantern heading towards the island. Iyena already on her way to meet him, he thought. Did he have time to wait for her? He tried to stand but his head spun so much he was forced back down. By the time the sickness and dizziness had cleared, he could see Iyena's glowing staff making its way through the trees.

'Hail, High Wizard Averen,' Iyena greeted him, breathing hard as she strode swiftly up the hill, fit despite her age. 'What has happened?' She gave him a half smile, clearly pleased to see him but sensing ill tidings as she passed him a flagon of water.

Averen took it gratefully and gulped it down.

'My apologies, Seer Iyena, I was dragged from my sleep and my bed with nightmare visions, and came here not a moment later. The elves are in terrible danger.'

'Naksu came to me with a vision just before I received the touch of your translocation spell. She was so distressed; I knew something was terribly wrong. Show me what you have seen.'

He licked his lips, keen to get going, but stepped forwards anyway and laid a hand upon her forehead. In his mind, he recalled everything he'd witnessed: the smoke and fire, the Under Flow, the terror of his people and Baelthrom's voice.

Iyena gasped and he dropped his hand.

'Naksu said over and again, "the elves, the elves".' Iyena's face was grim. 'Do what you must. You know where the elven tree is. Our promise to protect Sheyengetha will remain until the end of days and we are all dead and gone. This you know.'

'I hope it will never come to that,' Averen said, bowing.

'I'll alert the Trinity. They'll come with others to help in whatever way we can.'

Averen nodded his gratitude. There was no time to say more, and he whirled away, heading straight into the forest of oaks and evergreens without even trying to find a path. He ran where he could across the grass and earth, and used elven magic to assist his leaps over fallen boughs, crevices, and rocky hillocks.

He glanced up at the sky for a moment. The last orange sliver of Woetala's waning moon was barely visible. *Blessed Woetala, am I already too late?* He swallowed the lump that rose in his throat and pushed on faster until he burst into a clearing where what lay before him brought his flight to a halt so suddenly that he nearly fell over.

'Oh my!'

He stared in awe at the beauty before him. Fireflies danced around the giant blue oak tree. Its bark was a soft sheen of pale teal in the diffuse light of the quartz crystal. The tree was as wide as it was tall, its great branches—themselves as big as trees—stretching across the grass. Every leaf was perfectly formed, rich green and free from disease or blemish. Irises clustered around its base, bowing gracefully in the breeze.

An elven tree planted here eons ago by the elves as a symbol of peace and unity with humans. How funny that it was here where the elves had left for the Land of Mists. He wondered if the humans back then had known it was a gateway—open to chosen elves only, but a gateway to another world nonetheless.

The crystal glowed brighter as he, an elf, came closer. Blinking back tears for the exodus of his race, he laid a hand on the tree's illuminated bark. The ancient tree acknowledged him with joyful, welcoming feelings. He leant forwards, pressing his forehead against the bark, feeling great wisdom and gentleness far exceeding his own emanating from the tree.

'Great, wise Sheyengetha. I know the way is sealed against me for choosing to remain and not follow my kin. But, Sheyengetha, remember I said when they left that I would enter should there ever be dire need? That time is now. My people are in terrible danger and I beg you to let me through to do what I can before it is too late. I am the only wizard on Maioria who might have the power to save them.'

'Averen,' the tree spoke in a voice deep and whispering and filled with the ancient knowledge of the Wild Wood. Averen bowed his head in honour. 'Perhaps it is already too late.' There was deep sorrow in its voice as its great trunk began to shimmer and glow bright, becoming less substantial as the gateway opened.

'Thank you, Sheyengetha,' said Averen, bowing deeply. He held both hands up and reached into the light within Sheyengetha's trunk. The air tingled as he stepped forwards.

Averen emerged into a world of chaos. Gone were the Land of Mist's beautiful gold and silver trees he'd longed for centuries to see again. Gone the gentle sunlight, the crystal clear streams, the peace and the serenity.

Instead, the trees were raging furnaces of death and black rain fell from the darkness seeping across the sky. Where it fell the ground hissed, smoke billowed and the grass wilted and turned grey.

Averen whirled around, eyes wide in disbelief. Elves screamed and ran in all directions, darker silhouettes against the flaring yellow of a giant furnace, scrambling away from falling boughs of fire, trying to shield themselves from the devastating black rain. Where it touched, skin blistered and blackened.

A Dread Dragon screeched overhead. Averen collapsed onto his knees, his guts trembling. He couldn't see the beast for the smoke covering the sky. Within the flames, he heard the growls of death hounds, the shouts of Maphraxies.

The Under Flow moved. Baelthrom was near. Averen was too late. He had to focus on saving those he could. Whatever he did in the Flow would quickly draw the Immortal Lord's attention to him. His hands shook.

Risking his own life, he raised a finger and drew the Elven Shield symbol in the air. The Flow crawled beside the Under Flow to do his bidding. A shimmering purple shield flickered before him, rising and expanding, pushing back the fire and the black rain.

'Elves, come to me! I am Averen,' he used the Elven Voice, feeling it boom and reverberate through the chaos. All elves would hear him, he prayed Baelthrom would not. Those closest faltered and looked about. Seeing the purple shield, they pointed and ran to it; parents struggling to carry their children, others staggering with terrible wounds, exposed bones and dripping with blood. Desperation drove them on, all tried to get to his oasis.

'What are you doing?' a voice screamed from the trees.

Averen turned. The King of the Elves ran towards him, his pastel robes in tatters, his hands clenched into bloodied fists, his face a mask of fury.

'Daranarta,' Averen smiled.

'You are banished from this place, traitor!'

The hatred in Daranarta's eyes made Averen take a step back and his magic shield wobbled. He refocused his attention on it. A young elf girl, her dress smoking, staggered into the safety of the shield, followed by her parents. They were all blackened and bloody, their eyes full of a terror they hadn't known in centuries. At least they were still standing.

Daranarta rounded on him and pushed him.

'I came to warn you about a terrible premonition but I am too late,' said Averen, seeking to calm the livid king. 'Why have you not abandoned this place?'

'Abandoned? You fool! This is our home. There is nowhere else to go!' Daranarta screamed.

'Are you mad? You'll all die here!'

More people staggered into the safety of his shield, and it was swiftly becoming crowded. He tried to expand its reach, pulling the sluggish Flow into the shield.

An explosion rocked the ground, knocking everyone to their knees. The shield trembled violently. Getting back onto his feet, Averen grimaced and doubled his efforts to keep the shield up and enlarge it. The black rain fell harder, pinging off the top of it like hailstones.

More people arrived, some carrying those who couldn't walk, their legs nothing more than agonising blackened stumps dripping blood. They would not last past the hour and Averen knew he would never forget their howls of pain. He longed for the hour to end so they might find peace.

Daranarta grabbed a hold of his shoulder and shoved him. 'Get out!

We do not need or want you here. Get out!'

Averen shoved him back with the Flow, and the king staggered. 'You are mad, truly.' Averen could not believe what the king was doing. Had he gone insane? 'You want to die here? All of you?'

'How dare you,' Daranarta hissed. 'We'd rather die here than return to Maioria.'

'You would condemn your whole race because of pride?' Averen snapped, disbelieving what he was hearing. What had happened to the elves? Had they become consumed with selfish insanity? 'Isn't that why you came to the Land of Mists anyway? To protect the Elven race?'

'Death is better than returning,' spat Daranarta.

Averen stared at the king, searching for a glimmer of reason or sanity in his glaring eyes. Was he injured or had he hit his head? There was no injury that he could see. The king stood strong and proud—and was surely insane.

Averen tried to reason with him again, a ridiculous thing when the world was on fire and Dread Dragons hunted them. 'Daranarta, I've come to help you and our people before it's too late,' he pleaded. 'Why has your hatred of me not lessened in all these years?'

The elf king narrowed his eyes. 'If all the elves had done their duty to their people and not betrayed us by staying in Maioria, Baelthrom could never have found us. This is your fault! Yours and that witch, the Raven Queen,' the king snarled and spat on the ground. 'We've lived here in peace and abundance for hundreds of years—proving that without the diseased races of dwarves and humans, it can be done. Go back to your wars and your violence.'

'Daranarta, war and violence are upon you whether you wish it or not. Centuries away from the wars ravaging Maioria have made you weak. Look around you at Baelthrom's might! The elves will not survive unless you flee, and the only place to go is Maioria. You cannot divorce yourself from the world and pretend evil does not exist by hiding from it. When evil is ignored it festers and grows, it will find you in the end and eat you alive. You must stand and fight!'

'All you know is war and fighting. You have become like a human!' Daranarta sneered.

Averen ignored him. 'Baelthrom hunts for the Orb of Earth. He can smell it like a wolf on a scent. He has taken the Orb of Air and grows ever more powerful. It is only a matter of time before he has them all. The Dragon Dream has been destroyed, and soon too the Land of Mists. Where is the Orb of Earth? It must be protected for the sake of the elves and all Maioria.'

'You shall never have it!' Daranarta screamed, his pale, dishevelled hair a mess around his dirt-stained face. Averen had never seen the king look so wild and uncontrolled.

Another explosion, this time much closer, sent them sprawling. Averen fell to his knees, bruising them. Ignoring both the king and his own safety, he set his focus fully on the shield. The Under Flow surged towards him, the sickening wooziness made him swoon and he would have fallen had he not been on his knees. Baelthrom had detected him. He groaned and battled for control of the Flow that was slipping through his fingers like silk. Through the fog of the Flow, he was vaguely aware of Daranarta hitting him and then others trying to drag the king away.

The shield, don't let it drop. Focus only upon the shield! Sweat dripped down his back. Someone helped him stand. Blackness covered his magic vision, the shield slipped. He growled and fought through the blackness. He grabbed hold of the shield again, pouring every ounce of his magic and concentration into it, barely able to breathe with the strain.

'You cannot hide from me. You cannot fight me,' Baelthrom's voice boomed all around, even inside his head.

The Immortal Lord was right, Averen could not hope to fight him. Red eyes opened in the black sky directly above him. The people beneath the shield screamed and hugged each other. Howling wind tore at him, forcing him to hook a foot around a tree root just to stay anchored to the ground.

He looked back at Daranarta. Two elves restrained him but his eyes glowered at Averen.

Still more elves were falling into his shield. Several hundred clustered under it. He would not be able to protect many more. Women and men clung to each other and their children, their faces masks of terror and pain. None of them were ready to fight. They'd been so long away from the world and all its troubles, they had forgotten how to. The realisation horrified Averen; his people were doomed.

Dark shapes bounded through the flames, Death Hounds on leashes of chains held by Maphraxies. Thick tongues lolled out of fang-filled mouths. Eyes alight with only the need to kill and eat the flesh of the living. Maphraxie faces, grey and deformed, dead-eyed and soulless, barked their guttural orders to each other.

A terrible scream ripped through the sky. Averen's heart pounded in his throat and the dragon fear forced him to his knees again. The Under Flow surrounded his shield and squeezed. He could not fight that force. He lost himself in the world of the Flow as he struggled to maintain his control. His magic was a great ball of purple surrounding him and the elves, and beyond it, a deluge of black magic trying to break him.

A wave of earthen power came from behind him, a golden light flowing into his shield, strengthening it. *Sheyengetha, bless you.* The golden magic thickened, pushing back the Under Flow and creating a tunnel between him and the tree. The tree was opening up a safe passage through which he could retreat. He could hold no more people in his shield.

He tried to scream, "Follow me!" but wasn't sure if he had in the din of the Flow. In the raging battle of magic, he could not make out any people.

Fire raked across the sky, blood red in his magic vision. His shield began to crack. He stepped backwards towards Sheyengetha, dragging the shield with him, praying the elves would follow. He stepped back again. Each step seemed to take an age. Sheyengetha's light cooled his burning back, offering strength, calm and salvation in a world of chaos. He stepped back again. The shield fractured as the Under Flow thundered against it.

He stepped into Sheyengetha's light and took a great breath of pure, cool air. The Under Flow could not enter Sheyengetha's purity. He pulled the failing shield to him and poured the remainder of his energy and strength into it. Only he had the power to protect the elves fleeing from Baelthrom as they fled towards the gateway that was Sheyengetha.

Willingly, he lost himself to the Flow, pouring so much of himself into his magic that his body began to turn into light, losing its material, physical properties. The magical light filled him with ecstatic, tingling energy as he became a tunnel of living energy within the body of Sheyengetha.

He felt the first elf move through him, pass through the fibres of his being, into Sheyengetha and beyond. He smiled and sighed, a sound that echoed and soothed.

More elves passed and he began to cry with joy. The elves would survive, just. He would remain here for as long as it took to ensure Baelthrom and his horde would never make it through. He had to protect the elves and he had to protect the seers, just as they had protected great Sheyengetha and thus the Land of Mists for all this time.

'I give my life to protect this place,' Averen commanded in the Elven Voice, loud and booming in the light as he sealed his oath. 'Sheyengetha and I are one. Only the Orb of Earth will have the power to release me. This I decree.'

With a cry, he sealed the gateway shut.

CHAPTER 11

Elf in Limbo

DAWN brightened the skies.

Issa stared at the elves pouring through the most beautiful tree she had ever seen. With rich green leaves untouched by autumn, and a thick, strong, pale blue trunk around which flowers bloomed, it was the most perfect tree she had ever seen.

The stillness and beauty of the morning here in the glade was a stark contrast to the bloody, wounded and sobbing people that staggered onto the grass. Asaph's arm around her shoulders tightened at the spectacle. The growing cries of agony made them leap into action.

It seemed all the seers in Maioria had come to help and hundreds of blue robed women and men of all ages rushed forwards to assist the injured, helping those too weak to stand and laying them on the grass.

Issa, Naksu and Asaph with the rest of the Trinity had been the first to arrive after Iyena. Iyena was telling her about Averen's panicked arrival when the tree started shimmering and people began pouring through. Her dream and Naksu's similar vision now all made horrible sense. The Land of Mists had been discovered by Baelthrom and attacked.

'I don't know what to do, there are so many of them,' Issa said in anguish, opening her hands and feeling helpless as she watched Iyena direct the seers. At least a thousand elves now filled the glade and forest, and all carried injuries. She noted every face emerging through the light of the tree, but none of them were Daranarta, and none of them were Averen.

'Issa, Asaph, help me,' Naksu called, struggling to hold up an elven man nearly two feet taller than the seer was.

Blood soaked the cloth he held to his head, the bright red drops vivid as they splashed onto his pastel tunic. A small elf-girl clung to his leg, her dress covered in burn holes and her skin red and blistering.

Asaph took the man's arm and wrapped it around his shoulders. Half carrying him, Asaph set the man down on the grass at the base of a tree. Issa hugged the child and lifted her up. Naksu went to work immediately, pulling everything out of her sack from bandages to candles to bottles and ointments.

Issa tended the girl whilst Asaph found his best use in helping carry those who could barely walk. The elf girl trembled all over and would only stare wide-eyed at the grass. Issa placed a hand on her sweaty forehead and murmured soothing words to calm her.

'Now then, you're a brave girl, because I bet you saw a Dread Dragon.' Issa smiled as she hovered her hands over the girl's burns. The girl nodded but did not look at her.

Issa directed the Flow from her hands over the girl's skin. The most severe blistering burns soon calmed and the skin lost its angry redness.

'Now then, brave one,' she said, picking up a tiny pot of Naksu's balm. 'The pain has lessened, hasn't it?'

The girl nodded but continued staring at the ground.

'It won't come back either, but you'll need to rub this on your skin morning and night until the burns are gone. I can't promise they won't scar but they should heal with time. Now, you see that lady over there?' She pointed to a red-haired seer standing before a table laden with food and jugs of water. 'She'll give you food and water. Why don't you go get yourself something whilst we look after your friend.'

The girl nodded again and Issa helped her up. On hesitant feet, the girl walked to the red-haired seer. Issa turned to help Naksu with the man's ghastly wounds. He lay with his eyes closed, breathing lightly.

'I've managed to stem the bleeding from his face and neck, but he's not good,' said Naksu, shaking her head as she began to stitch together the gashes on his face. 'What you did with the girl was impressive. See what you can do with his burns. Some are very bad.'

The seer was right, carefully pulling off a piece of the man's blackened tunic revealed a horrible mass of bleeding, weeping, burning flesh.

Issa took a deep breath and pooled the Flow into her palms until they glowed blue, then she ran the cooling energy over the burns, wherever she found them. The elf man visibly relaxed, his muscles no longer twitched and his breath came deeper and slower.

When they were unable to do more, they left him to rest. Iyena swiftly pointed them towards a young elf woman and her sister; both in shock and one with a broken arm and the other with fractured ribs. Naksu and Issa helped them to sit or lie down. Issa used the Flow to set the bone whilst Naksu splinted and bandaged them.

They worked without pause and with barely a break for food and water until the sun began to set. As soon as they had tended one person, they moved on to the next, and there were still many more to tend.

Whilst they worked, those elves who could walk were taken to the mainland where they could be sheltered, fed and watered more easily.

All through the day, seers, Asaph and any others fit and able to assist, erected tents down by the port. Slowly, all the people were moved through the forest to their temporary accommodation, limping, on stretchers or holding on to people.

Every time she finished with one patient, Issa looked to Sheyengetha hoping Averen would emerge any moment, but he didn't.

When the last of the elves were finally carried away and dusk covered the forest, Issa stood and stretched her aching back with a groan. She watched the seers leave, reluctant to go herself in case anybody else emerged.

'Come, let's get some food,' said Asaph, his face and clothes were smeared with blood and dirt, and he looked exhausted. 'No one has come through since midday, and we need to look after ourselves, too.'

Issa, nodded, her stomach had been rumbling for a good hour. 'Averen never returned. Does that mean he's gone?'

Asaph looked away. 'I don't know.'

Issa walked towards the tree. It stood silent and serene, bathed in the soft light of the crystal. She couldn't believe the High Wizard was dead, it just couldn't be. Would the tree know? She was Daluni but it was said only elves could talk to trees.

'Sheyengetha,' she said the tree's name and laid a hand on its pale trunk. She felt or heard it sigh as if it were weary and wanted rest.

'Is Averen still alive?' Issa tried the Daluni mind-speak, wondering if it would speak to her. There was a long pause and a strong feeling of reluctance. She tried again.

'Please tell me. I pray to Woetala that he is. Does he need help? Is he trapped in the Land of Mists? Does Baelthrom have him? If you let me through, maybe I can help.'

'None but elves may pass,' Sheyengetha replied in a deep sighing voice that was filled with sorrow. Issa leant closer to hear. *'Averen and I are as one. We protect the gateway. Alone, I cannot. When the time comes, only the elven orb can part us.'*

'Is Daranarta with you? Is the orb safe?' asked Issa, but the tree remained silent and still.

'Thank you, Sheyengetha. May Woetala bless you.' She felt an acceptance of her blessing but no more. She dropped her hands and looked at Asaph.

'Averen lives, but within the tree. When the time is right only the Orb of Earth can release him.'

'What does that mean?' asked Asaph, his brow knitting together.

Issa frowned too. 'That's all Sheyengetha said.'

'Is the orb safe?'

Issa shook her head. 'I don't know. What if it's stuck beyond the tree? If Baelthrom has captured another orb...'

She felt faint at the thought and must have looked it for Asaph pulled her close. He didn't say anything though. What could he possibly say to ease her mind under such dire thoughts? He put an arm around her shoulder and turned her towards the path.

'Raven Queen,' Sheyengetha whispered in her mind, in a voice filled with knowing. Issa paused and looked back but the tree said no more.

The next day, Issa and Asaph were up before dawn to help the refugees. Of the three thousand or so elven souls who had made it through Sheyengetha, scores had died of their injuries in the night. The sorrow of it was swept away by the sheer number of others who needed their help.

At least they passed away peacefully on Myrn with the seers at their sides, and in as little pain as possible. Thankfully, those remaining were mostly recovering or at least stable.

At daybreak, the wizards arrived. Issa hurried over to them as they stepped off the boat on to the main dock at Oray. It was a relief to see Freydel's friendly face under the dire circumstances. The wizards stared, aghast at the temporary tents filled with elves stretching up and down the coast, and clustered around an exhausted Iyena, their purple robes a compliment to her pale blue one, as she explained everything that had transpired. Issa came to stand beside her.

'Where is Averen?' asked Freydel, worrying his beard.

'We've tried to reach him but can't,' Drumblodd shook his head, planting his axe between his feet.

'He's in the tree,' Issa said, just as Iyena was about to speak.

Everyone looked at her. Iyena had also been shocked when Issa told her about Averen and that the tree had spoken to her. Usually, only seers trained in Tree Whispering could do so—which had left Issa wondering all evening whether her mother been a trained Tree Whisperer and maybe even spoken to Sheyengetha herself all those years ago.

'In great Sheyengetha,' Issa continued. The wizards murmured, eyebrows raised, except for Domenon whose face remained impassive. 'The tree told me. It was the only way Averen could both keep the gateway to the Land of Mists open long enough for the elves to escape and then seal it shut against anything bad that might follow. Only when the time is right and with the elven orb will he leave the tree.'

'The orb,' Freydel gasped. 'Where is it?'

Issa looked at the ground, that same terrible feeling rising in her stomach. 'We don't know.'

'None of the elves have it and they don't know where it is,' said Iyena. 'Unless they are hiding it to protect it.'

'We must find it,' said Haelgon, his face drawn.

'It could be trapped within the Land of Mists,' Issa tried to sound hopeful.

Freydel took a deep breath, turned away and leant on his staff. 'If we lose another… It's all over. It is barely hanging on as it is.'

Iyena laid a hand on his shoulder. 'We must hope for the best, that's all we can do. Come now, there are hundreds of injured people who desperately need the help of wizards.'

'We will ask Truth Questions as we help them,' said King Navarr, looking determined.

Freydel nodded and rubbed his eyes. Iyena led him away and the wizards followed, except for Domenon.

'Did Sheyengetha say anything more about the orb?' asked Domenon, an intense look in his eyes.

'Don't you care about Averen?' Issa spoke her thoughts aloud and immediately wondered why she'd said it. She was tired and emotionally wrung out from all the pain and suffering, but still, the wizard's lack of caring never ceased to irritate her. He gave a surprised half-smile.

'Averen is more than capable of looking after himself, but the orb is not.'

Issa tutted. 'It may not be so obvious to the other wizards but it's obvious to me that your loyalties don't lie with the Wizard's Circle. I just wonder if you care about anyone else in this world other than yourself.'

A flicker of anger passed across his handsome face and was swiftly replaced with a cool smile. 'I'm pleased that you think of me so much, Raven Queen.' He gave a slight bow, whether mocking or not, Issa couldn't tell.

'As a Master Wizard it is my duty to help the needy. Like King Navarr suggested, I will ask every elf I treat about the orb and consider their responses. They won't be able to hide the truth from me. Later today I would like you to take me to Sheyengetha so I can get a feel for the situation, if it's not too much to ask.' He turned away to follow the other wizards without waiting for a response from her.

She shook her head, feeling strangely that he'd been both flirting and arguing with her. He was a confusing man; powerful yet sowing discord wherever he went, handsome and mysterious and yet irritating and dangerous. No wonder Freydel found him so difficult. Perhaps she would take him to the tree later…and perhaps she wouldn't, she thought with a grin.

For the rest of the day, she busied herself by healing the injured; changing bandages, easing pain with the Flow, salving wounds, distributing armsful of new clothes—the list was endless. She only stopped to rest when Asaph brought her a sandwich in the afternoon. She raised herself from the woman whose bandages she'd been rebinding and smiled at him.

'I'm so tired,' she sighed, thanking him for the sandwich as they walked towards seashore.

'Me too. I've erected at least twenty tents this morning and my shoulders are aching.'

They sat down on the edge of a jetty, their feet hanging over the water, and ate lunch. Ehka swooped down from the trees to join them. Issa crumbled up some of her bread for him. He gobbled it down in moments and looked up at her for more.

'I saw all those wizards arrive,' said Asaph. 'They looked impressive.'

Issa laughed. 'Well, it's mostly show, but they are nice enough, apart from Domenon. He's just so odd.'

'The dark-haired one?'

'Yes.'

'He's the one who hurt you.' Asaph glowered.

'Well, not really. He grabbed me and Ehka went crazy, but he didn't hurt me. He was just… emotional. He's not so bad, really, just difficult.'

'Hmph,' was all Asaph said, though his scowl remained.

'He wants me to take him to Sheyengetha later, to see if he can reach Averen. I'm not sure if I'll go, though.' Issa brushed the crumbs from her lap to Ehka.

'I'll come with you if you do,' said Asaph, finishing his sandwich and staring across the harbour. 'I'll make sure he keeps his manners.'

Issa smiled to herself, liking his protective nature.

Driven by intrigue, Issa decided to meet Domenon at the dock. The wizard was dressed in his usual thin, black leather trousers and boots, white shirt and dark purple wizards' cloak. He watched her approach, dark eyes never once blinking or wavering.

Issa self-consciously tightened the collar of her robe, wishing she'd worn her Dread Dragon armour. It just didn't feel right to wear her armour and sword here in this sacred place amongst the simply-robed seers. Neither Ehka nor Asaph were anywhere to be seen, annoyingly. At least the raven could have come. Maybe he was busy doing his favourite thing; bothering the crabs as they scuttled over the rocks.

A squeeze of her talisman tucked into her belt reassured her. She had the orb too, but she wished she'd left it at home, knowing how Domenon desired it. *That time he grabbed me was a one off. He's not going to harm me,* she reassured herself, feeling silly and almost guilty for assuming he had ill intentions.

'I had to help someone,' she said by way of an apology for keeping him waiting, then stopped. She didn't need to apologise for anything.

'On the contrary, I was early,' Domenon said with a smile. 'Shall we?' He offered her his arm and she hesitated before taking it, thinking of Asaph.

'Asaph wanted to come. He won't be a minute.' She didn't think Asaph would like her holding Domenon's arm, but the wizard laid a hand over hers and she felt it would be rude to pull away.

'Unfortunately, I don't have any time to wait. I must be back within two hours for a meeting. I'm sure he'll understand.'

Issa glanced behind them. Scanning the tents, Asaph was nowhere to be seen. He knew where she was going and he could catch up. Besides, she was more than capable of looking after herself, and this Master Wizard had a reputation to uphold. He'd never really done her harm other than just be irritable. She sighed and let him lead her away.

A middle-aged boatman with long brown hair tied back with a cord, dressed in a shirt and simple woollen jerkin helped them into the small boat and hoisted the little sail. There were many little boats and boatmen and women always ready to take people to any of the other four islands. Their services were free whilst they received teaching and learnt skills from the seers.

The wind picked up as they moved farther from shore and they navigated the short distance to the north island rapidly. At the jetty, Domenon jumped out first and offered his hand to help her. She refused it.

'I'm not a princess. I *can* do things for myself,' she said, smiling thinly.

'Indeed. I forget you are a queen,' said Domenon.

Again, she couldn't tell if he was mocking her or not. She chose to ignore it and led the way along the path. All of the elves had been provided with shelter on the main island now, but a handful of empty tents remained here, the white tarp flapping in the breeze.

They reached the trees and she glanced back before she lost sight of the coast, half hoping to see Asaph running up behind them. He wasn't and there was no other boat in the channel. With a sigh, she carried on. Clouds covered the sun now and then, and it was cold whenever they were plunged into shade. She lifted the collar of her robes higher. The smell of pine was rich in her nostrils and white squirrels jumped here and there, carrying and burying acorns in preparation for the coming winter.

'So what is this Asaph to you, then?' Domenon asked.

Issa almost stopped in her tracks. 'That's rather forward, don't you think?' She felt her cheek grow warm. 'Are you married? Have children? What's your wife like in bed?'

Domenon raised his eyebrows and laughed heartily. 'No, I'm not married. Nor do I have a wife or children, so I couldn't know what she is like in bed. My one devotion is to the Queen of Davono, but we are far from lovers. Respected acquaintances, you could say. She gives me power and excellent food and accommodation, and I give her protection and all the services a Master Wizard can provide.'

'Sounds like you're very successful,' said Issa, and hid a half-smile when he scowled. 'How old are you?'

'You know I'm older than humans thanks to my—' he began.

'Yes, because of your mixed heritage,' Issa cut him off, not wanting to hear it again.

'Anyway, you evaded my question,' Domenon broke in. 'Are you embarrassed? Don't you like the man's obvious attentions towards you?' Domenon said.

'Asaph and I are not married,' said Issa, getting cross.

'Still not answering the question,' said Domenon.

She pulled up short and leant towards him speaking firmly. 'Look, what's between me and Asaph is none of your business, nor anyone else's. Given that Baelthrom hunts me to no end, I find it unwise to get too involved with those who might be killed just because they are close to me. My adopted mother was murdered and my friends. I don't want to see any more die because of me, all right?'

'You can't stop people getting themselves killed, you can only protect yourself,' said Domenon, his face serious.

'Is that supposed to make me feel better?' she said, her temper making it difficult to control her tongue. 'I'm not surprised you'd say something like that. You do, after all, only look after yourself, isn't that right?'

'Perhaps,' Domenon shrugged, completely unruffled. 'But you can't help others if you can't help yourself. I'm merely questioning your relationship with the man. Men don't like to be led on.'

'Pah.' Issa stalked onwards. Domenon followed, matching her pace easily with his long legs. 'I'm not leading him on…I'm simply trying to get on with things. Just because I'm female, my life isn't all about getting married and having children, you know.' She was almost running now but he kept stride easily beside her.

'I like that it isn't,' said Domenon.

She side-glanced at him. Was he laughing at her? He gave a wide smile that lacked any mockery. She looked away feeling her cheeks get even hotter. Unable to keep the pace up, she hugged her chest and slowed.

'I think you don't know what to feel about him and perhaps you are even scared of your feelings,' intuited Domenon. 'He should help you feel confident and strong. And I'm sorry about those you've lost. Sometimes I forget to think about the impact of my words. I spend a long time away from people surrounded only by my studies. It can make you a little socially inept.'

Issa nodded, accepting his humble explanation and masking her surprise at his admissions.

'He does help me feel strong. And it's not like you to admit to a weakness,' she muttered.

'Everyone has a weakness. Perhaps one of mine is unmarried women,' Domenon said, his face nothing but innocence.

'You desire power and the orbs above all else. Even I can see that,' she said it with a laugh.

He didn't disagree.

'Look, there's the tree.' She pointed to Sheyengetha as they rounded a corner. 'It's so beautiful.'

The vivid green, majestic canopy moved gracefully in the breeze and the late afternoon sun diffused and spread a golden light around it. Songbirds sang and jumped amongst its branches, and a squirrel scooted up its trunk. Bright irises cast vivid indigo spots around its base.

'Some say it's the most beautiful, wisest tree in all Maioria,' said Domenon loudly as if he wanted the tree to hear. 'I remember when the tree was young.'

'That must have been hundreds of years ago,' said Issa, shocked.

Domenon simply smiled at her. She found herself searching his face for any hint of elven. He was handsome, yes, although she hated to admit it, with his chiselled features, dark hair and sultry, brooding eyes—but they weren't elven. He was taller than most men, though not slender like an elf but broader. The mystery around him deepened and she looked away.

He laid a hand on the tree, closed his eyes and seemed to be trying to communicate with it. She, too, laid a hand upon it and was surprised to find the pale blue bark warm.

'You don't fool me, Domenon,' Sheyengetha whispered, in a deep, calm voice. A sound like a low wind rustling through leaves. 'Or should I call you by your real name? I know who you are, *what* you are.'

Issa dropped her hand with a gasp. She could hear the tree speak so clearly. She glanced at Domenon wondering what Sheyengetha meant but he was scowling and looking only at the ground. She placed her hand back on the tree and heard them speaking again.

'I am your friend, as always. We need to know where the orb is,' said Domenon.

'From you and Baelthrom, the orb is safe. Before Daranarta left his mortal body, he bound it to another,' said Sheyengetha.

'You don't know my plans, Sheyengetha, no one does. And I am changing them even as we speak,' said Domenon.

'Deceit is never honoured by Woetala's trees,' said Sheyengetha. 'Soon the light will shine through your disguise and pretences.'

'Like the seers and elves, I simply keep myself protected,' whispered Domenon harshly.

He clearly didn't want Issa to hear any of this and she wondered what on earth he was hiding. Should she fear this man?

'That is understandable in these times, but trees see the truth of things and cannot be fooled,' repeated the tree.

'Where is the orb? We can help bring it back if it is trapped the other side,' said Issa. Regardless of Domenon's shadiness, he was right—the orb needed to be found and protected immediately. Baelthrom might even be the other side of the gateway still hunting for it.

'The orb is beyond the gate, Raven Queen, held by an elf who is in limbo,' said Sheyengetha.

'Then let us enter and retrieve it… and him,' said Domenon.

The tree was silent for a long time. Issa fidgeted. The Master Wizard clenched his jaw impatiently. Then the tree spoke. 'Only one may enter, but with the knowledge, they might not return.'

'Then let me pass,' Domenon hissed.

The tree was silent. Issa looked at him then back at the tree. Perhaps it had been a stupid idea to bring Domenon here so close to an orb in this state. Why hadn't she thought to bring the other wizards? Even Sheyengetha didn't seem to trust the man.

'You said there's an elf in limbo,' said Issa. 'If he's between the living and the dead, I can reach him.' Domenon glowered at her. 'You know my gifts, Domenon.'

'As you wish, Raven Queen,' said Sheyengetha.

Before she was ready, Issa felt her hands sinking into the tree as its trunk dematerialised into light and the gateway opened. She stumbled forwards.

Golden light surrounded Issa and the rich smell of earth and forest filled her nostrils. Sheyengetha's great presence was all around and her body melded with the tree. She felt her feet becoming roots digging deep into the cold, dark soil. Her head and arms reached up to the heavens, soaking up the life giving light of the sun, and her body was infinitely strong and rigid.

She moved forwards and felt her human body return to her as she emerged into a perfectly round space. Her breath caught in her throat at its beauty. Golden brown roots and branches entwined around, above and below her forming the walls of the circle and the air sparkled with light. She appeared to be standing in an inner space within the tree itself, although the area was surely bigger than the trunk of the tree. The air here was thick with the smell of wood resin.

She took a few steps forward. White and purple light flared and covered the wall of roots in front and above her. A figure formed in the light above, pale hair spread out around him like a sun, arms stretched wide and welcoming like a statue of the divine. His eyes were closed and his face, with its gentle, knowing smile, was the picture of serene bliss.

'Averen,' she breathed.

'He cannot answer. Together we both hold and guard the gateway,' Sheyengetha's voice echoed around her.

Remembering her mission, she walked forwards beneath Averen and towards the light which became a slow moving vortex of white. What would she find beyond it? Baelthrom? A hundred Dread Dragons? She swallowed and lifted a hand. She should have let Domenon go instead. *Think only about the orb, it is safer with me.* She nodded to herself. A man hung in limbo and she had the chance to save him. She took a deep breath, closed her eyes and stepped forwards.

The momentary peace and silence in the white vortex were destroyed by raging winds and an inferno of red flames. It was so hot she lifted her arms to shield her face and stepped back so she was half within the safety of the vortex.

In front of her, great tornados of fire whirled between earth and sky. Her hair and clothes whipped around her, trying to tear themselves from her body. Red and black clouds raced above. The ravaging fire was burning on nothing. There was only ash at her feet and no trees, houses or anything else. Was this what had become of the beautiful Land of Mists? Were there Dread Dragons somewhere above?

Baelthrom could be here. Sweat trickled down her brow and her hands trembled. She was too shaken to form control over the erratic Flow and it slipped out of her grasp. She placed the talisman on her chest and screamed the spell to enter the realm of the dead.

The roar dimmed to silence and, for the first time, she was relieved to emerge into the silent and empty Dead Realm. Gone were the raging winds and towering infernos. Instead, in the grey world, there were lots of something else—ghosts. More than she had ever seen. She gasped and clasped her hand over her mouth to keep from making a noise.

Ghostly elves floated between the trunks of massive grey trees. Others stood still, bunched together in clusters and turned inwards to each other as if in conversation, their shoulders hunched and hands clasping.

Issa's heart hammered in her chest and she swallowed. *All the recent dead.* The grief was palpable, suffocating and she blinked back tears. *Zanufey, please find them, gather them and take them to their endless forests of Woetala.* She wanted to help them, but what could she do?

I have to find the orb, she reminded herself, wrapping her arms around her as a form of protection. She closed her eyes and focused on the Flow. It was grey and sluggish, a ghost of its former power like the Dead Realm itself, and it revealed nothing of the orb's whereabouts. She opened her eyes with a sigh. A black shape landed at her feet, making her jump.

'Ehka, where have you been?' she whispered, utterly relieved. 'Thank the goddess you came. Do you know where the orb is?'

The raven hopped in a circle, cocking his head now and again. Then he flew off ahead. Shivering, she rubbed her arms and followed him, trying to tread carefully around the huddling souls of elves. They did not even look up. Perhaps she was just a ghost to them?

Ehka flew through the trees but didn't go far. He landed on the ground beside a huddled shape. Issa came closer, tiptoeing silently. The shape was a man sitting with his head buried between his knees, and hands clasped over his head. His long hair was draped around him and he appeared to be sobbing or groaning. Though everything about him was grey—his cloak, trousers, hands and pale hair—he looked as solid and real as Ehka beside him, and not ghost-like at all.

Licking her lips, she dared to touch his shoulder and jumped back in alarm as she felt his solidarity. He looked up at her, his face ravaged by sorrow and covered in cuts and dirt. *How can he be here?* Was he alive or dead? His face was ashen, even his lips and eyes and hair, unlike a real, healthy, living elf. He looked dead and yet he was solid. He looked like she had in the Shadowlands. She shuddered. *He's in limbo, just as I was...* The concept unnerved her.

'Who are you?' The elf man demanded, jerking himself up to tower above her. He lifted his arm as if to shield himself from her. 'Leave me alone!'

'Don't be afraid, I've come to help.' Issa sought to soothe him, hoping to push back the crushing loneliness she knew he would be feeling in this place.

'Who are you? Where am I?' He opened his arms a little to peer at her between them. His eyes went wide. 'I know you, you're the one who saw it coming! You knew he'd come, why didn't you help us?' He lunged forwards and grabbed her shoulders in a surprisingly strong grip.

'I tried to,' she said, pushing his hands off. 'But you wouldn't listen to me and sent me away. Zanufey cannot help those who refuse her aid. You're lucky anyone has come back here to find you.'

'Where am I? I am dead. Sometimes I see ghosts. Sometimes I recognise them. I run from them...' The elf man's eyes darted around. 'Are you a ghost?'

'No. And you're not dead, not fully. You're in limbo. Through the grace of Averen and Sheyengetha, your life may have been saved. Where is the Orb of Earth?'

'Is that what this is all about?' He scowled. 'You're one of them in disguise, come to take the orb from me like you tried to take it from Daranarta. Hah! Daranarta was smarter,' he grinned wildly. 'He gave his life to protect it—'

'Daranarta was a fool who caused the Land of Mists to fall and thousands to die,' Issa cut him off. 'I don't want the orb but if you don't let me help you, either you'll stay in limbo forever or Baelthrom will find you. Many of your kind have escaped to Maioria and you alone are being given a second chance to do so.'

'Stay here? Forever?' The man shook visibly.

'Come with me.' She held out a hand. 'I can help get you out.'

She didn't expect him to take her out-stretched hand, but fear must have got the better of him and he did.

'Follow me and try to be quiet. They won't see us if we don't draw their attention.'

Gripping his hand tightly, she followed Ehka back to Sheyengetha. Even in the Dead Realm, the great tree was impressive. It was grey like the others, but it wasn't wilted and instead stood proud; its huge round crown covered in grey leaves, and its thick trunk solid and strong.

She paused before the swirling light in Sheyengetha's trunk and turned back to the man.

'What's your name?'

'Orphinius,' he told her.

'Orphinius,' she said, her face sombre, 'I don't know what state your physical body will be in when we return but we will do everything we can. Expect it to hurt.'

He nodded and licked his lips. Gripping his hand tightly, she pressed the talisman against her chest.

'Return us to the living,' she commanded and stepped into Sheyengetha.

There came living warmth and pure air. Her physical body solidified. A world of colour replaced the grey. The golden light in the centre of Sheyengetha was so vivid and bright after the Dead Realm she blinked and squinted. For one horrifying moment, she could feel nothing and thought she had let go of Orphinius' hand.

He appeared moments later beside her and sagged. She pulled his arm over her shoulder, struggling to hold him up. Now no longer in the realm of the dead, the wounds on his face bled freely and blood swiftly soaked his midriff. Staggering under his weight, she tried to drag him forwards.

He had the orb, she could feel its power in the Flow. It was pulsing green light even through the fabric of his pocket. Relief washed over her. She became aware of tinkling music, like fairy songs. With a start, she realised Sheyengetha was singing to the orb. Images formed in her mind; flowers moving in the breeze, leaves rustling in autumn, the rich green of spring pastures. The music was so gentle and pure it brought tears to her eyes.

Sweating and panting under Orphinius' weight, she glanced back one last time at Averen. His eyes flicked open and flared purple light. He was smiling and she wondered if he could see her.

'Come back to us, Averen,' she pleaded, her voice breaking with emotion.

'Not yet, Raven Queen,' his melodic voice whispered in her mind. *'Fear not Domenon.'*

Wondering what he meant, she nodded anyway. Orphinius groaned, bringing her back to reality, and she moved with urgency back the way she had entered. Roots and branches faded into pale light as she drew close. Everything became very dense and the air thick, earthy and hard to breathe. Then she stepped onto green grass.

CHAPTER 12

Tree Whisperer

ISSA fell through the other side of Sheyengetha, unable to hold up Orphinius' sagging weight any longer.

She rolled the elf onto his back on the grass. He was in a bad way, shaking uncontrollably and all his wounds bled freely, as if they had been held in stasis in the realm of the dead and now were reopened. Blood matted his long, platinum blond hair and his clothes were in tatters.

'Where is the orb?' Domenon's panicked voice caught her attention. The wizard reached down and grabbed Orphinius' shoulders, lifting him up.

Orphinius groaned, too weak to protect himself. He flopped uselessly in Domenon's grasp.

'Domenon!' Issa shouted, grabbing his arm. 'The man is badly injured and has been through a lot, can't you see that?'

Domenon either ignored her or was so intent upon the man, he didn't actually hear her. She pushed herself to her feet, her legs feeling like jelly, and tried to pry his fingers off Orphinius' shoulders.

'Where is the orb?' repeated Domenon. 'You'd better have it! That's the only reason we brought your sorry hide back out.'

Issa fumed. She was the one who'd brought him out and this was no way to treat a man who had just returned through death's door and looked about to go back in. She felt Domenon enter the Flow and she jumped in ready to protect Orphinius if needed.

'Get off him!' shouted Issa, yanking on his arm.

Domenon flung his arm back at her, swiping her off her feet. She landed on her back, the wind knocked out of her lungs.

In a blink, Domenon was bending over her as she gasped for breath. 'Or have you got it?' He demanded.

The Master Wizard's anger and desperation took her by surprise, leaving her totally bewildered. His eyes narrowed and for the briefest moment, she thought they changed shape, becoming slits like those of a cat, and in the next instant they were normal again.

She didn't hear the other man arrive. All she saw was the blur of a fist smashing into Domenon's face and then blue sky above and the sound of someone roaring. She sat up and saw Asaph grappling with the Master Wizard, his thick muscles bunched and his face scowling. He landed two more blows before Domenon thrust him back and swiped his legs from under him. Asaph rolled but Domenon leapt upon him, as fast and graceful as a cat, and hammered a furious blow. Issa looked on in shock.

Asaph forced himself up and the two men struggled for balance. Asaph looked to be the stronger and broader of the two, but Domenon had been trained in special techniques and was able to dodge Asaph's blows, yet swiftly land his own. Blood already streaked from Asaph's split lip and an angry bruise swelled on Domenon's face.

The two men circled each other.

'Stop it,' shouted Issa, feeling utterly useless.

The men ignored her. She got the very strong sense that she shouldn't get involved.

'You've hurt her before, you won't do it again,' Asaph growled.

Domenon simply laughed, further enraging Asaph. His face was red and his blue eyes flashed, making her worry he might turn into a dragon at any moment.

'Stop it!' She shouted again. 'Asaph, I'm all right!' But he didn't seem to hear her and went for Domenon again.

His right swing missed but his left-handed blow connected. Domenon staggered but recovered fast—incredibly fast—and lunged. Asaph was ready. They both moved so quickly, it was sometimes hard to see who was who. Issa had never seen people fight with such speed.

Asaph stumbled and Domenon got him in a headlock.

'You know what dragons call you? Half-breeds,' Domenon sniggered.

'Not all dragons,' Asaph rasped, and flung them both forwards.

Issa licked her lips and tried to think of something that would make them stop before they really hurt each other. She couldn't even think of how to use the Flow to stop them without harming them. She entered the Flow anyway and what she saw astounded her.

Asaph's form was a whirling mass of yellow flames flaring wildly, passionately. And so was Domenon's. Both men's forms were filled with fire rushing through and around them. Asaph's flame energy was larger but Domenon's was smoother, more concentrated and controlled. Suddenly Domenon's energy spewed forth and surrounded Asaph entirely.

Issa shook her head and blinked in time to see Asaph crumple in the physical world. She yelped and ran to him, expecting Domenon to continue his attack, but the Master Wizard just stood calmly staring at the fallen Dragon Lord, his cheek cut and bleeding.

'What the hell are you doing?' Issa screamed at the wizard.

He raised an eyebrow, but there was a hint of guilt there. 'He attacked me first.'

Her own rage got the better of her and she jumped up and swung her own fist at him. He caught it easily and held it there. She swung her left but he caught that too. She struggled but he was far stronger and held tight to her wrists. For a moment she pooled the Flow, felt him do the same, and remembered the terrible sin of using magic against your fellow wizards, especially against the leaders on the Wizards' Circle.

She glared at him, daring him to hurt her, but he just held her and stared into her eyes. The rage drained out of him and confusion flickered across his face. He frowned, dropped the Flow and looked away, whether in guilt or not, she couldn't tell.

Orphinius groaned, then so did Asaph.

'Let go of me,' she hissed. Domenon released his grip and she yanked herself free. He turned to look across the forest, raising a hand to touch his bruised cheek.

As he was the closest to her, Issa fell beside Asaph first. Holding her hands over his bruised face, she used the Flow to stem his bleeding lip and nose. He groaned and rolled his eyes beneath his closed eyelids, but did not open them. He would be all right.

She ran to Orphinius and did the same, holding her hands over his cut face, using more of the Flow to stem the bleeding and ease his pain. She should have left the men to it and attended the elf. His wounds needed cleaning and stitches, and maybe his arm was broken, but she couldn't fix those things here. The elf began to breathe deeper and slower and she relaxed.

Domenon bent down over him and wiped the man's bloody face with a cloth, almost tenderly. Issa recoiled from the wizard but he did not look at her or speak.

'What did you do to Asaph?' she asked levelly.

'He attacked me first,' Domenon repeated flatly.

'Because you were attacking me,' she growled.

'I simply responded to his attack as I have been trained,' Domenon shrugged. There was no malice in his voice, possibly even weariness. 'I did nothing but show him a trick a Dragon Lord should already know.'

Issa snorted and returned to Asaph who was rolling onto his side, looking dazed.

'Are you all right?' she said gently, helping him to sit up.

'I don't know,' he moaned. 'I feel like my brain's spinning inside my skull. What did he do to me? Maybe I can't protect you after all.'

Issa laughed and wiped his bleeding lip. 'Looks like you won't be able to kiss me for a while.' She smiled.

Asaph tried to grin but that hurt his lip and he grimaced. 'I've never lost a fight before.' His eyes settled briefly on Domenon who was busy wrapping the elf's clothing closer around him and deliberately not looking in their direction.

Issa remembered losing all those fights to Grast'anth. Pride was a bitter thing to swallow. It was hard to accept defeat. But, for losing a fight, Asaph didn't seem too mortified.

'I know how you feel. Thankfully it was amongst our own kind and not the enemy,' she said.

'Hah! I don't think he's one of us,' Asaph said loudly, but if Domenon heard, he didn't show it.

At least the wizard was trying to help now, *or more likely checking for the orb,* she thought. She didn't need to worry. If it were bound to Orphinius then any ill intent to remove it from him without his permission would kill the taker. Domenon knew this.

'He has the orb,' Domenon said, confirming her thoughts.

'Thank the goddess,' Issa sighed in relief.

'So, that's what you were up to, coming here,' said Asaph. 'Sounds like another story to be told.'

'We thought the tree might know more about the orb,' Issa explained.

'Let's get him to a healer,' Domenon said.

Issa felt the Flow move and a sheet of white light slid under Orphinius. Domenon bent and lifted the man easily, the light somehow making the elf weightless.

Issa helped Asaph up. He limped a little. With her arm around him, they started walking back to the jetty in silence, following Domenon a good few paces behind. She noticed Asaph's eyes never left the man's back.

'Wait, I forgot to grab some foxbane for Edarna. I promised. Can you rest here on the tree? I'll only be a moment.'

'Sure,' said Asaph and leant against the pine tree with a sigh.

She turned back towards Sheyengetha.

Domenon continued walking as if he hadn't heard.

Issa spied the short round leaves of foxbane clustered in a patch at the tree's base. She carefully plucked two stems then stood up straight and looked at the tree. The plant wasn't the only reason she'd come back. Closing her eyes, she laid a hand on Sheyengetha's trunk.

'Thank you for letting me pass. I wanted to free Averen, but he said it was not time.'

'I know, Raven Queen,' said the tree in a slow soft voice. 'For a time, Averen and I are one, our minds and bodies linked. We have made a noble agreement of the highest order.'

Issa raised her eyebrows. 'A soul agreement?'

'If that makes it easier for you to understand, then yes.'

'What is its purpose?'

'A wise question,' said the tree. 'To return the pure knowledge of trees to the elves. It has long been diluted since the Dark Rift came. Many trees have forgotten who and what they once were. Many have become evil with Baelthrom's taint.'

'So you have hope, then? Hope that this will all end?' Issa asked.

'Always, but it is not complete. If the Dark Rift is not healed and Baelthrom wins, Averen will never be freed and we shall fall into oblivion together.'

'I pray that it does not come to that,' Issa swallowed and changed the subject. 'Is Domenon one of them?'

'It is not for me to discuss another's chosen path, but no, he is not in league with the Immortal Lord.'

Issa let out a long, slow sigh. She had never really thought he was working with Baelthrom, and it was a relief to hear it, but now the man and his nature seemed even more mysterious.

She was surprised Sheyengetha talked to her openly now, and she felt none of its former reluctance. Answering her thoughts and startling her, the tree said, 'I know who you are, Raven Queen.'

Issa held her breath and leant closer. 'You know my mother?'

'Yes, and that you carry her gift, Tree Whisperer.'

Issa began to cry.

Feelings of love emanated from the tree. She wanted to ask a thousand questions but couldn't speak past the lump in her throat.

'She was kind and strong, like you, like her mother,' said Sheyengetha. 'She was a powerful seer who was being trained to be one of the Trinity.'

Using mind-speak, the tree placed an image of her mother in her mind. She was just as Fraya had described her; long, dark brown hair, tall slender figure, and sea-green eyes that were a darker version of Issa's own. Issa's breath caught in her throat and she thought her heart might break.

Another image was placed in her mind; her father. He was broad-shouldered and had long, dark hair he wore tied back. Beautiful, green, bardic tattoos wound up his arms. He had a kind face and green eyes. She wanted to run to him and hug him, to pinch his stubbled cheek and have him lift her up as if she were a little girl.

'Your father was an accomplished bard of great renown,' said the tree in its soothing voice. 'A follower of the Old Ways before the Temple destroyed the old teachings. He was very learned for his age.

'They both left Myrn to protect you. If they had not gone, Baelthrom would have hunted them down and destroyed the Isles of Tirry and all the seers. I would have been destroyed, and so, too, the gateway to the Land of Mists. Worse, the Elven Realm may have been discovered and destroyed as well. This your mother had seen in a vision given to her by the Night Goddess. What happened after they fled, you already know.'

'But there is more I don't know,' said Issa, her voice little more than a whisper. 'Where did they go? Where are they now? Are they alive?' A feverish need to know burned within her.

'I do not know where they went, Raven Queen.'

Issa's heart fell and she stroked the foxbane leaves in her hand.

'But, that you are alive means they succeeded in keeping you safe,' said Sheyengetha. 'And if they succeeded, then it's most likely they, too, are alive. If Baelthrom had captured them, he would have found you long ago and you would not be here now.'

Issa's heart lifted but the world now suddenly seemed huge. How would she ever find out where her parents were? Now she thought about it, something didn't add up.

'Why do none of the seers know?'

'There is a secret that is yours by right to know but not to tell,' the tree said, making her frown. 'There's a witch's spell called the Web of Forgetting. Those upon whom it is cast forget anything the caster desires forever or until the spell is reversed. It is illegal to cast any Spells of Webbing on the Isles of Tirry or upon any seer—punishable by the stripping of one's powers and permanent exile.

'Your mother and father made a powerful combination, as any coupling between a bard and seer might. And especially as both of them were of Tusarzan ancestry and thus had strong magical abilities. They cast this Web of Forgetting most potently, knowing all the while that what they did was terribly wrong and forbidden, a crime against their people. But your parents cast it for the greater good, to save you and the seers, and a great many things.'

Issa listened in enraptured silence, feeling immense relief as the pieces of her past fell into place. She imagined her mother and her father singing and playing instruments and casting the Web of Forgetting over all the people. Where they ran to after, she could but wonder.

'You have a right to know what happened to your parents and why, but it is not for you to tell their secret. Even to tell the seers of what you have learned would be to bring shame upon them, and they alone must answer to their actions.'

'I guess, for me, it doesn't matter what they did, it only matters where they are now,' said Issa, her emotions a mix of joy at knowing who they were, and sadness wondering where they were. 'I pray to Zanufey that I will one day find them.'

'I hope that you will, too,' said the tree softly. 'Remember; it is not your secret to tell.'

Issa nodded. 'I could never betray them. What were their names? Fraya didn't even know their names.'

'Eritara of Jaya and Thanon Bard,' said the tree. Just hearing their beautiful names made Issa sigh and smile. 'Jaya was an ancient city in Tusarza, now long forgotten. Your grandmother was a witch. Quite a famous one. Or perhaps, infamous.' There was humour in the tree's voice.

Issa wondered as a child what it would be like to have a grandmother, to bake cakes together and listen to her singing old fairy tales, just like Tarry's grandmother used to do.

She closed her eyes as the tree showed in her mind an image of a strong, buxom woman, so unlike her and her mother's slender frame. Her long hair was a frizzy, uncontrollable mass of white, despite her young face. She looked formidable and utterly untamed, but her smile was of one who was fiercely protective and kind.

'She looks wild,' Issa murmured in fascination.

The tree laughed, a sound like the wind blowing gently over glass bottles. 'Yes, Belledyn faced demons and had *them* running in terror. Her darker dealings turned her hair white.'

The tree fell silent. A chill wind blew and Issa shivered.

'Thank you, Sheyengetha. It means so much, I cannot say. I want to learn more, but I should go,' she said, her voice hoarse with gratitude.

She wanted to sit and talk with Sheyengetha about her parents all night and day, and dream about the life they might have had together—a life Baelthrom had taken away from her. How could one being cause so much suffering?

Asaph had started to limp back up the path towards her, a frown of worry on his face. She wiped her eyes but the tears fell. She turned back to the tree to hide her tears.

'Goodbye for now, Sheyengetha,' she said and almost dropped her hand from its trunk before the tree spoke again softly.

'Whenever you pass into a tree there is a moment where you and the tree become one. You will have felt this, though forgotten. In that moment I learned much about you that even you do not know. There is wizard blood in your veins, Raven Queen. Where it comes from, I know not. Seer, bard, witch and wizard—do you see the importance of these things? For we always choose our parents and they their parents—even trees do this.'

'In you, all things are made whole,' Issa breathed in wonder, remembering Zanufey's words. 'I have to make whole what has been broken?'

The tree didn't answer, she sensed it did not know.

Issa didn't tell Asaph the details of what Sheyengetha had told her as they made their way home. Instead, she sat quietly, chin resting on her hand as she stared at the sea over the side of the boat. Domenon sat at the prow with his back to them, next to the boatman. No one said anything.

Every now and then, Issa frowned and tears filled her eyes. Asaph knew she would talk to him when she was ready, so he just held her hand and mulled over everything that had happened.

He'd arrived late to meet Issa, having had to reconstruct a tent whose beam snapped just as he was about to leave to meet her. He hadn't expected her to go without him and alarm bells started ringing when she wasn't there on the jetty waiting for him. He didn't want her to be alone with Domenon. Although he didn't know the wizard, he could see that the man was handsome and could use his charms well on any woman. He was also clearly untrustworthy to be left alone around Issa or the orbs. The thought of him even touching Issa made his blood boil.

After fixing the tent, he'd taken a boat to the island and run nearly all the way to the tree. What he saw made him stop short. Issa, and a badly wounded elf-man, emerged, no, fell out of the tree's massive trunk. Domenon had grabbed the wounded man roughly then Issa intervened.

When the wizard flung Issa back, Asaph saw red and ran at him, whilst putting up a mighty struggle to prevent the dragon within from awakening. But Domenon had reacted with such speed and skill, he had been utterly unprepared.

He'd assumed the man was just a wizard with little to no fighting skills. But the man was strong, uncannily strong, tumbling Asaph as if he were a child. He was also faster than Asaph, faster than a Dragon Lord. Domenon had clearly had training, lots of it, and Asaph wanted to know where he'd got it from. Despite his dislike of the wizard and his chagrin at losing the fight, he was forced to respect him.

The boatman guided the boat to the nearest jetty on the main island. Several seers must have spotted the prone elf and were waiting anxiously to assist. They helped carry the wounded elf to the medical tent where healers and physicians were busy working. Asaph waited outside whilst everyone else went in. It was crowded and he didn't like any kind of hospital.

'How did you do that?' Asaph said when Domenon re-emerged alone.

Domenon looked away and gave an exasperated sigh. 'Do what?'

'You know what. Fight like that. I didn't think wizards were trained in fists.' Asaph's hard gaze was met with an equally hard stare.

'There's probably a lot of things you "didn't think" about the world, given your lack of…training,' scowled Domenon, touching his bruised cheek and grimacing. 'My advice would be to not start fights with those you can't beat, otherwise, you're in for a bashing.' Domenon smirked.

He stood almost the same height as Asaph. The man's dislike of him was odd and went deeper than the fight they'd just had.

'You don't even know me, so why do you hate me? Why did you call me a half-breed? Humans don't generally give a damn.'

'Most humans are quite dumb,' said Domenon. 'That's why the world is in the mess it's in. Let's just say, I know full well that an untrained Dragon Lord is a danger to everyone. And, unlike most humans, combining dragons with humans creates nothing but abominable half-breeds.'

'I can't help what I am and, besides, how can you be against what Feygriene has ordained?' Asaph folded his arms.

Domenon glowered. 'Why don't you go tend to your love?'

'Why don't you teach me what you did back there? I've almost worked it out anyway. There's more you could teach me. I can pay you,' said Asaph.

Domenon laughed loudly. 'How ridiculous. You think I've got time to play around with fools?' The wizard stalked off. Asaph watched as he disappeared down a side street. A small smile of victory spread on his face.

CHAPTER 13

Orb of Earth

FAINT stars twinkled in the darkening skies.

Issa walked towards the makeshift healing tent where the seers attended Orphinius. Miraculously, the elf was sitting up on his bed pallet, his wounds were stitched and bandaged, and a little colour had returned to his face.

Dar knelt on one knee by his bedside holding his hand, and Iyena and Suli rested their hands on her shoulders. Everybody's eyes were closed. Issa watched silently as Orphinius began speaking in a quivering voice, recounting what he had witnessed when Baelthrom invaded the Land of Mists. Issa knew the seers were witnessing what he had seen as he relived it through their communal touch.

'The Dread Dragons came, bringing fire. Very quickly everything was burning, there was nowhere to run, no place to hide. We couldn't get away.'

Issa imagined the beautiful realm with its gold and silver trees and sparkling rivers turning to fire and ash. She shivered when he spoke about Baelthrom and tried not to think about the terror the people witnessed. Nowhere to go, no way of escaping. Trapped and knowing they were going to die. She shook away the fear and focused upon what Orphinius was saying.

'I saw Daranarta fall. We tried to get him to Averen's shield but our king was mad with fury. Then a tree fell on us. Daranarta was trapped and my friend was…killed.' Orphinius struggled with his emotions. When he next spoke his voice was unsteady.

'Red eyes opened in the sky above us. I tried and tried but I couldn't free Daranarta's legs. He said not to bother because they were broken anyway and the Death Hounds were coming on fast.

'He told me to take the orb and run. I said I didn't want it and that I wouldn't leave him, but he made me. I'm no magic wielder but he bound it to me with magic and thrust it into my pocket.

'I tried to stay with him but he screamed at me like a madman. He wanted me to save the orb. So I ran and didn't look back. I'd almost reached Averen and his shield when a blast threw me off my feet. There was terrible pain...and then nothing.' Orphinius swallowed, his features were alarmingly grey.

'Speak only if you want to,' said Iyena softly, still keeping her eyes closed.

'I must,' said Orphinius. 'There is more and everyone must know. When I awoke I was in a dead world. Everything was grey. There were ghosts; some of their faces I recognised...' his voice dropped to a hoarse whisper and he struggled to continue. 'It felt like I was there for days. I couldn't get out, and the sorrow was consuming, this feeling of the world swallowing me... Then she came. The Raven Queen. She brought me back and here I am.'

He opened his pale green eyes and smiled weakly at Issa. She shifted awkwardly. The seers opened their eyes and Dar stood.

'Relax now, Orphinius,' she said. 'You survived and saved the orb, and that's all that matters. You're safe now.'

'May the Night Goddess find and carry Daranarta's soul,' Issa whispered and was surprised when everyone echoed her prayer.

She looked at the floor. This would never have happened had Daranarta listened to her. It was his selfishness that had caused the death of millions. But her feelings for the misguided, indifferent elf king now lessened with his death and she felt deeply sorry for him.

'The orb must be protected at all costs.' Domenon's voice behind her made her jump. He stood in the doorway, his eyes shadowed, his bruise angry looking. How long had he been there?

'Indeed, Master Wizard Domenon, but look, the man needs rest first,' said Iyena, motioning to Orphinius who had slipped into a doze. 'We'll remain here with him all night casting our strongest shield over him. You needn't worry.'

This seemed to be good enough for the man, Iyena had a way of placating the difficult wizard. Domenon nodded his thanks, his face softening a little before he turned away. Issa followed him out. The wizards were soon to have a meeting and she was excited to have been invited. Without talking, they took the short walk through the town centre and down a side street to a small white house at the end.

All the wizards were already there and she was surprised to see Naksu seated amongst them at the big round table. She returned Issa's smile. The wizards were already in a debate, so Issa and Domenon quietly took the remaining empty seats.

'If we're targeted like this, all the orbs are in jeopardy.' Drumblodd shook his head.

Many wizards spoke at once, all saying different things about what to do with the orbs.

'At least he named another its Keeper before he passed,' said Drumblodd.

'We must separate ourselves from each other at once,' said Navarr.

'We are safer in numbers with our combined powers,' said Haelgon.

Luren didn't seem to know what to think and looked only at Domenon.

'It doesn't matter what you say, Orphinius is not strong enough to hold that orb.' Domenon's quiet voice cut through all of them. Everyone turned to look at him. 'I've analysed his energy fields, his aura—everything. He is not even a magic wielder. Daranarta gave the orb to him as a last resort before he lost his life.'

'He should have given it to Averen,' Issa agreed with Domenon. Another mistake made by Daranarta. 'If he had then maybe he would be with us now.'

'Those elves who left so hate the elves who remained.' Drumblodd sighed.

Issa remembered that the dwarf and Averen were good friends.

'I saw Averen,' she said, smiling at the dwarf. A spark lit up in his eyes. 'He's all right—more than all right, in a way. He seemed in bliss. Sheyengetha said they had made a soul agreement.'

She glanced at the others. A look of wonder spread across Freydel's face.

'I offer to be Keeper of the Orb of Earth, though I know it's a great burden,' said Domenon abruptly, making everyone start. 'It's clear to me that none of you want me in possession of the orb, but may I remind you that I am the only other Master Wizard here and I have elven blood, no matter how small.'

So, he admitted his elven heritage was minor, noted Issa.

The wizards looked thoughtful, apart from Freydel who scowled. Naksu's face remained interested, though she said nothing.

'Your audacity never ceases to shock me,' said Freydel, sighing.

'Who else has the power to hold the orb? You know I'm the strongest. Coronos was certainly not strong enough,' Domenon hissed.

The mention of his name in this manner hurt, and though Issa had a growing dislike for the man and his rough manner, she couldn't deny the truth of what he said. There was an orb that needed protection and he was the only Master Wizard without one.

The wizards exploded into heated discussion. It felt like a power struggle and Issa drew back from it as they argued. They were all afraid of everything that had happened and so was she.

"In you, all things are made whole." She recalled the things Zanufey had said to her, the ones giving her clarity and direction

'We should recombine the orbs, the ones we have left,' said Issa. She spoke quietly but captured everyone's attention. They looked at her and she shrugged. 'A power divided is weak. Perhaps now is the time we become one and Maioria's magic is united, however that is done.'

'And risk Baelthrom being able to take greater power?' said Drumblodd.

'Or fight him back with greater power,' said Issa. 'Look, I don't know what the answer is now, I only know that in the end the orbs must be recombined, just as magic wielders must become as one. Seers, witches and wizards must one day soon become one school and learn each other's wisdom. I *know* this is what we must do.'

Domenon glowered at her.

'And how would we combine them?' asked Haelgon, his smooth, shaven head glowing in the candlelight.

Issa shrugged again. 'I don't know. Murlonius and Yisufalni are still with us. The Ancients broke the magic of Maioria, so I think the answer is with them.'

King Navarr nodded. 'Yisufalni was the last Ancient and female to sit upon the Circle. She was once a High Priestess and a wizard too. I wonder if she still has the power and the knowledge to do this.'

'I would think her knowledge greater now than ever before, but her power?' said Freydel. He shook his head. 'It's a grand idea but I don't think such things can be done,'

His doubt surprised Issa. Was he reluctant to try? She noticed his hand was in his pocket where he kept his orb. Maybe he didn't want to give up the orb of power. She glanced at Drumblodd. He was looking into the centre of the table, frowning. Would he give up the Orb of Fire just like that? Would any of them?

She realised then the magnitude of what she had just asked. All the wizards hungered after the power the orbs gave them, and another wizard almost had one in his clutches. Whereas she would willingly give up her orb to make whole what had been broken.

'Without the other orbs, the magic cannot be recombined anyway,' said Freydel.

'Until that time, the Orb of Earth needs protecting,' Domenon pressed. He sighed heavily, his fingers brushing the bruise Asaph had given him. 'Fellow wizards, I am very tired. Please think long and hard on what I propose before it's too late.'

Issa was surprised when he stood up and left the table without adding more. She thought he would have tried much harder to get what he wanted. She watched him shut the door and turned back to the discussion.

Asaph was staring up at the stars and leaning on a garden wall when Domenon emerged from the house where the wizards were having their meeting. He enjoyed the surprise on the wizard's face.

'What are you doing here?' Domenon asked.

'I came to look at the stars and walk Issa home,' said Asaph. 'You can't trust anyone these days, not even here on the Isle of Myrn.

Domenon snorted. 'I'm not interested in her.'

'That's not the impression I get, but maybe I'll take your word for it,' said Asaph, pushing himself off the wall and following the wizard as he stalked past.

'What do you want? Another fight? Want to learn some new tricks?' Domenon grinned, his eyes hard.

'Yes, to all,' Asaph grinned back. 'But maybe not tonight. I've been thinking about it a lot and there is something oddly familiar about you, though I'm certain we've never met before. They say you're far older than you look, so maybe this familiar feeling can be found in the dragon's shared memory—'

'I know all about the Recollection, you don't need to bore me with an explanation.' Domenon wafted his hand.

'Do you know about the sleeping dragons?' asked Asaph, ignoring the man's manner and excited that he might discover something.

Domenon stopped and turned to him. 'I know a lot about a great many things. You'd be surprised. Whatever it is you want from me, you're not going to get it. Why don't you run back to your little missus?'

Asaph folded his arms. 'You called me a half-breed. Only one other has called me that before.'

'I didn't call you a half-breed, I said dragons call you people that,' said Domenon.

'Yes, it was a dragon who said it. Not all dragons hate humans,' said Asaph. *Or did they?* The thought that he might be hated by the very beings he'd dedicated his life to finding, chilled him to the bone. 'How do you know so much about dragons? Do you speak with them? They've been sleeping for decades.'

Domenon nodded. 'And long may they continue. When the world and all this madness has ended, they will rise again to be what they once were.'

Asaph frowned. 'If they stay sleeping, they won't be waking up ever again for Baelthrom will destroy us all. I didn't realise you trusted in Issa so much.'

'I don't.' Domenon snorted. 'I don't think she or any human can save this world. Look how easy it was for Baelthrom to control even you, with all your Dragon Lord powers.'

Asaph refused to react to his goading. 'I believe it is as she says. If we come together, we have a chance to defeat the darkness. Divided we fall—and that includes dragons. Soon, I intend to find the Sword of Binding and awaken them.'

Domenon's face darkened. He seemed about to say something then changed his mind. He nodded behind them. Asaph turned. The door of the meeting house was opening, spilling light onto the cobbles. Wizards emerged, chatting.

'Looks like the meeting's finished,' said Domenon. 'Why don't you go look after her before she gets attacked. I've got work to do.' The wizard whirled away, his satin cloak shimmering as he disappeared into the dark.

Asaph sighed, turned and waved at Issa. She came over.

'What are you doing here?' she asked in surprise, lifting the collar of her robe.

'I'm just your man-servant come to walk you home,' he bowed.

She laughed and took his hand.

CHAPTER 14

Worlds of Dominion

'I feel as strong as a young man here in your crystal palace,' said Freydel, lightly stroking his blue crystal staff.

In this magnificent place from where it was cut, the staff hummed with power. The power filled him almost to the point of trembling.

'Your travelling here has become seamless.' Ayeth nodded. 'You're a fast learner and skilled to be able to navigate across time and dimensions so quickly.'

'I would not be able to do it without the power of the staff you created, and your tutelage.' Freydel looked up at Ayeth, feeling in awe of the majestic being.

Ayeth's face gleamed and his dark blue eyes shone. He was standing perfectly still before a wall of glinting blue crystals. His cloak was the same blue making him appear to blend into the wall.

Ayeth had used his magic to strengthen Freydel's portal connection to the crystal caverns across the vast time and space over which he had travelled. As a result, this visit from Freydel felt stronger and less ethereal. His body held more density and he could breathe easier without feeling nauseous.

Yes, Ayeth was the most powerful wizard he had ever, or would ever, know.

'With your vast knowledge I could do so much more with the energies of Maioria,' said Freydel.

'Power can be a dangerous thing,' said Ayeth. 'Especially if one learns a power beyond one's means. It can destroy you. I say this not to anger you, but we all have limits that are tied to our physical bodies and the planets from whence we came.

'Hmm, so you say I destroy my beautiful home planet Aralansia.' He held his palm up and a dark blue planet the size of an apple appeared, turning slowly on its axis. 'And the question is why. What in the light could make me do such a thing? The Yurgha say the Rorsken have the power to move planets and the Anukon the technology to destroy them utterly.'

Above his hands, two more planets appeared; a tan coloured one with patches of blue and a darker one covered in white swirls that Freydel assumed to be clouds. He looked at his own palm, wondering how to create such an illusion and hungering to learn.

'I don't know the why of anything, but I believe whatever happens to destroy you and Aralansia can be halted, which is why I return—' Freydel stopped as an oblong light about five-feet high appeared between the crystal pedestal and the wall.

Ayeth turned to it and smiled as someone stepped through the light into the cavern. The light faded and Lona stood there. She was dressed in black; shimmering leggings and a tunic that floated around her. The black clothing made her bald head and pristine, alabaster face appear even whiter.

She looked up at Ayeth, smiling, and lifted a hand to caress the back of his neck. Ayeth stroked her cheek. She glanced at Freydel, her all-black eyes shining. Her strangely beautiful but disturbing features were impossible to read. Freydel shivered in spite of himself.

'Your friend has returned,' she purred.

'Yes,' said Ayeth, taking her hand and leading her over. 'As I told you, together we are learning a great many things.'

A deep smile curved Lona's colourless lips as she looked at Freydel. He felt very uncomfortable. Which was irrational, he told himself. Maybe he found her beautiful alienness just too much to take. But it was more than that; the magic flowed darkly around her. He couldn't quite call it the Flow, for here on Aralansia it moved and felt different to Maioria's energy. From that, he assumed that each planet's life magic behaved differently.

'Then maybe I should go,' she said, her eyes never leaving Freydel.

'No, please don't. Stay with us. You can teach him things too,' said Ayeth, much to Freydel's disappointment. He wanted Ayeth to himself and didn't feel comfortable talking about the future with her there. But she was a completely different, fascinating species and she might be able to show him something wonderful, he consoled himself.

'We were discussing again the destruction of our beloved Aralansia and searching for how it might come to pass. Can you believe he says I will do this? Hah! Unbelievable. The human doesn't lie. If this is a possible timeline, then it must be explored and understood if it's to be stopped. Freydel, please continue,' Ayeth gestured with a smile.

'Yes, where was I,' Freydel tried to recall their prior conversation and remembered seeing the planet crumbling. It tied in with the vision Issa had shared with him. He wanted to change the subject now Lona was here, but the expectation in Ayeth's eyes drove him on.

'There is a great cataclysm which destroys the planet, and maybe others too. It has something to do with the pyramids, or maybe they were being used to try to stop it, I cannot be sure. But after—how long after is anybody's guess—there exists what we call a Dark Rift created in the fabric of our universe.'

'An empty hole,' Ayeth nodded thoughtfully. 'These holes are created when planets unnaturally disappear or are destroyed.'

'The Anukon have threatened us with it. We have seen it in our shared dreams,' hissed Lona, her black eyes turning even darker.

Ayeth laid a comforting hand on her arm and continued speaking. 'Destroyed planets create a vacuum, an emptiness in the fabric of the space and time where they once had been. This sounds like the Dark Rift of which you speak. It is possible to fix them by sewing it together with powerful magic. The crystal pyramids can be used to do this.'

'They can also be used to create them,' said Lona, tossing her head proudly.

'They have the power to create holes in the universe and then mend them?' asked Freydel, trying to imagine anything with the power to destroy entire planets.

'Yes. They are powerful technologies which can be used to do great and marvellous things,' said Lona, sweeping her hand high. The keenness in her eyes disturbed Freydel.

'The Anukon,' she growled the name and scowled, her pretty face turning ugly, 'dared to use them on us and invade Yurgharon. But we, the Yurgha, with our superior intellect, reverse-engineered their technology and fought them back.'

'Then perhaps that is how Aralansia is destroyed,' said Freydel.

The Aralan stood silent. Pain and confusion passed across his features. Seeing Ayeth upset offered Freydel some relief. He was still a long way away from becoming the beast Baelthrom.

'We must never fear the future,' said Ayeth. 'Especially not now when we might have the power to change it. Time is a malleable thing, and there are many timelines spanning out from a single moment.'

Freydel nodded, pleased to have someone agree with his concept of time. 'Indeed, what we do now could change the course of history. The Dark Rift grows in Maioria's skies day after day, year after year. No one has the power or knowledge to stop it. Many more will die if we allow it to consume us.'

'Die,' Lona mouthed the word, a frown on her face. 'The Anukon make us weak and the Rorsken make us die.' A mad rage flickered across her features and was gone just as quickly.

'You will overcome the sickness they brought, I promise,' Ayeth said, casting a look of such love at Lona that Freydel felt moved.

Lona slid a sideways smile at Freydel. 'Neither magic nor technology are evil, they just are what they are. It's how they are used that dictates their purpose.'

'No. Where I am from, some magic is evil, though I cannot speak about technology for I am no technician,' Freydel argued. 'Certain magic comes from demons, others from the black arts and some from what we call the Under Flow—that which comes out of the Dark Rift.'

Ayeth sighed. 'There is something missing, something not quite right. I don't disbelieve anything you say, you speak the truth. I can see it in your aura. But I still don't understand. You talk about your ancient ancestors as if they are not within you. Your physical records were destroyed, yes, but each race carries its race memory within itself, in its blood and the tiny parts of which we are made.'

Freydel frowned then realisation dawned. 'Ah, racial memory. Only dragons and Wykiry still have the ability to read their race history. Not beings like me. Our most ancient legends say we lost it when we began to die. I guess we have fallen very far indeed.'

'That's so awful,' said Ayeth, shaking his head and leaning on his hands upon the crystal pedestal. 'What being can forget itself like this?'

'A race who does not know itself is weak and easily ruled, like an animal,' Lona scowled.

Freydel was surprised at the venom in her voice. Ayeth gave her a softening glance and her scowl faded into a look of such pain, Freydel was taken aback. The female hurt deeply, she was mad with it.

Ayeth turned to Freydel, concern on his face. 'How can you know anything if you don't know who and what you are? It is incredible to think that this can be done to a race. To think that I might have done... Forgive me for talking plainly, but a race without knowledge of its history—how do you even know who you are?'

Freydel shrugged. 'I guess we don't. Our days have grown dark and they turn darker still. I think we are in our last moments.'

'You say I come to your planet out of this Dark Rift?' said Ayeth.

Lona moved away into a darker part of the cavern but Freydel could feel her eyes watching him. When he glanced in her direction, he saw their gleam. As he spoke, she appeared undisturbed by the things he was saying, unlike Ayeth who struggled.

'It's hard to say, but you arrived like a falling star. The history we do have is incomplete and confusing. The Dark Rift appeared first at some point, and out of it, you fell.'

'I came out of an empty hole? Is that possible?' Ayeth's eyes were wide.

'The Anukon travel through them when they have drained enough energy from a host planet,' said Lona, stepping forwards slightly so the blue light of the cavern fell on her face and gleamed off her shiny black clothing. 'As we continue to fight them and the Rorsken, we learn more about their technologies and magic.'

'You arrived scattered, so the legends say,' Freydel continued. 'There were certain beings on Maioria who prophesied your coming. Not good beings but those who live in the shadows and work black arts. They study the darkness and revel in death. They found your scattered parts and put you back together again. Your consciousness, once whole, chose a mix of physical forms and created an incredible, abominable chimera in which to put itself.

'You don't remember who you are because of the scattering, but you know why you came—to destroy races. You persecuted those we call the Ancients. It seems they are descended from the original Aralans who came to Maioria. They are all gone now, apart from two.'

Ayeth covered his eyes with his hand. Freydel felt immense pity for him. How hard must it be to discover you will become a monster?

'I don't know what would make me do this,' Ayeth said.

'Why you end up hating your own people? I do not know,' Freydel said quietly.

Lona nodded. 'They are always difficult with you, even now. They forget that you are chosen.'

'Why would Arzanu choose me if I am to fail?' Ayeth shook his head.

The name made Freydel start. 'Who is Arzanu?'

'Arzanu is the great being who made us, our creator and guardian,' Ayeth's eyes shone with reverence as he spoke. 'Arzanu is our Great Mother created by the One Source to create us.'

Freydel felt faint and leant against the cool crystal wall.

'What is it? Are you sick? Here, let me help,' Ayeth came over and laid a cool hand on Freydel's forehead. The dizziness stopped as energy flowed into him, giving him strength. Knowledge seemed to flow from Ayeth's hand as well, again rekindling his insatiable desire to know more.

'We call her Zanufey,' Freydel said after a moment. 'The Goddess of the Night. She has come to Maioria. She has awakened with the rising indigo moon.'

Freydel glanced at Lona as she stepped back into the shadows. She wasn't looking his way but her perfect features were creased in deep concern. Did talk of this Arzanu worry her? Perhaps the Yurgha feared other peoples' gods.

'Then she must be one and the same,' Ayeth nodded, wonder in his eyes. 'By Arzanu's blessing, I was given great power—power to heal others, not to destroy. So you can see why the things you tell me cause me great pain.'

'I'm sorry. I don't want to be the one to tell you,' said Freydel, moved. 'Perhaps they will never come to pass.'

'How can I be chosen, only to fall?' Ayeth whispered to himself.

Lona moved fully out of the darkness this time and came to stand beside Ayeth, laying a pale hand on his arm.

Ayeth looked at her and seemed to grow stronger, calmer. He turned to Freydel. 'You say that it is the wisdom of the orb you carry that brought you here. To somehow undo what will happen. You call it the Orb of Undoing. But there is something I see that you do not seem to. Did you know the orb is undoing you too? It is destroying you in some way.'

Freydel dropped a hand to his pocket, fear gnawing at him. 'How do you mean?'

'Your physical body is strong enough but I can see your soul is weakening—it's being drained by the orb every moment. Sometimes objects of power require a price to be used, a cost. I can help you reverse the drain of magical objects on your life force. I can show you how to draw back the power it has taken from you so it does not bleed you dry. This orb's magic is very potent, yes, but it is incomplete, somehow.'

Freydel couldn't believe what he was hearing. He took the orb out and stared into its shimmering black surface. Both Ayeth and Lona came close. Could the orb be destroying him? He didn't feel anything obvious. Nothing in the texts about the orbs said they took anything from their Keeper. Could it be a side effect the Ancients never knew about? Was it unique to only the Orb of Destruction by its very nature? Ayeth could be wrong but he doubted it. Perhaps he would be better without it, but he knew he'd rather die than give up his object of power.

'I don't feel any different, but it *is* incomplete,' Freydel murmured. 'To protect the life-magic of Maioria from falling into Baelthrom's hands, the Ancients split it.'

Lona licked her lips as she gazed at the orb, making him nervous. Ayeth looked away as if struggling with something but his eyes were soon drawn back to its shining black surface.

'The link to me now and what I will become in the future lies in this orb for it can reach through time and space,' breathed Ayeth, his eyes full of wonder. 'I must stop this Dark Rift from ever being created.'

Lona's eyes widened and she took a step back as if afraid. Catching Freydel's gaze, her features smoothed over and she looked serene again.

What did she know of the Dark Rift and why was it important to her? Was she afraid of losing Ayeth?

'Perhaps if I can reach the being I will become, I can stop myself becoming it,' Ayeth said in barely a whisper. 'With the orb, we can try, for both you and the orb and I are anchored there.'

The thought of Ayeth meeting Baelthrom filled Freydel with foreboding. 'I don't think meeting your future self is a good idea,' Freydel shook his head, trying to reason through why it was a bad idea and struggling.

'You will be horrified. How you look now is very different to the monstrosity you will become. Just seeing yourself could destroy you. Baelthrom will also try to consume you and your magic.'

A frown passed across Ayeth's brow and he dropped his eyes in disappointment. 'I would do anything to stop the terrible destruction you have shown me. I will pledge my life to stopping it. I was given the gift to heal, not to destroy.'

Freydel saw nothing but deep concern and honesty in Ayeth's dark blue eyes.

'Baelthrom desires this orb and its sisters, like nothing else,' Freydel explained. 'He knows that when he has them all, he controls the life-magic of Maioria. Even if I could get close to him—which is nigh on impossible anyway—I would not for the safety of the orb.'

'I am certain that within this Baelthrom, a part of me still resides, *must* reside,' Ayeth continued. 'I just have to reach that part. Perhaps from here, with the power of the crystals, we could reach him in safety. I would pledge myself to you so I can never harm you.'

'If an Aralan pledges themselves to you, they are incapable of bringing you harm,' said Lona, her eyes glittering. Freydel raised his eyebrows. Lona shrugged. 'To harm the ones to whom they are pledged brings the same harm upon themselves. It is just the way they were created.'

Freydel considered this for a long moment. There were old Maiorian legends and fairy tales about beings who, once pledged to another, would be incapable of harming the other without harming themselves. Could these ancient stories be from the Aralans who reached Maioria so long ago? Witches' familiars were similar; they could not harm their owners.

A thought occurred to him that was both worrying and seemed like an excellent idea. After the terrible murder of Coronos, worry for the safety of his orb still consumed him. What if he was murdered and lost the orb in a similar manner? He desperately needed a Second Keeper for safety's sake. He'd chosen Issa but when she mentioned recombining the orbs, he'd hesitated. Her idea chilled him to the bone.

It was very dangerous to combine objects of magic even if one knew how to do so. The power of just one orb was too much to hold, but the power of two? Who could hold it? It could be catastrophic. And who, then, would be its Keeper? It was far harder for Baelthrom to chase several orbs rather than one. No, they should not be combined. But the decision had left him with a nagging feeling and no suitable Secondary Keeper to name.

He glanced at Ayeth and Lona who had finished talking amongst themselves and now were watching him. 'We have decided that, no matter how painful it might be, we should see this Baelthrom,' said Ayeth, his pale, gleaming face unreadable. 'Just an image in the orb…Maybe I can in some way understand it.'

Freydel beheld Ayeth, seeing everything that a noble being of great power and influence should be; intelligent, gracious and valiant. Here was one chosen by Zanufey just as Issa was—one chosen by a goddess to hold the power to help others. If he could not trust Ayeth, he could not trust anybody. He worried his beard.

Baelthrom was twisted and corrupt, just as Keteth was. If he showed Ayeth the horror of what he would become, maybe that would be so repulsive and disturbing Ayeth would never be able to become it. Could it even be enough to change a timeline?

'All right,' Freydel nodded. 'I will show you Baelthrom from the orb's memory. Maybe it will give you understanding.'

Freydel watched as the crystal pedestal rose underneath Ayeth's outstretched hand, unease riddling through him. The pale crystal slid smoothly and stopped at waist height without making a noise. With an encouraging motion of Ayeth's six-fingered hand, Freydel placed the orb upon the pedestal. He reluctantly drew his hand away from its cold black surface. It was the first time it had left his touch in this world.

'I give you my word, on my life you can trust me,' Ayeth said. 'I will not try to take your orb and I refuse to become this Baelthrom.'

A wave of sincerity emanated from Ayeth, leaving Freydel in no doubt that he would be true to his word. Freydel dared to relax, his inner turmoil easing. He was saving the world, he reminded himself. He was saving two worlds.

'Show us a shielded *image* of Baelthrom,' Freydel commanded the orb, emphasising the word "image" for added safety. He held his breath as triangular red eyes formed upon its surface.

Ayeth waved a hand, magic moved, and the red eyes were projected and enlarged two feet out from the orb. Freydel jumped back.

'We are safe,' Ayeth quickly reassured.

Freydel gripped his staff, not quite believing it, then stared in awe as the orb projected life-sized images in front of his face. His awe turned to horror as the tripartite helmet and metal face of Baelthrom formed around the eyes. His massive, black-armoured body materialised, leathery black wings spread wide, and thick-clawed, lizard legs bulged muscle. The projection was so real it seemed as if he stood in the room. Freydel took another step back and held his staff before him, his heart pounding.

Ayeth held up his hand for calm. 'No vision can harm us, and especially not here.' He turned back to the image, his slanted eyes impossibly wide as he looked at his future self. Freydel took his expression to be one of horror as he stared at Baelthrom.

'I become this?' Ayeth breathed.

Freydel nodded, unable to speak. The difference between Baelthrom and Ayeth was vast but there was one thing that remained the same. The stone amulets that hung around their necks, whilst different in colour, were the same in size and design.

Lona chuckled, somehow finding it funny as she stared at Baelthrom. 'He's as powerful as you are, though far more ugly and massive. I don't know, I find him impressive. The Rorsken would be terrified of him. The Anukon would try to fight him.'

'He is a Lord of War,' Freydel said. 'Where he passes comes death, destruction, sickness, and sorrow. We either fight and die, or assimilate into his world. The latter is most terrible for our souls are plunged into inescapable oblivion. It is as if we never were and never will be again.

There is no hope for those who have been touched by him.' Unable to take anymore and fearing the looks in Lona and Ayeth's eyes, Freydel changed the image by saying, 'Show us Maphrax.'

The image of Baelthrom melted away. Instead, the orb showed the mountains of Maphrax, projected large into the room, with its two giant peaks curved towards a central one.

'He destroyed a once beautiful land and torched the sky,' said Freydel, pointing with his staff to the barren plains ravaged by heartless winds and a sky that boiled darkly with blood red clouds.

'He's feeding off the world and all it contains, just like the Anukon and Rorsken do,' said Lona.

Ayeth nodded. 'Great swathes of Yurgharon look like this, only their storm sky is grey and the land bleeds red ore. I can see the energy of your planet feeding him. Those mountains are great conduits, like the pyramids. Where is the life energy going?'

Freydel frowned. 'What do you mean?'

'The mountains,' Ayeth pointed at the image. 'Hmm. They are taking the magic. Can you not see it? The energy beaming above them?'

Freydel peered at the Maphrax Mountains and the image focused closer upon them. 'I see nothing but the torched sky.' Was there something he was missing?

'Look,' Ayeth said. He murmured a word and drew a symbol in the air with his finger.

The image changed colour, or more accurately the colour leached out of it leaving it grey and white. The contrast intensified until there was only black and white. The starkness hurt his eyes.

Freydel gasped. Out of the top of the central mountain, blinding white light beamed.

'Where does the energy go?' Ayeth asked again.

'I don't know, I've never seen that before,' Freydel blinked shaking his head. Then he nodded. 'Yes, I guess I do know. It surely goes into the Dark Rift.'

The realisation made him feel faint. He tore his eyes away and leant heavily on his staff. Ayeth wafted his hand and the image returned to its normal raging red skies and black mountains.

'Your planet is being eaten alive and bled dry,' said Lona walking towards Freydel. He looked into her black eyes seeing truth there and a hint of something predatory. 'Unless you stop your planet bleeding, you will all die, and soon. We have seen this before. This is what is happening to Yurgharon.'

'Those mountains are crude, but they function as pyramids nonetheless—with incredible power,' Ayeth said.

'Legends say the mountains are not from Maioria, they are from the Dark Rift,' Freydel closed his eyes, wishing he hadn't learned anything today. Ignorance was better.

'How long have they been leaching your planet's life?' asked Ayeth.

'I don't know, no one does for sure. At least a thousand years,' said Freydel.

'Depending on the strength of its sun, a planet might last no more than a thousand years bleeding like that—a very short time indeed for the normal lifespan of a planet,' Lona said, bending closer to the image to stare at the mountains that betrayed no sign of what they were doing. 'Whatever it's feeding, it lives in that Dark Rift.'

Freydel swallowed. 'What *lives* in such a place as a Dark Rift?'

Ayeth glanced at him then at Lona, then looked into the middle distance, his face turning pale. 'What lives in the blackness of the empty holes is the same wherever they are found. Twisted worlds of dominion and submission. Suffering and powerlessness. Blame and hatred. It is not life, but slavery and servitude.'

'Slavery to whom?' asked Freydel, feeling a chill run down his spine.

'Slavery to an evil and twisted ideology, to all-encompassing thought forms and beliefs. Slavery so complete it binds you, body, mind and soul.' Ayeth's beautiful voice was low and sorrowful.

'The idea is that the One Light has abandoned you and hates you. The emptiness that idea breeds leads to hate; hatred of what you are, of what you have become. The belief that the One who made you has discarded you and you are not worthy. Hatred becomes blame, blame becomes powerlessness—each destitute feeling rolling one to another. Beings within it don't know what they are, they only know *that* they are and that they must feed. They think they are entitled to feed on anything and everything.'

'The Anukon,' Lona whispered.

Freydel imagined grey worlds filled with pain and suffering and emptiness. A place where the One Light did not reach and all beings were consumed by hatred and emptiness. Where any evil could exist and flourish unchecked. That was what the Abyss was, and all the worlds on the way down to it were various levels of degradation. The Shadowlands were but a glimpse of the anguish these worlds contained.

'Beings there are twisted beyond recognition,' Ayeth continued, a hopeless expression on his face. 'They can no longer feel the light—and so it does not exist for them. There is no hope of getting out, they have fallen so far. Energetically they are eaten alive by the strongest. Like this thing you humans do with food. The One Light can no longer reach them to feed them with the eternal life flows.'

'That is what we are becoming. We are falling into the Dark Rift to…' Freydel couldn't complete the sentence for the lump of fear that appeared in his throat.

'To be food for what exists there,' Ayeth completed it for him. 'Beings who cut themselves off from the One through the poor choices they make, no longer have the ability to care for the suffering of others. They have no empathy, which allows them to do terrible things without a care. So you see, I can never become one of them. I will not!'

'No,' Freydel agreed. 'Oblivion is better.' He hadn't meant to speak aloud.

'Oblivion is the final stage, the merciful end, when a being becomes so fragmented they no longer are. That is when the pain stops,' Ayeth said. 'As hard as the lessons were, I have learned these things in order to help heal them. That is my soul purpose.'

Freydel looked at Ayeth and saw his eyes wide and sparkling with need. 'If we heal the Dark Rift, none of this will happen,' said Freydel, asserting the fact to himself. He swallowed and nodded, his decision made. He had to do this, the world and many others depended on it. Right now he trusted Ayeth more than he trusted any other.

'There is something I can do to help you harness the power of the orb. With your greater wisdom, perhaps you can unlock its secrets.

'Ayeth of the Aralans, by all that is right and good in your world and in mine, and by the blessing of the Great Goddess and the One Light, the One Source of All, I name you Second Keeper.'

CHAPTER 15

Orphinius

FROM a hillock, Issa watched the elves as they assembled in a wide ring around Asaph and Orphinius.

The two men held wooden swords and were rolling up their sleeves preparing to fight. Everyone had gathered in a flat, grassy field, just north of the village. Mainly elf-men, Issa noted, but there were a few women dotted amongst them. All shared the same fierce and determined expressions on their beautiful, aquiline faces. Some sat on blankets whilst others stood, arms folded expectantly over their chests.

Many had cuts and bruises on their faces but most were fit and strong and of fighting age, or at least able to swing a sword. The other elf women would be looking after the children, the elderly and the more seriously wounded who could not practise fighting today, she supposed.

A chill autumn wind blew, tumbling fallen leaves over the grass around those assembled. The sun was out and the sky blue but it was cold. Issa wrapped her scarf tighter around her neck. Asaph was dressed in just a shirt and breeches and he stamped his feet to keep warm, clearly keen to get going.

Orphinius wore dark brown leggings of an elven design and a half-length seer's robe. His long, platinum hair was tied back and his green eyes sparkled with excitement as he addressed the crowd. As soon as Orphinius was out of his sick bed, he'd started his training school with a feverous passion. Those fit and well enough had flocked to it. Issa stepped closer to hear him.

'A long time ago, we elves had an army. An army that humans and dwarves fled from! We lost that army when we left this world of war. But war has found us again and we are weak. Now, if we want to survive, we must again learn how to fight and protect ourselves.'

The crowd nodded and murmured. Issa hid a smile, how different these people were now to when she'd first met them in the Land of Mists; shy and hidden in the trees, abhorred and disgusted by the very mention of war. Now, after seeing their beautiful haven destroyed and their loved ones eaten alive or burned to death, they wanted vengeance. Baelthrom's threat could no longer be ignored.

Orphinius slowly turned in her direction, his eyes gliding over everyone, taking them all in, challenging them to be a warrior. 'I used to be one such fighter in our armies and I would ask those of you who also were to reach back into those memories and rekindle the fighting spirit. You may not have wanted to fight before, but now I see the fire in your eyes, your raw need to avenge. Take hold of that fire! Nurture it, let it burn bright and dream of our ancient homeland; Intolana.'

Murmurs flowed through the crowd. Orphinius continued.

'Yes, I have been given a vision, a wondrous, incredible vision of a time when we take back the land that belongs to us and has always been ours. I see it rising from the ashes to become glorious once more! I see our ancient forests coming alive again and elves filling its borders from sea to mountain.'

The looks of wonder on the elves' faces brought tears to Issa's eyes. Orphinius' words ignited a fire in her heart too. She clenched her jaw. All the lands would be theirs again, one day. For the first time, she dared to believe her homeland would be restored too. Not her home on Little Kammy; her ancestral lands of beautiful, serene Tusarza—the first place to be subjected to the terror of the Immortal Lord and laid waste.

She closed her eyes, imaging the red clouds of Maphrax racing away, the ravaged earth filling with forests and flowers, the poisoned streams running clear and pure, and the Mountains of Maphrax exploding into nothing but dust, blown away by the wind.

"Dare to dream and dream big." So Fraya used to say to her.

'Oh, Fraya. Mother,' Issa muttered under her breath. 'I'll dream big! I'll dream the biggest dream.'

Orphinius finished speaking. He turned to Asaph and they began circling each other, their swords raised, and big grins on their faces. Asaph lunged first but the elf was naturally quick and stepped aside. Asaph attacked again and dodged the elf's strike with effortless speed. With a flick of his wrist, Asaph landed the first blow on the elf's side making him sigh.

They resumed their starting positions. Orphinius went in for a quick attack driving Asaph back. The elf dragged his right leg a little betraying his injury. Dar had tried to stop him doing the training camp but it was impossible—the elf was on a mission and was too enthused to listen to anyone. Issa hoped Asaph would notice and be gentle with him.

The elf began to move a little easier as he warmed up. The slap and crack of their swords rang out over the crowd. Neither man made a sound—not even a grunt. They were far too civilised for the brutality they were enacting, or perhaps they were conserving their energy. For someone who had not fought for hundreds of years, Orphinius was remembering quickly. The two men began to move with such speed that many of their moves were a blur. Too fast for normal men, Issa thought, stepping closer to get a better view. Too fast even for a Karalanth.

Asaph and the elf almost seemed to dance. Orphinius had all the grace she had seen in Marakon, only more, and Asaph moved with dominating speed and accuracy that only the dragon blood in his veins could give him. There was a smile on Asaph's face, and she wondered if he were holding back. When he landed a gentle swipe on Orphinius' good leg, she decided he must be.

A cheer escaped her mouth and those elves closest turned to look at her, grinning. The crowd clapped as the two men stepped apart, breathing hard. Asaph unbuttoned his shirt and threw it to one side. Orphinius took off his seer's robe and stood in a sleeveless tunic. They eagerly resumed their positions again.

Issa admired the way Asaph's muscles rippled over his shoulders and back and found her cheeks growing hot. His tanned skin glistened with sweat, and she realised she loved to watch him fight. The way he moved with an easy power and grace that could never have been taught to him.

'Er, Lady Issa, I wanted to say thank you.' A young man's melodious voice startled her out of gawking at Asaph.

Smoothing her hair and composing herself, she turned and looked up into the clear mauve eyes of a young elf man. He could be no more than seventeen years old in human years, impossible to tell in elven years. His hair was past shoulder length and a beautiful pale purple colour. His long, oval face was just losing the softness of youth and · his chin and cheekbones had a slight angular cast to them. Like most elves, he was tall and slender.

'I'm Velonorian,' he introduced himself with a boyish grin and an outstretched hand which Issa hesitantly shook.

'Forgive me, but thank you for what?' she said. She didn't remember helping this man and he didn't seem injured in any way. She cast her mind back over the past few days but nothing came to mind.

'I've been meaning to talk to you for a while, but it always seemed the wrong moment,' he said, almost stuttering with nerves. He dipped his head closer, the grin fading from his lips. 'You saw it coming and you tried to warn us. I knew you were right, but I was forbidden to speak about it to anyone, even by my mother. People shunned me if I tried. I'm sorry for how they treated you. I would have listened, but we have to do what King Daranarta tells us.'

'Had to,' Issa corrected him gently. 'You are free to follow your own guidance now, though I did not wish for this to happen. However, you are wrong and you have nothing to thank me for. I didn't do anything that helped.'

She looked back at the men fighting, a heavy feeling in her heart. How many elves had died? She couldn't bring herself to think about it.

'I failed, Velonorian. Had I convinced Daranarta to return to Maioria, all the elves would still be with us, and the Land of Mists would remain for you to return to. Now look what has happened.'

'It is not your fault, it's Daranarta's,' Velonorian said, coming closer so he was only a foot from her. There was a strange look in his eyes, one of awe she supposed—awe she didn't feel she deserved. 'I see the goddess in you.'

'The goddess is in everyone, Velonorian. Everyone is blessed and sacred.'

'Yes, but I see her moving within you, walking with you. That is why I know you can do it. I know you can drive Baelthrom and his horde from our lands, from all of Maioria. And that is why I will follow you.' The earnestness in his eyes moved her.

'I wish I had your conviction,' she smiled. 'Sometimes I do. Although sometimes, when this happens,' she motioned to the elven refugees before her, 'I doubt we can do anything.'

'It will make you stronger,' the young elf man nodded. 'Your resolve will become harder and harder until you know only your single purpose and you believe in nothing else.'

'You have wise words for someone so young,' Issa said, wondering if all young elves were this clever.

He blushed, either with pride or embarrassment. She hoped it was the former.

'I heard that you are forming an army of knights,' he said.

Issa's eyes went wide. 'Wow, rumours spread fast. Yes, I am. Well, Marakon Si Hara of the Feylint Halanoi has already formed the Knights of the Raven—'

'I want to join! With your grace of course,' he blurted before she could finish.

Issa blinked then was horrified when he took her hand gently in his own and got down on one knee before her.

'My Lady Issa, my Queen of Ravens, I pledge myself to your service. I will be your knight, your most loyal chaplain.'

So caught up in the moment, Issa was only vaguely aware of a squawk as Ehka landed on her shoulder. She stared at the elf. She didn't even know him and his devotion to her came as a complete shock. She would have felt embarrassed had the conviction, the faith in his eyes not moved her deeply. Did she deserve this young man's devotion? She would only get him killed.

'Should I die in service to you, it would only be an honour,' he said, making everything she was feeling ten times worse.

'Velonorian, you shall do no such thing. Now get up. I can't make you a knight, only Marakon can. I don't even know how.' She felt her cheeks redden as elves began to turn in her direction, looks of surprise spreading over their faces.

Velonorian stayed on his knee. 'Then I shall wait until there comes a time when you alone will knight me. My Lady Issa, all my family have been murdered and the best of my friends. I have no direction, no trade, no life purpose—except the deepest, goddess-given desire to serve you, my Queen.'

Issa wanted to say no and tell the man that he was being silly, but only because she was embarrassed and this had never happened to her before. To deny this man would be a crime and the ultimate insult to his pride.

'Please, be my liege. I will never fail you.' He bowed his head.

Tears filled her eyes and she blinked them back. She gripped his hand and pulled him to his feet.

'That is not what I am worried about, Velonorian. I fear that it's I who will let you down. Many whom I loved have also been taken from me. If you choose to be in my service, you must realise how dangerous that is. Baelthrom hunts me and already so many have died.'

'I know all of this and more, my Queen.' The devotion in his eyes didn't lessen with her words, it only seemed to increase.

'Let him,' Asaph whispered in her ear from behind, making her jump. She hadn't heard him arrive and Velonorian's eyes never strayed from her face to hint there was anyone else there.

She hesitated for a long moment then found herself saying, 'I would be honoured, Velonorian.'

The young man's face split into the broadest of smiles and his eyes sparkled. He held up her hand and kissed it.

'My Queen,' he said.

'Do you know how to use a sword?' Issa asked.

'Not yet, my Lady Issa,' he said.

'Just Issa will do. Well, why don't you start learning from Orphinius?' She gestured to the elf who was waiting for a new sparring partner.

'Yes, my Queen Issa. Right away.' Velonorian nodded vigorously.

Asaph passed him his wooden sword and the young elf clutched at it. With an exultant laugh, Velonorian whirled away through the crowd towards Orphinius.

'What have I done?' Issa asked, feeling confounded.

'Made a young man very happy.' Asaph laughed.

She turned to look at him as he wiped the sweat from his chest with a towel. The flame marks there were a vivid red and she found herself blushing when she looked at them, remembering when their two marks had touched.

'Aren't you jealous?' she said slyly.

He grinned and pulled her close. 'He's too young for you.'

'Oh really?' She laid a hand on his hot shoulder.

'But I do think you need to be watched day and night,' he said and bent his head to kiss her lightly on the lips. 'You should have a whole army protecting you whilst you sleep, like any other queen.'

'I certainly would like a bed to call my own, and a castle. Just my own house would do.'

'Maybe Raven Queens live in trees…'

She laughed and pushed him away. 'You're all sweaty, now go and wash.'

With a grin, he left her and walked towards one of the water fonts besides the houses on the edge of Oray. Issa took a deep breath and placed her hands on her hips. There were three pairs of young men in the ring now, Velonorian included, all fighting with wooden swords. Orphinius directed them, shouting out what they should be doing and correcting them every moment.

Issa wished she could wait for them to be fully trained before she left Myrn but she could not. Very soon she would be leaving for Davono to rendezvous with the Karalanths who were amassing on the borders. Scrying for Triest'anth had been easy, formulating their plan had not.

King Navarr had returned home a day or so ago to organise his army and prepare units to send to Davono. Drumblodd and Luren had also returned to the dwarf king's home in the central Everridge Mountains between Davono and Lans Himay. The dwarf planned to catch up with his army that was already marching to Davono. Reports had reached them that Lans Himay had managed to organise itself to send its own mercenary factions for a hefty fee, of course, footed mostly by King Navarr.

Luren was tasked with organising the affairs of Lans Himay where Averen left off. All of them planned to be in Davono ready for the offensive. There was a lot going on and a lot that could go wrong. The only thing Issa knew they had to do was attack.

Thinking of all these armies moving at her request made her palms sweaty. She was no war leader. Was she marching them to their deaths? It didn't bear thinking about. But it had not been her decision alone, everyone had agreed to it.

Domenon had already sent messages to Queen Thora explaining the situation, preparing her for the thought of foreign armies moving through her lands. The wizard was keen to return to his queen and explain in person, and yet he lingered here, spending every available moment with Orphinius.

'Aren't you going to fight?'

Issa jumped and looked up at Domenon, surprised to see him there as if her thoughts had made him appear. He nodded to the elves.

'I'd like to see you fight.' He grinned down at her. There was nothing but humour in his voice.

'Well, I guess I should practice, but I've been too busy helping the wounded and learning what I can from the seers before we leave.'

'Yes, I shall be leaving soon,' said Domenon. 'Depending on when the merchant ships from Atalanph arrive. They could be here as early as tomorrow and they next dock at Davono.'

'So soon?' Issa said, shocked. The wizard had changed his tune. Last time she'd made plans to leave he had procrastinated. She couldn't turn up in Davono without the Queen's advisor. What had changed his mind?

The wizard continued. 'A lot has happened. Drumblodd's army has nearly reached Davono's borders. Baelthrom may strike again at any time hunting for the elven orb he knows has escaped the Land of Mists. If Queen Thora agrees to act on this plan of yours and invade Venosia, we must do it quickly.'

Issa nodded. 'That's what I have been saying. But now the time has come, I don't feel ready to leave. I don't want to go to war.'

'It is the way of the Isles of Tirry to make you want to stay,' Domenon said. 'But we can do no more here for the elves. They are in the best place possible.'

Issa glanced at the elves training; fighting, dancing and striking each other, and wondered if they would become the fabled and feared warriors of old. 'And the orb will remain here in safety.' Issa nodded, feeling immensely relieved.

Domenon smiled. 'We can worry less about it now. Certain security measures have been put in place.'

'How?' said Issa instantly suspicious.

'Orphinius, in his greater wisdom, has made me Second Keeper,' Domenon's eyes sparkled as he whirled away.

Issa's heart pounded.

Issa realised her mouth was open and shut it. By the time she thought to run after the Master Wizard to question him further, the man had disappeared into Oray. She searched the cobbled streets but he was nowhere to found.

Instead, she decided to find and tell Freydel immediately. He was not going to be pleased. She hurried past a row of round houses all of which had little gardens filled with various herbs and flowers. One garden boasted a fountain with a giant fish that spurted water from its mouth.

She stopped at the house with a green gate; Freydel's guest house which he was sharing with Haelgon. She knocked on his door and went inside when no answer came.

Freydel turned to her, startled. He stood in the centre of the room holding the Orb of Death up to the sunlight that was spilling through the skylight. She noticed the bags under his eyes and his pale demeanour with worry.

'Orphinius named Domenon Second Keeper,' she blurted, hanging on to the door handle.

A look of horror spread across his face. 'How? Why?'

Issa shrugged. 'He's spent a lot of time with him. Maybe Orphinius got scared about its safety. We'd better ask him ourselves.'

Freydel dropped his arms and slipped the orb inside his robes, looking drained. 'It cannot be undone.'

'What is it, Freydel? You look exhausted. Is something bothering you?' She entered the room fully, shutting the door behind her.

In response, he sunk down into a red fabric chair. Issa knelt on the pile of large cushions that were set beside it. Freydel muttered to himself, cast her a glance, then looked away again.

'I did what I said I would. I shouldn't really speak about it...' he waved a hand.

'No, tell me.' She leant forward. What on earth had happened?

He took a deep breath. 'I've been visiting Ayeth.'

Issa inhaled sharply.

'It's not easy but under his tutelage and the power of this crystal staff…'

'How can you keep going to him?' Issa demanded. 'How can you endanger the orb?' She couldn't believe what she was hearing. The thought of being able to *time-travel* was staggering enough. That he was going back and forth to their enemy…

'I go to him to stop him becoming Baelthrom. There is no other option!' Freydel barked, spots of colour appearing on his cheeks. He turned away and tugged on his beard.

Issa leant back. She had never seen him so ragged and exhausted. He was always the epitome of calm wisdom—eccentric, yes, but always in control of his emotions.

'I'm sorry.' His shoulders slumped. 'I'm deeply tired.'

If he hadn't looked so worn, Issa would have hounded him. Instead, she worried. 'You should rest and not visit him ever again. He is right on one thing: the Orb of Death is doing just as its nature dictates—it is killing you! If we combine the last remaining orbs, it will not be able to drain you like this.'

'No!' Freydel almost shouted, making her jump.

'No,' he repeated more softly. 'Combining the orbs is too dangerous. He has made an oath to me.'

'Pah! Some good that will do,' Issa laughed.

'No, it's not like that. When an Aralan pledges themself to another, they cannot harm them. This Ayeth is not a monster. I cannot see how he becomes Baelthrom. Perhaps everything we have done together has already changed the timeline.'

'Then why is that bastard still here?' Issa asked, her hands balling into fists. 'There is only one way to make sure, and that is to kill this Ayeth.' She only half meant it, to see what his reaction might be. To see if she could trust him.

Freydel looked at her. She held his gaze.

'Ayeth is an amazing, powerful being who does not deserve to be destroyed. The very thought is terrible,' said Freydel. 'He has already taught me so much. That knowledge I can pass on to others.'

The awe and devotion in his eyes shocked Issa. Was he being

charmed? No, it was virtually impossible to charm a wizard. What, then, was going on?

'Have you lost your mind? That being becomes a monster who slaughters millions and destroys entire planets,' her own voice rose to shouting. Freydel flinched, instantly making her feel bad. She backed down.

'He's not what you think he is. He, like you, was chosen by Zanufey to help,' said Freydel.

All the fight drained out of her at his words and she sagged. He *was* chosen. To even consider that this Ayeth deserved to live was hard to swallow. She needed to hate him to destroy him. *But he is not Baelthrom,* she reminded herself.

'I know,' she whispered. 'But destroying him is the only way to ensure millions live. You have become infatuated with him and the power he has taught you. It has blinded you to your purpose.'

'No, it has made me strong.' There was a hard determined look in his eyes.

'Then what are we to do?'

The wizard was nearly three times her age and steeped in learning and experience. It felt wrong to assume she knew more than him, but still, her instincts nagged at her. Him visiting Ayeth, especially with the orb, made her feel sick.

When he didn't answer, she said, 'Let me come with you. I will meet him, if he is so nice.' She tried to keep the sarcasm out of her voice.

'It is too draining. The orb cannot take two. You need your strength to lead the people,' he said.

'I've got enough strength and my own orb. Let me come with you. Teach me how.'

'Out of the question, it's too dangerous. There is one beside him whom I do not trust—' he broke off as if he hadn't meant to speak.

'Who?' Issa frowned. The bad feeling in her stomach grew.

'No one, it doesn't matter.' He waved dismissively.

'Who?' Issa repeated, her eyes narrowing. She knew who it was, the black-eyed woman she'd seen in the star portal, but wanted Freydel to say it.

Freydel dropped his shoulders. 'Her name is Lona. She is of a different race to Ayeth, from a different planet.'

As Freydel told her his experience with the black-eyed female, a cold creeping sensation spread up Issa's back.

'But she has never done anything. I just don't trust her,' said Freydel. 'Ayeth is besotted with her though. He is so committed to helping her and her people, I feel he is blinded.'

'Likewise, I can see you have become quite attached to Ayeth,' Issa said in a tight voice, trying to reason through her emotions. 'Ending Ayeth is the only way to stop Baelthrom.'

'We cannot kill an innocent being,' said Freydel.

'He's not innocent,' she began, but knew he was right. Remembering Ayeth, his beauty and power and ultimate innocence, could she simply kill him? She would be killing Zanufey's chosen before he'd even committed a crime. It would make her the sinner and no better than Baelthrom.

'Well, you're going to have to trust me on this one,' said Freydel.

Issa said no more. She didn't want to get into a long debate and inevitable argument with her friend and teacher so she decided to let him rest.

Walking alone along the pale cobbled street deep in thought, she took a road that led out of Oray and into the forest. She stopped when she came to a small brook and watched the tinkling water. The sun was dipping into the trees, casting its long rays of light through the falling autumn leaves. With a sigh, she squatted down upon a rock jutting out of the earth and blew into her cold hands.

No matter how she turned it around in her head, Freydel's friendship with Ayeth was deeply disturbing. Ayeth could be working powerful magic to twist Freydel's mind, or he was as the wizard described him; honourable and kind. If he were killed, all their problems would disappear and millions of lives would be saved. But was it right to kill an innocent being? Of course not, but what choice did they have when not killing him would destroy them all.

Issa did not like these thoughts at all. She knew she couldn't kill Ayeth. The very thought was despicable. She slipped out the Orb of Water from her pocket. It sparkled turquoise and aqua as the sun hit it. The brook tinkled with music and shimmered more brightly. She smiled; the orb was talking to the water.

Could she use her orb to travel across time too? The thought made her stop. It was an uncomfortable question. She'd assumed that peculiar ability was specific to the Orb of Undoing, but now she wondered.

Freydel had just looked so exhausted. Maybe, when he'd rested, he would think more clearly and she'd be able to talk to him then. If the orb was draining him, was the Orb of Water draining her too? She couldn't feel anything but then neither could Freydel. The orbs held magic in an unnatural state. Even now she could feel the pull of it in her hand, like a gentle tug towards something. Towards being combined with the other elements. Things in an unnatural state always sought to rebalance themselves.

There was a lot she had to do. Soon she would be travelling to Davono and she needed to prepare herself for meeting the queen and organising the first offensive committed on enemy lands for a very long time. She didn't have the luxury of worrying about what Freydel, Domenon and the others were up to. She needed a single point of focus and the support of all those around her.

Slipping the orb back in her pocket, she pushed herself to her feet. She would have to trust Freydel knew what he was doing, for now.

CHAPTER 16

The Calling

ASAPH took the long road home, winding between the edge of Oray and the trees as the setting sun turned the sky golden.

The rich smell of the forest filled his nostrils and he felt good after his sword training. Orphinius' skill with the sword had come back to the elf fast and Asaph really had to put the effort in towards the end. The elves, what remained of them, would soon be a powerful band of warriors.

The elf had invited him to practice archery tomorrow but no matter how he looked at it, the thought of attacking the enemy from afar with projectiles rather than getting up close and whacking them with his sword felt somewhat cowardly and un-Draxian. So he'd politely declined.

It would be good for Issa to hone her skills with the bow though, he thought. Rhul'ynth said she had a natural talent with it, and it would help to keep her further away from the edge of a Maphraxie's blade.

The sudden darkening of the sky made by a passing cloud brought him out of his thoughts and he looked around, wondering where he was. Ahead was Feygriene's waterfall, the golden rocks gleaming, behind him, down the hill and just visible through the trees, were patches of white houses. He'd been so wrapped in his own thoughts he'd missed the path leading to his house.

He turned back the way he had come when a flash of something caught his eye making him pause. For a heart-stopping moment, he thought about Cirosa and his hand dropped to his sword. He scanned the trees but there was only a red squirrel jumping amongst the fallen leaves, an acorn lodged firmly in its mouth. It stopped and stared back at him. He relaxed his hand. Cirosa couldn't reach him here through Myrn's protective shield. Besides, after Faelsun had removed her chains, he was free of her grasp.

He glanced back at the waterfall and did a double take. There, suspended above the water's surface, surrounded by a halo of yellow light, hung the Sword of Binding. He inhaled sharply and walked towards it. The blood red pommel gleamed and the grey-blue blade looked as if it had been freshly sharpened. He glanced around but there was no one here; no seer or wizard to create this magic. Slowly he reached out a hand and touched it, stunned to find his finger slide across cold steel.

The Recollection snapped open.

Roaring fire blinded him and filled his ears so fully he thought they would burst from the noise. There was no heat—just light and sound. The raging flames calmed and he saw the sword suspended in its dark chamber somewhere beneath Castle Draxa, just as he had always seen it in the shared memory. The pages of the Recollection flipped fast in his mind but this time felt different to every time before. These memories were emotionless and absolute. He had a shocking realisation: this wasn't the memory of a being or dragon; it was the memory of the sword. Was it even possible for a sword to have memory?

Pressure filled his head making him groan in pain, then the walls of the sword's chamber exploded outward. Black magical fire filled the room, torching and melting anything that was not the sword; the ropes, the reeds on the floor—even the chains surrounding the blade and the stone dais beneath it began to melt and wither. *Fire hot enough to melt stone!*

But nothing could destroy the sword, it didn't even buckle.

The fire receded and diffuse light fell, whether daylight or from a torch, Asaph couldn't see. Shadows crowded close, tall things in robes that only seemed half-real. Fear prickled his skin. Were they necromancers? The thought of them being close to the sword, his sword, made him furious.

Thick blackness blanketed everything, shutting out the light. He couldn't see the sword. He strained and pushed against the black but it was absolute. The feel of it made him queasy. *Black magic.* The Recollection began to dim as if being forced to close.

'Find me.' The whisper that scoured his ears was harsh and grating, not made by a human throat. Had it come from the sword? Urgent need filled Asaph, so intense he wanted to cry out, and then it was gone.

He stood blinking beside the waterfall. The sword was gone. The black magic and necromancers—gone. He stood alone, apart from the squirrel rustling in the leaves. It looked up at him, made a squeak as if laughing, then scampered up a tree trunk.

He rubbed his eyes. What had he witnessed? Was the vision a message from Feygriene or from the sword? Whichever it was, the message was clear; he had to get the sword and he had to get it now.

Something in his pocket grew hot. He reached into it and grabbed the thing burning his leg. The three enchanted keys to the sword chamber flared into red fire. He yelped and dropped them. The keys turned white and the grass beneath them blackened. He cautiously bent to pick them up but the keys crumpled into white ash and the wind took the remains.

Drawing a shaking breath, he stood. The chamber had been destroyed, and so too its protective magic. He didn't need to be a magic wielder to understand the keys were void now the chamber itself had been obliterated. What use were enchanted keys and secret chambers now? There was nothing to protect the sword…

He clenched his sore hand into a fist and rubbed his chin, thinking hard and trying not to panic. Necromancers had discovered the sword. Baelthrom would have been hunting for the sword that bound dragon and human together since he invaded and took Drax. If he were Baelthrom fearing an uprising, he would have done it too. The sword was the key to awakening the dragons. Without it, it could not be done. They would not awaken and he, Asaph, would not lead them. If the hottest magical fire couldn't destroy the sword, then hopefully nothing could. But it could be lost and hidden, just as the black magic had hidden it.

An awful dilemma struck him; he could not go north to find the sword *and* accompany Issa south in her campaign. The thought of leaving her now when she needed him by her side was gut wrenching, he couldn't do it.

…But not going north and not finding the sword; to risk losing the sword forever, was far worse.

Asaph finished the rice on his plate, set down his fork and took a deep breath. 'As much as I want to, I cannot go south with you.' He clasped Issa's hand firmly as she tried to pull away.

'Your vision of the sword did not say you couldn't come south,' she said, her eyes wide.

'I know it's not what either of us want to hear but let me explain,' he said. 'That vision was a message so powerful I can't ignore it. If I don't find the sword, I may never find it again. Without it, I cannot awaken the dragons and they will sleep forever until their doom. If I find the sword, I will rouse them and bring them south. We can be there fast to join you.'

'Then let me go with you. I'll put the campaign on hold—'

'No, you cannot come with me. I will be facing *dragons*. Dragons that might not like me, like Morhork. You are needed here much more than with me, you know this. You have gathered the armies—only you can lead them. Marakon looks to you, the wizards and seers look to you. Hell, even the demons look to you. This offensive is just too important. I have to find the sword alone and I've no idea where it might be now its chamber has been destroyed.'

She opened her mouth to protest but her words died upon her lips as she took in the logic of what he was saying.

'I don't like it either. The thought of leaving you, after so much. After my father...' he blinked back the tears that suddenly welled. 'It's like you always said; our calling in this life is far more than just what you and I want. Even if I never win back Drax again, to awaken the dragons for one last battle is what I was born to do.'

He'd expected Issa to fight and rail against him, but she must have seen the determined passion in his eyes, understood the logic in his words. Silently she nodded with a joyless expression.

'There's a chance you will make it back to us before the offensive?' she asked.

'Possibly. I pray that I will,' he nodded and lifted her hand to his lips. In her other hand, she toyed with a green grape, rolling it between her fingers.

'When will you go?' She didn't look at him. 'And where?'

'Tonight,' he whispered, a lump in his throat. 'And I don't know where but as a dragon I hope to find the answers within. Perhaps Morhork can help me. I wish to all the world that I didn't have to go.'

'Why so soon? No, wait. I know you have to go. We've stayed here too long already but we had to help the elves. I just don't want you to go,' she admitted.

He pushed his chair back and pulled her onto his lap. 'I don't want to go without you either,' he said softly, hugging her. 'If I succeed or if I fail, it will be over quickly and I will soon be with you.'

'Or I'll never see you again,' she said.

'I worry that it's *you* who will disappear leaving me alone here…' said Asaph. 'But you know we both have to do what we've got to do.'

Asaph waited until Issa was asleep before he left. He stared at her black hair spilling over the pillow, at her pale flawless skin catching the light of the moon as it came through the skylight. He wanted to kiss her but didn't want to wake her. His heart was heavy. It always seemed that as soon as they'd come together after something terrible, they had to part again. He knew he was doing the right thing but he didn't feel good about it. He'd be leaving Issa with Domenon and that thought worried him more than it should.

Quietly, he slipped on his boots, buckled on his sword and wrapped his cloak around him. Silently, he slipped into the night. A cold wind blew from the Everridge Mountains far to the west making him shiver but the sky was clear and the light of the half-moon Doon lit his way. In the distance, he could hear ropes slapping the masts of the boats in the harbour.

He'd hoped for a strong, warm wind coming south from Atalanph, but at least the cold wind from the west wouldn't be blowing against him, slowing his flight north. He took the path that led straight into the forest, wishing for all the world that Coronos was with him.

He swallowed a lump in his throat. *I do this for you, Father. I do it for Mother and my blood-father also.*

His resolve steeled, he opened himself to his dragon form. It came easily but with a twinge of pain, as if he'd kept it bottled up for too long and it was bursting to get out. He filled his great lungs with cool air and let it out smokily. With a yawn and a stretch of his wings, he beat powerfully down, lifting himself easily into the air. He circled higher and higher, looking down at the shrinking patch of land that was Myrn below him, lit only by a couple of street lamps at the harbour.

He turned his attention to the Flow and saw the silvery protective shield covering all the islands against Baelthrom. He turned north, setting his gaze into the darkness and angling his wings against the western wind, his mind filling with thoughts of Drax and the sword that called to him

Hours later, the west wind gave in to a frigid north wind as he left the north shores of Lans Himay, and his cold reptilian blood longed for the warmth of Feygriene. His wings ached and his body felt heavy and slow. As he left the safety of the Frayonesse continent and neared enemy-held lands, he cloaked himself in shielding magic. This would surely be his most dangerous mission.

All the sword had told him was it needed to be saved, not *how* it could be saved or even where it might be located. It wasn't going to be easy to find.

A vague plan rattled in his brain, find Morhork, then find the sword. The dragon might know where it had gone, or at least be able to help him find it.

The dragon had saved him by taking him to Faelsun, hadn't he? He can't hate him *that* much. What if he didn't know where the sword was? If the sword had called to him, surely he would feel where it was. But what if it was cloaked in black magic? Asaph didn't like these questions, they filled him with doubt. He had nothing to go on but faith. *The sword will lead me on.*

The dark expanse of ocean below him became dotted with darker patches of islands. After a time, a larger chunk of land loomed on the horizon, spreading east to west as far as the eye could see.

Drax.

He could smell its snow-capped peaks even from here. A mix of awe and anger settled in his heart. Awe that his homeland was before him, anger that it was his no longer.

Double checking his cloaking magic, he slowed and dropped lower in the sky, hunting the islands for a suitable resting spot. He deliberately avoided the larger ones for fear they might be inhabited by Maphraxies.

As he banked around a small island with a single high cliff, he spied a black spot at its base where the sea didn't crash white against the rocks. A sea cave, though cold and wet, would be perfect to rest in if it were deep enough.

He circled lower, scanning the island for enemies, but there was nothing to be seen, not even a tree, just a barren rock against which the ocean pounded. A swoop past the cave entrance revealed it to be deep enough to not be able to see the end. There was a tight edge along its side which he might be able to land on.

Careful not to get himself wet in the freezing water and stiffen his already aching muscles, he dipped into the cave and scrabbled onto the tight ledge. Pausing for a moment to get his balance, he peered into the cave, his dragon eyes adjusting to the dark.

The ledge widened further into the cave and led far back out of the waves. He blasted fire from his nostrils, illuminating and heating the cave and destroying anything that might be lurking there. There was nothing. Enjoying the warmth of his fire on his scales, he blasted the cave again sending a shoal of fish darting this way and that in the sudden light.

Seeing the fish made his stomach rumble. *They wouldn't be enough to feed a dragon,* he thought. *But enough for a man.*

Setting his snout close to the surface he breathed fire, almost instantly making the water boil. Most of the fish got away but three unlucky ones bobbed to the surface, steaming. He fished them out and moved to the back of the cave.

With a sigh, he let go of his dragon form and set about eating the fish, grateful that feeding a man was far more economical than feeding a dragon. He didn't dare rest in his human form, however, and changed back before settling down, wrapping his tail around his body.

As dawn began to turn the sky pink, he fell asleep.

When dusk came, Asaph roused. The cave was frigid and he blasted it with fire again until the walls were dry and warm. As the sky outside the cave darkened, he caught and ate more fish, then moved to the entrance in dragon form.

Why couldn't he feel the sword? It must be hidden in black magic. Morhork was no Dragon Lord, maybe he wouldn't have felt the sword's desperate calling. And given how the dragon felt about "half-breeds" he was unlikely to care, let alone help him. Finding the old dragon seemed pointless. Asaph sighed. He was well and truly on his own.

He clambered out of the cave and up the rock to the level surface. In the grey twilight, the dark hunkering land that was Drax loomed close and menacing. He recalled Coronos' maps. The capital city, Draxa, lay on the west coast beyond the Grey Lords. If he took a wide berth and kept out to sea, he would have less chance of being detected.

He stretched his wings and beat them to get airborne. It was dark tonight, clouds covered the sky and would further hide his presence. *That was good,* he thought, as he lifted up through them, shivering as their icy wetness engulfed his body. Turning north-west, he kept the dark bulk of southern Drax to his right.

The land rose higher and higher from the coast until the enormous sheer peaks of the Grey Lords spiked up into the sky like dragon teeth. Beyond them, the land flattened into a plateau. It was still relatively free from snow this time of year.

He felt Draxa long before he saw it. The memory of it was in his blood. From a distance the city and immense fortress loomed, bringing strong emotions with it as it matched the memory in his mind. It looked majestic, belying the fact that only enemies inhabited the place now, the original inhabitants having been brutally murdered or fled. He tried to imagine it was his home and inside its vast grey walls were his people; working, feasting, laughing…

A shadow moved on a turret. Giant Dread Dragon wings spread wide into the air then settled back. A Dromoorai was stationed on his home. His dream shattered. He shuddered with repulsion.

Surrounding Draxa Castle and the city were several giant turrets—at least six that he could count—and each one was topped by a Dromoorai guard. Asaph swallowed and put greater distance between them, banking higher into the clouds. He couldn't get any closer and risk his cloaking magic being detected. He still couldn't feel the sword either. His plan suddenly seemed stupid and reckless. Perhaps if he looked into the Recollection, he would see where the sword had been.

A memory came to him, one of his own: Coronos carried him down dark and winding steps. The cold, damp, stone walls dripped with water and only a little wizard's light lit the way. The smell of the sea and human panic was heavy in the air. They emerged onto a shingle beach at the base of towering cliffs far below the castle.

Asaph blinked and dipped out of the clouds, glancing behind him to see Draxa now far away in the distance. Turning back, he dropped very low and glided only a few yards above the ocean's surface until Draxa was close again. With the memory of it clear in his mind, he hunted for that shingle beach at the base of the cliffs. There were several. He reached the first but it didn't match his memory; too many overhanging rocks making it difficult to land. The second was too wide, the third too small.

The cliffs curved away and as he lifted to try again, he spied another beach, virtually hidden by a spit of rock jutting out of the ocean. Glancing upwards to check there were no Dromoorai scouts, he glided towards the shingle beach.

He timed his landing as a wave crashed against it to hide the noise of his claws upon the pebbles. The surf receded, dragging stones with it, paused, then pushed the stones back again. The deafening noise was welcome.

Asaph stood there for a long time, all senses alert, waiting for imminent attack.

None came.

He snaked his head up. The sheer cliff rose so high it disappeared into the night sky above, the rocks slick and wet and treacherous. From this angle, he spied the narrow stairs cut into the cliff face. They vanished behind a jutting rock.

He stared at the steps, seeing in his mind's eye Coronos rushing down them with him, a tiny baby, in his arms. For a moment he was mesmerised, trapped in the past. This was where he had left Drax over twenty-five years ago. Now he had returned but Coronos was no longer with him. It was not how he wanted it to be.

He walked towards the base of the stairs. They wound up and disappeared somewhere above. Would the wooden doorway still be there? Would the secret tunnels leading all the way up into the castle still be whole? Did he dare go up them and find out? And to what end? He couldn't sneak around Baelthrom's castle, it would be crawling with necromancers and Maphraxies.

He let go of a long-held sigh. His mission here had been stupid and futile. He laid his great head against the rock. If the sword was near and able to, it would have spoken to him. Now it was stolen, he would never find it. Perhaps it was already far away deep in the fire chambers of Maphrax.

He rested against the cliff face wondering what to do. When pink brushed the sky, he was surprised by how long he had been loitering.

The sword blazed in his mind so blindingly bright he fought not to cry out. The red pommel swirled, the blade hummed and a flaming aura surrounded it. Whatever dark magic had been shielding it had gone. It was near, somewhere in Draxa, he had to get it!

In his need, he almost forgot about his magical shield as he began the change into a human. He regained himself. *I cannot use magic in my human form, but neither can I climb these steps and enter the castle as a dragon!*

A cackle came from above. His eyes darted upwards and spied something flying above the cliff tops. It was joined by many more, perhaps even twenty.

Harpies. He could feel their magic and smell their stink even from here. A raucous cackling came from the brood. He could flame the lot of them before they detected his presence—and almost leapt into the air to do just that when the huge dark shape of a Dread Dragon loomed into view.

Asaph wedged himself against the cliff face, praying his cloaking magic wouldn't be detected. The harpies and the Dromoorai circled lazily in the dawn light as if waiting for something. *Waiting for orders.*

Whispering filled his head, low and indistinct but urgent. He tried to focus on what was being said but couldn't make out the words. It seemed to be coming from the Dromoorai. He squinted upwards and his jaw dropped open. A glimmering sword was attached to the Dromoorai's belt—a sword with a blood red pommel.

'It cannot be...' Asaph breathed. Only a Dragon Lord could hold the blade. *The Dromoorai was once a Dragon Lord,* he reminded himself, feeling sick. Perhaps that was enough.

Another Dread Dragon appeared heading straight south. Asaph's great heart skipped several beats as his eyes fell upon its rider; a blonde-haired woman dressed in white. *Cirosa.* For a moment it seemed her chains still held him and his mind fogged over. If it hadn't been for his dragon form and cloaking magic, she would have detected him for sure.

She killed my father. Rage made his heart beat strong. He would willingly die killing her. His muscles bunched and it took all his willpower not to leap into the air and attack the woman. If he attacked her now, he would fail his mission and fail Issa.

The harpies and Dromoorai holding the sword fell into line behind her and disappeared from view. Asaph unwedged himself from the wall. He would have to follow them.

A cold, slithering feeling stroked his back, the fine scales of his neck itched. Something was watching him. His eyes darted left and right then rested at the top of the stone steps, the horrid feeling intensifying.

The necromancer's gaunt grey face matched the rocks so well, Asaph didn't immediately spot it peering at him. Asaph froze and stared at its sunken, unblinking eyes. It couldn't see him, surely? He didn't move but the necromancer was looking straight at him.

'My, my,' it said, its voice slithering around Asaph and making him shiver even in his dragon form.

It moved forward, its feet invisible beneath its long black robes, making it seem as if it floated. It paused. Long white hands folded over its chest. Its milky eyes were hungry and utterly unafraid. Dark spots flecked its aura and swiftly grew as it drew upon the Under Flow.

CHAPTER 17

Teramides

ISSA stood on the jetty dressed in her dragonscale armour and wrapped in a cloak.

She held the reins of Duskar and Ironclad, and Ehka perched on her shoulder shielding her face from the cold breeze. The sky was brightening with the dawn and the rippling clouds were a beautiful pink.

The merchant ship before her was large, the biggest she'd seen, and the Atalanphian crew scurried this way and that, hefting boxes and barrels as they took the cargo below deck. Others scaled the rigging, adjusting sails and tying ropes. They seemed to know exactly which each of the thousands of ropes did what.

She sighed. She missed Asaph already and imagined him flying into the frigid north. He had to go, and she had to go alone, for now. *Beloved Zanufey, I pray for the time when we no longer need to be separated. Together we are stronger.*

She turned and saw Iyena, Domenon, Haelgon and a handful of heavily armed elves chatting to each other as they walked towards her along the wooden jetty. Iyena gave Issa a warm smile and took her hand.

'You will always have a home on Myrn,' said the seer.

'Thank you for all that you have done and all you've taught me,' said Issa. 'I hope that you can manage with all the elves until they find their own place. At least you'll have your first ever standing army.'

Iyena laughed. 'You could put it like that. Already Orphinius is deciding where to settle them. If your campaign is successful, he has his eyes on Intolana with a legion of elves at his back.'

'I want to take all our lost lands back,' said Issa, setting her jaw. 'Hmm, where is Freydel?' She suddenly realised the wizard wasn't with the others.

'Oh yes,' said Iyena. 'He said to tell you that he's deeply sorry he can't make the journey to Davono because he has to return to Carvon to assist the king.'

Issa let out a silent sigh but said nothing. She would be making the journey without even her most trusted friend and tutor. King Navarr was more than capable of managing his own army. Was it an excuse so Freydel could secretly return to Ayeth? The thought was disturbing but she couldn't know for sure. Perhaps she should give him the benefit of the doubt.

'And do not worry for the manner of Queen Thora,' said Iyena. 'She is an austere woman who demands respect and truthfulness above all else. Qualities which you naturally possess. Speak frankly with her and she will be your loyal friend. Somewhere in there, there's a warm and loving person despite her coldness.'

'Thanks for the advice,' said Issa, wondering about the nature of the queen. She'd gone over and over the things she wanted to say to her, but nothing seemed quite right. She planned to play it by ear.

'Looks like it's your time to board.' Iyena pointed to the captain who was waving at them.

The Atalanphian captain was a short, stocky woman as wide as she was tall, and looked to be made of muscle. Her long hair was braided back and her smooth black skin made it impossible to tell her age. Her wide-brimmed hat shielded her blue eyes from the low sun and her above-knee dark boots rang out on the deck as she paraded back and forth shouting her orders to the crew.

Issa turned and hugged Iyena. The older woman patted her back.

'Trust in yourself and follow Zanufey's guidance. That is all the advice I can offer you,' said Iyena.

'Please look out for Asaph,' said Issa.

'We shall watch for him in our sacred pools,' the seer replied. 'Now you look after yourself and remember, trust in spirit.'

Issa nodded and turned to follow the wizards and elves onto the gangplank.

'Lady Queen Issa! Lady Queen Issa!' a voice called out.

Issa paused and peered over Duskar's back, her eyes widening. Velonorian was pelting towards the ship, his pack, bow and quiver bouncing madly on his shoulders. Iyena stepped aside with an amused grin as Velonorian stopped abruptly beside Issa. He bent over, panting to catch his breath.

'Sorry I'm late, my lady. I couldn't find my knife,' he said.

'Velonorian, why are you here? You can't come with me, you should be training with Orphinius,' said Issa.

'I've pledged myself to you, my Queen. I'll not leave your side. Especially now the Dragon Lord has left you.'

'He has not left me for long, Velonorian,' Issa sighed and caught Iyena grinning.

She clearly wasn't going to get rid of the elf, not that he was really a bother. Now she thought about it, perhaps having him along would make her feel safer. He could help clean weapons and look after the horses.

'Very well then,' Issa said, breaking into a smile. 'Then you can help me by taking Ironclad. He can be your horse until Asaph returns.'

'Thank you, my Queen,' Velonorian bowed deeply then grinned up at her, his eyes filled with devotion that was as flattering as it was unsettling.

'Issa,' said Issa, passing him the reins.

'My Queen Issa,' Velonorian said, standing tall and proud. He took Ironclad's reins as if he'd been given a grand task.

'Horses below,' the captain hollered as they stepped onto the deck.

Ehka hopped off her shoulder onto the railings to watch the sailors work. Several young deckhands came to take the horses' reins. Duskar tossed his head, making the boy who reached for him pause.

'It's all right, Duskar,' she patted his neck. 'He's not too fond of boats. When he was a foal, the ship he was on sank.'

The sailor swallowed, nodded and pulled on the reins but Duskar planted his feet firmly. Issa sighed. It was going to be a long journey for him if he already hated the ship. Speaking softly, she rubbed his neck and looked into his big brown eyes. Using the Flow, she focused on calming his nerves but he still tossed his head.

'I'll take him,' said Velonorian, and the sailor happily passed him the reins.

The elf stood close to Duskar and stroked his neck whilst whispering words in Elven. Duskar immediately stopped tossing his head and stood calmer.

Velonorian smiled at her. 'It is our way with horses.'

Issa returned the smile. 'You're the only person other than me able to calm him.'

He began to lead the horses away but Duskar stopped and turned to look at her. 'It's all right,' she said. 'You can trust him and I'll be right on board with you. You'll have a nosebag of oats if you follow him.' This seemed to satisfy the horse and he followed Ironclad down below.

'Miss?' said a young deck-hand with freckles scattered across his nose. 'I'll take you to your cabin.'

She followed him down one flight of narrow stairs and along a corridor of closed doors. He opened one of them and passed her her saddlebags.

'Thank you,' she said. He nodded and turned away.

Her cabin was tiny with a short, hard bed, a single shelf, a privy bucket and a bowl and jug of water for washing. It was all she needed and she squeezed inside and dumped her bags on the bed. A small porthole looked out across the ocean. She would be several days at sea, probably a week, but despite being cramped and not able to do anything, she liked sailing and being on the open ocean. It would give her a chance to relax, think and plan.

Not wanting to stay in her room, she went back up onto the top deck just as they were casting off from the jetty. Iyena still stood there and waved at her. Issa waved back. *Will I ever see Myrn again?* Celene was lost and gone and her Little Kammy was crawling with Maphraxies. It struck her that, since most ships sailed from Myrn to Davono, her mother must have made this same journey, decades ago. Knowing she travelled in her parent's footsteps brought tears to her eyes. Her parents had never returned to Myrn. *Yet,* a determined voice within said.

Keeping out of the way of the busy sailors, she made her way to the prow of the boat. The sails filled with air then became slack and filled with air again as the captain turned the ship through the wind towards Davono. Even Issa could tell it would be a long journey against this wind.

'Want a few lessons in Weather Magic?' asked Haelgon, coming to stand beside her.

She looked up at the tall Atalanphian wizard and smiled. 'Sure.'

'All right. Now, we can't change the direction of the wind, at least not for long and not without abusing the natural state of things,' he explained. 'Always we must try to work with, rather than against, the forces of nature. It's far less taxing too. So, with the wind coming almost straight from the direction we want to travel in, you want to use the Flow to part the wind so it flows past on either side, then swirls around and back into the sails, much like a heart shape.'

Issa frowned, trying to imagine what he was saying.

'Think of the flow of wind moving like water,' he said. 'Just like this ship is ploughing through the waves and parting it. We need to divide the wind so that it diverts around the ship, then bring that same wind forwards to push into the sails.'

'I think I get it.' Issa frowned.

'This is the hardest so if you can master this one, you can master all weather magic. Now, watch me in the Flow.'

She nodded and entered the Flow, seeing the wizard's buzzing, rainbow-coloured aura. He pointed forwards and she could see the wind rushing around them. It was a pale grey-blue. The ship was a fuzzy brown when she focused on it. Haelgon drew the Flow to him and lifted his arms.

'Part Wind,' he commanded. At his words, the wind divided into two streams and flowed past them. She felt the ship lurch a little at the sudden drop in resistance.

'Wind Forwards,' said Haelgon making a circular motion with his hands. The wind circled behind them and then came forwards. The ship tilted as the recircling wind filled the sails fully. The sailors cheered and the captain adjusted their course accordingly. Soon the ship's sails were straining and the sea-water surged against the prow.

'It really works' She laughed with delight.

Haelgon grinned, his blue eyes becoming even brighter as he used the Flow. 'Why don't you focus on parting the wind, and I'll work on circling it?'

She looked into the Flow and mirrored what Haelgon had just done. The wind parted at her request and she laughed at how easy it was. She revelled in the rush of air and magic around her. The ship was really ploughing through the waves now and already they had lost sight of Myrn. She could just see the captain at the helm, a huge grin on the woman's face.

Someone else entered the Flow, startling her. She blinked and saw Domenon standing behind them. In the Flow, his powerful aura flared all colours.

'Wave Forward,' he commanded.

The Flow beneath her feet became deep blue and undulating. Raucous laughter and cheering made her look outside the Flow. The sailors up the rigging were laughing and pointing. She noticed then how the ship was leaning forwards and gasped when she realised they were riding a huge surge in the ocean.

Domenon grinned at her and she smiled back.

'If you wizards keep this up, we'll be there in days rather than weeks!' Laughed a sailor hanging off a rope thicker than his arm. He wasn't wrong, they were literally surging through the sea.

'I hope Baelthrom won't detect this,' Issa said, the thought frightening her.

Domenon shrugged. 'The sooner we get to Davono the better. He will hunt your orb and you anyway. And besides, wizards using weather magic aboard ships is a common thing and also signals a dangerous target to attack.'

Issa allowed herself to relax.

On the evening of the fourth day, the sailors spied Davono's coast long before Issa could see anything and their excited hollers rang out across the ship. Issa, Haelgon and Domenon grinned at each other, each of them had eyes that were luminous from using the Flow.

'You can't beat three weather wizards,' said Haelgon.

Soon after the hulk of green land slipped into view, they spied the major port city, Teramides. The wizards calmed their weather magic and the ship slowed to an easy pace. Issa watched the huge port loom ahead. Even though it was late in the day, merchant ships, fishing boats, and dinghies were coming and going through the narrow harbour entrance. She had never seen so many ships. It was so busy that they had to queue behind a couple of smaller Frayonesse galleons whilst the harbour master directed them to suitable jetties. Ehka landed on the railing beside her to watch their approach.

Endless rows of warehouses and shops circled the harbour which disappeared into the distance. A hill rose beyond it, covered in houses that ranged from hobbles and shacks to terraces, and then palaces with turrets. All were constructed out of the same pale red stone. The countless streets were paved with dark grey cobbles along which donkeys and horses pulled carts and carriages.

A small white temple stood to the west of town, its spire poking up through the red houses. The site of any temple now left Issa feeling uncomfortable, bordering on angry. Perhaps this one was different, its priestesses diligently serving the spiritual needs of the people, but she doubted it. More like they just drained their hard earned money.

To the north, at the furthest and highest point of the city, was an enormous palace. It was long and thin and marked at points with round turrets. It was huge and seemed to stretch across the entire hill, its great red walls circling down around the city, hugging it like two arms.

Within the hour, the gangplank was down and they were disembarking. Ehka had disappeared off on his own to inspect the city. Duskar was so keen to get off the ship Issa had to hold his halter firmly. Velonorian followed with a more placid Ironclad. The young elf gawped at the city with his mouth open. Every now and then he would murmur "wow" making her grin.

'Have you never seen the world outside of the Land of Mists?' asked Issa. The very thought was shocking. The younger elves would know nothing of the real world.

'No, my Lady Issa. It's incredible,' he said.

'Well, it's infinitely more dangerous than anywhere you've been before,' said Domenon as he squeezed past them. He gave a cautionary glance at Issa. 'This is the busiest port in the Free World, and all sorts disembark here. I'd keep your weapons and your wits about you at all times.'

Issa nodded but found the thought of danger exciting.

'It's too late to make it to Rebben so we shall stay at the palace, courtesy of Duke Beddan,' said Domenon. 'It is possible the queen is already there since she will have received message of our plans, so be prepared. Now follow me.'

Their unusual band of wizards and elves caused people to stop and stare. Domenon received several nods of respect; being advisor to the queen, he was well known in Davono. The Davonians tended to be shorter than Domenon but stockier. The men were Issa's height and the women were smaller. Their hair was often black, and their skin tanned and olive. Their quick, dark eyes seemed to miss nothing and everyone wore some kind of weapon whether it be dagger, sword or crossbow.

Amongst them milled dwarves, not too many but more than she had ever seen in Carvon. Their bearded faces and hard eyes stared long at the elven warriors. The elves paid no one any attention and talked only amongst themselves. Sometimes Domenon would say something in elven to them but Issa did not understand what.

Domenon lifted his hand and beckoned to a standing of horse-drawn carriages waiting for passengers on the other side of the road. The carriages were black and decorated with gold painted swirls along the rims. Their wheels were the biggest she had ever seen and nearly as tall as she was. The drivers were dressed in tall black hats and coats with tails that came past their knees. They tapped the horses' rumps with their long whips and moved the carriages over to them. One driver jumped off and tied Duskar and Ironclad's reins to the iron loop on the back. He then opened the ornate wooden doors for them to embark.

Issa climbed in excited, she had never been in a carriage before. Velonorian tried to climb in after her but Domenon grasped his shoulder. 'No, we need to chat. If you don't mind, please go with Haelgon or the elves.' He pointed at the others climbing into their carriages. Velonorian shrugged and went to the elves.

Domenon climbed in and shut the door. Issa gave him a questioning look but the man said nothing. His dark grey eyes simply watched her as the carriage clattered along the cobbles.

'What is it?' she asked, quite used to his odd manner. 'Are you going to apologise for throwing me aside? For one who wants to chat, you don't have much to say.'

'There is something about you that I recognise deeply,' he said, rubbing his clean-shaven chin.

'What do you mean?' she asked. He didn't answer immediately so she looked out of the window at the streets, noting how dirty and crumbling they were. Perhaps proximity to the sea eroded stone faster here than in other cities. The architecture itself was rather ornate and would have been stunning once. Most buildings had beautifully carved cornices with inlaid sculptures of people and animals adorning the roofs. Ironwork decorated otherwise plain brick walls and delicate gates and chains marked the boundaries between houses and the street.

People lurked in dark, narrow alleys, their hats pulled low. Tramps and drunks sat or lay on the steps of boarded up houses. Issa wanted to jump out and kick open the door so they could at least shelter inside. But Teramides didn't care. Twice she heard someone yelling 'Stop!' but peering through the window she only glimpsed a street urchin running before disappearing down one of the dark alleys, no doubt with someone's stolen purse.

She compared the city to Corsolon. Teramides was certainly bigger and had an older, more crumbling feel to it. She decided she liked its rugged beauty, fancy architecture, its dirt and its grime. It had a darker side to it whilst Corsolon was pristine and almost stuck up. Corsolon had never really known hardship, Teramides knew everything about backbreaking labour and low pay, of over-population and street crime—things which seemed mostly non-existent in Corsolon. Oddly, she liked it here. She could hide, she could plan, and she could move more easily as a stranger along its bursting streets.

She looked back at Domenon who still hadn't answered. He genuinely seemed perplexed.

'If your mother was a seer as you say she was, then I will have known her. If she was on Myrn, that is,' said Domenon.

Issa stared harder out of the window, chewing a finger. *Not my secret to tell.* She reminded herself of what Sheyengetha had told her. But the desire to know more about her parents was overwhelming.

Domenon squinted at her. 'Something isn't right. When I try to imagine what your mother might have looked like, all I get is fog, as if a spell has been cast over me.' The wizard frowned and Issa swallowed.

I cannot reveal their secret to him, it would endanger their lives as well as mine. Had he been there that night they'd cast the spell? Is that why he couldn't remember? What harm could telling him do? She knew about her parents now, what more was there to know by talking to this untrustworthy wizard about them? *He might know where they went or where they are now.*

'Well, if you remember them, I'd love to know,' she forced herself to say.

'There are certain spells that open up our childhood memories, you know,' he said. 'Within our minds are all our memories of everything that had ever happened to us. The only problem is the pathways to those memories gets corroded and lost with time. A hypnotic spell can reforge those pathways. It's fairly straightforward and painless if you would like to try it.'

'I don't like the sound of hypnosis, of not being in control of who I am or what I'm experiencing,' she said. She felt hypnosis was dangerous too, opening the mind to let just anything in.

'As you wish.' Domenon shrugged, though his frown deepened.

'Why didn't you ask the Wizards' Circle before you were made Second Keeper?' she asked.

He grinned genuinely at her. 'Miss Issa, you forget yourself. I am a Master Wizard. No one can tell me what to do. And besides, they would have said no, as they always have done, stifling my growth and my power at every turn.'

'Soon, no one will have any orbs,' she said. 'They will be combined to return the life-magic of Maioria back to its natural, powerful state.'

'How are you so sure that is what should be done?' said Domenon.

'Because that is the natural state of things, and all things desire to return to their natural state one way or another.'

'I can see the seers have been teaching you,' he muttered and looked out of the window, falling into a moody silence.

The road wound up the hill towards the palace. It opened up into wider streets and emptied of people. Here there were larger shops with fancy, colourful or polished wares on display in their windows. Carved steps led up to bars and restaurants with ornate signs. On their doorsteps stood burly, well-dressed men ready to keep out any ruffians or pickpockets.

As the dusk deepened, a handful of men carrying ladders began to

light the tall lanterns lining the main street. The palace loomed into view
and they entered its grounds through a huge gateway. It was even more
impressive in size this close up. The smaller buildings were constructed of
pale red brick and turreted roofs. These turned into medium buildings of
the same design until they came to the main section.

Being square, the main building was more castle-like, so Issa thought.
It stood three stories high with one round turret to each of the four
corners, reminding her of Freydel's study on Celene, only these conical
roofs were covered in grey slate and not windowed to the stars. A swathe
of pale grey steps led up to the entrance; a black double-door with a huge,
shining, brass knocker. Outside it, two guards stood to attention, hands
on their swords, eyes staring straight ahead but missing nothing.

Their carriage ground loudly on the white shingled road. When it
stopped by the entrance, Issa realised how noisy it had been. A servant or
butler opened the carriage door and she took his hand and stepped out.
Domenon followed and the butler bowed to him.

'Greetings, Master Wizard Domenon.'

'Good evening, Eveson. Nice to see you again,' said the Master
Wizard as he swept up the steps. 'Please have the servants bring our packs
and saddlebags. The horses can be stabled with the others. Careful with
that black stallion.' Several servants appeared and began unloading the
carriages at his command. Issa was reminded how much power the Master
Wizard had here in Davono.

'I'll take him,' Issa said as a servant went towards Duskar. The man
nodded dutifully and she untied Duskar's harness from the carriage. He
snuffled her thigh.

'Ah, there you are, Master Wizard Domenon.' A rather fat, balding
man appeared at the entrance. His straggly grey hair was swept over his
head in a vain attempt to hide his baldness, and his moustache was short
and bushy. He had a humorous face and stood at least six feet tall—
uncommon for a Davonian—and wore a simple, royal blue suit with a
white shirt underneath.

The man came to stand at the top of the steps, took out his glasses
and squinted down at the new arrivals. 'Queen Thora warned me that you
might make a visit. I'm sure my cousin's spies are everywhere for they said
you would indeed arrive today.'

'Duke Beddan, how good it is to see you and thank you for accepting us into your home,' said Domenon, shaking the man's hand.

Issa was surprised that the wizard could turn up unannounced and assume hospitality for several guests.

'Elves, I see,' Beddan nodded approvingly. 'Well, this is quite an honour.'

He squinted at Issa and she felt like a horse being measured up. 'And who is this? Interesting clothing—intimidating for sure. Hmm, my-my, she's certainly of Tusarzan heritage.'

Issa arched her eyebrows, surprised at the man's observance.

'This is Lady Issa,' said Domenon.

The Duke walked down the steps, bowed and kissed her hand, tickling it with his moustache.

'Greetings, Lady Issa—or is it the Raven Queen? We've heard so much about you,' Beddan said, straightening.

'Only good things, I hope,' said Issa. The Duke smiled indulgently and winked, making her laugh.

'We will only stay one night then we must be off to Rebben, to see the Queen,' said Domenon.

'Why, of course—Ah, High Wizard Haelgon! We are doubly honoured and shall have a banquet!'

The Atalanph wizard smiled as he exited the carriage. He clasped the duke's outstretched hand. 'Good to see you, Duke Beddan. It's been many years.'

'I'll take him, my Queen Issa,' said Velonorian, taking Duskar's reins from her hands. Issa waited for the horse to protest but the young elf again whispered in Elven to him. Duskar pricked his ears forwards and snorted as if he had just heard a joke.

Issa smiled. 'I forget elves have a greater affinity to creatures than us mere humans.'

Velonorian winked and followed the other stable boys.

Inside, the palace was equally impressive and spotlessly clean. White and teal marbled tiles swathed the floors. High ceilings sported ornate coving, and impossibly large crystal chandeliers dangled above. Two young, female servants approached, dropped their eyes and curtsied before Issa. They wore simple, white and blue dresses and blue kerchiefs covering their hair.

'They will show you to your room, it's one of the best,' said the Duke, smiling at her and nodding to the huge staircase with a gold-painted bannister flowing up from the entrance hall. 'And then we'll have a dinner fit for a queen.' He winked.

The wizards and elves were soon surrounded by several male servants who led them in different directions to their rooms. Only Domenon remained, talking with the duke in Davonian. Issa didn't understand the somewhat clipped tongue as she followed the servants up the stairs. They led her along wide corridors with cherry wood floorboards and white walls adorned with pictures of stately looking people.

Her room was so huge it made her gasp. The rounded walls on the far side told her she was in one of the turrets. There was a four-poster bed, a chaise lounge and a couch all upholstered in beautiful, flower-covered fabric. Great windows on two sides revealed the darkening sky. Her bags were, miraculously, already laid out beside the couch. The ladies busied themselves drawing shut the heavy curtains and drapes and lighting the lanterns. A fire already crackled in the hearth making the room warm and welcoming.

'Would your ladyship like a bath? We can have it brought to you immediately before supper,' enquired the youngest looking servant.

'I'd like that very much,' Issa beamed.

They curtsied and hurried out of the room.

Barely moments had passed when two large men entered, sweating and panting as they carried a shining copper bath into the room under the direction of the servants.

CHAPTER 18

Interdimensional Metaphysics

WITH a deep and satisfied sigh, Issa sank deeper into the copper bath which was filled to the brim with hot water.

She gently blew the soap bubbles off her fingers and watched them float back down. Her thoughts filled with Asaph and she wished he were here, bathing with her. The memory of his hand on her breast made her blush. The feeling of their marks touching and igniting so powerfully within the Flow …what had happened? She wanted it to happen again.

Where was he now? Was he safe and warm? After a thought, she reached over the side of the bath and pulled out the water orb from its sack. It glimmered in her wet hand.

'Asaph,' she whispered, staring into its swirling turquoise surface and feeling magic move.

The orb turned dark and an endless ocean appeared beneath her. The sky was pale as if the sun had just risen or set. The image began to flicker and fade. She sighed. He must be a long way away. Perhaps he was still flying and using cloaking magic. She prayed he was all right.

Cupping the orb in her hands, her thoughts turned to Freydel and Ayeth. She chewed her lip. Could she travel back in time and to a different planet like Freydel had? Surely all the orbs held the same power. Could she trust Freydel to do what he must to stop Ayeth and protect Maioria? Was it even possible to change their timeline by going into the past? She had a feeling that it wasn't. There were too many unknowns and she was too frightened to try.

'Ayeth,' she whispered into the orb then held her breath.

Slowly, the strange being's image formed. His alien golden skin, huge slanted eyes and long aquiline face mesmerised her.

'Chosen by Zanufey,' she breathed. Was that what would happen to her if she failed, if she succumbed to the powers of the fallen? She shivered as she thought about the black-eyed woman.

'Lona,' she whispered her name.

A flawless, white face formed in the orb—beautiful but cruel, as if hate lingered there, barely hidden. Issa stared at the alien woman, in awe. Her onyx-black eyes opened wide and gleamed. ...*As black as the Dark Rift. She's the one who caused his downfall.*

"The eyes are the windows to the soul," Zanufey had said. Was Lona's soul black like her eyes? She didn't doubt that Ayeth loved her, but as she looked into Lona's face it was clear the being could not love, not properly. Issa stared harder, willing Lona's eyes to reveal her secrets. The woman didn't want Ayeth's help or to be healed, she only wanted his power.

Why would anyone not want help when they were sick and suffering? Baelthrom was sick but he certainly didn't want help. Neither did any of his evil hordes of Maphraxies. The very thought of them asking for help made her laugh. They were beyond help. Any creature who was too sick to be healed and a danger to others had to be destroyed. Ayeth would have to destroy Lona before she became too powerful. *And he will not be able to do it because he loves her. Therefore, the timeline cannot be changed.*

The truth hit Issa like a hammer-blow—nothing would be able to convince Ayeth that Lona was evil and beyond help. Not even his own people had managed to do that—so an outsider like Freydel certainly wouldn't be able to do it.

Issa sunk deeper in the bath, still holding the turquoise orb. She gazed at Ayeth and Lona pictured within, a very tall being and a small and slight being. She didn't doubt that the Yurgharon had been good once. Evil had been done to them too, hurting them and twisting them. Domination, fear, and revenge was what made a being fall.

The Rorsken and Anukon may have been beings of light but they, too, turned. Evil was like an infection spreading. How far back did it go? It was an eternal question, one she would have to ask Zanufey.

Was the same thing happening to Freydel? Was he becoming blinded by the good being that Ayeth was and all the power he was teaching him? He was devoted to his teacher whom he thought could still be saved, but it seemed the wizard would not be able to change what was going to happen. Forget about stopping Ayeth—she had to stop Freydel before he was in too deep. His orb was in terrible danger. She had to tell him immediately.

'Orb of Water, scry for me Master Wizard Freydel,' she said and watched the orb expectantly as magic moved through it. She entered the Flow and, through the orb, started searching for Freydel. The orb, in the presence of its water element, was stronger and its magic purer. It was easy to reach Freydel's study in Carvon but only an empty room filled with his scrolls and maps formed on the surface of the orb. He wasn't there. She focused her mind on his house in Myrn and swiftly it appeared but it, too, was empty.

Frowning, she wiped the steaming condensation off the orb. It was unlikely he would be blocking her. Could he have gone to Ayeth again? The thought made her shiver. How often did he meet with the Aralan? Travelling over such vast distances was going to destroy him physically and mentally long before Ayeth would have a thought to hurt him.

She pulled more on the Flow and concentrated harder, closing her eyes so she could better see the magic. Waves of light moved around her and she felt her mind lifting with it as the orb searched for Freydel.

Outwards, beyond the dimensional field of Maioria, it reached. She felt dreamy as it moved through the Astral Planes where everything was pastel ribbons of light. It seemed to know where he had gone, following his trail as if he'd left a scent along the way.

No, it's not following Freydel, but where the other orb has gone, she realised. It began to reach far beyond the Ethereal Planes and she pulled back, fearful of going too far and losing herself. The orb tried to pull her on but she resisted. She could have ended the search with a command but intrigue dampened her caution.

Something caught a hold of her and the orb, dragging them sideways. Cold darkness flowed over her as if she'd been swimming and suddenly entered a cold patch of water. She felt the faint presence of another consciousness.

'Return now,' Issa commanded, sitting upright with her eyes still closed. Something had detected them and was trying to latch on. The orb did not respond. Its magic became faint.

The darkness gathered in the distance and began to form into giant, humanoid shapes. The shapes turned and stalked towards her through a grey fog. Issa's heart leapt into her throat and she tried to see outside of the Flow but her consciousness was trapped within it.

The beings were at least ten feet tall. Black, wispy veils covered them from head to foot and billowed like smoke. She could see no faces. They reminded her of the wraiths in the Shadowlands only these were much bigger, faceless, and they could clearly see her.

The cold thrill of impending danger shot down her spine as the figures clustered around her, moving on feet she couldn't see. They communicated with each other in garbled tones that reminded Issa of a toad's croak only deeper. Over the top of this, at the periphery of her hearing, she became aware of other noises, horrible grating sounds overlaid with moaning voices that were too low to be human. They grew louder until the awful noise vibrated right through her, making her heart thump erratically.

She tried not to listen to the voices but the harrowing grating noise of metal scraping on metal at different pitches was the opposite of harmony. The din was chaos, scattering her senses and fragmenting her thoughts.

Her fear showed itself by forming cold beads of sweat on her face. Her breath came fast and shallow, filling her lungs with air that was cold, wet, and clammy as her strength drained. The enormous beings towered before her, their long heads lost behind black veils. They spoke in dark whispering, slithering voices and now Issa was able to understand what they were saying.

'One of them has come.'

'Trap it before it gets away.'

'Follow it to find its home.'

She tried to back away. They weren't Aralans or Yurgharon or even demons, so what were they? Gathering all her strength, she called the sluggish Flow to her, filling herself with it so she shone brightly. The creatures fell back, as if hurt.

'Return me home, now!' she shouted at the orb and released the Flow.

Issa held her breath and prayed frantically as the orb struggled to regain control of itself. It fought against the chaotic noise and seeping darkness until, after an indeterminable amount of time and with almost an audible snap, she was pulled into a fast but controlled fall.

Gratefully gasping air back into her lungs, Issa found herself in the bath again—but she wasn't alone. The orb in her hand became heavy and cold. It pulsated as black streaks shot through the swirling turquoise. The magic in the air around her suddenly lunged directly into the orb which became as heavy as lead. The orb plunged to the bottom of the bath. She tried to let go but her hands were stuck to its surface. Issa barely had time to suck in a breath before she was dragged under.

Her eyes smarted as she blinked through the stinging, soapy water and saw the Flow pouring into the orb as if it were being sucked through to somewhere else. She thrashed against it, fighting for control of the magic, and to push herself up and out of the water. As she desperately tried to pull the Flow back towards her, she could feel her mind being dragged along with it, into the orb, into the elemental power of water. The orb felt *wrong* and she battled against the taint and dirt, trying to push it out, but it seeped this way and that, evading her grasp.

She convulsed but forced her mouth to stay closed though her lungs burned from her body's desperate need for air. Drawing upon all her strength, Issa tried to control the absolute panic that threatened to destroy her concentration.

As she calmed herself she became aware of a strange sound, like a blade sliding on a whetstone. Intonations whispered making her shiver. Words were spoken in an alien voice. She recoiled at the sound but focused harder on the voice, needing to know what was being said as it could be the key to breaking the black magic attacking the orb. The more she focused, the more clear it became. A female voice. She caught some of the words as they slithered into her mind, filling her with ice cold dread.

Ezzu t' menarx yek gestiara.

The words were creating the blackness which fed off the Flow. A frozen numbness spread through her body and she could no longer feel her hands gripping the orb. The need for air was becoming a distant thing.

The blackness in the orb grew and began to order itself into a spinning vortex. *Vortex's become tunnels*, she thought dimly. But where would this tunnel go? A vague sense of panic clenched her stomach and was gone. The centre of the vortex spun faster as she watched in paralysed mesmerisation. What would happen when the vortex connected and a tunnel was formed? She stared into it.

The voice grew louder. Behind it came other voices chanting in unison but not as loudly. Their words were harnessing and draining the power of the Flow, feeding it into the blackness and making the dark magic stronger. The vortex pulled on her strongly. Part of her wanted to go into it to see where it led, but another part viciously resisted and dragged her back. Her body convulsed violently, but her mind was so detached from it, it felt like a faint jerking sensation.

Powerful magic engulfed her. The vortex exploded into shards of black and the magic snapped, ripping her mind from the Flow. She screamed in agony, bubbles and soapy water filling her mouth. She lunged for the Flow to protect herself in some way but was blocked from it. Helpless, she floundered.

A strong, vice-like arm wrapped around her chest and arms and dragged her upwards. She opened her mouth and sucked in air, air which burned her throat even as it filled her lungs. She couldn't seem to get enough of it. The shattered shards of vortex piercing her mind began to dissipate. Her lungs heaved out water and she coughed violently, expelling what she could before she greedily inhaled the life-giving air. Moments passed where everything was pain and chaos in her body and mind, and within the Flow.

The massive face of a dragon appeared just inches in front of her own, its snout long and nostrils flared. Black onyx horns sat like a crown upon its head. Ice-blue scales gleamed. Huge golden eyes with black slits glared at her. Powerful magic surged—the magic that was blocking her from the Flow. She was too weak and disorientated to fight for control of it.

She closed her eyes and when she re-opened them the dragon face was gone. Instead, the bleary image of a man with shiny black hair and a chiselled jaw looked back at her. She blinked again and the vision became clearer. The man had intense grey eyes ringed with luminous turquoise, perfect lips and the shadow of stubble. Water ran down his face and soaked his white shirt, sticking it to his body.

She realised he was holding her tightly against the back of the bath so she couldn't move or sink into the water. She sucked in more air, trying to get her bearings. He relaxed his grip a little to let her breathe but did not let go.

'What happened?' she gasped, trembling. *Domenon, that was his name.*

'Maybe you should tell me,' he said, his face only inches from her. 'Stupid girl. Don't do that in Castle Rebben otherwise you'll be thrown into the dungeon.'

'I didn't *do* anything.' She shook her head and tried to release his grip but he only tightened it.

'Yes, you did. I felt it. Which is why I came in here. I had to kick in the door! Lucky I did too, otherwise you'd have drowned. You created a dangerous thing. An unstable vortex, like the Storm Holt, only smaller. Before you play with magic like that, you need to know *exactly* what you are doing and where you are going. That's why dimensional gates exist; to control the pathways and the magic.'

'Yes, that's right, but I didn't create it. I was only scrying for Freydel!'

'You scryed beyond Maioria's natural boundaries—a very dangerous thing to do, especially with the likes of Baelthrom always watching.' He growled and gripped her harder, to push the point home.

'How do you know all this?' she glanced at him and struggled against his grip. 'And where is that dragon I saw after the magic broke? I only know one dragon and his name is Asaph.'

'I've exhaustively studied inter-dimensional metaphysics,' he said, loosening his grip. 'And Asaph is *not* a real dragon. Do you normally scry for people in the bath?'

She shook her head. 'No, it was just…important. And the orb is more powerful when in contact with its element.'

Domenon eyed her suspiciously. 'What could be so important that you couldn't wait half an hour? Where is Freydel? And what is he up to?'

Issa swallowed. She couldn't tell him about Ayeth. That was a secret between her and Freydel—a dangerous secret, it seemed. If Domenon knew Freydel was travelling back in time and between dimensions to meet the being Baelthrom once was, the dark-haired wizard would certainly take it before the Wizards' Circle. Freydel might lose his standing for fraternising with the enemy. Worse, he might lose his powers and his orb. She couldn't confide in Domenon, he was not a man to share secrets with. But he had just saved her life, and she owed him. She forgave him, just a little, for knocking her down over Orphinius.

'Listen, I did not create that tunnel! I was merely using the orb to look for Freydel. I could not find him where he should be so I looked further afield and then something beyond Maioria attacked me.'

Domenon was staring into her eyes as if trying to gauge whether she was telling the truth. He gave a slight nod.

'Then *something* attacked you? It might be wise for you to find out what.'

Issa nodded, still deeply shaken.

'I felt black magic surge into the Flow,' he said. 'It was happening in here. Look what you made me do to the door.' He motioned to the hunk of wood which was now laying flat on the floor. The doorframe was broken with splintered wood evident around the bolt and lock.

'You were drowning, physically and mentally, and I had to box you out of the Flow. It wasn't easy, you were thrashing around so much. Everything is soaked, including me.' He suddenly grinned and used his other hand to wipe the water from his face. His hair was dripping and his white shirt was plastered to his chest, revealing just how muscular the man was—unusual for a wizard who was dedicated to the study of magic, and a Master Wizard at that, who dedicated more time than anyone else.

'Oh dear,' said Issa, staring at the puddles surrounding the bathtub for several feet. There was as much water out of the tub as there was in it.

With an awful realisation, it dawned on Issa that she was sitting naked in the bath. Only bubbles and soap concealed her submerged nether regions, but her breasts were pressed firmly against Domenon's arm that still clamped her to the back of the bath.

He smiled at her colouring cheeks but did not let her go. 'Forgive me for saving your life. You would have drowned,' he said in a quieter voice. His eyes searched hers for something and she would have felt undressed by them if she hadn't been naked already. She dropped her gaze in embarrassment. Nudity meant little when your life was at stake, she consoled herself.

'Thank you,' her voice was barely a whisper. 'You can let me go now.'

He released her slowly and gently and she immediately covered her breasts with her arms. He rose to his feet and looked down at her, a half-smile on his face. It annoyed her that she found him so handsome. He was the only person she had ever met who managed to disarm and conquer everyone.

'What?' she asked when he failed to stop looking at her.

'You really do remind me of someone... maybe it is your parents. It's coming to me slowly, hmm. Without your Dragon Lord, it's very clear you need someone to protect you. So many are hunting you, you'd need an army to keep you safe. I'll do what I can if you accept my humble services.' He spread his arm and bowed slightly.

She didn't know if he was mocking her weaknesses or genuinely being helpful but she nodded anyway.

'We'll be safer in Castle Rebben where I have created far stronger shields. Until then, don't scry for Freydel, or anyone else for that matter. I suggest you shield this room tonight. Inter-dimensional vortexes have a nasty habit of hanging around even if they aren't formed properly.' He gave a lingering look at her then turned to go.

'Wait. What about the dragon?' she said, realising he hadn't answered her.

A frown of what could have been read as either worry or irritation passed across his face. 'Dragons can travel dimensionally too; but no dragon was attacking you. I would have felt that for sure. You have no Secondary Keeper for your orb. I suggest you get one and I suggest you choose me.'

'It clearly should be Freydel,' she said, challenging him.

He half turned away, his straight nose and sharp chin silhouetted in the lamplight.

'I am not stupid, Issa. Your orb should not have been compromised like that tonight. They are not keyed to any dimension other than Maioria's, and when taken outside of that dimension they are wildly unstable. From what I've seen, I know far more about the orbs than any on the Wizards' Circle, and yet I am the one who has none.'

'They don't trust how you will use it, Domenon. You seem power-hungry.'

He smirked and looked at her. 'And Freydel is not?'

She paused, forgetting what she was about to say. Wasn't the most powerful wizard in Maioria also power hungry? Look at how he talked about Ayeth, the way his eyes lit up when he spoke about the magic the Aralan was teaching him. She suddenly felt cold and uncertain. No one seemed to be who they really were; not Freydel or Domenon. At least Asaph seemed more normal now Cirosa's clutch on him was gone. She swallowed, realising there was no one she could fully trust any more. The thought concerned her deeply.

Maybe it was because of the worried look on her face that Domenon came back to her. He laid his hand on her shoulder. 'Look, goosebumps. You're shivering and will catch a cold.' He picked up a fluffy pink towel and held it up for her, turning his face away. 'I won't look, I promise.'

Sighing, she turned her back to him and stood, clutching it from his hands as he draped it around her shoulders.

'We need to talk about this once I have thought on it,' said Domenon. 'The orbs are being compromised, and there is something you and Freydel are not telling me. I can't protect you if I don't know what is going on. If I suspect people themselves are becoming compromised, that Baelthrom might be reaching them in his myriad of evil ways, then it will be brought before all the councils of the Free Peoples. We must protect ourselves at all costs from Baelthrom's spies.'

Domenon's hard gaze softened. 'Why don't we talk about it another time when you've recovered? Perhaps in my library at Castle Rebben. We shall be there tomorrow evening if we set off at dawn.'

There came the sound of footsteps pelting on floorboards and then Velonorian burst into the room, his long knife drawn and a sheen of sweat on his face as he fought to catch his breath.

'Lady Issa, are you all right?' he gasped. 'I had to run all the way here. They've put me at the other end of this stupid house. I felt dark magic and knew you were in danger.'

Domenon looked at her with a raised eyebrow. 'You're already gaining an army of protectors.'

She gave him a withering smile and turned to the young elf. 'I'm all right, Velonorian. Domenon broke the black magic.'

The elf nodded vigorously. 'Oh good. Thank you, Master Wizard.' He bowed. 'I shall have the maids house me closer so I can keep watch all night.'

A loud bell trilled from outside the room.

'Ah, dinner,' said Domenon rubbing his hands together. 'I'll send someone up to fix the door whilst you're dining.' He patted the elf's shoulder as he left the room.

Issa smiled weakly at Velonorian. 'Honestly, I'm all right. Why don't you wait outside while I get dressed? Then we can go to dinner together.' Though she didn't want to be alone at all right now.

'Yes, my Queen,' he bowed deeply and slipped outside.

A tapping came from outside the window and she opened it to let Ehka in. As she did so, the shadows behind the curtain moved. Jumping back, she ran for her sword then wondered why Ehka was doing nothing but preening himself?

'Miss Issy?' Maggot hissed and his ugly face and big yellow eyes formed out of the shadows.

'Uh, Maggot,' she sighed, setting her sword down and slumping onto the bed. 'Tonight, I can't take any more surprises.'

'I came before the wizard but had to hide from his magic. I saw he was helping you.'

The demon fully materialised out of the shadows and hesitantly stepped towards her. He laid a tiny cold hand on her bare calf. 'The magic that had you was dangerous, Issy. Undoing magic. Magic like Karhlusus used.'

She smiled, reached down and picked him up. He squirmed and moaned in her grasp. She realised he had never been picked up before. Laughing, she plonked him in her lap.

'Oh Maggot, what is going on? I'm beginning to feel I can't trust anyone. I worry for the two most powerful wizards on Maioria; one is losing himself to magic and the other is hell bent on getting it for himself.'

'Something hunts you, Issy. I saw it in the black vortex. It's an *Eater*.'

'What do you mean?'

'An Eater. It eats things, alive. Lesser demons eat things alive as punishment but we prefer eating dead things. Greater demons eat things alive for fun. That was more than a greater demon.'

'Is it from the Pit?' Issa asked.

Maggot shook his head. 'It's not even from the Abyss.'

Issa frowned. 'Where was it from then?'

Maggot shook his head, paused for a moment, then pointed upwards, confirming her deepest fears. *From above, from the Dark Rift.* She chewed her lip, finally accepting the obvious. Freydel had gone to Ayeth, and the orb, dutifully doing her bidding, had tried to reach for him. Remembering the Orb of Water, she set Maggot on the bed and went to the tub.

The orb was floating now, its beautiful turquoise surface sparkling once more. She picked it up and dried it on her towel. The bell rang again and, though she had now lost her ravenous appetite, she thought it would be utterly rude not to join everyone for dinner. She quickly dried herself and pulled on her tunic, leggings and seer's robe that had been gifted to her by Iyena. She finished combing her hair and turned back to the little demon who had been watching her curious preening behaviour all the while.

'Is that where the dragon came from, Maggot? From the Dark Rift?'

'No, Miss Issy, that came from the wizard.'

CHAPTER 19

Temple of Sacrifice

MORHORK lifted his head and growled.

He found himself listening for something, but there was nothing to hear. His sleep was often disturbed and he had trouble reaching the deepest slumber where he could stay for hundreds of years. The energies of Maioria were becoming increasingly erratic and he increasingly sensitive to them.

The part of his consciousness within his human body was harder to shut off since that foolish half-breed had awoken him. It worried him how strong that connection was becoming. Perhaps it had been a bad idea ever forming such an alliance with a human. It was clouding—infecting—his perfect judgement with thoughts and feelings he did not want, and which certainly did not belong to a dragon.

At odd moments he found himself wondering about humans and even feeling *concerned* about his human body that was out there, far away. Was he becoming like those human dragon half-breeds he detested so much? He snorted a cloud of smoke into the dark cave and ground his claws into the frozen rock beneath him, making deep grooves within it.

Never. I'll never be like them and I'll never like them.

He laid his head back down and blinked into the blackness, his tail tip flicking. That girl intrigued him, he wanted to know more about her. He fancied himself mating with her but that might cause trouble. He enjoyed trouble.

If he was restless, would the other dragons be too? What if they all woke up? The Dragon Dream was no longer there to hold them. Baelthrom would hunt them down and enslave them. Baelthrom had become too strong. He growled again and lifted his head. The Immortal Lord's power should have waned but it had only increased. His plan was taking longer than he'd anticipated. Could it be *failing?* The thought made him angry.

It was a simple plan. When Baelthrom's war had ravaged and weakened Maioria and both enemies, he would awaken the dragons and finish both sides off. Maioria would once again be for dragons to rule. Getting the orbs was part of that plan, but it was taking far longer than he'd anticipated.

Could he defeat the Immortal Lord? *Of course I could!* He snorted soot, but human anxiety seeped into his great heart, making him irritable. His brother had been destroyed, and Faelsun had been immensely strong. *My brother was a fool.* But the thought lacked the feeling behind it and he actually experienced a twinge of loneliness. *Me, a dragon, lonely? Pah!*

Maybe it was time to get rid of his human body before it weakened him any further with its thoughts and feelings. But then he would lose his spyhole into the world of men, and with it the chance to gain an orb of power.

The source of Baelthrom's strength was the Dark Rift. If Morhork closed his eyes he could feel it out there, a great sucking darkness on the outskirts of Maioria, bigger and closer than it had ever been before. It touched everything on the planet. Could he fight that? His talons paused their scraping into the rock. He knew he could not.

There were things in the Dark Rift just waiting to get out. A long time ago he'd travelled close to it simply to look. Dragons, like ravens and other magical creatures, had the power to travel through dimensions. Dragons, unlike wizards, could do this easily. He'd travelled there in the Astral Planes, not daring to try the Ethereal.

The darkness had substance. Things had reached for him and tried to pull him in. Powerful things. He felt them drinking his soul, his life force, like Maphraxies consuming the Black Drink of Oblivion. Rather than empty blackness, he quickly discovered the Dark Rift was a reality field filled with all manner of twisted consciousnesses feeding upon themselves and each other without thought or regard. A ravenous, hating, all-consuming hunger.

When he pulled away he felt their extreme panic. Their food source was being taken away from them and they would die if they did not sustain themselves. That overwhelming sense of mortal terror had shaken him to the core. He had never dared go close to the Dark Rift again.

He lay his head back down and closed his eyes, willing the disturbing thoughts away. Perhaps if he slept a plan would come to him.

He snorted and fidgeted and tried for hours to sleep. Just as he drifted on the edges of consciousness, a flash and crack of brilliant light exploded before him, jolting him awake. He snapped his head up, alarmed. A bright light assaulted his eyes and within it was the Sword of Binding. Its red pommel flared and he saw the green, majestic face of Slevina looking back at him. Her face grew bigger and bigger, engulfing the sword. Her silver eyes were wide, pupils narrowed to mere slits, demanding his servitude to his queen, demanding he be what his Goddess decreed.

'The sword was not made willingly,' he growled at the image. 'It has *nothing* to do with me or any true blood dragon.'

Slevina's face grew larger, sharper and more perfected. Her green scales began to glow and turned a brilliant gold. Fire flared and surrounded the most beautiful dragon face Morhork had ever seen. Great golden horns framed her head making her look like the sun. Her eyes were a lighter white gold that saw straight into his mind and soul. Life-giving warmth flowed through his bones and muscles, easing all tension.

Morhork dipped his head in respect. 'My Goddess,' he breathed.

Power, strength and passion filled him, coursing through his veins in a torrent he couldn't control. The goddess knew everything that he was, every thought and feeling he had was laid bare before her. Feygriene knew and understood his plans of dominion—she had always known—and she did not judge.

They were good plans, powerful dragon plans, he nodded to himself. He was dragon, born to rule, but now those plans seemed so small and puny in the face of the goddess, and compared to the immense and terrible reality unfolding upon Maioria.

The Sword of Binding hovered between him and the Sun Goddess. Darkness flooded around it. Morhork entered the Flow, thinking black magic had entered the chamber but it flowed only around the image of the sword. The black magic thickened and rose, smothering the sword and extinguishing its light.

The vision went and the chamber turned cold and empty.

'A dragon has awakened.' The voice that spoke was weak and airy.

The necromancer floated further down the steps and paused, its watery eyes never leaving him so Asaph had to concede that it could see him. Quickly, he assessed the situation. To his relief, it wore no Shadow Stone amulet. He could just turn and leave. The sword was why he was here and it was getting away. But necromancers had powerful magic and he had never faced one to know how to fight it. No matter what, his presence was known and would be reported back to Baelthrom, one way or another.

'I sense not an *ordinary* dragon,' its milky eyes grew wide with hunger. 'I see a Dragon Lord before me!' It rubbed its unnaturally long-fingered hands together.

Maybe other necromancers were already on their way. In a few moments, Maphraxies could be pouring down the steps. It left him only one option: kill the necromancer quickly, if he could.

Asaph moved with great dragon speed, but the necromancer was already gathering the Under Flow and drawing a symbol in the air. Fire burst from Asaph's mouth only to flare uselessly against an invisible wall protecting the necromancer. Asaph lunged, dropping his dragon form and pulling his sword free. He ran through his own flames swinging his blade.

The necromancer's magic wall had been created to stop magic, not a man, and Asaph plunged through it, feeling the cold touch of the Under Flow trickle over him. His sword came smashing down, slicing through the necromancer's left shoulder as easily as paper. It squealed a horrible sound and collapsed spurting watery red blood from its awful wounds. It kicked and writhed then crumpled in on itself as if an unseen hand crushed its body. Moments later, there was nothing left but its stinking black robes.

Asaph stamped on the robes to be sure it was gone, then picked them up and threw them over the side and into the sea. He backed away down the steps, his heart pounding in his ears as he waited for more necromancers or Maphraxies to pour down the steps, alerted by the dying screams.

He backed all the way to the shore, turned and plunged his sword into the sea. The necromancer's blood hissed as the water touched it. A grim smile curved his lips. He had taken his first revenge killing on his own homeland, the first of many. Justice was finally being delivered and it felt good to do it with Coronos' sword.

He sheathed it and resumed his dragon form. Cloaking his presence, he leapt into the air in the direction the sword had gone, keen to get away as fast as possible. Hopefully, they hadn't flown too far ahead.

The harpies and Dromoorai were no longer to be seen and a heavy bank of clouds made the night sky even darker. It would be hard to find them in the clouds, Asaph thought grimly, but they would also hide him too.

He lifted into them then cautiously poked his head above them. Starlight bathed the tops of the clouds in white. Great swathes of white hills and valleys rose and fell as far as the eye could see. *A true Land of Mists,* he thought. There were no dragons or harpies to be seen so, for a moment, he flew above the undulating, white starlit landscape, revelling in both the magnificence of the scenery and the joy of flying.

Focusing his mind and eyes into the realm of magic, he saw the world as great swathes of energy; the clouds were pristine white and the stars flaring orbs in a sea of dark blue. Far ahead flew dark patches marring the beauty of the Flow. He streamlined his body and tilted his wings to a keener angle. When the dark shapes began to descend, he did too.

Passing through the clouds he blinked into his physical vision. There, far away, were the dark specks of Dromoorai and harpies. He dared not get too close. What was he going to do when they landed? He couldn't face that many. He only needed to know where they were taking the sword. *His* sword.

Hours passed and the coast of northern Frayon came into view. A large town or city sprawled across a wide inlet. Perhaps it was Nordastin, he thought. Surely it was daring for these beasts to travel so brazenly across their enemies' lands? Had Baelthrom become so bold? It certainly seemed so. Asaph ground his teeth. They were not done in yet. As far as he was concerned, the real battles had only just begun. Issa's invasion would show them their strength and it was only the first of many.

As they dipped even lower in the sky, he felt the Under Flow slide beneath the Flow, drawing together around the enemy ahead. Harpy magic moved too, clearer and easier for him to read. They were cloaking themselves heavily and they did a good job because he couldn't see them at all anymore, forcing him to focus on the Flow again.

Blinking his vision between the world of magic and the physical, Asaph saw they were dropping lower and lower as they neared Carvon. It worried him. Were they going to attack? That would be foolish; there were too few of them. Should he alert King Navarr, Freydel and all the guards? He knew he ought to, but he smelled a rat. Something was going on for them to be taking the sword to Carvon—into the heart of their enemies' lands. If he attacked them now he would never discover what they were doing. He should follow them and find out what they were up to. He didn't like it and his human reasoning did not sit well in his fierce dragon heart that wanted to fight with teeth and claws and sinew.

With horror growing in his heart, he watched the dark shadows descending towards Carvon. The city rose high above the swathes of dark forest while the frothing Arin Flow surged around the castle and keep.

Keeping his distance so no enemy or magic wielder could detect him, Asaph hovered high in the sky, half in the base of the clouds, and watched as the enemy slowed above the grounds of the Goddess' Temple which glowed white in the Flow.

There came a flash of black light so fast that had he blinked he would have missed it. The temple itself disappeared for a split second, then reappeared and the Dromoorai and harpies were gone.

Some black magic that is! Asaph growled, looked outside the Flow and dipped lower. The grounds were heavily patrolled by temple guards walking in pairs, he could see their white tabards through the foliage. There were more than he'd ever seen before and they weren't running about in alarm, which made him deeply suspicious. Did the Temple *know* the evil party was arriving? Could they be in league with them? He didn't want to think it, let alone believe it.

Outside the temple grounds, the City Guard also stood watch, but Navarr had posted them there to keep an eye on the temple. They would not be magic wielders, so they wouldn't even sense something was up. It was unlikely King Navarr and his guards were in on it too. From his elevated position, Asaph doubted the king's guards would even be able to see the temple guards, hidden as they were by the trees.

The flash of black light came again and he felt the touch of a twisted dragon mind, the foul stench of a diseased beast. He blinked into the Flow and saw two dark shadows rise above the temple.

Swiftly, he pulled back into the cloud. The Dread Dragons were leaving. Was the sword with them? He couldn't feel it. Perhaps they had left it behind. His guts told him it was still in the temple.

He watched the shadows disappear into the east, then dropped out of the clouds again to survey the temple that crawled with guards. How was he going to get in there? He couldn't just land in the grounds. He circled as low as he dared, close enough to make out which rooftops were closest to the temple wall. There were several houses clustered close at the eastern edge but their rickety slate roofs were too low and far away and he wouldn't be able to jump from them onto the wall.

Further up from them was a clock tower which had long since fallen into disrepair. The clock face was green with moss and the hands were frozen at a quarter to midday or midnight. The top of the tower was much higher than the wall, too high to jump, but a long thick branch of an oak tree extended towards it. It looked strong enough to take a man's weight but it was a good two or three yards away from the roof. If he didn't make the jump, he could kill himself in the fall if he landed badly. He considered his options.

If he went straight to the City Guard and told them about the suspicious activity, they would certainly demand entry into the temple to investigate and then he would never find out what was going on in there. He might never find the sword. It was worth snooping first then raising the alarm later if things got messy.

Decision made, he swiftly descended towards the clock tower. His wings billowed great gusts through the streets sending leaves and garbage tumbling. The city guards nearest looked around at the sudden squall and Asaph held his breath. They didn't spot the great dragon just above them in the sky. Doing something he had never done before, he changed form in mid-air several feet above the clock tower's roof.

He hit the slate with a thud, just missing skewering himself on the weather vane, and tumbled alarmingly to the edge. He thrashed, trying to grip anything for purchase but the slate tiles were wet and slippery. As he rolled over the edge, his right hand found the stone gutter and clenched into a vice. Hanging by one hand he watched slate tiles tumble past him and smash on the ground some forty feet below.

Voices came from somewhere. Quickly, he gripped the guttering with his left hand, swung up a leg, and heaved himself up. Flattening himself on the roof, he lay still, feeling like a thief in the night.

Candlelight appeared in the window of a house below. The window swung open and a night-capped man peered out. He looked down at the tiles, then up at the clock tower.

'Bloody cats!' the man growled, shook his fist, then slammed the window.

The light went out and Asaph let go of his breath. He crawled around the roof to the edge closest to the tree. The branch seemed a long way away and anybody who looked up would see him in the light cast by the street lamp. There were no guards here but he'd noticed some circumambulating the walls earlier. It was only a matter of time before they reached here.

Licking his lips, he got into a crouching position. At most, he had a run of three steps before leaping. Slowly he stood up, backed to the edge of the tower, and launched into a run. Barely containing a howl of terror, he leapt.

The branch surged towards him closer than he had planned. His chest smacked into it knocking his breath away. He struggled to wrap his arms around it. The tree shook violently and he hung there dangling, his legs illuminated by streetlight. With a swing and a grunt, he wrapped his legs around the branch and, like a monkey, scrambled upside down into the shadows.

'What was that?' asked a man.

Asaph could just see the helmet of a city guard over the wall.

'I didn't see anything,' said another man. 'It's probably a cat, this city is crawling with 'em.'

'The whole bloody tree shook!' said the first.

'They've been getting huge. Some are the size of dogs! I think witches have been feedin' 'em,' said the second.

'Witches, eh? Someone said they were back in the city. Seemed pleased about it too. Tsk, tsk,' said the first.

'Aye, there've been posters popping up everywhere looking for "Women of the Metaphysical Arts" and stamped by a certain "Higglesworth Enterprises",' said the second. 'I'll tell you, between witches and the priestesses, something's afoot in this city and it ain't good. More work for us is all I see. Someone ought to keep these crazy women in check.'

'Pah,' said the first. 'No one could ever control a witch or a priestess. We're best off trying to play them off against each other. I'll be honest, it's not the witches I'm worried about. Not yet anyway. With people going missing every day, some are pointing their finger at the Temple. Now I don't mind the tramps and criminals disappearing—less work for us, aye? But it's the children that's downright worrying. Something's going on in there and I can't wait for the King to go inside and overturn the place. It gives me the creeps.'

'Aye,' said the second. 'The Oracle has refused to see anyone now and some have seen priestesses dressed in red robes not white. Blood red.'

The guards' voices faded as they walked away. Asaph let go of his breath in a long, silent sigh. Something surely was going on in the temple. Even the city guards thought so. He crawled closer to the tree's trunk and wedged himself into a nook, wiping the sweat from his forehead.

Looking down, there was nothing but exotic bushes with wide flat leaves and various shrubs. There were no temple guards that he could see. He inched his way down the trunk and jumped the last few feet to land in a patch of yellow flowers. Feeling bad for trampling them, he hoped no one would spot the damage tonight.

Hunching low, he made his way through the bushes towards the white walls of the temple. There had to be a side entrance rather than the brightly lit and heavily guarded front.

Two temple guards, hands resting on the pommel of their swords, walked the path towards him. He ducked into a thick patch of ferns. He glanced the other way along the path. A priestess and priest were coming from the other direction, their robes blood red and swishing around their legs. Why had they stopped wearing white? The guards and priests paused together near Asaph and he flattened himself against the earth holding his breath, ears straining to listen.

'They have arrived. Double the watch and let no one in or out until dawn,' said the priestess. She had long dark hair and a glint in her eye that made Asaph shiver. He noticed a thin, sickle-shaped knife dangling from her belt. It didn't look like a letter opener. Since when did priestesses start wearing weapons?

He watched them part, going back the way they had come. Good, the priest and priestess were headed straight towards the temple, hopefully to a side door. He followed them on silent feet, careful not to move a leaf or make a rustle, never once forgetting his keen tracking skills that the Kuapoh had taught him.

The pair paused at the back of the temple on the darkest part of the path. Looking left then right, they turned and stepped lightly across the grass as if trying not to flatten it but Asaph could see the imprints of several feet. Many had come this way. They stopped at the smooth base of the temple. The woman brushed her hand over the wall and, to Asaph's horror, traced the mark of Maphrax upon it. A portion of the wall faded to reveal a sconce-lit passageway that glowed red. She stepped inside and disappeared but the priest paused and looked around, frowning.

'Who's there?' the priest commanded, his voice harsh.

Asaph's heart leapt into his throat.

'What is it?' said the woman, appearing again.

'I can sense something. The Under Flow is unhappy,' said the man, sidling back across the grass.

'Come, we are late for the sacrifice. The guards are on their highest alert,' hissed the woman irritably. She turned away and went back inside.

Frowning, the man ignored her and carried on his search. Asaph's mind went into overdrive, both at his predicament and what was taking place in the temple. Sacrifice was black magic. The situation of the Temple in the heart of Carvon was far worse than anybody realised. They really were in league with Baelthrom. Was the entire Order of the Goddess now the enemy as well? Had the Free People been betrayed from within? The thought was heart stopping.

The man was now walking straight towards him. Asaph wished he could detect and use magic in his human form. He inched back behind a tree trunk, racking his brains. Play innocent, he decided, that way he would know their true intentions. Unbuckling his sword, he dropped it amongst the ferns, took a deep breath and wobbled out from behind the tree.

'It was my friends' fault,' he said, swaying slightly and putting on his most sheepish expression. 'We all got waaay too drunk, see? They played a prank and pushed me over the wall. Now I can't find the way out. I wasn't causin' any trouble.'

The man's face turned from one of anger into a sly smile. 'They don't sound like very good friends to me. Surely a man of your musculature would be able to fight back?'

Asaph grinned foolishly, his heart pounding in his chest.

The man stepped closer, moving like a predator. Asaph wished he hadn't dropped his sword.

'Why don't you come inside and have a hot drink before you go?' said the man.

Asaph realised then that he was covered in dirt and foliage and must look like a peasant. Getting inside was all he had wanted to do, but now faced with the prospect he wanted to run a mile.

The priest reached a companionable arm around his shoulders, making him shiver. There was a loud clap that seemed to come from within his skull, followed by intense pain. His consciousness scattered into the blackness.

CHAPTER 20

Karalanth Army

FINDING her hunger again, Issa hurried after the maid to the dining hall and took the only empty chair left which was opposite Domenon.

She was late, everyone was already seated around a long table laden with food. A bowl of green soup and warm, crusty bread sat waiting for her. The Master Wizard smiled at her in a way that made her cheeks burn. She tried not to remember that just moments ago he'd had his arm around her in the bath.

'Ah, Lady Issa,' said Duke Beddan standing to greet her.

Velonorian leapt to his feet and ran to pull her chair out for her to sit before the butler could get there.

'Thank you,' she said to the elf and turned to the Duke. 'Apologies for my lateness. There were things I needed to attend to.' If he was angered about the broken door, he didn't show it. Perhaps Domenon had, thankfully, not mentioned it.

'May I introduce my wife, Duchess Emiline,' he said, gesturing to the slight woman with rouge cheeks seated beside him.

Her long face and full, painted pink lips were quite distinguishing. She had a shock of golden curls held up by a band. Her back was straight and she held her head high but she toyed with her fingers constantly, hinting at a nervous disposition. She smiled warmly at Issa.

'Pleased to meet you,' said Issa politely and turned to her soup.

A servant poured her a glass of fine Davonian rosé wine. She took a sip but, although it was delicious, she didn't feel like letting her guard down tonight and instead stuck to the water.

The elves were talking quietly amongst themselves in Elven, as they often did. Some might call it rude but Issa tried to see it as just their manner along with a distrust of any human or dwarven folk. They left for the Land of Mists for a reason and were forced to return, mostly against their will. It might take many generations for them to trust humans again, she thought. It was also a sign of their nervousness in this violent world.

Domenon had turned back to his conversation with the Duke, speaking in Davonian and leaving her to wolf down her soup. As soon as she'd finished, the servants whisked away the empty bowl and placed a huge pie with roast potatoes and peppered vegetables in front of her.

'Are you all right, Lady Issa?' asked Velonorian who was seated to her right. He was already half way through his pie and showed no signs of slowing.

'Yes, thank you,' she half-lied. The recent commotion had left her shaken. She didn't feel like chatting and wanted nothing more than to eat and think upon everything that had happened. She was relieved that everyone else was engaged in their own conversations and that the duchess was too far away to engage in polite chitchat.

'I don't feel much like socialising, mind. I think I need a good night's sleep.'

'With me guarding you, you can rest easy.' Velonorian smiled.

She returned his smile. She did feel better knowing Domenon and her elf chaplain were looking out for her but the thought of going back to her room where she had been attacked made her uneasy.

As soon as she had finished desert—a delicious honeyed sponge cake—she made her excuses and left the table. Velonorian scraped his chair back to follow her, but she made him sit and finish his second helping of dessert. Thankfully, a maid showed her back to her room saving her from getting lost in the maze of corridors.

In the short time she'd been away, the bath had been removed, the water mopped up and the door fixed. Ehka perched on the bed-frame dozing and Maggot had gone.

Once alone, she slipped into her nightshirt, put out all the lanterns except the one on the bedside table, and sunk onto the bed with a sigh. She got under the covers, intending to sleep but as soon as she closed her eyes, her mind went into overdrive.

Neither of the two most powerful wizards in Maioria trusted each other, and now she was beginning to distrust them both. No one was who they said they were. Even Baelthrom wasn't what he seemed. *No, Baelthrom is a twisted abomination.* It was Ayeth who caused the confusion.

What were those things she had seen earlier, the veiled beings that had tried to feed off her? The Dark Rift ate the living light of planets. These veiled *Eaters,* as Maggot called them, consumed the energy of beings. Was that what inhabited the Dark Rift? Remorseless, twisted, fallen beings—beings like Baelthrom. They didn't care what they did to others and, worse, they felt entitled to. The living were simply their food. She shivered. Did the solution to destroying the Dark Rift lie within the Dark Rift itself? Such thoughts hurt her head.

She opened her eyes and looked at her flame ring that gleamed in the low light of the smouldering hearth. She wished Asaph were with her. All she wanted was for someone to trust. Someone to tell her what to do. She wished she were flying with him. When they were together she felt stronger. He wouldn't be gone long, she reminded herself. She should worry about herself first before she started worrying for a Dragon Lord's safety.

I have a war to command. I must turn my mind to the task at hand and think like Marakon thinks, like a battle commander thinks. And lying here was simply wasting time. She threw off the covers and her nightshirt and pulled on her dread dragon armour, strapping her blacksmith's belt and sword over the top of it. The orb she slipped into its usual sack and hooked it around her belt then held the raven talisman up. Ehka hopped closer, wondering what she was doing.

'I can't sleep, so I think a visit to the Karalanths is long overdue,' she said to the bird. 'You know where they might be? Good.'

Undoing the window latch she let it swing open and a cool breeze blew in. She took a deep breath and focused on the talisman.

'Make me raven,' she commanded, pulling on the barest bit of the Flow so no magic wielder would feel it. She didn't want Domenon running into her room again.

The change was fast. There came a brief moment when the wind seemed to blow through every particle in her body, and then she was perched on the floor staring up at the bigger raven, Ehka. The thrill of the wild filled her and she wanted nothing more than to rush to the window and jump into the air.

Ehka squawked and hopped onto the ledge. She landed beside him, the wind ruffling her feathers. With another squawk, he leapt into the night. With a crying caw of delight, she followed. The wind filled her wings pushing her into the air. The night was bright with the white light of Doon and an orange sliver of Woetala. Clouds hurried across the sky but never enough to cover the moons for long.

She glanced back at the palace. Most of the lights were still on since she'd gone to bed early. Below, the pale shingle road leading up to the palace was stark as it wound through trees. The port city seemed far away, its lights glimmering.

Ehka was a dark smudge ahead. With her acute avian senses, she could feel her companion's presence better than she could see him. He angled right, towards the dark forest and away from the city lights. Across the forest and far away, she could see the white tops of the Everridge Mountains. The permanent snow at their very tips caught the moonlight and led them on. Somewhere in the forests at the base of those mountains, the Karalanths gathered. She had scryed for them some time ago now, and she wondered how many had gathered there, preparing themselves to invade their own land and take back what had once been theirs.

Everything depended on Queen Thora allowing them, and all the armies and mercenaries, safe passage to the coast. Marakon would lead the Feylint Halanoi and the Knights of the Raven. Even though he had tried to pass the knight's leadership over to her, she knew she wasn't ready to. They needed an experienced military commander and she doubted she would ever be that. Much depended on the queen allowing her country to become a staging post; but Issa doubted she would agree to let in a legion of demons. Hopefully they wouldn't ever need Gedrock's demons, but she doubted it.

It struck her, then, how she had mobilised most of the Free World for war. *I didn't do it alone*, she reassured herself. Still, how many would die because of her plans? They would *all* die if nothing was done. She was doing the right thing; it was the only thing she could think to do short of facing Baelthrom herself. *Would it come to that in the end? Must I face Baelthrom myself?*

The wind turned increasingly bitter and she was very glad when Ehka finally dropped into the darkness of the forest towards the warm glow of a distant campfire.

'Soon I meet with Queen Thora,' said Issa to Cusap'anth and Rhul'ynth. The Karalanth leaders clustered close, their impressive antlers catching the light of the fire. They were decorated in the warrior symbols of Woetala and in the flickering light they looked quite menacing. 'I cannot imagine the Queen refusing passage to our armies through her lands given what we propose. And I hope she sends her own army to join us, and quickly before the enemy suspects anything.'

Issa passed a glance across the vast crowd of Karalanth warriors resting in the forest. There were two thousand, Cusap'anth had said, and another two thousand on the way. The monumental reality of what they had planned—to attack Venosia—made her mouth go dry.

As if sensing this, Rhul'ynth placed a hand on Issa's shoulder. 'Look, friend, we will do this with or without you. Our time has come. Woetala has gathered us. We will fight to take back what is ours or die trying.'

Issa nodded and squeezed her friend's hand. 'Thank the goddess you made it this far. But there are a lot of unknowns ahead of us, which is why I plan to scout Venosia's western coast with Ehka. That way we can draw up maps and attack where the enemy is weakest. Yes, it will be dangerous, but not so much for a raven.'

Cusap'anth grinned. 'Then perhaps I shall send my owl to do similar, and any of our totems that will make suitable scouts. Where is Asaph?'

'The Sword of Binding called to him and he has gone to rouse the dragons. He had to go alone. I pray to Zanufey that he will make it back to us safely and in time for the invasion.' Issa took a deep breath and tried to push her fears aside.

'A Karalanth army, a dragon army—what could be stronger?' He laughed.

'There is more,' Issa said. She'd already told them about her trials within the Storm Holt, much to their shock and awe. 'It's possible I'll be able to call on the demons, should we have need. Although I don't want to run out of favours with them too quickly. This invasion is just a small battle, we have an entire war to win ahead of us.'

Cusap'anth's face turned hard. 'Then we will win it one battle at a time.'

Issa hoped there would be enough of them left when the last battle came. 'After I have spoken to the queen, I will send Ehka to you to let you know. Gather as many as you can as far south as you can. Don't harm any Davonian scouts and I'll tell the queen you simply seek passage. With the goddess's blessing, I'll see you again at Port South Reach.'

Suppressing a yawn, she suddenly felt very tired and she still had an hour of flying ahead of her. Hugging the two Karalanths, she called the raven form to her and launched into the air. The eastern wind was frigid but at least it now blew her in the right direction.

'Lady Issa. I'm sorry to wake you, but Master Wizard Domenon is already waiting with the others by your carriage.'

Issa groaned. The maid threw open the curtains. The sky was dark and dawn looked at least half an hour away.

'Is it even morning?' Issa dragged herself out of bed yawning. She could only have had a few hours' sleep.

With the maid's help, she was packed, dressed and sitting in the carriage before the sun made it over the horizon. Duskar and Ironclad were tied on behind, and the carriages rolled slowly away from the palace.

'Busy night?' Domenon, seated opposite her, raised his eyebrow.

Issa didn't bother replying. Instead, she folded up her cloak into a pillow and leant against the window. The rocking of the carriage had her asleep in moments.

She awoke when they paused for an early lunch. The sky was dark and it was pouring with rain so there was no point leaving the carriage to explore. Domenon had said they would reach Rebben by nightfall and, as the drizzle fell against the window, it looked to be a long and boring ride. At least she could sleep for most of it, she consoled herself.

Domenon was busy sorting through official papers that bore the seal of Queen Thora.

'Do you think Baelthrom can be healed?' she asked. He looked at her with a frown. 'You know, can he be reached and made to see what he is doing is wrong?'

Domenon chuckled at first, then paused when he saw the look on her face. 'I can see you're serious, Issa, but if that were possible, it would have been done by the Ancients long ago. No, he is too far gone. Had he been Maiorian, then maybe a way could have been found. But we do not even know what is in the Dark Rift where he came from. We don't understand our enemy and that's what makes him so dangerous.'

Issa considered this for a time. 'I saw what is in there, that night in the bath…There are Light Eaters in there, like wraiths and Life Seekers. I don't know what else to call them. They sense the living and want to feed on them. Tall, formless things. Perhaps that is where he brought the Life Seekers from.' Issa shivered at the memory of the Light Eaters clustering around her.

Domenon considered this, seemed about to speak then changed his mind. 'So, where were you last night? I came to see if you were all right, and you weren't there.'

'I couldn't sleep and, rather than scry as you warned me not to do, I needed to see the Karalanths. They are ready to advance through Davono as soon as Queen Thora gives the go ahead.' She shrugged. 'They will advance anyway, one way or another, but I'd rather they did it with her approval.'

Domenon smoothed his hair back. 'I can't protect you if you are not here and you don't tell me where you're going.'

Issa was surprised at the genuine look of concern in his face. Or did he just dislike not being able to control her?

'You should not go off alone.' He sighed. 'But you seem to enjoy danger…Hmm, there's something else I have been meaning to mention. The more I've thought on it, the more something doesn't add up. There is an odd blank spot in my memory that I just cannot reconcile. So I decided to speak to Sheyengetha about your parents. If anyone knew about them, Sheyengetha would. Oddly, the tree would not say anything other than, "some secrets are not ours to tell." Knowing how keen you are to find out more about them, I assumed you would have talked to Sheyengetha about it.'

Issa watched the rain run down the window. 'You are certainly very clever to think that. Yes, I did talk to Sheyengetha but I will say the same, the secret is not mine to tell. The only thing that matters to me is where they are now—and no one can tell me that.'

'Perhaps I can, if I knew what they looked like,' said Domenon.

Issa chewed her lip. What if he knew where they were? She'd do anything to find them. But she couldn't betray her parents' secret and tell him.

'I have an excellent memory and the ability to recall even details from my birth,' said Domenon, watching her without blinking. 'So this 'blank spot' in my mind is terribly irregular. You are aware that any spell under the banner of "A Web" is illegal on the Isle of Myrn, as are many witches' spells.'

Issa caught her breath.

Domenon continued. 'There are no excuses. All casters of Webs are stripped of their powers and cast out for the protection of the seers and all of Myrn.'

'They are already cast out, Domenon,' Issa said quietly without looking at him. She traced a finger through the condensation on the window. 'I do not keep things from you deliberately. Some things are just not mine to tell.'

'Is that so? Hmm. You are also keeping things from me about Freydel.' Domenon's eyes were piercing and she found herself sweating. 'Why does he look pale and wasted these days? He's a learned wizard who has overcome all the difficulties of a novice new to magic and so should not be suffering like one. I'm sure he's lost weight as well. He struggles to control his emotions too. Why?'

'Everything to do with Freydel is surely the concern of the Wizards' Circle and not mine,' said Issa. 'I am merely his friend and his pupil, not his confidante. But I know what you mean. I'm concerned for him too.'

'Indeed,' said Domenon. 'Perhaps I'll discuss this with the other wizards at the next meeting.'

Thankfully he questioned her no more and went back to reading through and sorting his bag of papers.

As the sky darkened further, the only indication that the sun had set, the lights of Rebben appeared through the dark drizzle. They were taking the road around the outside of the city so, much to her disappointment, she didn't get to see a lot of the capital of Davono.

The castle looming on the hill was an imposing mass of square towers, battlements and impenetrable walls; or at least that's how it looked outside the city wall. They paused at a gate and the guards let them through. The carriage wheels clattered and slipped over the wet cobbles.

Servants dressed in shiny black shoes, white stockings, skirts and doublets came running from the castle entrance holding out umbrellas and covers for them. These protections against the weather didn't help though. The brief step out of the carriage to under an umbrella left her almost soaked through and wishing she'd worn her water-resistant leather armour.

She quickly checked on Duskar. The horse was as keen to get into a dry stable as she was the castle so she left Velonorian holding his and Ironclad's reins. The elf didn't seem nearly as uncomfortable in the downpour as everyone else was. The way he blinked up at the sky and smiled told her he was actually enjoying it. Maybe it never rained like this in the Land of Mists. This far south, it certainly wasn't cold rain, thankfully.

She rushed up the steps and halted in the reception room with the others. They were all dripping water onto the grey flagstones and beginning to shiver as the wind gusted. The reception area was just a draughty, plain room where they waited for the next set of heavy doors to open.

Someone entered the Flow and a brief wave of magic tickled her skin. With a shock, she looked down to find she was no longer soaking and neither was anyone else, even her hair was dry.

'My pleasure.' Domenon bowed slightly, grinning at their astonished faces.

A very useful trick, Issa noted.

The huge doors swung open and a welcome gush of warmth and light engulfed her. More servants spilled out to help the arrivals and Domenon briefly spoke to a senior looking woman with grey hair scraped into a bun and a straight back. He turned back to them and said, 'The servants will take your things to your rooms so we can go straight to dinner.'

Domenon caught her hand as she started to follow the servants. 'I have been informed that the Queen will see you as soon as you have finished your meal. And don't drink any wine until after. She cannot stand lapses in sobriety during business meetings.'

Issa nodded, intrigued but nervous.

The dining hall they entered was similar in design and layout to the one in Teramides, only much larger. Even the impressive, dark mahogany table was twice as long. Their large party only took up a third of it as they were seated for their meal.

Issa dutifully avoided the wine and made small talk with Velonorian beside her, all the while thinking about what she was going to say to the mysterious queen. It wasn't easy declaring impending war to the ruler of a land she had never met or been to before. The success of the meeting would all depend, she decided, on what manner of a woman the queen was.

CHAPTER 21

Bear Rider

'FION'DAR, Fion'dar!'

Voices screamed in Elven, crying to Woetala, the Life of the Forest, to save them.

A terrible roar shuddered through the earth and sky, and raging fire drowned out the screams of the dying. Maphraxies lumbered through the flames, dragged along by blood-hungry death hounds, drool and gore dripping from their fang-filled maws. Gut-wrenching fear rattled through his bones, turning his muscles to jelly. There was nowhere to flee. Walls of flame blocked every turn and black dragons above shattered the will to survive. Screams echoed all around him. No one could escape. They burned alive or were eaten.

Marakon jolted awake, his heart pounding. The screams faded with the dream. He took a long deep breath, trying to relax his muscles and his mind. Dawn light filtered through the gap in the tent flaps along with a chill gust of autumn wind. He shivered despite the sheen of sweat on his face. Pulling the blankets higher, he slid an arm lightly over Jarlain who lay beside him. She made a soft murmur and then was still again.

The same dream had been haunting him for over a week; the entire journey back from Carvon to the front line. Every night he watched elves flee for their lives in a world filled with raging fire. He was not alone, all the elves and any with elven blood in the camp had had the same dream. They'd all come to the same horrible conclusion as to what it meant: the Land of Mists had been attacked and they had witnessed the massacre of their kin.

King Navarr's couriers had reached them yesterday, carrying news from the king's wizards that confirmed the terrible news. Elven refugees now flooded the Isles of Tirry. Some of those in the army left immediately to make the long journey to Myrn to help them, but the Feylint Halanoi could ill-afford to lose many now they were on the offensive.

It was Daranarta's fault, Marakon clenched his fist. Half of him wanted to go and help too but the other half knew he could fight the enemy directly here and thus get his revenge. All those with elven blood had since fought with a ferocious rage. Their advance had been swift as they pushed the enemy back, pinning them to the very edge of the west coast in a few decimated towns, including Wenderon.

Marakon touched his aching, empty eye socket under his new, soft, tan patch. Sometimes the wound was agony, driving ice pick headaches deep into his skull. But he didn't want that eye back, even though his far-sightedness was forever lost.

He clenched his jaw thinking of Issa, the cause of his pain, then forced himself to relax. He knew why she'd commanded her raven to peck it out. After all, he deserved it and deserved to die for all the death and betrayal he'd unwittingly caused. But forgiving her was taking time. How many battles had Baelthrom seen him in, seen through him? Every time he'd lifted his patch, he'd betrayed his soldiers. The knowledge and guilt weighed him down. All his crew had died and only he'd been spared so he could spy upon, betray and kill others. The thought made him sick. How many other ways was Baelthrom spying on them all? Who was a spy and who wasn't? It didn't bear thinking about.

His good eye focused on the spear propped up in the corner of the tent. Unblemished by thousands of years, its surface gleamed as white as the day he'd first held it. *It's a shame it's only good at killing demons,* he thought. It seemed to have no great affect upon Maphraxies other than being slightly better than a normal spear at damaging their armour.

One day soon, when he received a message from Issa, he would use the spear to find and open the demon tunnels. He found the thought disturbing. He'd spent a lifetime destroying demons and closing their damned tunnels. Now, in this lifetime, he would have to do the opposite.

Ahh, the wondrous days of old. Charging with hundreds of his knights mounted upon their white steeds across green plains under a bright sun, their swords glinting in the light… The brief moments he'd so recently had with his precious eleven knights, reliving the glory days of old, he would treasure forever.

They were gone now, leaving him behind to live out his life. And before Jarlain had found him, he'd fought against the depression of meaninglessness and emptiness, finding the fighting only barely gave him a cause to exist, only just drowned out the loneliness. He'd thrown himself into battle with abandon, willing the enemy to kill him, stunned when they never could. But he had quickly grown sick of war, of waking up injured in jam-packed tents, of the cold and damp, of the boring food and the endless marching.

Jarlain stirred but her eyes remained closed. He rested on one elbow and looked at her, appreciating the smooth brown skin of her shoulder, soft chin and delicate nose. Her dark hair now reached her ears and he found her short, unruly curls quite becoming. She'd been so thin when he saw her, he'd barely recognised her. Thankfully she'd already gained some of her weight back and lost the gaunt look to her cheeks.

He gave a deep, reassuring sigh. How he'd missed her since he had left the Uncharted Lands—more than he would allow himself to feel. He tried not to think of Rasia, his wife so brutally taken from him. The pain was still too raw and deep. But now Jarlain was with him, just her presence was enough to heal the pain and the loneliness in his heart. He remembered when they had first made love and the healing she had brought to him then. She would keep him sane and happy, he was sure of it.

A deep snuffle came from outside and something big rolled over, alarmingly bulging in the side of the tent by their bed. Jarlain, too, rolled over and Marakon grinned. He could barely believe there was a massive bear sleeping the other side of the thin fabric of his tent.

'Is Fenn bothering you again?' Jarlain murmured.

'Not yet,' said Marakon, gently brushing the hair from her face. She blinked up at him and he smiled, feeling whole when he looked into her deep brown eyes. 'He doesn't like me taking you away from him. If he had his way, he'd be in the tent with us.'

Jarlain giggled and lifted a hand to his cheek. He took it and kissed it.

'So much has happened. I have such strange dreams…I've changed, grown strong and wise like an Elder,' she said. 'For so long in the wilderness I searched for you, blind and in nothing but rags. You know I would have died had Fenn not come to me?'

'Yes. And for that, I am indebted to him. Without you, my life would not be worth living.' He meant it and she smiled.

'I would hope you lived for more than just me,' she said.

'I've lived enough for everyone. Now I long for sleep and love and a long break from war,' he said, bending to kiss her long on the lips.

Interweaving her fingers in his hair, she drew him closer and sighed when he trailed a hand over her bare stomach.

Jarlain peered into the forest, gripping the hilt of her weapon and saw the gory remains of a deer, deep red splashed against the contrast of green grass. The smell wasn't coming from it but the undead that had been feeding on the carcass. Jarlain gagged.

Fenn growled, spotting a dark shape bounding through the trees ahead. He lunged after it. Jarlain held tightly onto him knowing the foltoy was unlikely to flee. She watched it circle through the trees, coming around to attack them. She scanned the forest looking for more but spotted none.

Fenn pelted forwards, gaining speed through a straight bit between the trees, amazing her with his swiftness. Jarlain gripped the fur at the base of his neck so tightly she wondered why it didn't hurt him. His muscles rippled beneath her legs that had now adapted to allow her to sit easily atop him. At first, riding him had left her legs so sore she could barely walk. Now it felt strange and awkward to sit atop a horse.

She ducked lower against him as he leapt over a boulder and lunged to the right. The foltoy was very fast and trying to get behind them to attack. Fenn wasn't letting it do that. She tilted with the bear, her body responding easily to his, perfectly balancing each other. Anger and adrenaline pounded in her veins as it did in his. His fury was her fury; his excitement was her excitement. They were one.

She lifted her spear but the moment to throw it was lost when the foltoy switched course through ferns. It leapt upon a rock, snarling bloodied fangs, green eyes blazing. Hunching, it launched into the air over

Fenn's head towards her. Inch-long razor claws gleamed, a rasping howl scoured her ears. She plunged her spear forwards, bracing against the weight of the foltoy. The spear sunk into its shoulder, a claw swiped to the left slicing her cheek as she fell back.

She felt Fenn rise on his hind legs, saw a huge brown muzzle open impossibly wide and engulf the foltoy's neck. She clung harder to him and the spear embedded in the foltoy. Then Fenn was dropping back down, his neck and back straining to hold the writhing creature. Jarlain regained her balance and screamed as she shoved her spear harder. There came a sickening, snapping, crunching sound and her spear was wrenched from her grasp as the foltoy fell beneath the bear, its neck broken.

Fenn pulled away. Jarlain sensed and felt his disgust as her own. He shook his head back and forth flinging undead blood from his mouth. Jarlain took a deep breath and slipped from his back to look at the shuddering foltoy. It twitched and then was still. Gripping her spear, she twisted and wrenched it free.

She touched her cheek. There was a little blood. Thankfully, it was only a scratch. Silently, they walked towards the river to wash their weapons; he, his teeth, and she, her spear. They didn't need to speak about what had happened, each had felt the others' feelings and thoughts. Squatting beside the river, she washed the blood from her cheek feeling it sting a little.

She glanced at the magnificent bear as he gulped down water. It struck her then what a powerful fighting unit they made, what a whole army of them could make. Human and beast working as one, feeling as one. This was their second foltoy kill today. The two had been in close proximity to each other. Grimacing, she washed the black blood off her spear. She sensed there were more and hoped to hunt them all down.

The afternoon sunlight fell through the birch leaves and sparkled on the river. They were alone scouting the forest but never strayed too far from camp. Fenn made the other soldiers nervous so they worked on their own. Jarlain feared nothing with him by her side. This was her and Fenn's task within the Feylint Halanoi now. Marakon wanted her fighting alongside him but he had to lead his unit west. He wanted to build his Knights of the Raven order, but the Feylint Halanoi needed him more right now.

A cold wind blew her short hair across her eyes, irritating her. She brushed it back only to have it blown straight back again. With a sigh, she shoved her helmet on, seriously considering shaving her head again. It was either going to be short or long, nothing in between was workable.

'What do bears remember of our alliance, if anything?' Jarlain asked Fenn.

He sat on his haunches beside the river. *'Only us brown bears paired with a chosen human, though most care little for it now given the way humans are to all creatures.'*

His thoughts came clearly in her mind. Their connection was strong since Doon had returned to her the gift of the Navadin and awakened within her the Daluni animal speak. Though she could only speak to bears, her talks with the elves had made it obvious that the translation was much clearer than any Daluni was able to forge.

The majestic elves told her animals used pictures to communicate, but she heard Fenn's thoughts as direct words *and* pictures. The elven soldiers did not remember a time of the Navadin. Jarlain wondered if that was because it was so long ago or because the two races had never come into contact with one another. Perhaps it was both.

She adjusted her plate mail cuirass, given to her by the Feylint Halanoi, and laid down her short spear wishing she had her Gurlanka knife. Marakon had tried to teach her the sword but she just couldn't get the hang of it and had done better with a spear, much to her surprise.

'Deep within my blood I remember they had spears,' said Fenn.

Jarlain nodded. 'Perhaps, then, that is why it comes more naturally to me than any other weapon.'

Fenn sat quietly, the sun dappling off his thick brown fur. He rarely spoke and when he did it was with few words.

From its sleeve on her back, she slipped out Hai's staff. *Not Hai's staff but the Gurlanka's*—the holder of the memory of her people. She sat down on the rock beside the spear and staff, her eyes lingering on the wood, remembering all that Hai had told her in his visitation. Just as the people here were being persecuted by the Maphraxies, were her people also being persecuted? Would there be any Navadin left to ride the bears as once they had?

'Ood says they will return,' Fenn said. Jarlain hadn't realised she'd spoken

her thoughts aloud. Or perhaps she hadn't and their connection was so strong he could read her thoughts. *'And when they do, the creatures of the forest will be free. Ood will be free.'*

'The Forest Guardian is not free? How can that be?' She looked at the bear, the pink scar on his jaw lifting his lip, his big brown eyes blinking.

'Ever since the darkness came, none of us have been free,' the bear said simply. *'Ood and his mate. All of us, sick. The dark moon heals us.'*

Jarlain looked down at the staff. How would her people return and become Navadin? She stroked the warm wood and a vision flashed in her mind.

Hai and Sharnu clinging to a palm tree, a sea of fire beneath them spread by black dragons. Her people burning alive. She shuddered. How many of her people still lived? How would she reach them? *The boatman.* The thought made her rise to her feet.

'I know how to bring them here,' she told Fenn. He flicked his ears back and forth.

Jarlain stared across the ocean, blinking against the bright sunset that turned the clouds into blazing pink and orange ribbons. Marakon hugged her closer against his chest as they stood on a wide, shingled beach watching the sun sink into the sea. The surf scraped the worn pebbles backwards and forwards in an oddly soothing monotonous din.

Behind them in the forest came the distant sound of soldiers training, their voices and clang of weapons faint. They currently camped a long way south of Wenderon with a thousand other soldiers tasked with freeing any Maphraxie captured farms and villages. Four farms and two villages had since been liberated and the Maphraxies burnt to nothing but dust.

She squeezed Marakon's arms. She finally had everything she ever wanted, and now she dared to risk it all by leaving him to return to her people.

'I am the highest ranking commander here,' said Marakon for the second time. 'I can come with you with a whole unit of soldiers if I choose to. I will be able to convince my officers.'

'This is not a war party but a saving of survivors, if any remain,' said

Jarlain. 'Of course I want you to come with me, but you are needed here. And what about Issa? What if the raven comes? If you're halfway across the world, that's even harder for it to find you. You left me once to return to your home, and I thought I'd never see you again. Now, it seems, I must do the same. It is my duty to my people and to Hai.'

Marakon sighed heavily. 'I just cannot stand the thought of you out there alone against the enemy. I don't want to argue about it again. I know why you do it, but I still hope the boatman won't answer your call.'

Jarlain smiled. His protective nature was touching. They had argued about her decision last night—their first—but he had given up quickly, seeing the determination in her eyes.

'Great Doon says the Navadin will return. I realise now that I must lead the Bear Riders of old, or at least awaken them to our ancient past. No one else can do it. Those who remain must be saved.'

She turned to look up into his violet eye and saw the protest on his face though he said nothing. 'I will return soon. Murlonius will know where to take me. You've said yourself he once carried a whole army. Whatever is left of my people, of the tribes of the ancient Navadin, I will find them and bring them back here to safety.

'I have seen in Hai's staff that not one tribe can withstand the forces of Baelthrom. They will fight to the death, yes. Until none remain. I cannot let that happen. Look to how you feel about your elves. Despite your anger at them, you still desire to save them. I must do the same for my people. I must!'

He took a deep breath. 'Why do I always pick stubborn, headstrong women?'

Jarlain laughed. 'Because you like a challenge.'

He held her hands, his expression serious. 'Promise me you will not leave Murlonius' boat if there is danger or enemies near. You get your people and you get out. Don't hang around.'

'I promise,' she said, and stroked the dark stubble on his cheek.

He looked at the ground. 'If you don't return, I shall come and find you.'

'I won't be gone that long,' she said, trying to convince him more than meaning the words. She didn't know if she would return and she didn't dare think about it. 'If I don't go now, who will be left of my people?'

He nodded. 'But I need more than just your word.'

He pulled out of his pocket the stone she had given so long ago decorated with a bear on one side and a sun on the other. He placed it on the ground. Unsheathing his sword, he put the point on the stone and struck it so it split into two perfectly shorn halves. Picking up the broken pebble he gave her one half. She looked at it curiously. He held his half next to hers, making the bear whole again.

'Always carry your luck stone,' he said. 'And I'll carry mine. It's a silly thing but it links us strongly together.'

'No, it's not silly,' Jarlain blinked back tears, remembering it was the only thing that had led her to him. 'It is the perfect thing.' She kissed the stone and slipped it in her pocket.

He embraced her roughly, running his hands through her hair. She breathed in his smell, her cheek pressed against the firmness of his chest.

'Don't let me bury another wife,' he said hoarsely in her ear. 'At least let us die together. I can't die alone again.'

'You won't,' said Jarlain as they pulled apart. She wiped the tears from her face and saw Fenn loping out of the forest behind. The bear slowed to a lazy walk, his great bulk swaying.

'I'll wait with you until the boatman comes, unless you want to wait until tomorrow?' said Marakon.

'If I go now, I'll follow the sun. It will still be light when I arrive.'

She struggled into her cuirass and Marakon helped tighten the straps. She had a blade concealed in each boot, a knife at her belt, and a spear in the sheath beside the staff on her back. Marakon kissed her one last time, a long, passion filled kiss that left her wanting more. Hooking her helmet under her arm, she looked at Fenn who had stopped beside the shoreline.

'I'm glad he's with you, although I've never seen a bear cross an ocean in a boat before,' Marakon grinned. 'Make sure he protects you.'

'I don't think he quite understands what he's let himself in for, but he won't leave my side,' said Jarlain. 'His presence will help awaken my people.'

'I'm beginning to think I need to swap my horse for a bear,' said Marakon, making her laugh.

They went to stand beside Fenn, Marakon eyeing him with a curious yet wary expression. He still hadn't got used to the huge beast. Jarlain laid a hand on Fenn's head and the bear gazed at her. With a sigh, she turned to the ocean and stilled her mind.

'Murlonius,' she said, loud and low.

Twice more she repeated the name. Fenn stared out across the ocean.

So slowly it was barely perceptible, the waves began to calm, the din of the surf dropped and everything became still. There was no wind and no sound of anything. A patch of mist formed on the horizon then flowed towards them. Within it, the carved, serpent-head prow of the boat appeared, an unlit lantern swaying in its teeth.

Not one person stood in the boat, but two.

Jarlain stared up at the boatman and woman, unable to take her eyes off the people before her whose beauty surpassed even the elves. Though clothed in thick, simple grey cloaks and tan breeches, their flawless faces were full of life and youth as if they had never aged a day past thirty.

Yisufalni radiated light; her pale, pearlescent skin gleamed and her slanted, violet eyes were wide and bright. Her faintly pastel blue hair was long like Murlonius', though his was tied back. The most disconcerting thing about her was her long, six-fingered hands that folded neatly over each other. Those hands reached to take hold of her own. The Ancient had a surprisingly strong grip as she helped Jarlain into the boat.

'You no longer age?' asked Marakon, his eyes wide as he held the boat steady.

'Well met, Marakon Si Hara,' said Murlonius beaming with joy as he inclined his head. 'Now we are finally together, the curse is weakened and I no longer age when I near land. But still, our energy dwindles the longer we spend on Maioria's shores. We have not found a complete cure for it yet, perhaps there is none.'

'Destroying Baelthrom will cure all ills,' said Marakon with a hard smile.

'Then let us pray that that time is not far away and we will be victorious,' said Murlonius. He turned to Jarlain. 'But what is this? I see another prophecy fulfilled, the awakening of the ancient Navadin.' His smile deepened as Fenn waded into the water to sniff the boat.

'The Navadin were old when our race was young,' said Yisufalni, her voice soft and melodious.

'I only remember parts. Fenn remembers more.' Jarlain nodded to the bear who was now on his hind legs and towering above Marakon. 'Don't worry, Fenn, it is big enough. It will stretch.'

The bear said nothing but leapt powerfully into the boat. They all fell back as it rocked violently. Marakon clung to the side to keep it from capsizing as everybody tried to hang on to something. The boat stretched imperceptibly to accommodate the bear. Everyone regained their seats, thankful for not being dumped into the sea.

'Now you will be inseparable until death takes one of you,' laughed Murlonius to Jarlain, though his eyes were on the bear.

'I'd do anything for a normal life and a normal relationship,' sighed Marakon, a wan grin on his face.

Jarlain laughed. 'Nothing can come between you and I. Fenn will protect you too, you know.'

'Just bring her safely back to me,' said Marakon to Fenn, and he pushed the boat into the still waters.

Murlonius nodded to Marakon then took his seat and began to row.

Jarlain did not take her eyes off Marakon. *How strange it is that once he left me to return to his home and I thought I'd never see him again. Now I leave him to return to mine. I will see you again, my beloved.* She kissed her hand and held it up. Marakon lifted his own.

'The journey of every life is a beautiful, complex dance. A dazzling vision of movement of the most perfect choreograph,' said Yisufalni. 'We should never be afraid of anything, and yet all of us lose ourselves in the dance of life.'

Jarlain pondered the Ancient's words as Marakon disappeared on the horizon, her arm resting on Fenn's shoulders beside her.

CHAPTER 22

Dark Light

ASAPH'S head swam to the sound of chanting.

Men and women's voices rose and fell in waves that were sickening, monotonous and frightening. He swallowed against the tight metal choker around his neck and tried to open his eyes. Everything was bleary and his head pounded with the after effects of whatever magic spell had hit him.

He tried to move but found his arms had been chained behind his back to a stone wall. Everything was very dark apart from the red glow of a light coming from somewhere ahead of him. He was seated on the cold stone floor, his legs bound in front of him and he was naked, which concerned him deeply. Why would they take his clothes? To both his left and right were the hunched forms of other people also chained and naked.

He blinked trying to focus through the fog. This was more than magic; he had been drugged. His thoughts scattered easily and his body sagged, feeling as if it were made of lead. The chanting made him feel worse. He didn't understand the words but maybe that was because of his befuddled mind. Water would help, he was desperately thirsty.

How had he got here? Where *was* here? *I was in the temple grounds, then the priest came…*

There came a whimper to his right and he realised the dark lump a few feet away was a child. A man coughed further along and there was the sound of a woman crying softly. His vision cleared briefly and in front of him were thick iron bars that reached from floor to ceiling. They were all in one long prison cell that curved around the rough walls and out of sight. He could see at least twenty people to his right and the same to his left. All were chained to the floor.

He must have drifted asleep then for his head jerked up to the sound of metal screeching on stone. The door to the prison was opening, creaking on its rusty hinges. He squinted up at two red-robed people, their faces hidden in their hoods. They weren't looking at him; instead, they grabbed the boy beside him.

The boy moaned as they roughly gripped his skinny arms. From the size of him, he could only have been around eight years old. He began to wail; the awful sound of a doomed animal. Asaph tried to move but his body wouldn't respond. He tried to shout but only mumbling came out over his thick tongue. There came a clap of magic and the boy slumped becoming silent and limp.

Asaph breathed hard as they dragged the boy away. Where were they taking him? He tried to speak but his mouth seemed full of wool. Beyond the bars appeared to be a room that was hidden from view by a stone wall. The room glowed red. He squinted and saw that there were several red-robed men and women clustered together before the room watching something that was out of his sight. *Priests and priestesses,* he thought, *but why are they wearing red robes? Am I somewhere in the basement of the Temple of Carvon?*

They parted to let the two carrying the boy through. The chanting began again and the priests moved out of sight. Asaph shook his head and tried to hum to get rid of the awful droning noise. It didn't help. The chanting rose in pitch and fervour. Asaph's heart pounded harder in response and he began to sweat with fear. Fear was thick here in this goddess-forsaken place.

From the red room there came a scream of absolute terror that drove right into his heart, scoured the walls and made it hard to breathe. He angled his head and tried to see around the corner. A deathly silence descended as the chanting stopped. Even the chained people around him made no sound, no crying or whimpering.

Asaph still couldn't see any priests or priestesses. He released a long held breath, cold sweat trickling down his temples. The smell of terror was rife, even without his dragon form. What was going on behind that wall? Some kind of awful ritual.

Two different red-robed priests—a man and a woman he could see clearer now—stalked from the red room, their cloaks swaying. They opened a prison door further down. Asaph strained his eyes, willing them to focus. They reached down and grabbed an old man. He had a very long, scraggly beard and curling fingernails that hadn't been cut in a long time. A homeless man dragged off the streets, or had he been imprisoned down here for years? The man moaned and shook, clearly drugged, but was unable to fight his captors as they dragged him away.

The chanting began again and, though Asaph didn't want to, he tried to focus on what was being said. *I know those words from the Recollection...it's Dark Dwarven,* he realised. He didn't understand what was said but it made him shiver and his skin crawled.

Another howling scream of terror and pain cut through his thoughts. It went on and on and he wished he could cover his ears with his hands. The scream ended in a sickening gurgling noise and then, again, there was the terrible sound of silence. He thought he could smell blood.

Asaph looked to his left. There was a woman beside him. Her long brown hair covered her face and her nudity as she curled up against the wall. He thought she might be drugged and sleeping but saw she trembled uncontrollably.

'Hey,' he whispered to her. 'What's going on? Let's try and get out.' His voice was hoarse and his tongue didn't work like it should but he managed to get the words out.

She just shook her head slightly and didn't look up.

'Hey,' he tried again.

'It's no use,' whispered a man beyond her. He seemed less drugged and more coherent than the woman. 'Talking will make them pick you next.'

Asaph blinked at him, trying to make out his features but he was too blurry. All he could see was that the man was slim, muscled and maybe of a similar age to Asaph. Something about him seemed familiar, but without focus he couldn't tell much more than that. From the man's position further along the wall, Asaph wondered if he could see into the red room and what was going on.

Asaph dipped his gaze and hung his head when two red-robed

priestesses stalked out of the red room. It seemed shameful but he was in no position to fight just yet. Maybe when the drug had worn off, he would. They opened a prison door opposite and dragged out a girl covered in dirt and grime. The girl hung limp and unmoving.

Was this really happening? Rage grew in Asaph, driving away the fear but making his head pound horribly. The maddening chanting began again and he clenched his fists and ground his teeth. This just couldn't be happening, shouldn't be happening. King Navarr would raze this place to the ground when he got out and told him. *If* he got out. What could he do? He couldn't even stand up!

The chanting stopped. There was no sound. Adult voices came, speaking in angry tones.

'They don't like it when there's no terror,' the man beyond the shivering woman whispered, then hushed and looked down as two priests appeared.

They opened the door closest to Asaph and he thought they were coming for him. He got ready to fight, bunching his muscles. A red-robed priest glanced at him, his dark eyes gleaming, piercing from within his hood. He had a feral, hungry look. Blood smeared his chin and lips.

Asaph curled back his lips and growled. 'Take me you bastard. Let's have some fun.'

'You're not ready to enter the Dark Light yet.' A cruel smile twisted the man's lips.

Asaph strained against his chains, trying to stand, to punch the priest, to do anything. He tried to yell but his voice was broken. The man placed a palm on Asaph's head and pain exploded there. His growl turned into a rasping howl. His head thronged as if a gong had been stuck inside it and he thought his skull would explode. Waves of agony convulsed his body and he slumped.

When Asaph came to, he felt worse than he had ever done in his life, far beyond drinking a gallon of Kuapoh Fire Wine the night before. Thoughts of water filled his mind. His head pounded painfully and he could barely lift it. It was so cold he shivered. His legs and bottom felt frozen to the floor and his whole body was stiff and sore from being in the same position for hours.

Light trickled in from a couple of tiny windows far above them. It looked like daylight. There was no chanting anymore and as he looked around he saw several empty spaces where people had been. The woman next to him had gone, but the man who had spoken was still there. He was curled over to one side and appeared to be sleeping.

The hopelessness of the situation dawned on Asaph. He was underground in a dungeon waiting to be sacrificed to some "Dark Light" and nobody knew he was here. There were many priests and priestesses, some with powerful magic. He was horribly outnumbered.

A cold wind blew from somewhere and his keen dragon senses smelt blood on it. He wrinkled up his nose and shifted, trying to find a comfortable position with the few inches his chains would allow. He found some relief but soon grew sore and had to move again. He tried to lie down but the floor was so cold he sat back up.

Finally, he brought his knees up and rested his head on them. Thoughts of Issa filled his mind. Would she sense what was happening to him? The flame ring she wore linked them and she had come for him when he was trapped in Keteth's prison. But that had been a prison of the soul. He was trapped here body *and* soul. The last thing he wanted was her coming here. The place was protected with magic too, no scryer could penetrate these walls.

How foolish had he been to get himself into this position? Foolhardy and arrogant, he'd been so sure of himself. His ignorance would cost him his life. Again, he'd underestimated the power of Baelthrom. No, this wasn't just Baelthrom, these were ordinary people turning to the darkness for some gain. There had always been people on Maioria willing to turn from the light, willing to hurt and kill others just to gain power and dominion. That they worked for Baelthrom made no difference. They would work for any fallen being who gave them power. They worked for death and darkness itself.

Well, he would not go without a fight, he determined. But he was so weak, could he even fight? He reached for the dragon, feeling for it within him, but it was not there. It must be the magic on this place interfering with his connection. Even the Recollection was too hazy to read. Was Cirosa here? The thought made him sit up straighter. He recalled everything that had happened, fuzzy though it was. No, he hadn't seen her, so perhaps she had left with the Dread Dragons. What about the sword? *Get the sword. Nothing matters, only that I get the sword!* The thought gave him purpose and having that helped to calm the horrible fear that he would die here.

'They've gone, for now. That's how I know it's day,' the man to his left said, shaking him out of his thoughts.

Asaph glanced at him, pleased to hear a human voice rather than the harrowing whimpering of terrified victims. The man was sitting up and staring straight ahead, nerves and fear making him tremble a little but at least his voice was sane and logical. Asaph noticed his own body trembled too, with cold and anger mostly.

The man looked at him. 'They only do the sacrifices at night. Some say they kill twice as many when there are no moons—no goddesses to watch and condemn them.'

Asaph stared at the man, noting his familiar fair hair that was tied back and his body covered in sinewy muscle. Though he was skinny, gaunt and wide-eyed, Asaph was certain he recognised him.

'Leaper?' said Asaph.

The man grinned and smoothed back his hair with a bruised hand. 'Yeah, that's right. I recognised you as soon as they brought you in. A Draxian with that mark on your chest. It's the last thing I saw when you knocked me out.'

Asaph remembered the fight and felt bad. 'Sorry,' he mumbled.

'Hah! Nah, don't worry. Taught me a thing or two. You might not be able to do it again,' Leaper winked.

'How did you get in here?' Asaph couldn't believe they'd been able to take the best fighter in Carvon. From the people he had seen here, they seemed to prey mostly on the weak and vulnerable. Asaph had stupidly given himself up so he could get inside.

'I was a fool, see,' said Leaper. 'Got drunk and fell asleep on a bench. Easy pickings for these vultures. They weren't expecting me to fight though. I killed two of them but then they all descended on me like a pack of wolves streaming out of the shadows. I ripped the throat out of one, snapped the neck of another and took the eye of a third before they took me down.'

The man grinned. In the dim light, Asaph noticed old cuts and bruises covering his face.

'When you're caught, that's it. They'll never let you go, it's too dangerous. My punishment is sitting here for days on end in full view, watching them sacrifice anyone and everyone, especially children.' His face had a strange look to it, bordering on grief and insanity.

'No one talks down here because you get chosen faster. They would rather cling to the last few moments of life they had left. Who can blame 'em, eh? I talk because I want them to pick me, but they never do. They hurt me though and the pain is more than I can bear. That magic makes it seem as if my skin is splitting and turning inside out. What he did to you when he put his hand on your head—well, it gets much worse than that.'

'How long have you been down here?' Asaph dared to ask. He couldn't bear being here another minute.

The man shrugged. 'Hard to say but I think three or four days. That's how I know they don't do sacrifices during the day. People in the temple might hear the screams. Most prisoners only last a day. They want me to suffer but I'm beyond it now. I'm so numb...' He dropped his head and his shoulders shook, though he made no sound.

Asaph had a hundred questions. 'How long has this been going on for? Does the king know?'

'Some says weeks, others say years. Who knows? It seems in the last month or so it's turned a lot worse. There are more red-robes than white now. I wondered where all the tramps in the city had gone. Jeffo disappeared two weeks ago, and he never missed the Monday free meal at The Black Horse.

'Some say people in the king's aide are part of it. I don't think the king knows or has anything to do with it though. I've never seen him down here.'

'What do they want?' Asaph frowned, he couldn't work out what it was all for.

When Leaper looked at him, his face seemed paler. 'Well, from what I see, they take a victim and tie them to the altar there. They do this horrible chanting, it's dark runic or dwarven or something. Then a black spiral opens, like a doorway to another place, a terrible place. Shadows reach out of it, these long hands like this, and touch the victim. Horrible things I can't quite describe but they seem to emanate terror itself. To see them makes me wet myself. It's uncontrollable. When they touch them, they begin screaming.' Leaper swallowed and struggled to contain himself. His voice shook when he spoke again.

'They hold their knives up, little curved sickle-shaped ones, and…you know. Ugh. They start cutting the victim quickly in many places. There is so much blood… it gushes into rivets on the altar and then pours out of little fonts. They catch it in those cups they all carry.

'The priests drink the blood and it gives them some kind of quickening or power. Shadows surround them, auras visible even to the naked eye—I can't use magic. Their faces look beatific for all the horrors they have just committed. I think they feed on the terror of the person. Fear does something to the blood. They feed on that.

'The black vortex bulges and sucks on the writhing victim, not their blood but something else, their life-force maybe. You can see their soul—a beautiful shimmer of light—being dragged into the vortex by the shadows. Then the victim's body, still convulsing, begins to turn black and fragment. It becomes dust that is also sucked into the vortex and then the whole horrible thing just disappears as if it never was.'

Asaph felt sick and fought not to retch.

'Just before you came they changed it though. Oh great goddess, I've heard of 'em but never seen one before. It was massive, this *Dromoorai*. Black armoured and terrifying, though not as bad as the things in the black vortex. At least this beast is solid.

'Well, instead of using their sickle-knives to kill the victim, now they have this Dromoorai with a sword to do the killing blow. They still cut 'em up for the blood letting, but the Dromoorai kills 'em. Why they changed it, I don't know.'

Asaph mind worked hard. 'What does this sword look like?'

'It doesn't look like black iron like the rest of their weapons, no. It's got this blood red pommel and blade that shines almost blue.'

Asaph held his breath, anger rising. He couldn't believe what he was hearing. They were using the Sword of Binding—a symbol of unity and peace—to do unimaginable evil. He said nothing, struggling to comprehend the evil of this place in the heart of Carvon. He wanted to tear it all down and fight them all to the death.

Leaper continued speaking though Asaph barely heard him through his anger. '...Now these sickle-knives, they're shaped funny like crescent moons. We all know the crescent moon is a symbol sacred to the Mother Goddess. I guess they like to use them to kill, to take away the life the goddess gives to us. Twisted bastards.'

'Why children?' Asaph asked quietly.

'They love children the most,' Leaper continued, quite matter-of-factly, though every now and then he trembled. 'All those ones you hear about going missing? Well, they come here. They use tramps and drunks for fun, but it's the children they want most. It's the purity you see. Young children have the purity of innocence. Their terror tastes sweeter. I don't think that vortex and where it goes cares what age the victim is though as it all happens the same. But when the priests drink the blood of children, it's more powerful. Makes me wonder about those awful rumours I heard, that they hold humans captive and breed sacrificial children underground, but I can't be sure of that.'

Quiet rage boiled within Asaph. He fought to control it, readying it for the time he would need it. 'That sword is the Great Sword of Binding. Forged from the blood of Slevina, and the symbol of unity between dragon and man. It marks the birth of the Dragon Lords.'

Leaper looked at him for a long time then nodded slowly. 'I remember the legend. Didn't believe it was real. That's why they use it then. A powerful symbol of good. Well, see, they love to desecrate, foul and despoil all pure, good and true things. It makes what they do more fun, more meaningful. That's why this evil infects those dedicated to the goddess. Turning a pure symbol to evil is part of their dark magic.'

'You know a lot,' said Asaph.

'I've seen a lot these past few days, enough to make me wish I'd never been born. And you don't stay ignorant for long as a fighter on the streets.' He grinned a little, but it didn't reach his eyes. There was pain there instead—a mad, torturous pain Asaph could barely imagine.

Asaph sat in silence for a long time thinking about what was going on here and wondering how on Maioria he was going to get out. It was hard to control his anger just so he could think straight. The sword was here, somewhere, maybe just beyond that wall. Why had they brought it here, to the centre of Carvon of all places? It made no sense. "If you want to hide something, hide it in plain view," so the old saying went. It was not a good saying. It spoke of evil and deceit. What else had been hidden in plain view? Spies and traitors. Even Marakon himself didn't know he carried the eye of Baelthrom.

They would hide the sword here because it is the last place anyone would ever think to look. The city of Carvon, the heart of the lands of the Free Peoples. *And the protective force around this place…No one would have ever felt its presence, certainly not me.* Thank the goddess he had come here when he had. It was a shame he was likely to die here.

Would he be killed by his own sword? The thought made him laugh. Let them try. He only hoped they didn't know he was a Dragon Lord. That Cirosa wasn't here was a huge relief. He doubted he could fight her even just one on one.

Perhaps, when his moment came, he would be able to reach the dragon within. It was a weak hope. He couldn't even feel the dragon sleeping. He thought through all his options, limited as they were, and considered all the outcomes. He hung his head. Was this how he was to die? Was this what Coronos died for? Would everything he had done up until now been for this, been for nothing?

Swallowing against his parched throat, he closed his eyes and leant his head back against the wall. What would Coronos do if he were here? *Coronos Avernayis Dragon Rider, my beloved Father, if you can hear me, help me find a way out of this.*

Slowly, Asaph recited the Fire Sight in his mind, over and again, seeking to reach the solace and guidance Coronos had always taught him to find. Each repetition instilled within him greater calm and clarity. He still had his rage but it was controlled and channelled. Beneath the burning thirst and weakening hunger, the Fire Sight finally brought him the strength that he sought.

CHAPTER 23

Queen Thora

ISSA waited in the anteroom seated upon a red velvet covered chair.

Highly polished dark green marble covered the floor and huge gold-gilded frames housed pictures of richly dressed Royals in seated or standing poses.

The chandelier above was lit by at least twenty candles that cast flickering light everywhere. Domenon hadn't left her seated there long when one of the massive, ornately carved, wooden doors opened and he reappeared.

'The Queen will see you now,' he said.

She smoothed her dragon-scale armour, which she had changed into after dinner, adjusted the raven talisman tucked in her belt and stood.

On the other side of the door was an enormously long chamber, easily large enough to fit several cottages within it. Issa reminded herself not to gawp. The floor was decorated with square blue and red tiles formed in a checkerboard style. Arched windows, like those of the Temples, reached from floor to ceiling all the way to the end of one side—which was almost hazy with distance. The heavy red curtains weren't drawn shut, surprising Issa since it was dark outside.

The biggest fireplace she had ever seen dominated the other wall. If she stood inside it, she doubted she would be able to reach the top. It wasn't lit, which was very strange because there was a definite chill in the air and she'd wished she'd worn her cloak even over her armour.

Giant floor gas-lamps flowed up either side of the room, creating a nice up-lighting effect. Her eyes travelled over to the blue and red marble steps that led up to two large thrones. The dark wood chairs were exquisitely carved with lion paws for feet and lion heads for arm rests.

Only one chair was occupied and Issa's eyes settled on an emotionless, white-faced woman who stared at her without blinking. Her pale face was a stark contrast to the swathes of black she was wrapped in. Black skirts covered her legs, beneath which poked black boots. Her high-necked, long-sleeved tunic was black as was her shawl. She even wore a fine black cowl with three small diamonds above the brow that served to keep her straight black hair back from her face.

'May I present to you Issalena Kammy of Little Kammy. Otherwise known as the Raven Queen,' said Domenon, bowing deeply. The queen made no movement, not even with her eyes. 'I shall leave you, my Queen. Please ring if you require anything else.'

The queen didn't speak as Domenon closed the door quietly behind him. Issa knew she should have felt uncomfortable under the intimidating woman's scrutinising gaze, but she didn't. It was her determination for the mission that made her brave. If anything she felt intrigued by the woman. Seeing the empty throne beside her made Issa feel sorry for the Queen too. Perhaps that was why she wore black and seemed so lifeless. Her beloved King Sott taken by death. She knew all too well what it was like having a loved one linger on in pain for so long and then, when they were gone, nothing. *Bless you, Ma.*

Issa took a step forward, remembered herself, and bowed deeply. She hated curtseying but saw no reason not to show respect.

'I'm sorry about your husband—' she began.

'No, you never knew him, so how can you be?' said the Queen matter-of-factly. Her voice was strong and, despite her words, lacked malice.

Issa checked herself and closed her mouth. The Queen sighed almost imperceptibly and produced from her pocket a thin, fluted black stick. Into this, she placed a shorter, thin brown stick. Issa saw that she wore long, black velvet gloves and on one finger was a gold ring with a bright sparkling ruby.

'I demand honesty,' said the queen. She held what looked like a round ball the size of an egg out of which protuded a silver lever. When clicking the lever, a flame appeared on top of the ball. Issa blinked, she could detect no magic. This device that created fire was some kind of clever mechanics.

The Queen pushed the brown stick into the flame and sucked on the end until it smouldered, just like Bokaard used to do with his cigars only without the extra black stick. It smelt the same as a cigar, only was much thinner.

'Come closer, child,' said the Queen, wafting her smoking stick. 'This is only an Atalanphian cigar and won't hurt you.'

Issa dutifully stepped forwards, suddenly feeling like a child. 'I have an Atalanph friend who also smokes these "cigars" and I quite enjoy that cedar-wood smell.'

Issa paused before the dais and could see the Queen clearly now. She looked to be in her fifties though she was supposed to be past sixty. Despite her grief, she was ageing well. Her dark eyebrows arched over clear brown eyes and her cheekbones were high. She might have been attractive had her hair not been pulled back so tightly and her face not drained of colour. Maybe laughter in her eyes would have made her prettier, but there was none.

'... "When the dark moon rises, nothing will be as it was before. Either we descend into darkness or we will ascend into the light." Do you know of the Prophecies of Zanufey?' asked the Queen lightly, her eyes never leaving Issa's as she twirled her cigar between finger and thumb.

'I have read some of them, Queen Thora. Mostly I choose not to think about them. I don't want to be ruled by something I did not write.'

'Hah!' barked the Queen, her voice echoing in the empty hall. 'Who does, Issalena? Or should I call you Raven Queen? Queen to Queen.'

'Issa is better. I do not presume to rule over ravens—they are my friends,' she said simply.

'You know how to call them and they come when you call?' asked the Queen.

'Yes.'

'Interesting. No one has ever done that before.'

'It's a small thing given what is required to save this world,' Issa shrugged.

The Queen's eyes sparkled with sudden humour. 'And have you come up with ideas to "save this world" when no one else has?'

'I will try, my Queen,' said Issa, lifting her head higher and feeling none of the confidence her words suggested.

'Then please speak.'

Issa nodded. 'You will no doubt have already spoken to Domenon about what I'm about to say... I ask that you let pass through your lands several friendly armies. One of Karalanths from the north and east, dwarves from the north, elves by ship from Myrn, and Atalanphians from the south. There will also be Feylint Halanoi from King Navarr, and mercenaries from Lans Himay—though these details I do not as yet know. There will be several thousand soldiers and warriors. We require them to have safe passage through your lands so that we might rendezvous at your southern ports before heading to Venosia.

'From there we will launch a full-scale attack with the intent to recolonise our lost lands. We would be overjoyed if you joined our armies with your own Davonian soldiers.' Issa finished, surprised at the succinctness of her words. The queen wanted frankness and that was as frank as it came.

The Queen's face remained emotionless as Issa spoke and then she burst into deep, rich laughter that echoed around them. 'My dear girl, if this is true, you have managed to do what no one in the world has done: organise a joint attack beyond simply the Feylint Halanoi. And how will you contain this rabble? Dwarves and Karalanths are bitter enemies, and elves despise everyone. Lans Himay is no friend of ours. A wary truce holds. How can I be sure all these armies won't then turn on us, their host, and take what they want for themselves?'

'I cannot offer any guarantees, my Queen. All I know is that if we do nothing, Baelthrom will soon take Frayon and all will fall.'

'Baelthrom will win sooner, don't you mean?' the Queen said leaning forwards, her eyes hard.

'If I did not have a shred of hope that we could fight this darkness, I wouldn't be standing before you now,' Issa said.

'If we attack now, will we not lose something undefended? North Frayon perhaps?' asked the Queen.

'It is possible, my Queen,' Issa conceded, 'but all the time we defend we are also losing. We must attack to show our strength, harry the enemy, and invade now.' She didn't add that the Karalanths were determined to attack with or without the queen's say, even if it was a suicide mission.

The Queen looked away and rested her chin on her palm. She stared into the middle distance, her cigar trailing a thin line of dense smoke above her. 'We have not been attacked by Maphraxie ships in a year. Peace has improved trade, allowed us to fix our defences and fill our army. I would be a fool to think Davono is still standing because of our might. Davono only stands because Baelthrom has his eyes on Frayon. Everyone knows this but dare not say it. I do not want to organise war, not when my husband...War was Sott's expertise.'

'We are all afraid of war,' said Issa. The queen side-glanced her, looking her up and down as Issa spoke. 'People are more afraid of fighting for their freedom than of living in a world ruled by Baelthrom. They do not realise the Immortal Lord's plan is to drag us into the Dark Rift—even though they see the scar in our night sky growing and coming ever closer. If that is allowed to happen, we will be food for those who live within it, our souls plunged into oblivion. Perhaps, for most, oblivion has become more desirable than the pain of fighting for what is left.'

Issa's own words unnerved her. They were words from the heart and having spoken them, she wished she didn't feel that they were true. Needing to end on a strong note, she said, 'I for one would rather die on the battlefield before I'll ever see that happen.'

'Well said,' the Queen nodded, a new kind of respect growing in her eyes. 'I see now what this Raven Queen is made of. Maybe I'll even begin to believe in her.'

Issa dared to take a single step up the dais closer to the queen. 'Will you do it? Will you allow them passage to your south-eastern shores?'

The queen held her gaze for a long time, searching Issa for truth and the strength to pull this off.

'You are too young to command this war,' the Queen sighed and sunk back into her chair, worrying her sleeve with her free hand. Ash from her cigar fell unnoticed to the floor as the Queen lost herself in her thoughts. 'You will need the very best and experienced commanders at your side.'

Issa's heart sank, feeling that the queen would say no, halt the invasion and risk battles with Karalanths and any others determined to still attack Venosia.

'I have a few already,' she murmured thinking of Asaph, Marakon, Bokaard and the small but growing Knights of the Raven. 'Won't you agree to this, my Queen? Don't you dare to make the first stand against the Immortal Lord?' Issa's voice was barely a whisper.

The Queen gave her a hard look, always measuring her up, working her out. 'All of me wants to say no, war is just too costly and their outcomes uncertain, but always a question niggles my mind: What have we to lose? Baelthrom will not stop, so to not attack is suicide in the same manner that attacking surely is. I just wish it didn't have to be me—to be Davono—doing the attacking. If we fail, Baelthrom's retaliation will be swift and brutal and we will bear the brunt of it.'

'But you will also have more than five armies converging on your lands and a number of knights and mercenaries to boot.' Issa thought of Asaph bringing the dragons but didn't say anything. 'So you'll say yes?'

The Queen pursed her lips, her brown eyes holding Issa's for a long time. 'Yes, but on one condition.' Issa struggled to keep her composure as the queen continued. 'My most trusted advisor, Domenon, will be by your side and you will hold Davono's safety in the forefront of your mind. If you fail, all returning armies will remain on Davono's soil to protect her from retaliation and they do not leave until the mess is sorted. Do I make myself clear?'

'Yes, my Queen,' said Issa, bowing her head dutifully. 'I will die rather than fail.'

'See to it that you don't.' The Queen sighed and looked out of the dark window. 'I will prepare the Davonian army so that they will be ready to leave within the week.'

'Thank you, my Queen.'

The Queen picked up a small bell from the table beside her and rang it. Domenon rather than the butler or guards entered the room.

'We are finished here,' said Thora.

Domenon bowed and beckoned to Issa. Issa bowed slightly to the queen, who stared unseeing at the glowing tip of her cigar, then followed the wizard out.

'You look like you need a drink. I have some of the finest wine in Davono sitting in my library,' Domenon said, folding her hand over his arm.

'I'm rather tired,' said Issa, though the thought of a glass of wine sounded good. 'After that meeting, I guess I could do with relaxing.'

Meeting the Queen, or any royalty for that matter, she always found rather nerve-racking. The Queen's manner and the nature of her request had left her rather wrought.

They took a winding, marble staircase overlaid with red carpet up to another floor and walked along a wide, wood-panelled corridor decorated with paintings of nature. Domenon paused by the door at the end, took out a key and opened it. With an indulgent smile, he spread his arm wide to let her pass through first.

'Your library must be very special to keep it locked,' said Issa, stepping inside.

'Oh yes,' said Domenon, his smile deepening. 'No wizard leaves magical books and artefacts just lying around for the cleaners to meddle with.'

She entered a mid-sized room and stared at the filled to the brim bookcases that lined every wall and, in several rows, reached from floor to ceiling. It certainly was a packed library. A brief scan of the titles showed many to be books of magic, history or science.

'You've read all of these?' asked Issa, open-mouthed. 'There must be thousands of books in here. No one could read this many books and still be alive, it would take a lifetime to read them all.

'Yes, apart from the row in the far corner beside the chaise longue. Those are the books I'm working through,' replied the wizard as he busied himself with a decanter and glasses, placing them on the wine table.

Issa looked at the red velvet chaise longue that had gold legs and was covered in soft-looking cushions. She sank onto it gratefully. Domenon smiled as he passed her a crystal glass full of claret and took the deep chair opposite. He sipped his wine and set it on the small table beside him.

'I suppose you want me to tell you what I talked about with the Queen,' Issa said sipping her wine. It was deliciously smooth and she felt herself instantly relaxing, despite being in Domenon's presence.

'No. Queen Thora will tell me later if she wishes. And she usually does,' he replied.

'Well, she agreed to allow the armies through her lands and add to it with her own soldiers. Tomorrow I will scry for Freydel and all wizards and seers—' Issa paused as Domenon cut her off.

'You will not be able to scry for anyone whilst within Castle Rebben. Only I am able to reach beyond the protective wards placed here by myself and only from within this room. It is for the protection of the Queen and the whole of Davono. After what happened to you in Teramides, I'm sure you can understand.'

Issa's initial scowl softened and she nodded slowly. She took several sips of her wine thinking on that. She'd wondered why she couldn't scry earlier nor even project her thoughts to Asaph to feel for where he was. Of course, protecting the queen and thus the kingdom was a priority for her key advisor and protector. Issa was foolish to think otherwise.

'I see that Queen Thora is very thorough, which can only be a good thing,' she said.

'*Very* thorough,' agreed Domenon. 'If you so much as touch the Flow, I will feel it.' There was a glitter in his eyes that wasn't menacing but proved that he meant what he said.

'I only use magic to do good,' she said, jutting her chin and meaning it as a challenge.

'Then that is all right,' Domenon smiled, not rising to it.

He reached for the wine bottle and topped up first her glass, then his. Setting the bottle down, he pulled out of his pocket a small black rock that shimmered with gold and silver specks. She breathed in. It was just like her raven talisman, the trilithon in the desert and some of the standing stones around the star portal. One side was smooth and polished but the rest was rough and jagged.

'Where did you get that?' she asked, wide-eyed.

'I see you recognise it,' he said and smiled, turning the rock over in his hand.

'You broke it off the sacred mound?' The thought was sacrilege.

'Not exactly. You think so little of me,' Domenon sighed. 'There was a storm several years ago. It was really quite epic and lightening even flared erratically against Myrn's protective shield. We can't be sure but we think it was Baelthrom's doing. The ground shook too, and one of the stones surrounding the sacred mound suffered when a tree fell on it. A piece was shorn off. This piece.' He tossed it to her and she struggled to catch it without spilling her wine.

She held it in her hand. It was the same stone as her talisman, its depths filled with beautiful stars.

'Farla in ah iot issalena,' Domenon spoke in a flowing foreign language.

She blinked and looked up at him. There was an enigmatic smile on his face.

'What did you say?' She frowned, there was something about those words she should know.

'Farla in ah iot issalena. Yissen en ah Sharafeya,' Domenon said easily, clearly understanding the strange language he spoke.

The words moved Issa and she stared at the wizard spellbound. The language was flowing and smooth, almost Elven in its sound but with less melody.

'I said,' Domenon leant forwards, his eyes sparkling. '… "Lady of the blue moonlight. Blessed by the Goddess.". It is Tusarzan. A beautiful language that is sadly lost like many others.

'You speak Tusarzan?' Issa asked.

'I speak most languages, even dead ones,' said Domenon.

'But it's ancient,' said Issa, wondering again how old Domenon was.

'Indeed. I am a voracious reader and an adept and fast learner,' said the wizard.

Issa felt uneducated and ignorant. The man knew more about her ancestral home than she did.

'I have books on it if you would like to read them and learn a little of your ancient language,' he said.

'What's the point in learning a dead language?'

Domenon laughed. 'Ah, the impatience of humans. Life is just too short for them.'

'You're human too, remember,' she scowled. 'There isn't any point lounging around learning dead languages when the planet is about to be destroyed, now is there?'

Domenon looked away and took a sip of his wine.

'There is power in words, and in every language,' he finally said, looking at her and folding a hand over his knee. 'You might find greater meaning to things when expressed in another language. Words *are* power.

Words control the Flow. Many of the spells wizards use are from dead languages, but the power remains.'

Issa felt even more ignorant as the wizard spoke.

'If you became my pupil, I could teach you many of these things,' said Domenon.

'You would teach me?' The thought excited her but then she realised Freydel wouldn't like it. Was that why Domenon was offering?

'Of course I would,' said the wizard. 'I will teach any with the ability and desire to learn.'

Issa stared down at the rock in her hand, working through her feelings. 'There isn't enough time. And besides, I don't think my calling is a wizard's calling.'

'Ah sena vey iot ena ah un drens phelan,' said Domenon.

Issa felt magic move and looked up at the wizard quizzically.

'..."The stone glows blue for the one who's true,"' said Domenon. 'Look.' He gestured to the stone in her hands with a grin.

Issa gasped. The stone was glowing blue; a beautiful, soft indigo aura sparkling with life.

'The stone is from Aralansia,' she breathed, tears filling her eyes.

The indigo colour suddenly spread over her arms like cool silk sliding over her skin. 'What is happening?' she gasped.

There was surprise on Domenon's face, and he perched himself on the edge of his seat. She sensed he was in the Flow.

Over her shoulders and face the blue spread, soothing and pure, calming the overwhelming emotions she suddenly felt. The blue cooled her cheeks that the wine had made red and she blinked back the tears for the destroyed planet and its people.

'This is most interesting,' whispered Domenon. 'Ancient seer scripture recorded an inscription on an even more ancient temple in Tusarza where a sparkling stone was kept. Both stone and temple were long ago destroyed. "Ah sena vey iot ena ah un drens phelan," is what it read. I have thought about it often. When I saw you with the raven talisman, I knew it was made of the same stone. I do not know what it means, but I know that your name means "moonlight," and I had a thought to try it. So tell me then, Moonlight, all about this Aralansia you seem to know about.'

Issa swallowed, realising she had put her foot in it. She set the stone on the table and watched as the blue faded away. Taking a sip of wine, she quickly set her glass down, suddenly realising she had almost drunk a second glass and it was going straight to her head.

'We can take time,' Domenon smiled. 'The night is early still.'

He seemed a little blurry in her vision but still handsome with his black hair and strong, chiselled features. Issa felt embarrassed for noticing these things. *I'm just tipsy, that is all.*

'It was just a place I saw in a vision once,' she tried to dismiss it.

'It sounds more than that,' Domenon said. 'Has anyone else seen this place?'

'Well, yes. Freydel,' she said, then cursed herself for blurting it out. Freydel had told her not to talk about this until he had spoken to the Wizards' Circle about his inter-dimensional time travelling. *But why hasn't he talked to the wizards about Ayeth and Baelthrom yet? It is of utmost importance. He probably wasn't ever going to,* Issa thought suspiciously. *Perhaps Domenon should know, but then again his story isn't mine to tell and Domenon is not a good or safe person to confide in.*

'Oh really?' the wizard said conversationally. 'So how did you both see this place if it was just a vision for you?'

'Well, he used his orb.' Issa tried to stop herself from speaking but it came out anyway. 'Hmm, I think I'm overtired and should go to bed. My tongue sometimes gets the better of me and I can talk nonsense after a wine.' Her voice was slightly slurred too. She began to worry.

Maybe Domenon spotted this too for he said, 'Well there's nothing to be concerned about here, in Queen Thora's castle. We're very safe and just chatting. But on the contrary, I think you need to relax a bit more,' said the wizard. He filled his glass then stood to reach hers.

'No—' she tried to protest but he insisted.

'Nonsense. You are a guest in my house and I promised myself to lavish you with the finest wine Davono can offer. You'll not find this quality anywhere else. You cannot turn down the best host in the land.'

He smiled and sat down next to her on the chaise longue. Perhaps this was his way of apologising for his roughness over Orphinius. He held his glass up and, with a defeated sigh, she picked hers up and they chinked glasses. It certainly was the most delicious wine she had ever tasted, if a little strong, and it would be rude to turn down her host. His eyes never left hers as she sipped.

He set his glass down. 'Now then, tell me some more. Maybe these stones all come from this place called Aralansia. Like the lettering marking the top of this sacred mound?'

'Yes,' said Issa, surprised. 'You've been to the sacred mound, or star portal as some call it?'

'I found it once a long time ago but I could not enter,' said Domenon, further shocking Issa. She thought only witches and seers ever found the star portal, and only women at that. But then again the portal was there for anyone able to find it.

'Did Freydel manage to enter?' Domenon repeated the question.

'Um, no, I don't know. He never mentioned the portal. But he went to Aralansia using his orb when he was trying to escape Baelthrom. It was all unintentional. Somehow, he travelled back in time. When he got there he met Ayeth—the being that will become Baelthrom.'

Issa found her tongue working even when she tried to stop it. Domenon's questions were so perfectly directed she found she could not deny him anything. Even when she wanted to hold back she couldn't. The wine dampened the panic as she spoke and she soon found herself finishing the third glass. Domenon continued to ask her questions and the answers flowed easily out of her mouth.

The wine was relaxing but with it came tiredness. At one point she suddenly felt her head drooping onto Domenon's shoulder. She lifted back in embarrassment.

'Sorry,' she mumbled, noting how slurred her words had become.

'On the contrary,' he said, and placed a supportive arm around her shoulders, making her blush.

She realised how close together they sat on the chair now, so close that even their thighs were touching. Domenon seemed not to notice at all. She suddenly felt very hot, most probably from the wine, and loosened the neck of her armour wishing she had changed into her lighter seer's robes. Domenon had already taken off his tunic and rolled up his shirtsleeves.

'So, Freydel has met this Ayeth, and he hopes to somehow stop him becoming the monster Baelthrom. Very interesting.' He topped up Issa's glass and she felt herself swaying. She wanted to slump back on the chair but Domenon held her close, supporting her. He didn't seem to want to let her, but why? Her thoughts were scrambled and vacant.

'I know you're tired, I am too, but I'd love for you to tell me all about what Sheyengetha said to you, especially about your parents,' said Domenon. His smile filled her vision and his face was very close, sometimes coming into focus so she stared into his dark grey eyes and then his features would blur. 'You see, I'm certain I'd remember your parents if only I knew a little more. You'd like me to remember who they were, wouldn't you?'

Issa found herself nodding and then her head sank onto his shoulder. A cool strong hand gently lifted her chin and held it.

'Just a little more talk, then we can all go to sleep,' he said, his breath brushing her cheek.

She nodded and felt herself slumping even more against him. All she wanted to do was lie down. Domenon's presence beside her was equally intoxicating and she found herself wondering what it would be like to kiss his lips.

'My parentss casst a Web of Forgetting to protect all of Myrn,' she began. She no longer cared what she said. Domenon was simply asking polite questions and there was no reason not to answer them. Not to speak would be rude, especially when he was being so nice to her.

'They knew it wass wrong but they did it to protect me and all of Myrn from Baelthrom. Then they fled sso no one would ever remember them or where they had gone.'

She finished telling him everything she knew about her parents that Sheyengetha had told her.

'Thank you, Issa,' Domenon said, smiling deeply. He held her cheek and lightly kissed her forehead.

'I shhhouldn't,' she slurred, now struggling to speak at all but too wine-filled to feel any panic. 'Asssaph wouldn't be happy,' she said then wondered why she was talking about Asaph at all. He wasn't here. She felt very confused.

'And what about Asaph?' asked Domenon keeping his face close and his hand on her cheek, half supporting her head. 'What is he planning?'

'He hass gone to get the Ssword of Binding. With it he will awaken the dragonss,' she sighed.

'I don't think he will do that,' said Domenon coming closer. 'It would be too dangerous.' His lips almost brushed hers.

She nodded. 'It'ss too dangerouss.'

'Just a kiss,' Domenon whispered. 'It won't hurt anyone.'

Issa nodded. Who could it hurt? Domenon's other arm wrapped around her waist pulling her close against him. She was glad he did because she found she could no longer support herself at all.

His lips brushed hers and she tingled all over. Was there magic in his kiss? He kissed her fully, his lips soft and then firm, gentle but dominating. She found herself swimming in a strange desire, completely at his mercy. She tried to look into his eyes but all she saw were swirls of grey and something blue forming in the swirls.

He released her lips and she gasped as he kissed her neck, each kiss making her tingle. When he kissed her lips again, she stared into his eyes and saw the same ice-blue dragon she had seen when she almost drowned in the bath. Everything swirled around her and she lost herself in the dizziness.

CHAPTER 24

Sacrifice

AS the daylight faded, the prison cells grew totally black.

The darkness didn't last for long—soon an ominous red glow bloomed in the chamber beyond the wall. Asaph could hear voices murmuring and imagined the repulsive priesthood in their red robes gleefully gathering for the evening's atrocities.

Leaper didn't even look up and stayed with his head bowed onto his knees, eyes staring behind into nothing. He seemed depressed and broken. Asaph fought against the despair. The sword was here; just knowing that gave him some strength.

The despised chanting began. The rage grew in the pit of Asaph's stomach and he held it there, honing it. In his head he sang the Fire Sight over and again, protecting his mind with it from their awful dark dwarven words.

He willed for them to take him, but the first victim was a child from the furthest part of the cell. The young boy screamed and wailed all the way. Asaph shouted but quickly found his temples pounding and his throat closing as dark magic subdued him.

Tears streamed down Asaph's cheeks. The absolute helplessness of the child and his inability to do anything were crushing. He focused on both his anger and the Fire Sight, pretending the chanting wasn't there, pretending the child's wailing was just the wind howling. Now he knew what was happening it was ten times worse. He could feel the black magic of the priests, the vortex, the evil beings that came out of it all around him, even though he couldn't see them.

He glanced at Leaper. The man still had his head on his knees but it was turned fully away so he couldn't witness anything. A subtle tremble of his shoulders told Asaph he was awake.

Asaph took a deep shaking breath when the screams ended and he murmured the Fire Sight out loud, praying to Feygriene to shine her light on this dark evil place. When the robed priests appeared, their hoods covering their faces, their sickle knives swinging from cords at their waists, he said it even louder. They paused, pointed at him and turned to his cell. His door opened with a great screech.

Asaph grinned up at them, defiant, the rage boiling within him. They smiled, almost tenderly as if he were a poor sick child, their lips stained red. Cold hands gripped his bare shoulder and he shook them off, ready to fight. They grabbed him roughly and dragged him up. He tried to head butt or ram his shoulder into them but his body sagged, he was too weak and slow and the priests were horribly strong.

The rage within him faltered and fear began to gnaw at him. Their magic had made him weak as a child. He doubted he could stand or lift his arms even if they hadn't been bound. He couldn't walk since his feet were tied and so they dragged him along the floor. His knees scraped along the stone and he soon felt blood.

He glanced at Leaper. The man was staring wide-eyed, reflecting the terror he'd dare not allow himself to feel. Asaph winked at him wanting to say he'd figure something out, but only a strange mumble came out. He had never felt at the mercy of something before and nothing he had experienced had ever been more terrifying.

Asaph stared ahead of him. The chamber they dragged him into was smooth and circular with a high, plain-domed ceiling. Lanterns stood around the edges and they burned a strange dark red, casting everything with a red glow. Red for blood, he assumed. Was this the Mother's Chamber? Had the once most sacred place of the Temple to the Goddess now been turned to evil?

There were so many robed priests and priestesses present that his befuddled mind couldn't count them all. At a guess, there were around thirty faceless people robed in red, hands clasped in front or behind their backs, all eagerly watching him with faces that were utterly pitiless. He wondered if the Oracle or Cirosa were amongst them. Cirosa would recognise him if she were there. If he told them he was a Dragon Lord, they would spare him—spare him for some other evil. *I will die here rather than become a Dromoorai!*

In the centre was a man-sized grey stone altar. It was covered in blood from the previous victim. Thin channels snaked over it all joining up to lead to one spout at the end where blood still dripped. Asaph retched, but his stomach was so empty nothing came up. Instead, his body convulsed. Their chuckles of amusement made him growl and struggle weakly. Two more priests grabbed his legs and he was swung into the air and dumped on the stone slab, almost winded. The child's blood was still horribly warm beneath him and he tried to arch his back away from it, tears filling his eyes.

He kicked out his legs sending a priest flying into the others. A fist smashed into his face as three more grabbed him and roughly tied him down. More priests loomed beside him, raining blows upon his face and head until his senses spun. Unable to fight, he had to take it. His lip split against his teeth and he coughed and snorted blood from his nose.

As the beating abated, he realised the constant growling he could hear was coming from his own throat.

The priesthood clustered close and the chanting began. Asaph strained and fought against the bindings with all the strength he could muster. The rope tying his right hand snapped. He lunged up, grabbing the throat of the nearest priest through his hood. The rage boiled up, and he gripped with all his might, crushing, yanking, shaking and growling. The priest's eyes bulged and rolled back. Asaph yanked downwards with all that he had, feeling flesh tear and warm blood flow over his hand. He became aware of savage blows pummelling on his body and head as priests and priestesses tried to pry his grip off, but it was too late. The priest crumpled to the floor, dead.

A palm struck Asaph's forehead. Immense agony flowed first through his brain and then his entire body. He arched his back and screamed. The pain flowed through him in a series of never-ending waves. He felt his bones bending from the agony of it.

After an interminable amount of time, the pain receded. Asaph shook and gasped, sweat rolling off his body, stinging the cuts and bruises that covered him. They tied him back down again and he could find no strength to fight them. His eyes were swelling from the beating, making everything fuzzy.

He felt a mind before him, a familiar, twisted, dead mind. *Dead brethren.* He peered through the bleariness at the huge Dromoorai now standing at his feet. The Dromoorai's eyes blazed red as it held the Sword of Binding, point downwards, in its gauntleted fists.

Asaph took great breaths as he stared at the sword. Its dragon blood pommel glowed even deeper and darker in the red light, the silver-blue sheen of the blade almost shimmering with its own aura. *Help me!* He screamed in his mind at it. The sword had called to him to save it, now it could help him, surely?

The chanting crescendoed. Asaph's eyes were forced from the sword to the spinning black hole appearing several feet above the Dromoorai's head; a dense black shadow that was darkness itself. It was opening to another dimension—his dragon self could sense that much.

"Like ravens, dragons, too, can travel to other dimensions," Coronos had said to him one night in Castle Carvon. As soon as he had said it, the Recollection had opened in his mind and he knew it to be true, though he didn't know how it was done. Just as they could go to the Dragon Dream, dragons could also travel to the Murk, though none ever did. They could even go to the Land of Mists, if invited, and to any fairy world, if they knew where the entrance was.

He had longed to try such travel, but now he stared into that spinning hole above him he wanted nothing to do with other dimensions. *It leads to the Dark Rift,* the dragon part of him whispered. All of these sacrifices fed whatever was in the Dark Rift. In exchange, power would be given to the priesthood. Evil power.

Shadows flowed out of the centre of the spinning vortex in long, indistinct blobs. Asaph swallowed the rising panic, determined to show no fear. The sword would do something, it had to. If he didn't survive, it would be trapped here forever. He was its only hope.

The Dromoorai turned and walked from Asaph's feet to stand on his right. It raised the sword up, its point hovering without wavering above his chest. After hundreds of years locked away, it still looked wickedly sharp. How funny it seemed that he would be killed by his own sword, by his own kind.

He spat at the Dromoorai. It did nothing. Its eyes simply continued to blaze that awful red. For the first time, Asaph realised the Shadow Stone amulet on its chest was not burning brightly. Was Baelthrom not watching this? Oddly, if he had been, Asaph might have been recognised, he might have been spared. *Not even the Immortal Lord can save me,* he thought bitterly. Why wasn't Baelthrom watching? Perhaps he had grown bored with these sacrifices. Perhaps they were just too unimportant.

The chanting rose to deafening levels making him feel woozy. He suspected the Under Flow was surging all around him and was thankful he couldn't feel or see the black magic directly. The shadow blobs came closer, growing and elongating. A cold wind blew right through his soul, making goose-bumps rise and his body shiver. Never ceasing their chanting, the priests and priestesses drew their sickle knives. They gleamed in the same manner that their eyes gleamed within their hoods— hungry and bloodthirsty.

Asaph began to struggle; but he was bound so tightly he could barely move an inch. A shadow hand reached for him and brushed against his chest. Deathly cold stole through him making him gasp. A piece of his soul drained away; a piece of vital energy. He instinctively panicked and fought violently, his mind scrambling to remember the words of the Fire Sight.

'I thought you dumbed him?' hissed a priestess.

'I did. This one is different. Stronger,' said a priest.

'We can't do it again now, it would interfere with the Dark Rift connection,' hissed another priestess licking her lips. 'Just get on with it. Kill him as we cut him, the blood will still flow.'

A knife plunged deep into his ankle and he screamed and bucked, feeling the binding come loose under a spurt of slippery blood. Another dark shadow passed a hand across his stomach. Daggers of ice filled his belly and he tried to double up with the pain even as hot blood flowed freely from his foot.

The one who had cut him was desperately trying to catch it in her cup as he kicked and thrashed. Too desperate to wait, she gulped whatever she had got. Her eyes widened as if she'd discovered something about him through the drinking of his blood. He kicked again, snapping the bindings that held that foot.

'He's a dra—' she began, but Asaph smashed his foot into her chin, whipping her head back with a sickening crack. She crumpled, her cup of his blood spilling over her.

'Kill him now,' screamed a priestess, commanding the Dromoorai who had remained motionless beside him. In response, it lifted the sword higher and brought it down hard. Asaph had no chance to move or free his arms. The sword glinted, moving in terrifying slow motion as it descended.

The point pierced his flame mark.

He didn't feel any pain. Instead, a cold rage flooded through his body filling him with the strength of ten men. Rage came directly from the sword and mingled with his own fury. The Recollection burst open—but it was far more than that. The lives of all dragons and Dragon Lords entered Asaph's mind, poured into his spirit, all at once, as though the entire Recollection was being fully installed into him in a single moment. It filled his heart, his blood, his mind, and his soul.

He reached into the Recollection and called out to the minds of those dragons still upon Maioria. The calling was involuntary; it came straight from his soul and was filled with all the power of the great Sword of Binding.

Asaph was suspended in time as the sword embedded in his flame mark and the Recollection filled his mind. The sword went no deeper into his body despite the entire might of the Dromoorai pushing down on it. In this state, Asaph could see and feel magic, and the Under Flow filled the room and flowed out of the vortex.

'Dawn Bringer,' a female voice whispered, the words reverberating around him.

Feygriene filled him. Golden light burst from his hands and then his entire body, surging up and surrounding the sword. The golden light turned to golden flames and engulfed the darkness of the Under Flow. Brighter flames burned directly from his body as if he were the sun. The feeding shadows fled back into the vortex. The golden flames followed them, illuminating the dark, and Asaph glimpsed briefly into the place from where they had come. In his expanded state, he didn't so much see as feel what was there.

There were beings and worlds, many of them, but each was wrong and twisted. Distorted consciousnesses fed remorselessly upon each other—like the priests and priestesses around him fed upon their own, even children, with no feeling. Hopelessness, vengeance, hate and rage filled that place—a place of no redemption. The One Source of All was far away, and no benevolent god or goddess trod there.

Asaph did not belong. Repulsed, he pulled away. He never wished to see that place again. *That is what will become of Maioria if we fail.*

He glanced at the priests and priestesses surrounding him, each momentarily frozen in time so that not even their robes moved. *Lost and fallen. This barbarism and evil is what will become of us all if we fail. Evil will spread through us and turn us against each other until we consume ourselves.*

The vortex flared and snapped shut. Time was still frozen. Asaph flexed his arms and legs, snapping the bindings as if they were made of paper. He pushed his chest up against the sword, forcing the Dromoorai which was still pressing down on it, back.

'My own sword cannot kill me!' he roared.

Knocking the tip aside, he ripped it from the Dromoorai's grasp. The hilt fit his palm perfectly, filling him with a sense of completion. He closed his eyes and took a deep breath, feeling the power of the sword. With his eyes closed he swung it with all his might. It clanged against the Dromoorai's metal helmet, passing through as if it were made of card.

He opened his eyes in time to see the blade slide through thick black iron leaving a thin red line of heat where it sliced. It eased through a red eye that flickered and went dark, through the nose-bridge and then cheek, the sound of metal scouring metal only just reaching him. The metal on the other side of the helmet bent outwards as his blade exited. Watery black blood spewed. The top of the Dromoorai's head slid sideways and then fell, slamming to the floor. Its body toppled and the dismembered thing writhed and screamed furiously, the noise shaking the walls, and then it was dead.

Time sped up. The priests and priestesses fell back from him, looks of horror spreading on their bloodstained faces now illuminated by his light. They turned to run, like the true cowards they were, feeding on the weak and innocent. Their time was over. Asaph had to act fast, he could not let them get away; not with their crimes nor with the knowledge of what he was.

He called the Sun Fire within him and let it explode through the tip of his sword. Golden flames burst from it all around him, striking every priest and priestess, even those furthest away by the exit. The light consumed them and their screams were deafening. They did not so much burn as become engulfed in the golden light which turned their bodies to dust and winked them from existence.

Silence fell. The Sun Fire within him withdrew. The sword, which he realised had been throbbing the whole time, stilled. Calm descended. Justice had occurred. Prophecy had been fulfilled. The sword had found its master and was bound to him. He was complete. The Recollection receded and he felt a thousand dragons yawn and stretch before it closed fully.

Asaph rolled back his shoulders, lowered his sword, and realised he was naked. He glanced back at Leaper, the only one who would have seen it all. There was a look of awe and incredulity on the man's face.

'No one touches this sword but me,' said Asaph, struggling to find the words to explain something he felt was very complicated.

Leaper nodded, gulped, closed and then reopened his mouth. 'Anything you s-say. Uh, l-look, your c-cuts have h-healed,' he stammered.

Asaph looked down. Sure enough, his foot, though covered in blood, was no longer bleeding and didn't hurt. His bloodied chest, where the sword had pierced, was healed and painless. *The Sun Fire, what was that?* He tried to remember how he had called it but his mind was blank. He still couldn't use magic in his human form. Perhaps it had been Feygriene.

People moaning caught his attention. Leaper's face was pale and he held his head in his hands as if he were too weak to hold it up without the help. The others were listless, hunched. Not one of them dared to look his way even though the sacrificers were gone. *Drugged and close to death,* Asaph thought. He had to help them. Not knowing what else to do, he hunted around for some water.

Near one of the exit tunnels that led into darkness, there was a large pail of water along with rows of white priesthood robes hanging up. He stared at the robes. So they got changed down here to hide what they were doing. All of the priests and priestesses had been adults, yet the Order of the Goddess took in novices of all ages, even children. Not everyone could be part of the disgusting sacrificial rites, maybe only a select few corrupt people were.

He slipped on a white robe and picked up the pail, struggling under its weight with increasing fatigue. He set it down in front of Leaper's cell. Metal sacrificial cups were strewn around the chamber, discarded in the fleeing priesthood's terror. Grabbing one, he rinsed out the blood in disgust then tried the water. It tasted fine. Forcing himself to trust it, he downed a cup, then hunted around for some keys—there had to be some somewhere.

Kicking at the piles of ash on the floor, all that remained of a priest or priestess after his Sun Fire, his foot clanged against a ring of black keys. Grimacing, he picked them out of the ash, along with a sickle knife, and opened Leaper's cell. Even after Asaph released his chains and bindings, the man couldn't stand on his own so Asaph passed him cups of water. It was awful to see such a fighter in this pitiful state. Leaper gulped down the water then pushed the cup away.

'Make sure everyone gets some,' he said, leaning his head back, his voice stronger.

Asaph unlocked the other prison doors and helped the people, giving them white robes and cups of water. There were twenty people in all, men, women and children of all ages, and he had to get them out.

Even after water, only a young woman and middle-aged man were able to stand, but the others and all seven children were far too weak. They huddled against each other, trembling, too traumatised to speak. What if more sacrificers came? What if there were other sacrificial chambers beyond this one? Where were the harpies who had come with the Dromoorai, and when would the Dromoorai's Dread Dragon return? *It would have felt the death of its rider.*

Asaph didn't like any of these questions. He licked his lips nervously. From what he had seen outside, the temple guard were involved, or at least ordered to guard the temple against any outsiders. Whether they knew what was going on inside was another matter.

He turned to the man and woman who were able to stand. The woman's face was bruised and she had trouble meeting his eyes as she clutched at the neck of her robe. The man leant against the wall rubbing his eyes.

'Collect all the sickle knives and any weapons you can find, give them out to everyone.' Hopefully a task would keep their minds busy. 'Leaper, take the Dromoorai's sword. I'll go scout the place to find a way out. I won't go far but do what you can to protect yourselves should you need to.'

Grabbing one of the red lanterns, Asaph turned away and walked towards a tunnel that led to a solid wall. It must be a hidden door like the one the priestess had opened on the outside of the temple, but without magic, he couldn't open it. He turned and went back.

Beyond the chamber where the robes had been hanging up, another tunnel stretched into the darkness. He made his way slowly along it using the light of the red lantern that glistened off the slick walls. It led a long way. There might have been other magical doors, but if there were, he couldn't tell. From the length of this tunnel, he assumed there certainly would be.

As he walked, he decided he must have left the grounds of the temple by now. There would certainly be secret passageways into the temple itself, wouldn't there? Surely walking blindly along a tunnel created by the enemy was stupid. He slowed, wondering what to do. He didn't want to leave the others on their own. Although he was weak from hunger, he was the only one still able to put up a fight.

It was with some surprise that he came to a door on his left. It was simple, made of old planks roughly nailed together, like the door of a farmer's shed, with a plain iron handle and a wooden bolt across it. It certainly wasn't strong enough to keep prisoners inside.

He held his ear against it. There was no sound. Tucking his sword inside his robe, he pulled up his hood to cover his face and knocked, his heart pounding in his chest. Nothing happened. He knocked again. Nothing. Carefully, he lifted the bolt and turned the handle. It wouldn't budge. Either it was very stiff or locked on the other side.

After a few seconds pause for thought, Asaph took a step back then threw his shoulder against it. The old door groaned and splintered under his weight. He fell through it into a room lit by a shard of light falling from the ceiling high above. Coughing in the dust he looked up at the eddies swirling in the light. Desperate for some form of normality, Asaph imagined it to be the light of day. Somewhere up there was a world lit by the sun.

Groaning and the sound of rattling chains came from somewhere out of his sight. Asaph froze, peering into the gloom. Slowly, he held the lantern up into the darkness and gasped. The room he was in was square and not that big. One wall was empty, but chained around the others were nine naked men. Their arms were tied above their heads to the wall and their feet to the floor. They hung limply on their chains, their heads flopping forwards through their arms. They were anything from twenty to fifty years old, fit, and of fighting age.

Two made slight groaning noises, but the rest were silent. For a horrible moment, Asaph's eyes rested on a man who looked completely grey. He went closer, lifting the lantern up. The man had a chiselled jaw and straight nose and would have been handsome under other circumstances.

Tentatively, Asaph lifted the man's deathly cold chin. His eye sockets were empty holes covered in gouges and dried blood. With a horrified yelp, Asaph dropped the man's chin. Mercifully, he was dead.

He looked around, glad to note that the others weren't grey—bruised and bloodied, yes, but not dead. Not yet. All had a raw, swollen mark branded on their chests. *Three mountains; the mark of Maphrax.* They were drugged and weak, just like he had been. He saw something on the floor and reached down to pick up a long, slick, brown feather—too big to belong to any bird. *Harpies!* He dropped it in disgust.

'Wake up!' Asaph commanded.

Two of the men groaned and lifted their heads. He ran to the first and struck his sword upon the chains. Sparks illuminated the chamber as the manacles splintered. Asaph caught the man as he fell and helped him to the floor where he lay moaning. He struck the chains from his feet then went to help the other man.

The second man had more life and blinked up at Asaph as he lay him down. Perhaps he was newer here. His head was shaved—all the men's heads were—and though he was bruised, his toned body was clean and there was a subtle scent on him. *Prepared for harpies,* Asaph grimaced.

'What's going on here?' Asaph asked, cradling the man's head. His eyes were glazed and he struggled to focus.

'Harpies,' the man said. 'They've drained our blood to give to the Maphraxies and make us weak. With their magic, they've raped our seed.'

Asaph felt sick, made worse in his famished state.

'What's your name?' asked Asaph.

'Danny.'

Hearing human voices, two more men stirred. They tried to lift their lolling heads as Asaph rose and sliced his sword through their chains in another shower of sparks, again amazed that no metal could withstand the blade of the Sword of Binding. By the time he had helped them to the floor, the first two men were on their knees and trying to stand.

'How do we get out?' asked Asaph.

Danny shook his head. 'I woke up here, I don't remember how I got here. In the beginning, I saw dark dwarves. I think they made the tunnels. The harpies use magic to make us forget who we are. When they return, they use magic to open the wall. I think they come from somewhere else outside of Frayon, but I don't know for sure.'

'Come, I can take you to clean water,' said Asaph. 'There are others here who were to be sacrificed; women and children too. I was amongst them but got free and killed all the priests and priestesses. When others find out, we'll all be killed. The temple guard are patrolling everywhere above ground, but we have a chance to escape in daylight. Are there any more rooms like this, with people trapped?'

'I don't know.' Danny shook his head. 'But the harpies will return when the light fades. Two will die this very night when they have finished with them. They always leave one of the dead chained here to remind us who owns us. In the end, we will all die.'

Asaph had no idea how much daylight was left so they had to get out now. He stood and cut the chains of the dead man, laying his body down respectfully.

'Why did they do that to his eyes?' Asaph asked, flinching back from the man's bloody, sunken lids.

'When they can't give them their seed, the harpies take their eyes,' said Danny, closing his own and swallowing.

'It's frenzied, the worst thing I have ever seen,' said the other man in a cracked voice. 'But it doesn't happen very often, this inability to perform. Harpy magic is powerful.'

Asaph took a deep breath. How many men had been sacrificed here when they could be fighting alongside the Feylint Halanoi? No wonder the army was dwindling.

'Let's go back to the others,' he said, breathing hard against his rage. 'We're safer in numbers. Help me carry them. We'll have to return for those who can't walk.' He indicated to the other two men who were getting to their knees.

'I'm Asaph,' he introduced himself.

'Jekk,' said the second man, taking Asaph's hand as he helped him to his feet.

Jekk and Danny moved to the others. One of the men was well over six feet tall and covered in muscle, so Asaph helped Danny lift him, dragging an arm each over their shoulders. Jekk helped the smaller man but all of them struggled.

'Go right,' Asaph instructed as Jekk paused to peer outside the door. He passed him their only lantern.

A low humming noise began.

'Oh no, the wall!' Danny wailed. 'Harpies are returning.'

Asaph glanced behind them. On the wall about waist height, an apple-sized ball of white and black light swirled and rapidly grew.

'Let's go,' Asaph growled and hurried forwards. 'Take him if you can. I'll try to get another.' He let Danny take the big man who was becoming more responsive and trying to take his own weight.

'Go!' he yelled when Danny paused. The man staggered after Jekk.

Asaph bent to help another man. He was lifeless and Asaph struggled to pull his arm over his shoulder. The ball of light grew brighter and now the whole wall was swirling. He dragged the man to the door and staggered. He tried again and almost fell. Cursing he let the man down. He was too weak to carry a dead weight and save himself.

'I'm sorry,' he whispered, feeling sick with hopelessness. He had to leave him.

Asaph stepped out of the door, raised his sword and struck at the doorframe. Sparks flew as stone cracked. He fell back as the doorway and part of the roof collapsed, blocking the exit into the tunnel. It would buy them time, nothing more. He hurried after the others and helped Danny with the big man, glancing back all the way.

'Leaper, it's me. There's trouble coming,' Asaph shouted ahead before they reached the sacrificial chamber.

'What's happening?' asked Leaper, setting the Dromoorai sword down to help the men. He gave them water and robes as Asaph spoke.

'A tunnel that goes on and on,' Asaph sighed and slumped against the wall, leaning his back against it. 'There is no way out apart from that tunnel, wherever it leads. Harpies will be here soon.'

'Great,' sighed Leaper stroking back his hair.

Asaph looked at them all and almost laughed. There were at least eight fit fighting men here armed with knives and swords and all of them were weak as kittens. Screeching echoed from a distance. Asaph pulled himself to his feet, cold determination steeling his nerves.

They put the children by the wall and the weak and old in front of them. The rest all brandished sickle knives, their faces a mix of fear and grim resolve. The screeching came closer. Asaph turned to face the tunnel, Leaper, Danny and Jekk clustered by his sides. They each had a wild, savage look in their eyes, along with a desperate need for vengeance.

Shouting sounded along the tunnel, men and women's voices mixed with harpy cackles. *More priests and priestesses?* Asaph's heart fell when he heard the sound of swords being drawn. The temple guards were here too.

Harpies burst into the chamber first. The bird women leapt onto the sacrificial altar, took a moment to survey the scene, then lunged at Asaph. He jumped to meet them, swinging his sword so fast the first harpy didn't even see it as her head flew off. The second took his return arc, the tip slicing down through her shoulder, severing a wing. He took one more down before the guards, more harpies and red-robed priests and priestesses poured in.

Screaming, screeching, shouting and the clang of weapons echoed deafeningly around the chamber. Leaper plunged his huge claymore first through a harpy, then a guard. Jekk and Danny took down a priest and priestess and their howls of pain made the Order hesitate and fall back.

Pressure built in the air and a clap of thunder sent everyone to their knees, temple guards and priests as well. His senses scattered by harpy magic, Asaph failed to lift his sword in time as a harpy jumped on him. Her talons tore into his arms. The burning itch of poison filled his wounds and he felt his energy draining. The dragon blood in his veins fought the harpy infection, driving back the weakness.

With a roar, he stabbed his sword through the harpy's chest and laughed as he heaved himself up with the harpy still writhing on his sword.

'Stupid bird,' he roared. 'Harpy poison is useless against dragon-kind!' He twisted and wrenched his sword free. The harpy fell, twitching.

Looking up at the number of harpies and guards filling the room, he realised the hopelessness of their situation. Well, he'd got this far and he wasn't about to go down without a fight. He placed himself as best he could in front of the others, determined to protect every one of them until he fell.

A priest lunged for him with a short sword, Asaph feinted and slashed. The priest fell. Two harpies came in, chanting a spell. He ran at them fast before they could cast it, taking one down and badly wounding the other.

Beyond the din of the vicious battle, there came another deafening sound. Asaph was too busy hacking and stabbing to focus on it at first until the sound of rocks cracking and falling grew too loud to ignore. The chamber trembled. Both friend and foe stepped back and looked around, weapons still raised. Suddenly, the wall behind the children cracked and started to crumble. The adults grabbed the children away as the entire wall collapsed outwards.

A giant, ice-blue claw appeared through the rubble and scraped back the bricks and boulders. Everyone stared open-mouthed, too shocked to be afraid. Two talons appeared, scraping back more rubble, then blinding daylight spilled down onto them. Asaph shielded his eyes and blinked up into the enormous golden eyes of a dragon.

'Morhork?' he said in shock. Everyone around him collapsed to the floor trembling in dragon fear. Even Asaph's knees knocked together.

'You and that sword are making a right bloody racket. Either you disarm or get some serious training,' said the dragon.

Asaph laughed a short sharp bark and waved his sword slightly, wondering what the dragon meant. Morhork seemed utterly irritated, which pleased Asaph because it made him more volatile—a good thing in their current situation.

A harpy jumped on Asaph's back, knocking him to the floor and winding him. Morhork reached in, plucked the harpy from his back and crushed the bird-woman between his claws in a spray of blood. The dragon tossed the body behind him, reached a giant talon over their heads and back into the chamber where he gripped a handful of temple guards and priestesses, crushed them and threw them behind him, too. The enemy turned and ran screaming.

'Please help us out,' Asaph said, his voice hoarse with exhaustion. 'The children first.'

Morhork stared at him a moment, then grimaced. He carefully scooped up a couple of trembling children and lifted them out of the hole he had created. One by one, and sometimes two, the dragon hoiked them out of the underground chamber.

After setting Asaph free, the dragon lay its giant body down almost languidly, crushing ancient trees and exotic bushes as it almost filled the eastern half of the temple grounds. Most things were flattened under his great bulk and a quarter of the temple had been destroyed in his digging. Asaph wondered how people would be feeling about a huge dragon in the middle of their city. Thankfully, it was still dawn and the clouds above were turning a paler shade of pink.

Asaph stared up at the dragon. 'You saved us. You came for me. Why? How?'

'I did not come for you! As I said, you and that sword made a right racket.' Morhork picked up the flaccid body of a harpy and tossed it into his mouth, swallowing noisily. Asaph swallowed too, trying not to vomit.

'But you were in the north, miles away. You couldn't have reached here in time.'

'Foolish half-breed,' scowled Morhork. He seemed in a fouler mood than usual. 'Dragons can travel through dimensions whenever we wish. But we don't like it. It makes us tired, hungry and thus angry.'

'So it's really possible. You really *can* travel through dimensions like ravens.'

'Yes,' said Morhork, bringing his face close to Asaph, his eyes narrowing to the barest slits. 'Like wizards and harpies and demons—all things with magic, though dragons are naturally masters of it. Idiot.'

'Can you teach me?' Asaph asked, ignoring the insult and awed by the prospect.

Morhork snorted, covering Asaph in black soot and making him choke.

The sound of shouting made Asaph turn to see the city guard spilling into the temple grounds. They were met with temple guards and the clang of swords rang out.

'Men,' Morhork said in disgust. 'Why have I come to this awful place?' He lifted up as if to go.

'Wait. You still haven't told me why you came,' Asaph said.

'When you picked up that sword, every bloody dragon in the world will have heard it. You've woken up every brood, you idiot. This is not their time. Now I've got to go and clean up your bloody mess again!' Morhork bunched his muscles and leapt into the air, magic shimmering around him.

'Thank you, Morhork.' Asaph waved up at the dragon, trying to understand what he had said. 'I owe you, *we* owe you, our lives. I'll come and find you.'

'Not if I can help it,' growled the dragon. 'It would do you well to remember that I was on Slevina's side.'

With a roar that probably had the whole city on their knees, Morhork shot towards the clouds and was gone.

Asaph stared down at the great Sword of Binding in his hands, noticing how the blood red pommel sparkled and then dimmed as Morhork disappeared. It knew a dragon was near. A grin spread across his face.

CHAPTER 25

Four Horsemen

ISSA opened her eyes and tried to focus on her bedroom.

The lampshades and curtains wobbled as if alive. Everything else was blurry and her head pounded horribly. With a moan, she managed to push herself up. Faint light trickled through the curtains so she assumed it must be dawn.

She tried to piece together what had happened. She had talked incessantly about everything, then Domenon had kissed her, after which she remembered nothing. She touched her lips, her cheeks growing hot as she remembered. *Too much wine…*

How had she got back into her bed? She quickly looked under the covers. She was dressed in her nightshirt—but who had done that? Her involuntary groan was cut off when, to her horror, realisation dawned. *It can't have been just wine. I was drugged!*

She reached for the water jug beside her bed and downed half. She had told him everything; about Freydel, her parents, Ayeth… Everything! Horror turned to fury. Feeling a little rehydrated she threw back the covers but the room still span. There came a knock on the door. A maid's voice called out even as the handle turned and Kay entered.

'It's past dawn, Miss, and I've been informed by Master Domenon to wake you.'

'What happened?' Issa mumbled, through a mouth that felt full of wool.

'Too much wine?' Kay winked. 'Master Wizard Domenon carried you here. You were fast asleep. And I put you to bed.'

The maid threw back the curtains, blinding Issa with the light and making her head ache all the more. At least Domenon hadn't put her to bed.

'Do you need help dressing, Miss?' asked the maid.

'No, thank you,' Issa said, biting back her fury. How dare he drug her!

Kay curtsied and left. Issa dragged herself out of bed and pulled on her clothes, grinding her teeth.

Through the maze of Castle Rebben's hallways, she found Domenon's library more by luck than anything else. Seeing the grim expression on her face, the maids fell out of her way as she stalked the corridors and staircases, her cheeks hot with anger and the remnants of wine and whatever else he had drugged her with. She did not respond to their 'Good Morning' greetings, in fact, she barely heard them speak. All she could think about was what Domenon had done to her. She stopped at his door and hammered her fists on it.

No one answered.

'Master Wizard Domenon is with the Queen, Miss Issalena,' said a butler who was passing by the room carrying a tray of cups and a steaming teapot.

'Right, thank you,' said Issa tightly. The butler gave a slight bow and hurried on.

Issa stalked back the way she had come, down the stairs, through the main hallway and towards the room where she had met the queen. Two pike holding guards stood outside the closed doors, faces emotionless as she approached.

'Is Domenon in there?' she growled.

'He is, but asked not to be disturbed,' said a guard politely.

'Let me pass,' Issa said, her scowl deepening.

'No one may enter,' said the other guard.

'Let me pass,' Issa repeated, the fury rising. She entered the Flow, not caring what Domenon had told her.

Maybe one of the guards could sense magic for he shifted uncomfortably and his free hand went to his sword. She pulled the Flow to her in greater waves, knowing the Master Wizard would feel it.

'If you don't let me pass, I will explode open these doors!' Issa shouted.

Quickly, she lifted her hands, preparing the command and getting ready to disarm the guards. The air crackled with latent energy. She felt someone enter the Flow but maintained her grip on it, not letting anyone take it away. The guards crossed their pikes barring her passing and gripped their sword hilts menacingly.

'I'm warning you!' she shouted.

The door opened and the Queen stood there regarding her coolly. Her black robes swathed over her body and even her head was adorned with a black lace cowl. Her pale face was stark and her lips pursed. The guards bowed but still lifted their spears ready to protect the Queen.

Issa did a double take; she had not expected the Queen to appear. Her grip on the Flow faltered and was suddenly ripped away from her, sending her reeling. She stepped back and eyed the velvet seats, wishing she could sit down but forced herself to remain standing.

'If your gripe is with my wizard then it is actually with me,' said Queen Thora. 'I asked him to do whatever was necessary to ensure you were not working with the enemy and that what you told me was the truth.'

'You authorised my drugging?' Issa's voice was high-pitched. The Queen herself had actioned all of this? Had allowed her guest to be abused?

'Do not act so surprised. When you enter my house you play my game and abide by my rules. I am pleased to say I can now confidently trust you and will offer my entire army to your cause.' The Queen's lips tilted into the barest smile—the first Issa had seen.

Issa opened and closed her mouth, the remnants of her rage battling with the good news. The queen trusted her fully. The army would be hers to command. Seeing the drop in threat the guards relaxed, but left their pikes crossed before Issa until a wave of Thora's hand allowed them to stand down. She motioned for Issa to enter. She slowly stepped forwards.

The room beyond was dark. No lamps were lit and the light of dawn had yet to reach over the trees to this part of the palace. Beside the throne stood Domenon, tall, draped in his purple wizard's robe, a knowing smile forming on his lips. He showed none of the effects of the wine they had drunk, but then, he'd probably protected himself against them.

'You drugged me,' Issa growled, her anger rising once again. She turned to glare at Thora, unable to control her fury even in the cold face of royalty. 'Did you tell him to kiss and ravage me too?'

The Queen considered her, a strange gleam in her eyes. 'I like a woman with temper and fearlessness.' The gleam left her eyes and her smile dropped as she turned to regard the wizard.

Domenon looked at the floor and, for the first time, Issa thought he looked guilty.

'Is this true, Master Wizard?' the Queen demanded coldly.

'I couldn't help but steal a kiss from such beauty, my Queen,' he said, casting his eyes sheepishly downwards; but his remaining smile proved he didn't really feel guilty at all.

'Is that all that happened?' barked the Queen, her eyes narrowing at the wizard.

'All that happened? Isn't that enough?' Issa flared, her eyes wide. How dare he even touch her.

'Indeed, my Queen.' Domenon spoke in frank tones and rolled his shoulders back. 'The Raven Queen is sensitive to Davonian wine and the truth serum. I misjudged how much she could take.'

'Sensitive? Truth serum?' squeaked Issa.

The Queen laid a cool hand on her arm. Issa went to throw it off then checked herself—she *was* in the presence of royalty.

'We live in dangerous times,' said Thora, her voice worried and low as if someone unwanted was listening. 'We have to be sure we are not letting the enemy into our house. Baelthrom's spies are everywhere.'

Issa couldn't disagree, but she didn't like the idea of being drugged. It took an enormous amount of effort to breathe deeply and control her anger. She needed the queen's army and her trust more than anything right now.

'My handsome wizard does not kiss just anybody,' she winked at Issa.

Issa felt her cheeks colour remembering the kiss. It had been a good kiss. Passionate and almost like a Dragon Lord. The thought made her pause.

'Who is the blue dragon? I saw it again,' Issa asked, arching her eyebrows at the wizard.

Domenon's face darkened and he frowned at the floor. The Queen looked at Issa quizzically.

'What dragon?' Domenon laughed. 'Surely your boyfriend must know. Come on, we must get going.' The wizard stood straight, pulled up the collar of his cloak and strode towards them.

Issa wanted to press the point but her memory of last night was foggy. Had she made it up? Perhaps the drug had made her hallucinate? Domenon didn't look at her as he breezed past them to the door. He had secrets. She silently resolved to get them out of him, one way or another.

'This truth serum,' Issa began, talking to Thora. 'If I am to have soldiers and others close to me as my aides, I would very much like some of it to be sure I can trust them with my life. Perhaps you can give me some?'

The queen pursed her lips and considered her. 'I don't see why not. I'll have my butler put a pack in your carriage.'

Issa nodded her thanks and bowed. 'I will not forget your generosity, or for drugging me.' She added the last under breath and gave a slight smile.

The Queen smiled fully before turning away. 'We shall get on well, you and I.'

Issa nodded to herself, pleased the Queen felt that way, and followed Domenon's cloak as it disappeared around a corner.

Outside in the courtyard, she patted Duskar then climbed into the carriage, politely refusing the butler's helping hand. Thinking about Thora, she listened to the clatter of hooves and wheels on cobbles and watched Castle Rebben disappear into the trees.

Issa squinted through the grey fog sure that up ahead something moved within it. She could just make out a large and wavering dark patch. The air was close and damp and silent. The fog was so thick she couldn't even see her feet and it was deathly cold. She shivered and hugged her shoulders. Not even her Dread Dragon armour could keep out the chill. Something snorted; it sounded vaguely like a horse, but not exactly. A horse-like head lifted in the fog but a billow of mist swiftly concealed it.

'Who's there?' Her voice sounded eerie and loud.

A heavy foot stamped, and then another, closer. The hairs on the back of her neck prickled. Something hunted for her presence in the fog just as she searched for it. Her hand dropped to her sword while the other rested on the raven talisman tucked in her belt. Another dark shape appeared beside the first and then two more. Four dark dense patches moving in the mist.

The cold crept into her heart and she tiptoed back slowly, silently, afraid. The four shadows turned in her direction, then made their way towards her, their feet heavy, unstoppable, the only sound in the silence. Thud, thud. Her heart thumped in time with it

Issa turned and ran, her feet scuffing loudly on stones she couldn't see. Stumbling, she fell, dropping her sword in order to catch herself. It clattered loudly. She rolled to get up but the shadows were now before her. Her breath stuck in her throat and cold sweat trickled down her temples.

She dragged herself back using her elbows and feet. The shadows followed, growing larger until they towered above her. She could barely breathe for the terror in her throat. They reminded her of the Light Eaters in the Dark Rift that lacked any form. Even as she thought it, their forms shifted. Long heads became denser and more horse-like in shape. On their backs were other shapes. Riders.

The closest horse-shadow bent to sniff her, its snout materialising out of the fog. Hairless dark skin gleamed; nostrils billowed black soot like a dragon. Its mane was a crown of spines and horns that rattled and clacked as it tossed its head. Thick lips pulled back to reveal blackened fangs, not blunt teeth for eating grass. Its black eyes became swirling pits of nothingness that tried to pull her in. Issa tore her gaze away, her heart pounding.

'What do you want,' she gasped, hunting desperately for the Flow— but it was not there.

'You,' breathed its rider. Its voice was low and airy; a wind howling through a graveyard.

The rider reached towards her, its huge, gauntleted hand materialised out of the fog and clenched. Her heart squeezed in her body and she gasped. A helmeted face formed and its empty eyes were like those of its horse; consuming, soul draining. The other horsemen reached towards her. Excruciating cold flooded every cell in her body and she screamed.

The carriage jolted and swayed. Issa gasped, blinking in the lantern light and trying to decipher where she was.

'Bad dreams?' asked Domenon who was seated opposite her. The wobbling lantern cast strange shadows on his face as he looked at her.

Issa rubbed the raven mark on her chest and took a deep breath. Her face and neck were sweaty and her hands shook. They were on the way to South Reach and had briefly stopped for lunch. Sometime after she must have fallen asleep. Her dream had been so real. Baelthrom was hunting her, maybe even in the dream-state. Were the shadow horses sent by him? They were undead and they drank her soul. Real night mares stalking her. She didn't feel safe even in her dreams.

'I must apologise, the truth serum can give you nightmares straight after,' said the wizard, closing the book he had been reading. 'I would not have used it had my Queen not commanded me to do so. I don't need potions to kiss women.'

Issa laughed incredulously and sat up in her seat, struggling to shake the terror of the dream away, feeling hunted even now.

'Unlike you to apologise,' she said and peered out of the window through the dribbling rain into the pitch black. Every now and then a light would appear beyond the trees. 'I guess you need them drunk and unarmed though.'

She grinned when he snorted.

'We are nearly there,' he said, also peering out. 'We're on the coastal road just east of the port. It must be a couple of hours to midnight by now.'

She'd been asleep all that time? It must be the dregs of the drug. She felt much better now, even if she was still shaken by the dream.

'I sent a rider ahead to check our lodgings at a good tavern big enough to hold our entourage,' said the wizard. 'Perhaps here we can rendezvous with your Karalanths for it lies on the edge of South Reach woods. The southern barracks at the port are already being prepared for the Queen's army. Some soldiers will already be there. The whole port town is quickly becoming a military base. How long it will take for

Drumblodd's army to reach us is anybody's guess.'

'Ehka told me three more days,' said Issa. The bird had been scouting for the armies and militias earlier that day whilst they travelled south. 'The militia party from Lans Himay will hopefully join them within that time, along with any of King Navarr's Feylint Halanoi. The Karalanths might join us tomorrow. The only unknown is Atalanph, although, after I scryed with Haelgon, it seems the king will send his army to join us on enemy soil rather than add to the sea journey by sailing to Davono first.'

She chewed her lip. She had no idea how to manage an army or conduct a war. All she had was a plan. After that, she had to place complete trust in the commanders and officers. She needed Marakon and she needed Asaph. Perhaps if she focussed her thoughts only on what needed to be done—and not how it would be done—she could manage. Thinking of Asaph instilled worry. She couldn't fight without him by her side, not this time. This was too big.

They crested a hill and the lights of a tavern came into view in the trees below. It was a huge building constructed solely of wood like a hunter's lodge and, it turned out, made completely empty for their party, except for the barmaids, chefs and housekeepers—as ordered by Domenon on request of the Queen. At three storeys high, it had many rooms and was very secluded and hidden, surrounded as it was by thick forest. A lantern shone in every one of its hundred or so windows, making the place blaze like a gem in the dark.

Their party had grown to fifteen carriages now that a small unit of Davonian soldiers accompanied them to prepare camp. The horses were quickly stabled and the people each shown to their rooms by maids.

Hers was small, warm and bright with only a single bed and tiny table in it. It was all she needed. She stuffed her packs under the bed and ran down to dinner in the huge restaurant. A blazing fire warmed the place and people milled everywhere chatting, eating, and drinking ale.

Dinner was simple; huge baked potatoes with a choice of fillings, and cider, ale or wine. The thought of drinking anything but water after the previous night's assault made her head hurt. She scanned the people but, oddly, Domenon was nowhere to be seen. She took the empty seat next to Velonorian—he always managed to keep one seat next to him free, for her, no doubt.

Her young aide talked incessantly—uncommon for an elf—mostly about his abilities with the bow and his people. She found his talkativeness amusing, perhaps a little endearing, but hoped his eagerness to please and impress her would lessen with time. She was grateful for his lessons in Elven, though. Learning Elven reminded her of her school in Little Kammy.

After dinner, he walked her to her room and she sighed in relief when she closed the door, glad to finally be alone. But when she lay on her bed, sleep scuttled away. Perhaps because she'd spent half the day sleeping, she was no longer tired.

With a sigh, she sat up and looked out of the window over the dark tops of the trees. No one knew anything about Venosia, so what were they really getting themselves into? The coasts might be crawling with the enemy, guarded by Dread Dragons and totally impenetrable. But if that were true, surely Davono would be under constant, relentless attack? Such attacks were happening on the north side of Frayon. Wouldn't it be good to finally know something more about the enemy and what they were up to?

We need to do what the enemy does; we need to scout deep into their lands. We can't send spies or Life Seekers, but we do have wings and magic. She chewed her nails. *Somebody* needed to scout out Venosia. *Only Ehka and I can do this without being spotted—or at least seen as easily as something like a dragon.*

Baelthrom was able to detect travelling minds in the astral, but he seemed less able to spot something physical. Could she do that? Could she really fly as a raven all the way to Venosia and scout it out? How else would they know what was there? How would they know where to land the ships and attack?

If they sailed all that way and then had to spend a week looking for a place to dock, the enemy would surely see them and have plenty of time to prepare. Stealth and surprise attacks were the hallmark of their enemy, so they must act the same way. Wandering ships were like sitting ducks to Dread Dragons.

She took a deep breath and closed her eyes. *Beloved Zanufey, if this is what I must do, then please protect me.* And when should she go? She stood up.

'Now,' she sighed. Her mind was made up. There just wasn't a moment to lose and if she spent more time thinking on it she would only dissuade herself from action.

She should go and find Domenon immediately, but the wizard had disappeared as soon as they had arrived. He hadn't even gone to his room, or so the maid had said. She couldn't tell Velonorian, he would be too worried and might try to stop her. She couldn't tell anyone else for that matter.

Quickly, she opened her pack, grabbed a pencil and scribbled a note on paper that had been left on the little table.

> *'Back soon.*
> *Issa.'*

Would she be back soon? How long did it take to fly to Venosia? What if she were spotted, or worse, captured? Venturing into enemy land was terrifying, especially when there were so many unknowns. It was exciting too. She grinned, tied back her hair and opened the window. If she went now, she'd have the night to hide her journey.

Rubbing her raven mark, she pulled on the Flow and called upon her raven form.

CHAPTER 26

Ruling the Dark Rift

'THE Temple of Carvon is ours and soon the rest of the Order of the Goddess will follow. The faith of the people—their hearts and minds—will belong to us to do with as we please,' said Cirosa.

'You will be impressed with our New Order.' She inclined her head dutifully, her platinum hair cascading freely down her black iron cuirass that the dark dwarves had made for her. An iron coronet adorned with spikes kept her hair back from her face and her dark red cloak kept off the chill of the chamber.

'Well done, my Priestess,' said Baelthrom. 'The religious order of humans was easier to infiltrate than anticipated. Faith can always be broken from within by greed and fear.' He turned from the priestess to look into the images within the iron ring. It showed what was occurring beneath the Temple of Carvon in the sacred Mother's Chamber. Harpies chained their new men, who knelt naked, listless and drugged on the floor, and wrenched them up by their hands so that they all but hung from the cell's walls.

The men were worthless human captives that the bird-women could do with as they pleased. It mattered nothing to Baelthrom so long as the harpies kept their allegiance and did as he commanded. He lifted a hand and the image changed to the Dromoorai carrying the Sword of Binding. Red-robed, New Order priestesses and priests clustered around its hulking form.

Baelthrom's eyes lingered on the shining blade of the sword, hating its indestructibility. He'd been hunting for the blade for decades, knowing the Dragon Lord Queen had hidden it. Only now, over a quarter of a century later, had it been found by dark dwarves tunnelling beneath Castle Draxa. The necromancers felt it first, the powerful magic shrouding the chamber. But magic could not stop them obliterating the room. The doors and walls were reduced to ash, the protective spells broken, but untouched and unscratched the sword hung defiant, blazing with anger.

The first necromancer to touch the sword died in agony, its innards boiling from within before its body turned black and crumpled to dust. No spell could lift the sword or undo the enchantments upon it. His black fire, cast through a Shadow Stone, did not even blacken the blade, much to his fury.

Two more necromancers died trying to touch the sword before a Dromoorai was brought before it. Painlessly, the undead dragon kin gripped the hilt. The sword had flared as if confused. The old scriptures were proven right; only those with dragon blood could hold the sword, and that included Dromoorai.

It was a source of power in Drax and so he'd decided to move it as far away as possible from its home. The Dragon Lord heir to the throne would be looking for it, it was only a matter of time before the sword called to its master.

'If you want to hide something, hide it in front of all the people to see,' said Cirosa rubbing her hands with a smile. 'The heir to the throne will never look for it in the Mother's Chamber beneath the Temple of Carvon and down there he will never feel it nor be allowed to enter. People are so stupid; they will not suspect. If there is any trouble, it can be hidden in the secret tunnels.'

'See to it that you are right, Priestess,' Baelthrom rumbled. 'If the last Dragon Lord and heir to the throne of Drax touches that sword, there will be an uprising of dragons. The alliance between man and dragon must stay dead and buried whilst both are still alive. We do not have enough Dromoorai to fight the number of dragons still sleeping out there. When we have subjugated the world of men, we will... *clean up* the other races.'

He turned to the dark dwarf. 'Your dwarves have done well to dig the tunnels beneath the city so quickly, Kilkarn.'

The dark dwarf stepped into the light cast by a brazier, his yellow eyes gleaming and his pale grey skin slick with sweat. Cirosa scowled at the dwarf who took no notice.

'Thank you, my Lord,' Kilkarn bowed.

Baelthrom turned back to the ring and watched the red-robed priesthood clustering in awe around the Dromoorai. His new priests were weak minded, little more than minions, but they could be used to control the swathes of people. They would be his slave owners. All it had taken to turn them to his will was the offer of a little power—magical power which they had never had—and wealth. Now they sacrificed to the Dark Rift, making it stronger, bringing it closer.

His eyes passed over the rows of trembling prisoners. He had been surprised by the outright cruelty of the priesthood. After their first kill, after the shadows had come from the Dark Rift and given them their first taste of real power, they had sacrificed with abandon as if all empathy had been driven from them. The more beings of Maioria that were given in his name to the Dark Rift, the more power he received from the place that was his home. He longed to return to it with his prize, Maioria.

'Now I understand the nature of what it is I most desire and remember that which I had forgotten on my journey here millennia ago. Everything is clear,' he breathed.

He watched the priests drag a screaming child to the altar and tie him down. Before now, Baelthrom had hated death, the end of things, the nothing he did not understand. But now he understood its greater purpose; the Dark Rift had shown him that not all beings or humans were good enough for the immortal life that he offered. The lesser beings must die to feed the greater beings. As the grass feeds the horse, so then must humans and those beings of light feed the greater beings of the dark. Those existing within the Dark Rift were the greatest, most powerful beings of all. Humans should be honoured they were giving themselves to them.

'If we do not feed the Dark Rift, it will die,' said Baelthrom. 'It has been starved too long, subsisting on the weaker things it could find, and now it's ravenous. It has to grow.' Indeed, the Dark Rift itself was an entity that needed sustenance like anything else.

The priesthood started to chant in dark dwarven and initiated the opening of the vortex to the Dark Rift. It began, as it always did, as a speck of swirling black. Even just watching it from within his chamber, Baelthrom could feel its energy reaching up into the sky and out across the vastness of space to the black scar. The connection was forged and the tunnel opened hungrily over the terrified boy.

The humans would not be able to see what Baelthrom could see. In the Under Flow the terror of the child was a real thing; a dark red light that seeped all around him, heavy and cloying like blood.

Shadow essences—a purer form of his Life Seekers—poured out of the Dark Rift. They hovered behind each priest and priestess who lifted the boy's terror-filled blood to their lips. When they drank, the priests allowed themselves to be inhabited. The shadows moved forwards, eagerly becoming one with them, billowing their robes, filling them with power and consuming the victim's blood just as the body they possessed did.

The priests and priestesses finished their cups, faces flushed, eyes almost black with the power of the Under Flow moving through them. The shadow essences stepped back, bigger and of stronger form than before.

The Dromoorai stood beside the boy and lifted the Sword of Binding. Baelthrom revelled in the protesting hum of the blade.

'Any symbol or relic used to do the opposite of what it was created for serves to weaken and break its power,' said Baelthrom, nodding approvingly. 'All wizards and artificers know this.'

'Yes, my lord,' said Cirosa, her eyes wide with morbid fascination as she watched the sacrifice unfold.

As much as he enjoyed seeing the sword broken, these sacrifices had grown tedious and repetitive. With faint interest he watched the Dromoorai make the killing blow, and the boy's terrified spirit lift from the body. A pure, shimmering, white light like that which Baelthrom had taught his necromancers to capture in the black drink.

The shadows descended upon the spirit like a pack of hungry wolves. A surging, starving mass snatched the light then dragged it into the vortex; another soul to feed the Dark Rift. He'd witnessed this a hundred times or more, ever since he'd first touched that which lived within the Dark Rift. Before, the rift had been too far away. Now it was so much larger, so much closer, he could reach it through the iron ring. He had come to learn that there were many beings within the rift, but he could only reach the ones without form, for only they could travel through the dimensions.

These shadow beings fed upon the light and were as insatiable as they were powerful. But such need for the sustenance only living things could provide, Baelthrom considered a weakness. So he'd struck a bargain with them. He would feed them if they gave him power. *And one day I will return to them as their master.*

'I'd despised death before now,' he spoke his thoughts aloud. 'Only the goddess's weak creations die. But look at it. It is a means to a greater end. I will feed them, and in return I will rule the Dark Rift. Each priest or priestess the shadow essence touches, their minds will be mine to further bend to my will. These *Light Eaters* from the Dark Rift are the purest form of Life Seeker I have ever witnessed, but they struggle to maintain their presence on Maioria.

'The more of Maioria and her life-forms we feed to the Dark Rift, the stronger we and the Dark Rift become and the weaker this planet grows. All it takes is for the majority of the people to serve me, then will the power be mine. Then, Maioria will no longer belong to those who seek to destroy us, but to those who have joined our ranks. It all comes down to what the majority of people desire, and look how easily their religion fell. They must be made to desire the "peace" they will be given in the Dark Rift. They must submit or suffer endless war and annihilation.'

'Then taking control of the Temple has been a huge step towards our goal,' grinned Cirosa. 'A superb plan, my Lord. I did not think they would submit so easily, but humans are weak.'

'We will continue to wear them down with war,' said Baelthrom. 'Many will fight bitterly towards the end. It will be a great loss to see their most powerful fall, for they will never submit and never turn to our cause. Which is what makes them so strong. Never forget, Cirosa, that you are a traitor to your race, and that will always be *your* weakness.'

Cirosa shut her mouth and quickly smoothed the scowl on her face. 'I am dedicated to you and you alone, my Lord.' She bowed her head.

Baelthrom gripped the hilt of his blade and squeezed. He admired those who would not fall to him. He knew they would rather die than do so—whether they be dragon, human, dwarf or elf. In that, they were like the Ancients. Those who did fall to him were betrayers to their own race and never to be trusted. Their greed for power made them weak. Traitors were dangerous to keep close and all he could find on this planet were those—apart from Hameka and the dark dwarves. In the Dark Rift, there would be no traitors.

'The New Order of the Great God will move amongst the people as them and work our agenda in the shadows, feeding the Dark Rift and spreading the Under Flow where they can,' said Cirosa. 'They will turn the people to our cause—willingly or unwillingly. The Temple Guard will soon outnumber the City Guard and then Carvon itself will fall. Once touched by the Under Flow, no one can resist.'

'You will lead this New Order, my Priestess, but remember, overconfidence is a dangerous thing,' warned Baelthrom. The cunning woman was ambitious, a good thing and a fault. 'There are still orbs of power beyond my control and great resistance to us which must be broken down.

'Anchoring the energy of the Dark Rift on this planet will diminish this resistance and turn the minds of the people to our will. The more of the Under Flow we can bring upon Maioria, the faster this will happen.

'The power of the Dark Rift flows fully into these Mountains of Maphrax. They are a conduit, a power in themselves. It is through these mountains—themselves from the Dark Rift—that the Under Flow reaches Maioria and flows into her core. And now the time has come to finally eliminate the last remnants of an old energy. The last of the Ancients have evaded me for many years but being only two in number, I let them go. They are a blockage to the Under Flow and their light must be removed forever from this world.'

He lifted his hands and commanded magic. The image in the iron ring became a grey fog.

'Come to me my Knights of Maphrax,' Baelthrom whispered, his voice so deep the ring vibrated.

An image formed in the swirling grey of the iron ring and the long muzzle of a horse appeared. The nose lifted, inhaled and snorted.

Cirosa stepped back with a gasp as the horse's head pushed out of the image into the chamber, all smoke and shadow that billowed and wavered.

The horse's eye opened, a pit of black. Its breath was soot like a dragon's. A shadow hand pulled on the reins and a rider appeared upon the horse's back, again all smoke and shadow. Three more ghost riders and their horses emerged out of the grey to stand beside the first. The chamber grew deathly cold and silent and there was a rank smell in the air.

'My beautiful horsemen, knights of the shadow, who can travel beyond the grave and between dimensions. Astral hunters, dream stealers. They can step into this chamber should I command them.'

The head of the first horse took solid form. Its furless skin gleamed metallic black like Dread Dragon scales. It shook its head, its mane of spikes clattering against each other. The horseman's hand solidified into a black iron gauntlet and its eyes within its tripartite helmet swallowed the light. These were eyes that drained the life of the living. They wore no amulets—they needed no Shadow Stone for Baelthrom to know where they were. He could find them in the Under Flow, the medium through which they travelled.

'My knights can pass into the realm of the dead, a place I could never go. A place where Keteth and now the Raven Queen evade me. But no longer. These knights are already dead, already cursed. You were commanded to bring me the other knights, Cirosa.'

'I lost them in the Murk, my lord. A place I could not reach,' she said stepping forwards, wringing her hands. 'From there, they never returned.'

'Karhlusus, also, never returned,' said Baelthrom. 'But the demon wizard was an imbecile. He was useful for a time, but his greed, arrogance and insanity were a danger. No being possessed by a demon ever thinks logically or acts reasonably. It is better that he is gone. The demon worlds can wait for our coming. They will be easy to dominate.'

Baelthrom wasn't bothered about the Murk and its inhabitants. Demons held barely half the light energy of humans and so were less sustaining. The Dark Rift was not interested in those who were half as bright.

'Let us hope that four knights will be all I need,' Baelthrom said as he walked towards the horseman which had partially materialised out of the ring. The horse lifted its head and the knight's black eyes stared at Baelthrom.

'My Shadow Knights of Maphrax. Hunt down the last of the Ancients and bring them to me. Only you can ride the places between dimensions. You will find them by their living light that burns brighter than any being on Maioria.

'Then hunt for the Raven Queen. You cannot trap her in Maioria, her magic will be too powerful even for you. You must wait until she enters the realm of the dead, where you will now be the stronger. She won't expect you to have power there and that is your chance. Bring her to me unharmed. Now go.'

'As you command, Lord Baelthrom.' The shadow knight's voice was a long grating whisper.

They turned their steeds away, dematerialising and dissipating into the grey fog.

'The last of the Ancients will be given to the Dark Rift. A great gift and the snuffing out of their kind on Maioria forever.' He turned from the ring and walked to the pedestal where two orbs glowed dully.

'With their death, the orbs can never be made whole again for they were the ones to split the magic. What happens then to the Orb of Life is an intriguing mystery.' He passed his hand over the multi-coloured orb. It glowed brighter. 'This orb is keyed to the Ancient's race. When they are gone, what happens to the energy of life? Kilkarn, bring to me the prisoners.'

'Yes, my Lord,' Kilkarn grinned.

The dark dwarf returned with two necromancers. Between them, they half-dragged a middle-aged man and woman, both scrawny and bent over in hunger and weakness. They wore rags for clothes and their unkempt hair had not been cut in a long time. Their arms and chests were covered in unhealed wounds where the necromancers had frequently syphoned their blood—living blood was essential to a necromancer's work and sustenance.

There were many prisoners in the dungeons of Maphrax, mostly for the production of Sirin Derenax, but Baelthrom rarely saw them. They were managed and processed by his necromancers.

The necromancers held the humans before the iron ring where they shivered and hunched listlessly, not even attempting to fight their captors.

Their pale skin was almost grey and their sunken eyes had long given up on life. They were already dead. Perhaps they were not such a great gift to the Dark Rift. Their pitiful state made him angry. Those who did not fight were worthless. He hated the way they cowered before him. *Merely food for the immortals.*

Raising his arms, the Under Flow surged, surrounding him in a glittering sea of dark. He directed the magic into the iron ring. It exploded into it then burst up through the hole in the ceiling. He felt it gushing into the sky and towards the Dark Rift, from where it came. A vortex of black opened in the iron ring. Howling wind filled the chamber, billowing his cape and Cirosa's hair. Waves of power returned to him and he breathed in the essence of the Dark Rift; the ecstasy of it, the immensity of it, the purity of it. He closed his eyes and let it become him.

Deep, long groans of pain or ecstasy came from the iron ring. They wound around the chamber, growing in crescendo then dropping; a soul-wrenching noise that carried upon the Under Flow. He felt the shadows come then, the eaters of the living light moving towards him in the vortex. When the prisoners whimpered, he opened his eyes.

Shadow beings emerged from the vortex and flowed rather than stepped into the room. They were tall, twice the height of Baelthrom, but thin, insubstantial and flowing. They had no proper form as yet, but one day they would. Every time they fed on the living they grew stronger and their presence on Maioria increased.

Four shadows descended upon the woman, smothering her. She closed her eyes and clawed the air. Baelthrom wondered if she could even see them. The man at her side stood stricken, his eyes wide with horror. The woman lifted her head, the veins on her neck and face bulging. Her chest heaved and she seemed to be trying to scream but no sound came out.

She blinked incessantly, her eyes becoming all black and then normal again. Her aura began to glow brightly; they were lifting her life force from her body. Her fear spread through the chamber, thick and cloying. The shadows fed upon that too, bending their insubstantial heads and feeding like animals upon it.

There came a ripping sound like fabric being torn. The woman howled as her soul was rent from her. Swiftly, her body sagged, turned black and became shadow. This, too, the Dark Rift beings consumed whilst still gripping her shimmering soul in their arms. The shadow beings stood and turned to Baelthrom.

The Under Flow pulsed strongly then surged into Baelthrom. Everything turned to energy around him; swirls of dark power were his to command, more than he had been able to hold before. There was nothing greater than this feeling of power, there was nothing he existed for more than to feel it. This was their return gift.

The shadow beings flowed back into the vortex, taking their captured soul with them. Four more beings flowed out to surround the shaking man. The fear of the second victim was always more potent, attracting more things to come out of the vortex and numerous smaller shadows followed.

The man didn't even manage to scream before the Light Eaters ripped his soul from his body, but he did lose control of his bladder, much to Baelthrom's disgust. Even this the shadows consumed. All the bodily parts and fluids of the living were a source of food for the beings in the Dark Rift. Nothing went to waste.

Shadow beings clustered in the ring, standing tall. They bowed silently to Baelthrom, then flowed away into the vortex. Baelthrom took in a great breath and let it go as the Under Flow receded. *Soon we will be together.*

'That is our exchange,' said Baelthrom.

The priestess's eyes were wide and keen with hunger. In the exchange of energy, she too had been given a little more power from the Under Flow. It was akin to sipping the Elixir of Immortality only purer.

'It is divine,' she breathed, looking up at him in adoration and fear, the perfect combination.

Hameka, his second in command, had already witnessed everything she had seen today. Now he wanted his priestess to feel the power of the Dark Rift, to taste the purity of the Under Flow, to keep her keen and hungry and under control. There was no escaping this power.

'In return for the power of the Under Flow, they receive sustenance from me and soon they will have form here.'

Baelthrom walked to a corner of the chamber and picked up the wizard's staff he kept there. 'It is amazing how the universe unfolds to my needs. When I found the wizard with the orb I desire most, he left behind this staff. Now it belongs to me linking us together, for a staff is tightly bound to its wizard.

'Leave me, both of you. Priestess Cirosa, go with Vornus and prepare our northern forces to attack. Hameka has secured Wenderon and attacks the Uncharted Lands as we speak. They will soon fall. We must be relentless now. The glorious end is near.'

'As you command, my Lord Baelthrom,' Cirosa bowed and backed away. Kilkarn followed her.

Baelthrom held the staff towards the iron ring and pooled the Under Flow around him. While the power was still rich within him and the connection to the Dark Rift strong, he cast his mind to the one locked in his memory. Through the Dark Rift and beyond he would find her.

'Lona,' he said, slow and low and loud.

The name echoed around the chamber vibrating the Under Flow and rippling across the surface of the vortex. The staff pulled and twitched as if seeking to find and return to its master. The vortex twisted and turned, searching. Baelthrom held his breath as an alien female face formed, made huge by the size of the iron ring.

How he remembered that face! Through all the fog of the past millennia, it came to him clear and sharp across the eons. Her eyes appeared first, shining black onyxes over which impossibly long eyelashes fluttered. The Under Flow came in stronger waves out of the iron ring and more of her was revealed. Smooth alabaster skin shone with ethereal light. Her nose was thin and tiny, and lips small and red. High cheekbones pushed up her large, slanted eyes. The collar of her strange clothing rose to spikes around her bald head, like a crown that starkly accentuated her beauty.

Baelthrom stared at her, enthralled. Only the Raven Queen had captured his attention as much. She'd appeared when he'd first made direct contact with the Dark Rift—something he had been striving for, for decades.

'Lona,' his voice was a whisper and he stepped closer, the staff pulling strongly as if sensing something there. Could it really be her? Had he really reached her across the boundaries that separated Maioria and the Dark Rift?

Powerful, disturbing feelings ignited within him, emotions he had not felt before: hurt, desire, obsession. He dropped his gaze. Those eyes. Those lips…he remembered naked flesh, softness, awe and wonder.

Then terrible pain, darkness, cold…rage. Why didn't he remember everything? Did she know? There was something wrong with this alien being before him, something in his memory he should remember but could not quite reach. This being was dangerous—but why? He clenched his fists. Such ignorance undermined his power. He forced the foreign feelings away and retained a commanding hold on the Under Flow.

'My Baelthrom,' the woman said in a voice that was deep, almost melodic. *That voice! He remembered that voice!* 'I have watched you from afar and endlessly tried to reach you before…Never mind, our time is short. I can see you still understand our language but remember little of who and what you were. It is no matter, for look at how magnificent you are. Your body is stronger than ever it was, powerful, dominating. My race will respect you very much. Do you remember us, the Yurgharon? We are not as physically magnificent but we are incredible architectures of entire worlds. Our intellect has yet to be surpassed. We will make a formidable alliance.'

Baelthrom said nothing. He searched the being for some sign, some clue, as to what it was he should remember. Vague, fractured memories filled his mind of a life lived so long ago, he could barely reach it.

Golden and silver-skinned beings screamed and fled from something in the sky. They were tall and aquiline featured, like the Ancients. Immense, destructive energy shuddered through his body although it was only his mind remembering. A world breaking. Deep, earth-shaking booms, felt more than heard, and then a terrible shattering. Blue sand spraying everywhere… Blue sand. A world destroyed.

'What is the blue sand I see in my mind. It is everywhere. An endless desert,' Baelthrom said, hard and cold. He reminded himself that the past was of no consequence. Everything to be his lay ahead in the future.

Lona paused, the barest uncertainty passing across her face before it smoothed into a knowing, soothing smile. 'The blue sand is from the cursed dark moon you see in your skies. It plagues you and distorts the energy of the Dark Rift. It must be destroyed. You cannot overcome the Raven Queen—Maioria cannot be yours to rule—without destroying that moon.'

'How do you know these things? Have you been watching from afar? And what if I would have her rule beside me—one with power and dedication such as she? I will not be surrounded only by traitors,' said Baelthrom, testing.

Lona's face hardened, her black eyes gleamed. 'I have the ability to see many things from afar. And then I found you…' She paused and dropped that line of conversation, focusing on the other. 'One such as she, one who is dedicated to and chosen by the goddess, cannot be turned to the power of the Dark Rift. It was the goddess who destroyed the blue planet you see in your mind. It was your beloved home, Ara—'

'Aralansia,' Baelthrom finished it for her. Many things he had suspected finally slotted into place in his mind.

'Yes, you remember and that is good,' Lona smiled indulgently. 'Through her, the one you call the Raven Queen, the goddess will destroy the Dark Rift and everything within it, including me. It cannot be allowed to happen. That is why I reach for you now, and why you reach for me.'

Baelthrom's eyes blazed from blue to green and then red as he sifted through a hundred thousand things at once, paradigms explored and outcomes decided. He cast them all away. This Lona possessed power that he desired. She, like them all, was not to be trusted, not until he could remember her fully. He would play along, for now.

Baelthrom spoke simply. 'I say she can be turned when she sees what I offer, or the alternative; the destruction of Maioria. Perhaps you are jealous of the power this woman holds? Afraid, maybe.'

Lona pursed her tiny lips. 'The risk is too great. There is something you must know. Through the orb of the wizard whose staff you hold, I first found you. That wizard has come to us from your time to try and stop what you will become. Within his orb of power, I have seen many things and our future, both yours and mine, is dire. If this Raven Queen lives, the Dark Rift will be utterly destroyed and all those within it. This cannot happen, which is why I come to you now, across time and dimensions, to ensure our very survival. I will stop this wizard and you will destroy the Raven Queen so that the Dark Rift can continue.'

Baelthrom considered her dedication and decided it was true. Her words of doom did not stir him. Nothing could halt what he had set in motion, not even the Raven Queen. It was only a matter of catching her and channelling her powerful magic to his means. Maioria and her people were too weak to resist his might.

Lona drew closer. A shimmering boot stepped out of the vortex and clapped onto the hard floor of his chamber. With another step, she fully materialised before him. Those eyes, those lips…utterly unchanged. He forced the disturbing feelings back, letting them anger him rather than entice. She paused a few feet away and looked up at him from beneath her long eyelashes. He was half again as tall as she, and could crush her with his fist but she was fearless and that unsettled him deeply.

'You turned your back on your goddess when she destroyed your planet,' Lona said.

She began to pace slowly around him, her black robes shimmering and clinging to her lithe body. He wondered what the material was, considered taking it and getting the necromancers to design one for himself. Other feelings and desires were also aroused; desires he had only used for domination and destruction of other beings. He could destroy her now and forget about her.

'Your goddess obliterated you and your people because you dared to be greater than the gods.' She almost shouted the last, her face becoming hard and her voice venomous. 'When you tried to fight her, your people turned against you. That is why you persecuted them across the dimensions.'

Baelthrom laid his wings flatter against his back. Distrust; that is what he felt. He should remember these things, they were important. Lona was concealing things from him.

'What occurred in the past has no meaning for me now,' he said, swishing his tail and forcing her to take a wider path as she circled around him. 'Old planets and their gods mean nothing to me. Only Maioria.'

'You set your sights too low,' Lona crooned. She paused to raise a hand, and the Under Flow moved. A universe of stars appeared in the iron ring instead of the vortex. No other being had been able, or ever dared, to affect the contents of his iron ring. He glowered at her dangerously, hand lifting the blade at his hip.

Her lips curved into a slight smile as if she enjoyed the danger. She lifted a hand and indicated to the universe. 'Every one of these stars and planets can be yours, can be ours. The Dark Rift has no bounds, like the great One Source has no bounds. This is the only place which exists for us alone without the rules of the One Source. Now, we get to be the gods of this place.'

Baelthrom's eyes glowed darkly. Did she want to rule beside him? He would not share his rule once in the rift. 'You come to me now to help you stop your own destruction? You hold something back and that is very dangerous. Who are your enemies?'

'It is complicated,' Lona snapped and whirled away. 'Either our future lies in the Dark Rift, or it does not exist at all.' Her face twisted into a scowl of pure hatred. 'Yes, we have enemies! The Anukon and the Rorsken. You knew this once. We must destroy them before they destroy us. If they are not stopped, they will become the rulers of the magnificent Dark Rift.

'We have many problems but all can be overcome if we act now. I come here now to help *you* stop the destruction of the Dark Rift at the hands of the Raven Queen. That is why we cannot afford *not* to help each other. Either we are rulers or we are nothing at all. I will not be a slave for my enemies' enjoyment.'

Her scowl softened and her alien beauty returned. She came to him and lightly laid a hand upon his armoured chest. 'Don't you remember me at all, Ayeth?'

The name and her touch sparked intense memory. Bright flashes hurt his mind. Lona's face from long ago. Immense pain. Betrayal. A loathing of all things in existence and a bitter, seething hatred of himself. He removed her hand resisting the urge to crush it. Resisting the urge to unleash his power and obliterate everything before him, her, his iron ring and chamber, the Mountains of Maphrax and even himself. His rage cooled.

'I am Baelthrom. Whoever this Ayeth is, is not me and died long ago with that planet. I am so much more. I am a God and I do not share power.'

Lona's eyes gleamed. 'Magnificent,' she breathed, withdrawing her hand. Her black eyes turned hard and glittering. 'I will do anything in my power to destroy my enemies and ensure my own survival. I have discovered knowledge and magic I've yet to share with anyone. We would do well to work together.'

She stepped up into the iron ring and the vortex spun around her. 'Do not kill the wizard. The fool is bending to our will and assisting our cause. Without him and his relic of power, we would never have seen the future or been able to reach you.'

Lona turned away and in a rush of wind, the vortex disappeared, leaving the iron ring empty and the dark chamber visible beyond it. That she had the power to travel in such a manner and he did not was not lost on Baelthrom. She was powerful, more powerful than he dared to admit, but he would not trust her. A being that existed to ensure the complete destruction of another was dangerous, unstable. Her power and ambition were concerning. Their allegiance would be tumultuous but useful.

Whatever he had been in the past was gone—long gone. All that mattered was that he ruled the Dark Rift and no other.

CHAPTER 27

Loyal Men

'ASAPH, here!'

Asaph turned at Leaper's voice. The man, still holding the claymore, was running after a group of red-robed priests and priestesses fleeing to a side door in the temple. Overcome with the flood of city guards, the Order were getting away.

Asaph ran towards them but he was too late. The red robes disappeared through the door and it vanished, leaving him and Leaper to smack up against the solid white walls of the temple.

'Shit!' Leaper threw down his claymore and bent over to catch his breath.

'Another secret door,' nodded Asaph. 'Clever. I guess many got away.'

He looked towards the front gate. There were only two fallen red robes unmoving in the bushes. Through the trees, he could make out the City Guard surrounding ten or so Temple Guards, but no red robes. Beyond them was a group of huddling, young, white-robed priestesses, clearly shocked and upset by what was happening.

'I think they ran as soon as there was trouble,' said Leaper. 'Cowards! They know they'll be hanged.' He spat on the ground.

'Where are the others? The children?' asked Asaph.

'They went to the gates,' Leaper nodded towards them and followed Asaph when he started walking that way.

'No, wait,' Asaph stopped. 'My sword!'

'You already have a sword,' said Leaper, pointing to the one in his hand.

'No, my other one,' he grinned and turned towards the bushes.

'How many do you need?' asked Leaper.

To his relief, Asaph found Coronos' sword where he had left it, concealed amongst the ferns. He picked it up, feeling as if a part of Coronos were with him again.

'My father's sword,' he murmured when Leaper stood beside him. 'He was murdered by the High Priestess of this despicable order.' Asaph clenched his jaw. That woman had taken too much from him and he'd nearly lost Issa because of her, too.

'Sounds like you got a whole lotta revenge to enjoy.' Leaper slapped his back, trying to cheer him up before events caught up with him and he sighed and slumped against a tree trunk. He was weak, exhausted and dehydrated, as were they all.

'Come, let's get food and rest,' said Asaph.

'With what?' laughed Leaper. 'They took everything, even my sodding boots.'

'Mine too. But, I know someone who will help us—a very powerful someone.' Asaph helped Leaper stand and wrapped the man's arm over his shoulders. Together, they walked towards the gate. Immediately, two city guards came running up, swords raised. They were closely followed by two more.

'Wait, we escaped. We were prisoners,' said Asaph, trying to nonchalantly hold two swords in one hand. 'I am Asaph Dragon Lord, a friend of King Navarr.'

Leaper looked at him. 'You know the king?'

The City Guard, seeing their bloodied, dishevelled state, bare feet and chests beneath their white robes, slowly lowered their swords, but their suspicion remained.

'I must help this man,' said Asaph, breathing hard and feeling faint himself. 'And those men over there are not to be harmed.' He pointed towards the four men he had rescued from the harpies. They were sitting on the ground by the wall, hands on knees and heads hanging low.

'You'll have to prove it,' said a guard. 'The king is on his way right now.' The guards escorted them to the gate, eyeing them closely.

'That's 'im!' squawked a woman from somewhere. 'Now let me through!'

Asaph squinted at the plump, older woman who was trying to push her way through the heavily armed city guards standing to attention at the gates.

'Edarna?' Asaph said.

He helped Leaper to sit beside the other men and went to the old witch, a guard following him.

'There you are!' she said, tiptoeing to see over the shoulder of a guard, a wide grin spreading across her face. 'I had a right terrible dream about a Dragon Lord being sacrificed to the black hole in the sky.'

'It was no dream,' said Asaph, wiping the sweat from his forehead.

She ducked under the guard's arm and looked up at Asaph, her face serious, her green eyes sharp and missing nothing. 'I knew they were up to evil in there, Mr Dubbins confirmed it, but you can't do anything in this city or accuse anyone without proof. Pah! The whole Order needs to be destroyed!'

'There are tunnels, Edarna. And magic doors. They could be everywhere, leading anywhere. This city is compromised. The king must be told, if he doesn't know already. There are harpies who come here through secret gateways. Even a Dromoorai landed but no one suspected. Those men over there were with five others. I couldn't save them all.' Asaph swallowed hard.

'The higher echelons of the Order have turned to blood sacrifice to feed the Dark Rift. They have joined with Baelthrom.' He couldn't quite believe his own words. Were people turned so easily? Was nobody loyal to goodness and freedom anymore?

'Then Baelthrom has finally found a way to connect to it, to the Dark Rift. Something I always feared,' sighed Edarna. She suddenly looked very old and weary. Asaph realised the witch knew a lot about a great many things.

'Always, the darkness needs to feed upon the light to survive,' she continued. 'It's not a balance that's needed between the two at all. And where is Issa? Is she safe?' The witch gripped his arm, worried.

'Yes, I left her on Myrn to start her mission,' he smiled and patted the witch's hand reassuringly. 'I had to because I came to get this. But rather, it came to me.' He lifted the Sword of Binding. It flashed in the morning light.

Edarna's eyes went wide. 'The Dawn Bringer has come,' she gasped. Her grip on his arm tightened. 'You must go to them, King Asaph. You must find the dragons for they will have heard the sword find its master. Go now while they awaken. You must hurry. The dragons *will* follow the Dawn Bringer, but if they fall back to sleep, no man can awaken them again.'

She brought the inner sense of urgency that had been nagging at him to the surface. He should go north this very moment.

'You are right. First, I must tell the king what has happened here and help the men, but then I shall go,' said Asaph.

'Look,' she nodded over his shoulder. 'The King is here.'

Atop a spritely chestnut stallion and surrounded by his knights bearing the Carvon tabard of a white castle on a royal blue background, King Navarr hollered orders and the City Guard scattered to obey.

'Go now. I need to start cleaning up the black energy of this place.' Edarna scowled and pulled up her sleeves.

'Take care of yourself, Edarna,' said Asaph as he turned to go.

'And you take care of Issa,' said the witch.

He nodded.

Thinking no one was watching, the witch looked left and right, sidled nonchalantly past a guard who was looking the other way, and tiptoed into the trees within the temple gardens.

Asaph grinned to himself.

'And all this has been going on for weeks?' asked an incredulous King Navarr as he paced before the blazing fire. He rubbed his short beard, frowning with worry.

It was too hot in the dining room and Asaph loosened the collar of his new shirt—generously given to him by Navarr. Stuffed full of a four-course meal, he pushed his plate of cheese and biscuits back and leant his elbows upon the table. 'Maybe months.'

'Traitors! They will all be hanged at dawn,' growled the King. He paused his pacing and looked out of the window at the night sky.

'I know the one who started it,' said Asaph. 'She was the one who killed Coronos. A High Priestess now serving Baelthrom. Don't worry, I will have revenge.'

'And I will root out this evil in my city and destroy the Temple!' said the King. 'Carvon will not fall while I'm alive.'

'I'm sorry to bring you this news,' Asaph sighed. 'Maybe Leaper and these other men will know more and can help you. I don't know from what walks of life they come, but please look after them. They have been to the brink of death at the hands of the harpies. From what I have seen, they will make good fighting men. For now, I have given them some money from my savings so they can get clothing and food.'

'Of course, it is incredible that any of you managed to survive. Your men are being fed as we speak. They can remain in nearby lodgings if they wish until they are strong and ready to go.'

'That's very generous, thank you. I recommend Leaper as a fine fighter. Perhaps he would do well to enter your service, my King,' said Asaph, broaching the subject.

'Indeed,' said Navarr, nodding thoughtfully. 'We could do with a few more in our ranks. I will have our master-at-arms test his abilities.'

Asaph leant back in the chair, feeling strength return to him after the mountain of food he'd consumed. His eyes travelled to his swords leaning against the wall. With plain, strong lines, Coronos' sword was beautiful in its solid, dependable simplicity, but beside it, the Sword of Binding was a masterpiece. With its red pommel, curved crossguard and bluish grey blade, it looked almost like a ceremonial sword but far more. Both broadswords gleamed in the firelight.

Navarr's weaponsmith was already working on a sheath for the dragon sword and he hoped it would be done before he left at dawn.

Navarr followed his eyes. 'So, that really is the fabled Sword of Binding? It looks like it was made yesterday.'

'It is and it does,' Asaph agreed. 'There is not even a notch in it— even after I smashed it through a door earlier.'

'There are strong magic enchantments on it, even after all this time,' said Navarr.

'Yes, they seem as unbreakable as the blade itself,' agreed Asaph. 'I cannot wield Coronos' sword as well. Please look after it for me. It is all I have left of…' He trailed off.

Navarr nodded. 'You sure you won't stay? You've been through rather an ordeal.'

'I would like to but I must go north. I should have already left.' Asaph stood up, feeling that same sense of urgency. 'As ever, my King, thank you for your hospitality. When I return, I will have a surprise and I won't be alone. One day soon, Drax will be free and mighty again.'

'May you have what you seek, King Asaph,' said Navarr reaching out his hand.

Asaph clasped his outstretched arm, king to king. For the first time, he felt almost the man's equal. At this very moment, he *was* a king.

Asaph followed a servant to a small dining room in the lower section of the castle where Leaper and the other men were having dinner.

It was obvious Navarr was deeply disturbed by what was going on right under his nose, undermining his power, but Asaph worried that the King could not fix this problem. It would bury itself deeper and go underground, much like the light dwarves could never destroy the dark dwarves and stamp out their practises—they just crept away into the shadows. Evil, when detected, hid.

The servant opened the door and Asaph entered. He passed his eyes over them, Leaper, Danny, Jekk, Renno and Blaise, all stuffing their mouths with cheese, biscuits and wine, just as he had been doing moments ago.

Leaper grinned, set down his wine and stood. The man had washed away the dirt and blood, shaved, and tied back his fair hair—which Asaph could now see was shaved from his ears downwards. Like the others, he was dressed in new clothes; a simple shirt and woven trousers, given to them by the King. There was colour in his face and he looked full of life.

The other men followed his lead, setting down their wine and standing, though more nervously.

'Sit, sit, and eat,' said Asaph motioning with his hands. 'The food is good and the King is generous, so eat it all if you can.'

'We wouldn't be here if it weren't for you,' said Danny. There were scratches on his face from harpy claws, and his green eyes were clouded with the horrors he had witnessed.

'And I would not be here without any of you,' said Asaph in all seriousness. 'Alone, I would never have escaped.'

'Is it true you are the long lost heir to the throne of Drax?' asked Jekk. The dark haired man fiddled with his spoon nervously.

Asaph took a deep breath. 'I see that servants talk. Well, yes, for what it is worth, it's true.'

'And he's a Dragon Lord—the last,' blurted Leaper.

'Then we are your men, loyal to you for saving our lives,' said Renno. He was tall and wide with heavy muscle stretching his shirt tight. To Asaph's horror, the big man stood up and dropped to his knee.

'My King,' he said.

'What? No, get up,' Asaph flustered, then stopped himself—a king needed men, men he could trust. These men could be his loyal entourage, his bodyguards and knights like King Navarr had. *No, I'm getting ahead of myself here. Just because I recovered the sword...*

But he found himself saying, 'In time, I will need loyal men. Will you be among them?'

The men looked at each other and, seeing no doubt, nodded eagerly. Asaph smiled. In their brief time together they had already fought for each other's lives—and survived. He knew he could trust them with his life. What more could a king ask of his men?

'For now, I have to leave to go on a quest,' Asaph said, finding the sword's pommel in his grasp and his thoughts turning to the dragons. He had stayed here too long already.

'Then we will come,' said Leaper. 'I lost my bricklaying job anyway. That's why those bastards found me so drunk. And I prefer fighting.' He stood up proudly and unashamed.

'No, no one will come with me. I must go alone,' said Asaph. 'I'll be going north—as far north as one can go.'

'To the dragons,' said Leaper under his breath, his face a mix of fear and awe.

Asaph nodded once. 'The time has come. Our world is plunging into darkness. Maybe they will help. They *must* help. I only hope it is not too late. When I return, I will need to form my own army. I intend to take back Drax.' He clenched his fist. The men looked at him, half in wonder and half as if he were insane.

'For now, stay here. Tell them everything that happened to you in the temple. King Navarr is a good man who values honesty. If he offers you training, take it. If he offers you a place in his guard, take it.'

'I would be honoured,' said Renno. The man's eyes were alight with prospects.

The others agreed.

Finding nothing more to say, Asaph inclined his head and turned towards the door. Leaper followed.

'How long will it take?' he asked.

Asaph shrugged. 'I don't know. I only know that I cannot fail. Without the dragons, we can never fight the Dromoorai. If I don't succeed, it is better I don't return at all.'

Leaper looked at the floor. 'I don't think you will fail. If you do, then we're all lost anyway. Thank you, for saving me back there. I still feel half mad from the things I've seen. Terrible things.' He looked at the floor as a tremble took hold of his shoulders.

'Time,' said Asaph, laying a hand on the man's shoulder. 'Time will help. And revenge. There are untold horrors occurring in this world as we speak. That is why we fight.' He cast his eyes over all the men. 'If we do not fight, evil will win. I will die rather than live in their world of barbarism and servitude.'

Whatever haunted Leaper passed from his eyes and the man clenched his jaw, vengeful. 'I mean it,' he said. 'And I'm sure they do too. We will fight and we are loyal to you now.'

Asaph dropped his voice for only Leaper to hear. 'Just look after them and be watchful. Baelthrom might attack at any moment. When we get the chance we'll destroy the one who started it all. You saw her; the blonde woman, the High Priestess.'

Leaper swallowed and nodded. 'She's not…human. She's one of them but filled with vicious, cunning hatred. And the things that come out of the black hole…'

'Leaper, don't think about it. Think on better things. Don't let the darkness in. A new dawn is coming; I promise you that while I still breathe. And with it a new age. We have to believe.'

'Yes, Sir,' he said, standing straighter

Asaph grinned. 'Just Asaph. We were beside each other stark naked in a dungeon not a day ago.'

Leaper smiled then wiggled his jaw. 'And I can still feel where you knocked me out.'

Sitting on the bed in his old room in Castle Carvon felt odd. Coronos was not here and neither was Issa. There was nothing here for him. Everything lay with the dragons in the north or with Issa in the south. There was no point staying any longer, and with this urgency burning within him he knew he wouldn't be able to sleep, despite sorely needing too.

He pushed himself up, grabbed his pack of water and food, and then took up his sword and left his room. Not really wanting to bump into anyone, he took the quieter corridor down to a back door and slipped out into the lamp-lit courtyard. Seeing light coming through a gap in the smithy door, he headed over to it and went inside.

Warmth and the red glow of the furnace hit him. Zeb was bent over the workbench working on something Asaph couldn't quite see, using tools he was unfamiliar with and had no idea what they were used for. The fair-haired man looked up, startled.

'I didn't think smiths worked this late,' said Asaph, smiling at the stocky man.

Zeb smiled and stood, running a hand through his fair hair as he arched his back. 'I'm usually done by sunset but I know you needed this by dawn.' He picked up what he had been working on; a scabbard for Asaph's blade. 'And it's Mary's birthday tomorrow so I was just waiting for this to set.' He picked up a hand-sized wooden mould within which was a molten silver ring.

Asaph raised an eyebrow. 'A blacksmith, weaponsmith, and a silversmith? You are a man of many talents.'

Zeb smiled. 'Not really. I'm only good at blacksmithing but I try my hand at the others and earn a bit extra on the side.'

'Well, Mary is a lucky woman. That ring is solidly made,' said Asaph, admiring its flawless sheen.

'Solidly made, yes, but I'll need a proper silversmith to inscribe it. I don't have the knack for intricate detail. Now then, try this for size.'

The man tossed him the scabbard. Asaph caught it, immediately surprised at its light weight, and began his inspection. It was edged in shining steel and made of some strange black material. Frowning in recognition, he stroked the toughened leather that gleamed metallic black. He took a sharp breath and shot Zeb a look.

'Dread Dragon scales?'

'Aye,' said the man, his face breaking into a tilted smile. 'There be a new shop in town. Higglesworth Enterprises. It's filled with all manner of interesting and exotic items collected from across the Known World. The most precious of which appear to be these dragon scales. So, the scabbard is expensive, but nothing will ever break it.'

'Incredible—and fitting,' Asaph said, admiring the stunning piece of work. Carefully he slid the Sword of Binding into the sheath and it made a soft ringing sound. As soon as it was in, the skin miraculously tightened around it to fit it snuggly. The weight of the sword in the scabbard was little more than before.

'My,' said Asaph, amazed. 'This scabbard is worth gold. All it needs is a good enchantment,'

The smith nodded, clearly proud of his work. Asaph pulled out gold and silver coins and passed them to him. Zeb's eyes lit up.

'With that, I can take Mary to Rosie's Restaurant, and fix my chimney and the stove,' he said.

'I know where to come when I need any armour or jewellery.' Asaph grinned, tying his sheathed sword onto his sword frog. 'Thank you, Zeb.'

The two men shook hands, Asaph almost wincing in the man's strong grasp.

'You look after that young missy of yours, she's a good one,' said Zeb, his face turning serious. 'In this world, a woman needs a strong man to look after her. I've seen them black dragons in the sky. Hoped I never would…Good luck to you.'

'I will, Zeb,' said Asaph, 'and good luck to you too.'

Asaph left the smithy and stepped out into the night. The greatest task of his life now lay before him. Everything he had dreamed of doing, of becoming, was finally in his grasp.

CHAPTER 28

Venosia

THE exhilarating rush of the raven form engulfed Issa and then she was ruffling her feathers in the cold breeze.

She hopped onto the windowsill and looked across the dark forest. Her sensitive hearing could just pick up the sound of the waves crashing on the shores beyond the trees.

Ehka squawked from a tree somewhere in the dark. At least she wouldn't be flying alone. She had considered sending just him but feared for his safety, plus she knew she needed to see the enemy-held lands with her own eyes. She wanted to know what a once beautiful land looked like after Baelthrom had ravaged it. Was it really true what the stories said, that everything was withered and dead? That red clouds scoured the skies and rivers had long since dried up?

It would be dangerous, of course. But if it took too long to reach Venosia, she could always turn back.

Before fear and doubt changed her mind, she leapt into the air and spread her wings, letting the joy of flying fill her and shut all else out. She wheeled lazily around the smoking chimney of the tavern, lifting higher and higher. Setting her mind upon Venosia she turned east toward the ocean with Ehka following below.

The night was mostly overcast but, between the clouds, Woetala shone down. An east wind blew against her but it wasn't strong and it was said to often change direction at night. She hoped it would change soon and blow her forward. The lights of the South Reach and its harbour came and went. Ahead there was only darkness and an endless sea.

In her avian body, she didn't know fear of the future in quite the same way. Yes, she was still her human self, but it was heavily overlaid with her raven self; wild, focused on the moment, and interpreting a world filled more with sounds, sights and smells than ever before. She could smell the sea like never she had, she could make out the white-tipped waves far below, and she could hear the ropes slapping against masts in the harbour, now far away. She could feel where she was in the sky relative to the sea or ground and she instinctively knew which way was north, east, south or west.

Ehka flew lower and a little ahead of her, keeping a sharp look out for danger. They were swiftly covering a lot of distance in darkness. How slow and cumbersome it was to walk on two legs. Flying was far more effortless. The Flow was different, however. It was there but wilder and harder to grasp and control. It also seemed a little weaker. Perhaps her human self had become adept at using it. Thankfully, it still responded to her will.

Not wanting to wait for the wind to naturally change direction, she drew the Flow to her, commanding it with her mind since she doubted raven squawks would be as effective as her inner voice.

'Wind be at my back.'

The wind slackened, then blew from behind. Tilting her wings to catch it, she cawed her joy, thankful for Haelgon's lessons in Weather Magic. Faster, she made the wind blow until sometimes it was hard to breathe as it gushed past. It was daring, using magic to enter enemy lands, but she counted on being high in the sky and small. Nothing would detect them easily. Besides, it was doubtful any necromancers or Dromoorai were watching for them. What if Baelthrom had already spotted their armies marching to Davono? That thought made her fly faster.

They flew for over two hours without slowing before she felt a change. Land was near. The scent in the air was different. She sensed danger, too, not a specific threat but more a general, dull sense that she should not go further.

On the horizon, a black layer appeared. Swiftly it approached and she dropped her control of the wind, focusing the magic on cloaking her and Ehka. Her wings ached and her belly rumbled. She longed to rest on a rock and eat the biscuits in her pocket, but these were enemy-held lands. Her hunger waned.

Clouds blanketed the sky, concealing the orange light of Woetala and, ahead, they glowed a strange dull red. Glancing down at the ocean, she saw things in the water around which the waves crashed white. She dropped lower to inspect them.

Enormous spikes of black rock struck out of the ocean, rising at least twenty feet and angled towards any approaching ship. There were hundreds of them, stretching out for a mile from the coast of Venosia, and north and south as far as the eye could see. Ehka circled the spikes with her and Issa squawked her dismay. No ship could navigate a course through them; they would be skewered and smashed apart.

The Devil's Horns. The shipmates had talked about them on the way to Davono. Issa shivered and her hopes dipped. They would halt their army before they even landed. Somehow they had to be destroyed before they reached Venosia's shores. But how did they do that without eliminating their element of surprise and tiring the wizards aboard?

Issa flew low over the spikes considering the attack, but no good ideas came to mind. She turned towards the coast. Ahead were mostly tall, dark cliffs, but here and there were long flat coves. Some of them had clusters of small buildings. *The old fishing villages,* she realised, spying the sad, crumbled rock walls of ancient houses and the lines of terracing that the weather, time or the enemy had not been able to erase.

Cautiously, she glided up the grey sand beach of a small cove and landed on a wall that was barely more than a line of rocks. Black cliffs loomed above her on either side of the village remains and a narrow pass stretched over the hill beyond. The wind blew and the waves scoured the shore, but there was nothing here. Not even any trees. She sensed no enemy. Some ships could dock here but not many.

She flew along the cliffs to the next cove and the remains of another village. This one was larger than the previous, and not as hemmed in by cliffs. She didn't pause but carried on scouting. The next cove was larger still. They could land many ships here and attack, assuming they made it past the black spikes.

She lifted into the air and climbed the cliff, heading north. A yellow light appeared on a bluff, followed by two more. *Danger.* She dropped low and hugged the base of the rocks, the waves crashed against it, wetting her feathers. As she rounded the cliff, more lights appeared.

A huge, smooth rock jutted oddly out from the cliffside. She landed on it with Ehka and stared at it through her claws. It had been carved into perfect, giant fingers and fingernails—each finger as big as her human body. She perched upon a giant, chiselled hand. She looked up to where it might have fallen from but there was just jagged rock. In the ocean below there was a tonne of rubble and huge boulders. Some of them were rounded and may have once been carved, but the sea had pounded them beyond recognition.

Whatever the hand had been part of would have been gigantic, certainly the largest statue she had ever seen. *Statues we no longer make nor know how to make.* Now it was nothing but rubble. A relic of a long forgotten age when her race had been skilled and powerful. *How far the mighty fall,* she thought. *We don't even remember who we are. Everything we had is gone.*

Movement caught her attention. Ahead, a long beach ended in the massive grey wall of a harbour stretching out to sea. Along it burned giant sconces illuminating Maphraxies marching in pairs, their black armour catching the light. She swallowed.

Adjoining the harbour was a large port. From her position, she could only see part of it but there were many lights illuminating scores of ugly, flat, square buildings. Even though it was night, Maphraxie guards patrolled everywhere. *This is dark dwarf land and dark dwarves live underground,* she thought. There could be thousands of them living beneath the port.

Her army would have to attack here first and hope that not too many escaped to raise the alarm in other settlements.

A tremendous screech cut through the air and she froze, her insides trembling. Ehka cowered and dipped his head. Cold fear trickled down her back. The Dread Dragon screeched again, closer. She didn't need to see it to know what it was. Surely it could see them it sounded so close. It was a good thing she couldn't move.

The Dread Dragon swooped over them, wind blasting past, its huge body snaking through the air, light gleaming off its slick scales. Dropping its hind legs, it landed on the harbour wall and gave another ear-bursting scream. Issa couldn't take her eyes off it as she flattened herself against the rock.

Another scream answered from further away. She squinted at the far cliff and saw a black mass moving and more lights. How many Dromoorai were there? Did she dare fly at all with these beasts so close? A part of her had imagined there being no Dromoorai and few Maphraxies. An entire empty coast just waiting for them to land. She laughed inwardly at the foolish thought.

On trembling wings, she dropped from the rock and flew low across the waves, giving the port a wide berth. She could see it clearly now, the strange, flat, grey buildings stretching back into land and over the hill. It was the perfect place to dock and attack but it was also teeming with the enemy.

She flew around the cliff, keen to put more space between her and the Dread Dragons. A shallow cave appeared half way up and she darted into it. Breathing hard she rested her wings. Ehka landed beside her. Her stomach rumbled as fear and exhaustion made her feel faint.

It took a good long moment and lots of convincing for her to release her raven form. Flattening her body against the floor, she sat listening to the crashing waves for some time, expecting for the head of a Dread Dragon to appear at the entrance any moment.

Nothing happened.

Reaching into a pouch tied to her belt, she pulled out a couple of sweet oat biscuits she had saved from dinner. She crumbled one for Ehka and chewed on her own as he gobbled it up.

'It'll have to do until we get back home, I'm afraid,' she whispered, feeling her own stomach rumble for more. She had no idea flying would be this tiring or that Venosia was so far away. She began to curse herself for doing things on a whim. What a foolish idea coming here had been. *Half an hour's rest and no more.* Then she'd go north a little further and head back to Davono.

Flying north, she found several smaller coves. Only one was inhabited with a small harbour and the same square buildings. There were flaming sconces but less than at the previous harbour. Their armies could easily take the coves and the main port unless there was an entire city of dark dwarves underground waiting for them—then it might not be so easy. It was a huge risk, but after so much had happened they had little choice. It had to be a risk she was prepared to take.

Lifting high into the air she turned inland and headed back south. A vast swathe of treeless, grassless land spread out before her. It went on and on into the horizon. In every direction as far as the eye could see there was empty, scoured dirt illuminated by the strange, dull red clouds above. It looked like there might be shrub or two here and there but she couldn't be sure. Perhaps it was just rubble.

This was once Karalanth land, swathed in ancient forests thicker and deeper than those in Frayon, stretching from the north coast all the way to the south. Now it was nothing and the trees were gone. There weren't even rivers; the beds had bled dry long ago, leaving empty ruts of rocks scarring the land. Occasionally she passed over huge piles of rubble and what may have been terracing or village walls. *This land was lost a long, long time ago.* Her raven form shielded her from the anger and sorrow she might have felt.

Low thunder rumbled above and the clouds became more heavy and oppressive. *What made them dark red like that?* she wondered. She had the feeling thunder always rumbled here—as if the sky were as sick as the land. Beneath the Flow, she could feel the Under Flow moving in the earth and in the clouds. She didn't dare focus on the black magic, not wanting to feel it or alert it to her presence.

A deep sense of foreboding stole over her. She should head back. Coming here was too dangerous. If she were spotted, there was nowhere on this barren landscape to hide. She took a keener angle towards the ocean in the distance. Once she reached the sea, she would be safe.

A ridge rose ahead, stretching many miles west. She crested it and wheeled back in shock, a muffled caw escaping her beak. Lifting high to hang just beneath the clouds, she surveyed the scene.

A great city sprawled below surrounded by a huge wall, thicker and taller than any she had ever seen and lacking any pleasing detail to break up its endless surface. The city was perfectly square and ordered in design, and contained the same flat square buildings that dominated the port. At its centre, a huge obelisk speared up into the sky, at least one hundred yards high. Red clouds clustered more densely above it and silent lightening flared down to meet it at odd intervals.

Construction was happening at the city walls. Giant blocks of black stone were being placed on top of the flat surface giving the wall a jagged appearance that also sloped inwards. Was the city still being built?

She turned her attention back to the giant obelisk, banking left to avoid flying too close to it. It wasn't a single pillar of stone, and there were many lights within it all the way to its top. With a gasp, she saw that what she had thought were turrets were actually Dromoorai, perched one to each corner. They stood so still, like statues. *No, they are real, they are just sleeping,* she thought, though she knew Dromoorai never really slept and were always ready for battle.

Long straight streets crisscrossed the city and along these tiny beings marched. *Maphraxies, they never sleep either, nor do they even need to rest.* She hated them all for that strength, especially now when her wings ached and she wished she were back in her bed. There were more Dromoorai too, positioned on massive square platforms at each corner of the city.

She racked her brain for any maps of Venosia she might have seen. From what she remembered, this city was far too close to the coast to be the main dark dwarven stronghold Diredrull—a place said to exist underneath the abandoned Tarvalastone city taken from the dwarves of light long ago.

No, this was a new, different city. Beneath it would be a cavernous realm made by the dark dwarves. How many such cities were there in Venosia? There would be more than one close to the coast. All it would take to alert them to an attack would be a Dread Dragon.

Even if they were able to take this city, would they be able to hold it against legion of enemies? Even if their armies successfully took the coast, there was no running water and no food. Maybe there was ground water somewhere. The Orb of Water would help her find it. And they would have food from the supply ships, and more would be brought from Davono and Atalanph. She sighed. It wouldn't be easy. She'd have to rely on experienced officers and commanders knowing what to do. All she had come here for was to scout the area, and now it was time to go.

She turned west into the wind. At the coast, she would have the rest of her biscuits and prepare herself for the return trip. The wind had picked up and blew so strongly against her that even getting to the cliffs was slow going. She scouted along the bluffs but couldn't find the shallow cave again. Instead, she was forced to land beside a pile of rocks a little back from the cliff's edge.

She felt exposed here, with the wind gushing up the cliff and tearing at her feathers. Ehka wedged himself between two boulders, his eyes constantly darting left and right, evidently feeling as uncomfortable as she did. It took a long time to convince herself to drop her raven form. When she did, the feeling of unease intensified.

'Just a short rest and some food,' she said, more to herself than Ehka, and pulled out her biscuits. As they ate she looked west. Out there, far away on the horizon, was the barest sliver of light. The lighter sky in the distance lifted her spirits. There would be no sunset here on Venosia, only a growing red sky with the same dark, thundering clouds. Neither the sun nor the moons had risen here for hundreds if not thousands of years. If they retook the land, would it push back the Under Flow and the overcast skies? She imagined the blue moon rising here, cleansing everything with its light.

Perhaps it was the sound of the surf drowning everything out, or the wind and the sea whipping away the foul stench of the Black Drink, but neither she nor Ehka heard the footfalls until a great cold hand clasped over her throat, lifting her into the air and pulling her backwards.

A meaty fist punched into her stomach knocking the air from her lungs. Issa doubled over, gasping for breath. A Maphraxie's arms wrapped around her in a crushing vice. The smell of the undead made her gag. Ehka cawed loudly, only just making it into the air in time as another Maphraxie swung a black iron axe at him.

Issa kicked and bucked uselessly. In her throes, she glimpsed the hidden doorway in the ground just a few yards away. A tunnel disappeared into the blackness, confirming her fears that the whole place was riddled with them and infested with dark dwarves. She sighed. None of this was ever going to be easy.

Lifting her feet, she booted the Maphraxie looming before her in the stomach, using the one clamping its arms around her as leverage. The surprised Maphraxie gasped a putrid breath and its watery white eyes widened. Ehka attacked the head of the one holding her, his talons and beak gleaming.

Feeling its grip slacken, Issa yanked her right arm free and managed to reach her sword. She pulled it free and stabbed down into the grey flesh of an exposed calf. The Maphraxie grunted and dropped her. Rolling to her feet, she just dodged the other Maphraxies' axe.

The Maphraxie laughed, a choking sound, and hefted its axe, its sharp edge jagged like a saw. Issa pursed her lips. She had to kill these two. Even if she managed to get away, they couldn't be allowed to live to alert the others, although eventually they would be found to be missing. She was an idiot for not finding a better resting place. Now there was even less time to return to Davono and bring the army. That element of surprise was all they had.

Ehka squawked loudly but she couldn't take her eyes off the enemy in front of her. She feinted left, spinning to avoid the axe and allowing her a glimpse of Ehka's predicament. He was scratching at the eyes of a howling Maphraxie who was trying to swat him and at the same time pull out his mace.

Issa lunged at her opponent, hoping to drive it back but it just stood there and parried, jolting her arm. She pirouetted back from its axe towards the other Maphraxie, daring to drop her gaze and glance back. The other Maphraxies' fleshy grey throat was exposed while Ehka attacked. Issa entered the Flow then remembered where she was. She couldn't use magic here; it would attract Dromoorai.

Her opponent ran at her. She ducked around the other Maphraxie and stabbed at its throat. Her sword sunk sickeningly deep into its flesh and black blood oozed. She stabbed again. Ehka leapt off its head. It gurgled and its hands uselessly grasped at the blood spilling from its neck. Issa would have vomited had the other Maphraxie not been running towards her, axe raised and howling at the demise of its companion.

She ran, dodged under its swinging axe and jumped at the other, wounded Maphraxie, planting both feet into its chest. The Maphraxie staggered towards the cliff edge, then toppled off, howling. Issa rolled to her knees. The move cost her time and she barely turned her chest away from the other's falling axe. It sliced across her left arm with sickening ease.

Battle fury kept the pain away. There was no agony yet just hot blood and weakness. Her fingers tingled but she still had her arm. There was no woozy feeling and she thanked the goddess it wasn't her sword arm and the blade wasn't poisoned.

Growling, she drove her sword forward. It clanged uselessly off the Maphraxie's armour. She ran back as the enemy pounded towards her. Ehka swooped to attack. She screamed as he narrowly missed its swinging blade. Stepping towards the cliff's edge, she glanced at the waves crashing far below. The fallen Maphraxie was nowhere to be seen. Pure white surrounded black rocks reminding her of the Shadowlands. The Maphraxie followed her, utterly fearless.

The axe swung. She ducked under it and leapt up, flinging herself onto the Maphraxie's chest. She grappled with its breastplate, pain bursting in her injured arm as she struggled to hold on. Clinging to its chest brought her out of range of its axe. With her good arm, she sliced her sword down, severing its left hand at the edge of its bracers. It only grunted, making her wonder if these beasts felt pain at all.

Awkwardly lifting herself off its cuirass, she swung her whole body towards the cliff edge, groaning against the fire in her arm as she tried to hang on. Ehka attacked its eyes again, and it stumbled and lurched. Finally, it dropped its axe to swat at the bird. For a moment the edge came into view and the frothing white waves crashed against black rocks far below. Then they were falling together.

Issa shoved herself off the flailing Maphraxie, closed her eyes against the rushing, tumbling world and embraced her raven form. Wind filled her wings thrusting her upwards. The Maphraxie fell fast and splattered upon the rocks, black blood oozing over them to stain the sea dark. The pain in her arm, now a bleeding wing, was unbearable. It took all her concentration to stay airborne and not fall out of the sky.

She cawed for Ehka. He was nowhere to be seen. Frantically, she searched the sky above and rocks below. Swooping lower, she spied a black speck struggling to stay atop a rock as the sea surged around it. She dropped towards it. Ehka looked up and cawed. His wing hung down but he was alive. Waves were almost crashing over the top of the rock he was on trying to sweep him into the sea.

She landed beside him and released her raven form, shivering as sea spray soaked her and stung her injured arm. Carefully she put him on her lap and touched his wounded wing. It was hot. He couldn't fly. Only magic was going to get them off this rock. Dropping her curses, she decided to use magic and entered the Flow. She lightly held his wing and closed her eyes, feeling out the injury. It was fractured in two places. Drawing on the Flow, it was pitifully weak in this place anyway, she moved the barest magic through her palm, spreading it into his wing, hoping to make it strong enough so he could at least get off this rock.

Issa opened her eyes. His wing was still hot but it drooped less. Hopefully he could fly a short way. Using the same technique, she held her palm against her own wound. It was wet with fresh blood though the dragon scale tunic itself had mended together.

Edarna's enchantments, she thought. *What a blessing.* The wound was too deep for the enchantment to heal her fully. Ely's bracelet was surely helping to stem the blood flow, otherwise she would have been in a worse state. Still, she needed rest and to tend it properly. She stared up at the cliff, searching for somewhere safe that they could reach.

'Ah, I recognise it now,' she said, and pointed up and to the right. 'Fly to the cave, it should be there somewhere.'

Ehka dipped his beak and launched uneasily into the air. Embracing her raven form, she overtook him and flew ahead, hunting for the shallow cave. Spotting it, she landed inside and released her form, immediately glad to be out of the cold wind. Ehka skidded besides her, listing weakly. It wasn't much of a shelter, but it beat sitting next to a dark dwarf tunnel filled with Maphraxies.

Carefully, she undid her armour and slipped it over her shoulder. Blood trickled from her wound but it was trying to close and ached dully now rather than with raging pain. She pulled from her pouch a tiny pot of potent healing ointment that Naksu had given her. With just two drops, she set about cleaning the wound then bound it with a strip of gauze Naksu had made her keep in her belt. She did up her armour then sat still, thinking. She couldn't rest, not just yet. That doorway to the tunnel had to be closed and the Maphraxie had dropped its weapon somewhere meaning it was just waiting to be found.

'*Stay here,*' she said to Ehka in Daluni mind-speak, resumed her raven form and launched back into the air, her wing protesting painfully.

Cautiously, she returned to the tunnel the Maphraxies had emerged from. There were no Maphraxies and no smell of the enemy near so she dared to land beside it.

Inspecting the rough entrance revealed no obvious door. Perhaps it had been a magical door opened by dark dwarven runes. If things worked in her favour, the enemy would think one of their own had left it open. It was a weak hope.

She hunted for the Maphraxie's weapon. There, on the ground beside the cliff was the dropped axe. She hopped towards it. Looking left then right, she resumed her human form and kicked the axe off the edge. It spun into the sea with a giant splash. Now there was no obvious sign that anything had happened up here.

She returned to the cave finding Ehka shivering and huddled against the floor. She sat down beside him and held him close, trying to give him warmth. What did they do now? His wing was temporarily better, but there was no way he could make the return journey home. She couldn't stay here in this hellhole until he was healed.

She felt his mind press upon hers and with it came images of the open ocean and sunlight.

'No. I'm not leaving you so don't even think it,' she said aloud and chewed her fingernail. 'But we can't stay here. Soon, they'll know two of theirs are missing and will send out a search party. Already our cover might be blown.'

An idea came to her—it was the only way out of here she could think of. Picking up a stone, she scraped the symbol of the Murk into the rock. With her knife, she nicked her finger and clasped her fist around it to catch the blood.

Carefully lifting Ehka, she stepped onto the symbol and let the blood fall, holding her intention to reach the Murk clear in her mind. The symbol flared green, then smoke and rushing wind became her world.

CHAPTER 29

Demon Magic

THAT moment between places, between dimensions, when everything was dark and fragmented and a rush of noise, wind and confusion, lasted longer than Issa remembered.

She felt the connection waver as if it wasn't as strong. It didn't last long enough for her to panic and in the next instance, she found herself swaying before the green crystal shard, wanting to throw up the biscuits that now seemed lodged in her stomach.

'Is it time?' the voice was so deep and gravelly it took her a while to realise the words were Frayonesse, not Demonic.

She blinked up into the huge, ugly, flat face of Gedrock. Yellow eyes with slitted pupils narrowed.

'Issy!' squeaked a voice and then something smacked into her calf and wrapped its arms, legs and tail around her. Ehka squawked in her arms.

'Maggot?' She reached down and scratched his head, but the movement made her so dizzy she stood back up and leant against the wall.

'I tried to come, but I couldn't reach you!' Maggot said, his yellow eyes wide and pupils mere slits.

'The connection was strange,' she said, catching her breath and wondering.

'She smells worse than usual.' Gedrock's advisor came to stand beside the king, heavily relying on his staff as he walked. His face wrinkled in disgust.

'She does. Where have you come from?' asked Gedrock.

'I come from behind the enemy line. Could that be why the translocation was weak?'

'It's the Other Magic,' said Wekurd to Gedrock. 'I can smell it all over her.'

'The Under Flow? Yes, it must be,' Issa said. 'No, King Gedrock. In answer to your question, it is not time and we are not at war, *yet*. I was scouting enemy-held lands and we were attacked. Ehka hurt his wing and we became trapped. We cannot stay there nor can we make the long journey home until his wing is stronger.'

'You have the spear. With it you can get to safer places other than the Murk,' said the King.

'Marakon has the spear. He is far away. Listen, I must leave Ehka here in your care until he can return to us. It will only be a day or two with the magic I have used. Water and maggots will suit him fine.' She smiled at Maggot. The little demon frowned, his skin wrinkling up on his forehead so he looked a hundred years old. Clearly, he didn't want to share his maggots with anyone.

Gedrock rolled back his muscled shoulders. 'We do not like... ravens.' He bared his fangs at the bird.

Ehka gave a defiant squawk, opening his mouth wide and sticking out his tongue.

'You will remember that it was he who risked his life to warn you about the greater demons.' Issa reminded him.

Gedrock eyed the bird suspiciously. 'Hmm, I suppose it is rather small. Perhaps it can stay for a short time. But I cannot vouch for his safety should any of our kind think it edible.'

'Ehka has ways in which he can look after himself,' Issa said, though she knew that Gedrock or Maggot would do whatever they could to protect the bird.

Gedrock turned his gaze upon her. 'And what about you?'

'I must return immediately.'

'Alone? To enemy lands? It is dangerous. All wizards can sense a portal being opened, whether from the Murk or anywhere else. Necromancers especially.'

'Too dangerous,' echoed Maggot still gripping her leg.

Issa chewed her lip. They were right, but she had to get back to the others. It would take her half a day to fly, even with Weather Magic. The battle could not wait, not when she had potentially triggered the enemy's suspicion. They could already be hunting for their missing Maphraxies. What if their death hounds could smell her presence?

Despite those worries, extreme tiredness nagged at her and she found herself saying with a sigh, 'All right. I'll rest here for a couple of hours.' Maybe Ehka would be stronger by then but she doubted it.

'Great. We shall have a banquet,' said Gedrock and bellowed. Wekurd snickered beside him, his long, red tongue lolling out.

Issa grimaced at the thought of a demon banquet. 'No offence, King Gedrock, but I don't think I'll be joining you. I'm too tired and it's probably not for humans.'

Gedrock considered this, his ears twitching, then nodded. 'So be it.'

'Maggot,' said Issa lightly, glad to have escaped eating with demons. 'Why don't you show me something interesting about this place?' She looked around the giant chamber. It was further illuminated by hundreds of smaller green crystals hugging the rock walls. This was the first time she had been in Carmedrak without fearing for her life.

'Maggot, show her the view from the turret,' said Gedrock. 'Humans enjoy views and it will keep her out of the way. I don't want her smell spreading everywhere and getting the demons excited.'

He wasn't being unkind and she found herself hiding a smile, especially when she struggled to cope with the rank, fleshy smell of the demons themselves.

The little demon looked excited. He flapped into the air, grabbed a lock of her hair and flew towards a huge arched doorway, pulling her somewhat gently along by it.

She glanced back at Ehka. He seemed quite happy dozing beside Gedrock's huge clawed feet. Gedrock eyed the bird with a frown. Issa tried not to giggle.

The view from the turret was breath-taking. The half-moon of Zorock beamed down upon the vast landscape. Miles below them, the Black Sands stretched in all directions to the base of the mountains several leagues away. Their black craggy peaks ringed the plane, protective and foreboding.

'Over there is where we came and you arrived with Demon Slayer,' explained Maggot, pointing.

Issa recalled the moment she had raced atop Duskar across the Black Sands, Pit Demons chasing her, and thrown the spear to Marakon.

'Have all the demons from the Pit gone now? Did any return?'

Maggot shook his head. 'No. They all disappeared when Demon Slayer closed the tunnel. King says none will ever be able to break through again. There is trouble with some Grazen though. They do not like having a Shadow Demon king and want their own.'

Issa sighed. Demon troubles appeared to be similar to human ones.

Issa rested in the corner of a chamber with several small crystal shards casting an eerie green light. She tried to find it relaxing. Ehka and Maggot slept beside her. Her arm hurt quite a lot, but she knew it was healing pain. To take her mind off it, she thought about the coming invasion, where best to land, how to overcome the Devil's Horns and retain their surprise attack—all of which made it even harder to sleep despite her throbbing shoulder.

She pulled the rank-smelling blanket they had given her closer, thankful at least for the warmth it provided. After a moment she surprised herself and fell asleep.

When she awoke, Maggot and Ehka still slept and Zorock had not yet set, though it was just touching the mountain tops. How much time had passed upon Maioria since she had been gone? Whatever the answer was, it was too long. She had to get going.

She sat up. Maggot stretched and Ehka opened his eyes.

'You stay here until you know you can fly home,' she said, stroking the bird. 'Don't return to Venosia, it's not safe. Go whichever way you ravens know best.' He dipped his head. She knew he didn't want her to go but understood their predicament.

'I'll come with you, Issy,' said Maggot.

'Just help me get back through the crystal. I won't need any help after that,' she said.

In the King's great chamber, Maggot placed his hands on the huge green crystal first, his eyes a mix of fear and wonder. 'I hate the human worlds, but being with you is exciting,' he said, twitching his ears.

Issa grinned and placed her hands on the crystal beside his, feeling at once the strange demon magic recoil at her touch and then hungrily fill her palms, seeking her soul energy. She didn't like the feeling at all.

Her body was pulled forwards, becoming light and insubstantial. Rushing air filled her being, the chamber faded away, and she felt herself lifting upwards. Maggot's face was lost in a sea of pulsing green. Focusing on Venosia, she could feel the Murk magic seeking the symbol she had drawn on the floor of the shallow cave. It connected and she rushed forwards.

The symbol appeared before her, a line of bright luminescence in a field of green. Soon she could make out the rock of the cave. Suddenly, the demon magic faltered and grew thin. Something was wrong. It jerked and stuttered.

Issa entered the Flow, finding herself able to reach it here between dimensions, and supplemented the Murk magic with her own. The ground materialised but dark clouds engulfed her, blotting out her vision. Refusing to panic, she pulled more magic to her. The Flow was driven from her grasp.

The rushing wind stopped and she crouched, feeling hard rock beneath her hands but there was no cave around her, she was in an open space. The black brightened into swathes of grey moving this way and that like a thick fog. Slowly she pulled herself to her feet, ignoring the knot tightening in her stomach.

'Maggot?' she called out, her voice heavy and eerie in the silence. He wasn't here; she was very much alone. She pulled out her raven talisman. It was heavy, cold and unresponsive to her commanding mind. She tried to reach the Flow again.

Nothing.

Then she heard a faint noise, as if from far away. She pricked her ears. It was a beat thudding into the earth. Horses? It sounded like there were more than one and they were getting louder. She unsheathed her sword. What could she do against several of anything with just her sword and no magic? Without the talisman, she couldn't even reach the realm of the dead!

In the billowing grey, black specks formed. The sound of hoof beats rumbled closer, soon becoming thunderous in her ears. Issa's heart leapt into her throat. The specks became definite horse shapes with riders—four dark shadows galloping through the fog straight towards her.

One of the horses lifted its long shadow head and neighed—but the sound it made was a scream, a scream that tore into her. She trembled, dropped her sword and fell to her knees. The Under Flow surged towards her, coming directly from the four horsemen. Paralysing cold engulfed her, chilling her bones. She tried to stand, to grab her sword, anything, but her body would not obey. It was bound by the Under Flow. All she could do was tremble.

Cold sweat trickled down her temples and back. They were only yards away. Another horse lifted its head and neighed. Agony filled her ears and she screamed. Her terror seemed to excite them and they came on faster.

She forced herself to look at the horsemen. They had no eyes; only black pits that leaked smoke. The pits drew her in, hunting for her soul, eating her alive. As her strength drained they grew larger and more substantial.

The horsemen separated to surround her, lifting their shadow swords high. She could not run; she could not fight. A horse bent its head towards her, its snout materialising into that of a solid beast. *Black metallic skin like the scales of a Dread Dragon.* It pulled back its lips and black fangs protruded.

Issa jerked away, trying but failing to control her trembling body. Beyond the shadow horsemen, other shadows formed, great pillars of darkness that began to take human form. Her breath came fast and she shook her head, disbelieving. *Light Eaters!* The same fallen beings she had glimpsed in the Dark Rift.

Issa was gasping so much she felt faint. She had never been this helpless before. The horsemen reached down to her, huge hands materialising from the smoke, gauntleted in black iron armour like a Dromoorai.

Gold flashed, catching her eye. One wore a ring. It seemed so strange upon the horseman's finger that she stared at it, noting the engraving of a horse. A fist clamped around her throat and a cold agony spread from there, right down to her chest, forcing the scream from her lips. By some miracle, her searching fingers found her sword and she slashed up. It clanged loudly and glanced harmlessly off impenetrable armour.

Beneath her, a green symbol flared, Murk magic surged and the Under Flow was shoved away. A foot-long spike with a wickedly sharp tip shot past her ear straight into the shadow face of the horseman gripping her neck. The horseman howled a deafening sound and released her neck.

She fell to her knees and stared in shock as the spike turned in mid-air and whizzed past her face again to strike another horseman. It screamed and the Under Flow lost power. The ground beneath her slid away and then she was falling. A horse screamed again, though from far away. The sound still tore at her mind and she writhed in agony.

She hit something hard, rolled and lay there panting as the pain receded. Her body shook and she kept her face pressed against cold hard rock. The air was damp and salty and there was a booming din as of waves against cliffs.

'Issy?' said a familiar voice.

CHAPTER 30

The Dawn Bringer

ASAPH paused at the edge of the forest.

Only the light of the city behind him pushed back the darkness. It was cloudy tonight, and cold.

The dragon form came easily to him in a rush of magic. Breathing in, he leapt into the air and beat his wings until the city lights were far below him. Cloaking himself in magic, he lifted beyond the clouds and marvelled at the wondrous sky filled with stars. They twinkled silently above and all around—he even saw two shooting through the night in a blaze of pure light. There were so many stars, he felt tiny and insignificant, even as a dragon.

His eyes drifted to the massive black scar of the Dark Rift in the sky to his right. It was, without a doubt, much closer and larger. *The largest I have ever seen it.* Maioria was just rolling helplessly towards it. *Or being pulled into it.* He forced his gaze away and focused on feeling for the dragons, rekindling again that incredible moment when he had gripped the Sword of Binding; the power, the memory, the magic. A shiver trembled his body.

'Hear me, great dragons. Awaken!' he called out with his mind across the miles. *'Feygriene's dawn is rising. She calls us to take back our world.'*

The wind soon turned to ice, bringing with it the keen smell of snow. He dropped through the clouds and a world of snow-covered mountains and valleys appeared. It was still a long way to the golden temple where he had met Morhork, and where Ark and Ralan Afisius had formed the First Code. That was where he intended to call the dragons. Initially, he thought he would call to them from the Grey Lords, where Qurenn had fought Slevina and they'd destroyed each other, where Dragon Lords had been born and the sword first formed.

No. He would go back to the start; where the alliance of man and dragon was mutual and respected, even loved. He had no doubt that Ralan Afisius loved Ark, and he, her. Why else would the magician kill herself after his murder?

It was with the first glimmer of the alliance between dragon and man in his mind that he touched down upon the snow-covered plateau before the frozen lake. The snow was deep, coming several feet up his legs.

At the opposite end of the great lake, halfway up the mountains rising above it, he saw a pinprick of gold marking the little temple where he had cremated Coronos' body and set his soul free to Feygriene's light. To his right, there was nothing but boulders and snow. The once magnificent castle that had existed there had been destroyed and sunk into the lake long ago by Morhork.

He did not know what to do about Morhork. The dragon hated humans, Dragons Lords, and any alliance between them. And yet he had saved Asaph—twice—for no benefit to himself. The dragon was a source of confusion and mystery. He certainly opposed Asaph awakening the dragons and leading them to war—another *human* war.

He took a deep breath, then, deciding he couldn't do this on an empty stomach, resumed his human form to eat the sandwich in his pack. When he finished he became still, considering the ancient place upon which he stood. Nothing he had been before mattered now. Nothing that had gone before mattered—and yet all of it had led up to now. Without Ralan and Ark, there could be no Qurenn and Slevina. Without them, there could be no Dragon Lords and thus, no Asaph.

Now they were all gone apart from him. Coronos was gone. Faelsun was gone. He was the last alive and awake to remember the Code and the Binding. And the only one with the power to reignite them. No wonder Morhork hated him. *And yet he saved me.*

'I am no longer the Asaph of old,' he said to the world that was slowly brightening with the coming dawn. It would be a short day in this place so far north. 'I am the last Dragon Lord and a king! And I have Feygriene's blessing.'

He unsheathed the Sword of Binding and held it up, staring into the pommel made of Slevina's blood. *The blood of dragons.* The blood through which he could call them. He walked towards the lake and stepped upon the frozen surface. The ice was so thick and old, it could probably hold a hundred men, he thought.

When he'd walked about a hundred yards, he lifted the sword, angled the point down, and plunged it part way into the ice. It didn't take much strength to penetrate such a blade into it and it slid easily a third of the way into the ice. Satisfied, he left the sword and turned back the way he had come.

Once on land, he resumed his dragon form and entered the Flow. Great swathes of magic engulfed him with a rush of excitement and dragon glory. He filled his lungs with air and roared, releasing the magic as he did so. His roar echoed across the mountains but the vast magic he expended was silent. Again, he filled his lungs and roared, releasing along with it another silent call on the waves of dragon magic.

On the third call, he felt something return to him, a gentle feathering at the corners of his consciousness. Another mind, faint but there. It was joined by another, and then another. He closed his eyes and heard whisperings.

'The Dawn Bringer,' they said. 'The Dawn Bringer.'

Asaph spoke to them in dragon, sending his thought forms far. *'Come to me, noble dragons. Awaken. The Dragon Dream is no more, Faelsun has been murdered—this you know from your dreams. Maioria is falling into oblivion. Feygriene calls to you now to awaken.'*

The whisperings ceased but the dragon minds grew stronger, more alert, though they were still far away. He sensed one approaching, fast, and then it was gone. He tried to find it again but there was nothing. He frowned. Was there some dragon trick he wasn't aware of?

There was no warning; no sound, no wind, nothing to alert him, but suddenly something big exploded into his back sending him flying through the snow and knocking the senses from him. Then the thing was on top of him, crushing him with his weight, and his throat was in its mouth. An ice-blue tail whipped into view. Morhork? He was in such a position that he couldn't see the dragon. One thing he did know, those teeth on his throat were sinking into his scales and shutting off his windpipe. They intended to kill.

With his tail and wings, he heaved himself up, lifting Morhork's bulk as well. It was an immense effort, especially when he could barely breathe. He had to get to his feet. He could not fight on his back and he would not die on it either.

Morhork growled and wrenched viciously. Agony exploded through Asaph, and his brain dimmed from the lack of air. Soon he would lose consciousness. He whipped his tail back and slammed it onto where he thought Morhork's head was. Magic crackled from his blow and Morhork's grip loosened a little.

Asaph smacked his tail down again, filling the blow with more magic. When Morhork loosened a little more, he dared to wrench his throat free, feeling scales tear. Asaph gasped and lunged, spouting flames upon the other dragon. A blizzard of snow blanketed his fire. He leapt through fire and snow to get to the dragon, breathing hard.

Morhork did not evade and rose to attack, his golden eyes blazing in mad fury. Such fury would make Morhork strong, he might even kill Asaph, but it would also make him unreasonable and hasty. Asaph decided to fan the flames of the other dragon's fury. He'd had enough of Morhork now.

'You thought I couldn't do it. Pah, look at you, traitor!' Asaph snarled. 'Faelsun should have killed you when he had the chance.'

Morhork roared and they fell upon one another, great jaws snapping, each seeking to find a hold on the other's throat. Talons tore into each flesh, slicing through the smaller scales, scouring off the bigger ones. Blood splattered as they heaved and strained but, in the depths of battle, Asaph was mercifully unaware of any injuries instilled upon him.

'The world is falling and all you can do is fight your own,' Asaph growled, feeling his own fury at the dragon rising.

'*Not* my own. Disgusting half-breed!' snarled Morhork.

Blue fire engulfed Asaph and he barely had time to shut his eyes. He lumbered forwards calling upon water and dampening the flames. His skin hissed as it cooled in the brief rain. He slammed into Morhork and they both rolled, snow flying up around them as each tried to get on top of the other. Asaph was momentarily pinned down but he bucked the other dragon off with his hind legs. Moving fast, he leapt into the air, spread his wings for lift, then closed them and dropped down. He crashed hard upon the other dragon, crushing Morhork beneath him.

'Without wings, you are nothing more than a deformed beast,' Asaph spat. Morhork roared and thrashed.

Magic built—a pressure on his mind. It built faster than he was able to react then exploded beneath him sending him spinning into the air. He barely had his wings open before he crashed into the mountainside.

Morhork was up and pelting towards him, murderous rage in his eyes. Asaph threw himself sideways, narrowly avoiding the hail of snapping teeth and clawing talons. He felt them rake down his side, searing between scales. He sprayed Morhork with fire, forcing the dragon to retreat.

Morhork roared, magic surged. Thunderous cracking echoed in the valley and then great boulders of rock and ice were tumbling towards him. Asaph scrambled into the air to clear them. Fire engulfed him. He beat his wings to get away and pulled on the Flow to shower his opponent with snow. Water hissed and smoke billowed as the snow doused the flames. Asaph choked, unable to see where he was flying.

A thousand daggers of ice shot towards him through the flames. He dropped low. One ice dagger passed right through his wing tip leaving a bloody hole. He could feel the air rushing through it as he beat his wings, his stability in the air compromised. He crashed below the smoke and into the snow. Morhork was on his back before he could get up, claws tearing into his scales.

Asaph threw him off, fatigue gnawing at him. The other dragon was far more experienced in magic and Asaph's use of it was draining his strength fast. The only upper hand he held against the other dragon, who was more experienced in every way, was that he had wings. His fatigue was swiftly dissipating that advantage and it was obvious Morhork was not going to give up until one of them was dead.

'You would have all the dragons die in their sleep rather than awaken and fight,' snarled Asaph. Maybe he could lead the dragon to reason.

Again, Morhork attacked, his bulk smashing into Asaph, sending them spinning onto the edge of the frozen lake. The ice cracked dangerously beneath them. Asaph beat his wings, lifting into the air while Morhork dragged himself to land. Asaph dropped out of the air onto Morhork's shoulders and clamped his jaws over the back of the dragon's neck, just behind his ears and between two horns. Blood dribbled into his mouth as he clenched harder. Morhork threw himself into a roll and Asaph lost his grip.

Something caught his eye as they rolled, a speck of red in the sky but he didn't have time to focus on it as Morhork clawed at his face.

'So, you found the sword and it gives you strength. When I'm finished with you, I'll destroy it utterly,' growled Morhork.

'My strength is my own. Only when I hold the sword does its power become mine. Nothing can destroy it.' Asaph bared bloodied teeth in a gruesome parody of a grin. They lunged at each other. Morhork's tail sliced across his face, and his own blood sprayed into his eyes. Asaph raked at the dragon's neck, feeling hot blood flow over his claws.

Both panting with exertion, they drew apart for a moment. Blinking through blood, Asaph stared in shock. There on the mountain was a slender red dragon watching them. He could smell she was female. She had dark red horns and very long wings. Her head was held high as she rested on her limbs, completely still, a blaze of red on the white and grey mountainside and the picture of majesty and beauty.

He reached out and touched her impassive female mind. The communication was broken off. She raised a barrier but not out of fear or disrespect. *She is watching the fight and waiting for it to finish,* Asaph realised. *Whoever wins she will respect. Was this some kind of dragon protocol?*

Morhork followed his gaze and roared in fury. Asaph glimpsed another shape in the sky, a trail of green, but he had no time to wonder, Morhork's fire exploded towards him. Too late to run, he flattened himself in the snow. The heat seared his back. Ignoring the agony, he leapt forwards but Morhork's tail flashed out of nowhere and smacked his head sideways. The whole world turned dark briefly.

In the few moments it took before he came back to his senses it seemed the entire mountainside rushed towards him. Boulders, ice and snow hurtled at him. Asaph jumped into the air, spreading his wings, but a giant boulder smacked into him and then he was rolling with the rubble. Another boulder smacked him in the face, turning the world dark again. His body twisted between ice and rock. He gasped for breath filling his mouth with dirt and choking on it. A boulder struck his chest; he thought he heard ribs crack and then the tumbling slowed.

A great weight crushed down upon him. He could barely breathe as every inhalation filled his nostrils with snow and dirt, and every exhalation made it harder to draw another breath. He could see nothing and heard only the sound of lesser rocks tumbling. He tried to push himself up but the whole mountain appeared to be crushing down upon him. He began to panic and reached for other dragon minds.

There was nothing there.

Being trapped like an animal in a cage filled Asaph with fury. How dare he end like this in front of the awakened dragons. He reached for the Flow but found it blocked to him. The loss made him violent and, opening his mouth, he roared his frustration in fire and soot. The snow around his face melted and stones fell away allowing him to breathe deeper. He thrashed savagely, feeling a boulder by his tail move and dislodge several others.

Smashing his head up and dislodging more rubble, a trickle of light filtered through. Energised by this, he did it again and a larger hole appeared, revealing sky. He caught a glimpse of several dragons now waiting on the mountainside; two reds, three greens and a grey. He would have cried out in joy had he not been so furious at his predicament. He paused, seeing Morhork come into view. The dragon was lumbering towards the others with his back to Asaph and he was covered in blood, gaping wounds and burns.

'Dragons, at last, I have awoken you,' cried Morhork. 'The world of man is still at war...'

Asaph heard no more as the rushing din of rage filled his ears. His bunched his muscles and *heaved*, roaring his fury in a hail of fire. With Morhork's attention now on the other dragons, Asaph broke the barrier to the Flow and dragged the magic to him. Snow, rock, ice and fire erupted into the air, and in the middle of it was Asaph. He hurtled into Morhork, taking the wingless dragon by complete surprise. The ice-blue dragon fell and sprawled in the snow beneath him. Asaph jumped off his back, lifted into the air and pelted him with magic; relentless showers of snow, rock and ice that had followed his explosion.

Morhork was knocked senseless and soon half submerged in the rubble. Several fangs were knocked out from flying rocks and blood dripped from his nostrils. Asaph landed before the stunned dragon and stalked towards him, intending to finish it once and for all. It was only when his chest suddenly burned with agony, making him roar and sit back on his haunches, that his need to kill Morhork abated.

Gasping smoke, he looked down. Upon his chest, the mark from his Trial by Fire blazed. The flame mark burned brightly, three licks of fire flickering yellow for all to see. What was happening?

He felt surprise spread through the assembled dragons and turned to face them, hoping for an explanation. They all had their heads lifted and were sitting up. He stared down at the mark, feeling the heat behind the flames cool. His raging fury melted away. Morhork growled from behind him, but it was the soft growl of one dazed and in pain.

Light flared on the lake, capturing everyone's attention. The Sword of Binding burst into a blaze of white. *What is happening?* Asaph forgot about his flame mark and went towards it, coming to a stop at the lake's edge. If he changed into his human form now to walk across the lake, Morhork or any of the other dragons could easily kill him.

The sword flared again and became a blazing pillar of yellow and white light reaching up into the deep blue sky that was still sprinkled with stars. Asaph's breath caught in his throat. The Flow surged towards the sword, filling it with power. The light grew larger and brighter and he realised it was roaring and flickering, like fire made of pure white and yellow. The light grew, becoming wider and wider until it was massive and engulfing most of the lake.

A form took shape in the light and the largest, most beautiful dragon he had ever seen appeared. She was made of the same yellow-white light and perfect in every way. Great golden horns spiralled high above a long, sculpted head. Her eyes glowed pure white as did her short, triangular spikes that ran all the way from the neck, along her spine and to the tail-tip.

The pillar of light vanished leaving just the enormous glowing dragon. All the other dragons had their heads and necks dipped in an s-shape, spellbound and reverent. The dragon of light turned to Asaph.

He lifted his head and, realising it was hanging open, closed his jaw. Divine power filled him, making him swoon. It was like liquid sunlight flowing through his veins. Painlessly, his cracked ribs snapped into place and mended. His torn wing stopped dripping blood and became whole. The rest of his many wounds closed as his scales and skin knitted together. The strain and fatigue left his muscles and his befuddled brain cleared. His battered aching body felt lithe and young and new.

'Feygriene,' he breathed. He had never seen her in this form. He closed his eyes and dipped his head in reverence, his sense of divinity and awe increasing.

The Sun Goddess spoke, her voice deep and rich and harmonious. With her words came a torrent of mental images, feelings, thoughts and emotions creating complete comprehension and leaving nothing to doubt.

'Behold the Dawn Bringer,' her communication said. 'The only Dragon Lord to survive the Trial by Fire where before only pureblood dragons have passed. Without this Dragon Lord, the world of Maioria will fall into oblivion—the black scar of emptiness you have witnessed in your dreams. He awakens you now so you may arise and decide whether you will fight for this world, your world, or not.'

The dragons around him shifted and murmured and a shared thought was spoken in unison. 'This is the Dawn Bringer we have been dreaming of.'

Asaph wasn't entirely sure if they had spoken aloud or only in his head.

'You have been awoken now so that you may decide your future,' said the dragon of light. 'No sleeper has the power of choice, and if you do not choose, others will make that choice for you. Do you want your fate decided by others? Those who would choose for you want to enslave you.

'My beloved son, Morhork. You are strong, stronger than all the others, which is why I awoke you first. Do not fall to the temptations of the Dark Rift and seek dominion. The Dark Rift will consume all; none on the edge can withstand it, and there are more powerful beings than you within it.'

Asaph noticed that at some stage during the Sun Goddess's communication the ice-blue dragon had come to stand beside him, his eyes half-closed and head bowed in reverence. Morhork's body was also healed of all wounds, and all the rage and hatred of him had now disappeared in Feygriene's presence.

'Great gifts await you if the race of dragons survives. For if Maioria falls, so too the sun from where you came which gives you sustenance. The Dark Rift touches and taints even here. If the sun dies, then all things in this solar system will wither and die. Thus will be the end of dragons. Remember the First Code. Remember the Sword of Binding. Do not undo that which is holy, and you will be king among dragons.'

The light began to dissipate around Feygriene and her dragon form melted away leaving just a beautiful pillar of undulating yellow and white. The light flared bright like the sun and Asaph could barely look at it, then it was gone.

'Behold, the Dawn Bringer!' Feygriene's rich voice boomed across the valley, vibrating through him and trembling the ground.

Dawn broke in a shard of sunlight that burst over the mountain and between the clouds. It struck first the Sword of Binding, making it flare, then streamed from the sword straight into Asaph's chest, igniting his flame mark. An awesome, overwhelming power filled him just as it had when he had become one with the sun in his Trial by Fire and when he had first touched the sword under the Temple of Carvon. All sense of time and place faded away. He was one with the divine power of the sun.

The overwhelming power spread from him into the valley. As it spread, it lessened in his body. The clouds parted to let more through, bathing all the dragons in warmth and light. Everything was hushed.

Asaph felt his human form return of its own accord. He stood as a man, beside the great bulk of Morhork, and the other dragons watched him. He took a deep, steadying breath, his whole body humming with the after effects of the power. Sunlight still illuminated the sword and he walked towards it on strong legs across the ice. Gripping the hilt, he found it warm as he pulled it free and stared at it in wonder.

'Behold the Dawn Bringer,' the dragons said as one, echoing Feygriene's words.

Although he did not speak, there was a growing look of wonder in Morhork's eyes as he gazed at Asaph; all hatred and malice swept away by the divine light of the Sun Goddess.

The ice beneath Asaph cracked alarmingly and a huge fracture splintered outwards from where he had plunged the sword. The ice groaned and split some more, then he was running to the shore, squealing.

He jumped the last yard as the ice broke under his feet and he only just made it to the shore, landing head first into the snow. He rolled, choked and wiped the snow out of his eyes. Blearily he watched as the entire lake's surface shattered and then began to melt.

'Look at the gold beneath the ice! Ark's ancient castle, it's rising,' said the closest dragon standing up on all fours. He was green-scaled and had heavy black horns.

Sure enough, huge golden blocks were rising from the darkness of the lake bed—hundreds of them lifted by some unseen hand into the air, dripping water and glimmering in the sunlight. They levitated across the surface to the place where once the castle had been and laid themselves gently down. Faster and faster the golden blocks moved and in stunned silence the dragons watched an entire castle rebuild itself—a massive structure soon complete with shining golden domes, turrets, and walkways. It was as big as the Tower of Flame and certainly as majestic—only this one had been built by humans and dragons together.

'Large enough for dragons too,' Asaph noted the gigantic archways and towering pillars holding up the roofs.

'It wasn't easy to destroy. It took six months to recover my magic reserves,' said Morhork, overhearing him.

Asaph would have laughed but he was too in awe of the unfolding spectacle. Another golden building was being rebuilt to their left on the other side of the lake, below where the red dragon female was standing. It was smaller but just as graceful with round turrets and sweeping spires.

'But I didn't destroy the temple to Feygriene. That was Baelthrom,' said Morhork.

'What was destroyed can be rebuilt,' said Asaph, placing his hands on his hips. The message from the Sun Goddess was not lost on him. He loosened the collar of his shirt; it was certainly getting warm for somewhere this far north. Blinking in disbelief, he noticed the snow and ice was swiftly melting and beginning to run down the mountainsides.

'Hey, look, it's getting warmer! The ice is melting.' Asaph pointed.

All around, the snow was turning into melt water and pouring into the lake. Brown patches of dirt began to appear underneath their feet, and the river running from the lake behind them was swiftly turning into a frothing torrent. Asaph's jaw dropped as green grass sprouted and tender new shoots pushed through the dirt.

Soon, great swathes of green billowed gently in the breeze where once deep snow had been. The air turned even warmer and he was certain he could smell the scent of spring on the air. *But it was autumn and surely winter was coming…*

The dragons on the mountainside launched into the air and glided down towards the now grassy plateau upon which he stood. They landed and peered at the ground. Flowers began to sprout all around them; delicate white, purple and yellow buds blooming in their thousands. *Mountain flowers,* Asaph thought, *marking spring.* He closed his eyes and breathed the cool, clear, mountain air. It reminded him of the valleys of Drax and it smelt just the same. If there had been two suns above, it could even have been the Dragon Dream.

'The Dragon Dream has come to Maioria,' said the red dragon, blinking her huge copper eyes as she echoed his thoughts.

The other dragons lumbered forwards until they surrounded Asaph. Seven enormous beasts, all watching him through eyes that were bigger than his head. He had only ever dreamed of this point and was more nervous than afraid. Morhork's expression was unreadable. They were all magnificent. But why were there so few?

'Are you all that remain?' Asaph asked, not knowing what else to say. Could there really only be seven dragons?

'No, Feygriene came to us in a dream and awoke us first,' said the red female dragon. 'We all dreamed the same dream. We have seen many things and the growing of the Dark Rift in the sky. Then we were led here by her golden light. We are the Six Chosen, selected to witness the Dawn Bringer and awaken the others. Many of us have given in to deep sleep and some have been in hibernation so long they are on the brink of death. Dragons need time to awaken and strengthen after such a fast.'

'Then you know about the breaking of the Dragon Dream?' Asaph asked, his voice thick.

The dragons dipped their heads. Morhork looked away, his long pupils narrowing in the sunlight.

'Faelsun has gone to the Fire in the Sky,' said the red female.

'Those who killed him will kill or enslave us all if they are not stopped,' said Asaph. 'That is why you have been awoken. Soon there will be a battle in the south of the Known World. I can only ask for your aid.'

The red female shook her head. 'We are not ready for war. We have not even had breakfast.'

Asaph would have laughed had he not felt so urgent. 'There is a little time,' said Asaph. He was going to have to try a lot harder to convince these dragons to fight, but they did need food and time to grow strong again. And the obvious question remained, why should they fight for human causes?

'But we will fight. What Feygriene has shown us is the truth. We must fight.' The red nodded her great head and stared out across the lake.

Asaph sighed silently in relief. Perhaps it wouldn't be so hard but he couldn't let them rest for too long. The sense of urgency Feygriene had instilled in them all was too precious to lose.

'First, we must gather the others,' said the green dragon with black horns, lifting his head.

'Some of them are so weak they are faint in my mind,' said the grey dragon, a female.

'But they are all here, in the frozen caves of the north. We can reach them,' nodded the green dragon, stretching his wings above him.

'Where do we go, Sire?' The slender red female asked Morhork, inclining her head as if he were royalty. Perhaps he was, if he were Faelsun's brother.

'Garna, you must do as Feygriene has shown you,' said Morhork. 'Awaken the dragons if that is what you have been guided to do. I have seen a…different thing. I must go south to complete it. It must be done alone.' Morhork looked away, his muscles twitching.

Asaph wondered why the dragon seemed suddenly uncomfortable. Despite the Sun Goddess healing their hatred, he couldn't trust this dragon yet. Even now, Morhork was being secretive. But then, he didn't really have the choice not to trust him. Perhaps Morhork had spent so long alone, he no longer knew how to think of anyone else, and certainly he didn't seem to care.

'What are we waiting for?' barked the third green excitedly. He was a young male and he'd already spread his wings and leapt into the air with a roar.

'Wait, we cannot leave this place unprotected,' said the other red dragon. He was big and heavy and his voice was deep to match.

'Rust is right,' nodded Garna. 'This place is sacred to Feygriene. Holy. It must be treated as such. Let us shield and protect it from the evil we witnessed in our dreams and remember in our past. The undead immortals must not find it.'

The other dragons agreed and then launched into the air one by one. Their beating wings sent gusts of winds battering into Asaph, nearly lifting him off the ground. Shielding his eyes, he looked up and longed to fly with them, but something told him that it would not be appropriate to join with them right now and besides, his immediate task lay elsewhere.

'Wait,' he shouted, ducking low and squinting through the swirling debris. The dragons turned and hovered, watching him. 'We haven't got long, two days at the most. Please help us in the south, just some of you.' He realised he was pleading and no dragon respected anyone who grovelled, least of all a human.

'At most, two days it will be, Dawn Bringer,' said Garna. 'We will return here with those who will, and can, help you.' The other dragons dipped their heads formally in unison. Asaph realised he had a lot to learn about dragons and how they communicated.

Morhork silently lifted into the air with nothing but a faint shimmer of magic where his wings should be. Without speaking, the dragon turned from them all and sped south faster than any dragon could naturally fly.

'Where on Maioria is he going?' murmured Asaph. With a sigh, he dismissed the wingless dragon from his mind and stared after the others, watching in awe as the six dragons landed on the tips of the mountains ringing the lake. Dragons of vivid colours perching atop snow-crested mountains... *What a majestic sight!*

He felt a tingling on his skin; all he could sense of dragon magic moving while he was in his human form. The dragons roared together, a deafening noise that shook the very mountains and echoed for ages after. When their roars fell to silence, they lifted into the air and flew gracefully in different directions to find and gather the others dragons.

Asaph watched them until they were all gone. He stood alone, realising how quiet and empty the lake valley now was.

'Hah,' he said to himself, looking at the Sword of Binding in his hand. It gleamed in the sunlight. He swung it and it made a whistling sound in the air. What was he supposed to do now? He couldn't leave in case more dragons arrived, and where would he go anyway? *What would Coronos do at a time like this on the eve of battle? He would sit and plan, and read and plan some more.*

Asaph's gaze wandered to the massive castle. But there was always time for exploring. He laughed and ran forwards. *Issa is gonna wish she was here!* He skipped and pirouetted across the grass, swishing his sword left and right, a grin spreading across his face as he approached the enormous, shining castle.

CHAPTER 31

Gathering Armies

ISSA lay curled up tight in a ball, trembling.

Maggot continually and reassuringly squeezed her arm with his tiny cold hands. She couldn't find her voice to speak and clenched her eyes shut. The terror just didn't want to release her.

'Issy, it's all right. We made it through,' Maggot coaxed.

Slowly, she opened her eyes and stared at the slick grey rock in front of her. They may be in enemy-held lands but, by the goddess, was she glad to be back on Maioria.

'They came out of the Dark Rift. They were … *Light Eaters* … I don't really know what they are! There were horsemen too, four of them. They were already there, waiting. I couldn't fight them.'

'Many things exist in the spaces between realms. That's why I told you not to enter the Storm Holt,' said Maggot, his voice scolding.

'I have never seen those *things* before.' She shook her head. All her confidence had been knocked from her. What other horrors would they face in the coming war? If she doubted herself now, then all was lost.

Perhaps it was the terror and sudden release, or perhaps it was for all the things she suddenly felt she couldn't do, but to her chagrin, she began to cry. She'd already nearly got Ehka killed. She couldn't bear the thought of losing anyone.

'I couldn't fight them, Maggot,' she sobbed.

He came around to the front of her and she pulled him into a hug. His bald skin was cold and he smelled like something rotting but she didn't care. His hand awkwardly pulled on her hair as if he were trying to stroke it. He'd never had to offer anyone comfort before.

The horsemen were surely Baelthrom's design with their black iron armour and helmets like a Dromoorai's, but the other things, the giant eaters who had no form, they came from the Dark Rift. The rift was growing and Baelthrom's power increasing whilst Maioria withered. And what the hell was Freydel doing? The more time he spent with that Ayeth, the worse things were becoming here, not better. Had he totally betrayed them? Maybe Domenon was right to be suspicious about Freydel. A part of her was glad that he knew Freydel was visiting Ayeth. At least *someone* knew and she didn't have to carry this burden alone.

'But you survived the Storm Holt and defeated the demons from the Pit,' Maggot reminded her.

She sighed, feeling spent, and pushed herself up. She wiped the tears from her cheeks and listlessly cradled Maggot in her lap, hopelessness sending a chill through her body. 'This is all an endless, futile struggle and I'm already exhausted before the battle has begun. Every time we defeat an enemy, a new, more terrible one springs up in their place.'

'And so, too, do friends,' said the little demon, his yellow eyes wide and seeking her affection.

Issa looked at him then laughed as tears blurred her vision. 'You're just full of surprise wisdom, Maggot.'

She took a deep breath and stared out of the cave entrance. Out there in the distance, it was day but dirty-coloured clouds darkened the skies. The sea rolled turbulent and grey, crashing white against the menacing black spikes of rocks a hundred yards from the shore. Everything they had to do seemed insurmountable against their relentless, tireless, formidable enemy.

Far away on the horizon, she glimpsed a sparkle of blue sea where the clouds had broken to let through a brief ray of sunlight, and then it was gone. It was a long way away and she might have been mistaken, but the thought of being away from this terrible place and flying in the sunlight lifted her spirits.

'I should go and you must return to the Murk. The enemy could be hunting me right now. What is that?'

She pointed to the stick hanging from his belt. It was the same thin spike that had pierced the face of the horseman.

'Jabber,' said Maggot, holding it up proudly. 'I made it myself. It doesn't throw very well but I can tell it where to go.'

Issa smiled and rubbed his head. 'Where would I be without you? Now, don't worry about me, I'm going west, into the sunlight where they can't touch me. And you must go and look after Ehka.'

'Urgh, sunlight,' Maggot wrinkled up his face. 'That stuff is the worst.'

She watched as he melted into the shadows, his yellow eyes the last to fade, and then his presence was gone. With a deep breath, she embraced her raven form and darted at full speed out of the cave, heading straight for the patch of blue water she had momentarily glimpsed. She imagined ten Dromoorai chasing her as she sped on.

Only when a hundred yards or so had passed did she dare use the Flow to cloak herself. After a hundred more she used weather magic to push her onwards, thinking only of a warm bath and a hot meal.

When Issa spied the grey coast of Davono on the horizon she squawked with joy. Her wounded arm, though healed well enough to fly, was throbbing and frozen in flight position. The sun was past its zenith now and her whole body ached. Gulls wheeled above and below her, cawing as if to welcome her home, and the sea sparkled in the sunlight. She wanted nothing more than to return to her human form and rest.

As she neared the coast, an incredible sight greeted her. Up and down the shore, filling the harbours and coves were hundreds of battleships. Most were Davonian, constructed of dark wood and appearing blocky but sturdy. They sported fat, squat masts and short wide sails. Bobbing beside them were many sleeker Atalanph merchant ships better suited to speed than attack. They were constructed of lighter wood and had taller masts and slender sails. Smaller ships built for shorter journeys also nestled amongst them and aboard all milled hundreds, maybe thousands, of soldiers, their polished armour reflecting the sunlight. White-capped sailors worked amongst them loading the decks and fixing ropes and sails.

They are using every ship they can spare, Issa marvelled, circling high above them. The port itself was teeming with soldiers as well. Most wore the yellow sun on a green background tabard of Davono but there were other colours amongst them too. She wondered how many soldiers in total would be going into battle, for there were several thousand in Port South Reach alone.

She turned towards the forest and hunted for the lodge. Velonorian was likely to be worried out of his mind, she thought, but at least her disappearance would have given Domenon something to think about. The notion made her grin.

She dropped towards the wooden building nestled in the trees and landed on her windowsill. Hopping inside, everything was as she had left it, apart from her note which was missing. She stood up and stretched her arms, feeling like they were about to fall off. Draining the pitcher of water to drown out her hunger, she flopped forwards onto the bed and fell deeply asleep.

'The Dragon Lord said you would be difficult to protect,' Velonorian said to Issa as they stood in the port, squinting in the morning sun. Autumn was milder this far south and a gentle breeze lifted her hair.

Issa grinned and adjusted her sword belt, her hand resting lightly on her short sword. She'd slept through the rest of the day before and right through the night until ravenous hunger woke her just before dawn. The kitchen couldn't keep up with her demands for breakfast. The wound on her shoulder was still sore inside, but it had healed externally, leaving a red scar.

Now, she stood in the port along with everyone else because the queen herself had arrived. Wearing black from head to toe, Queen Thora stood regally with her back to Issa, surrounded by her entourage.

In front of her, stretching from the stadium upon which they stood all the way to the harbour walls, were row upon row of immaculately armoured soldiers standing to attention, their round helmets a sea of silver baubles gleaming in the sun. All held pikes, their wicked tips freshly sharpened, and all wore swords strapped to their sides. Many held standards of various colours depicting beasts, weapons or symbols. Some were just single colours and very long. They billowed in the breeze like delicate ribbons.

There were at least two thousand soldiers here and more would be tending the ships. Velonorian had said all the southern harbours and ports were full. Still more soldiers would be arriving, for she spotted only one small unit of dwarves far to the left. Their helmets did not gleam for they were of roughened metal and their short stature made them hard to spot from this far away.

There would be at least five hundred more dwarves coming, a thousand Karalanths, and several thousand Feylint Halanoi. And what about the elves? Orphinius had been determined not to miss the battle before she had left Myrn. His elven archers and fighters would be most valuable. Then there would be the Lans Himay mercenaries too. And what about Asaph? Would he bring dragons?

Issa swallowed. It was finally happening; the offensive she had been hoping to launch for so long was finally happening. And she was frightened. People would die. She might die. But that mattered less to her than Baelthrom discovering their attack and later launching a counter attack. Speed and surprise were of the essence. She gripped her sword, suddenly keen to get going.

But how many would die? She took a deep breath. *They fight because they want to, because they have to,* she reassured herself.

'Are you all right, Lady Issa? You haven't heard anything I've said,' said Velonorian, smiling when she looked up at him. 'Unless you are an animal or have elven ears, I doubt you can hear the queen from back here, either.'

'Sorry, I was lost in my thoughts. I do not want to go to war, but we must. I don't want anyone to die for what I have caused.'

'"You" have caused? Baelthrom caused it when he arrived out of Oblivion,' said Velonorian. 'This was coming one way or another. You have given us something to believe in. I'd rather die for something than nothing at all.' He gave her a reassuring smile. The devotion in his eyes only served to deepen her worry. If he should die, she would never forgive herself.

'You'll feel better when Asaph returns,' said the elf. 'The two of you will be formidable. Ah, the wonder of seeing a Dragon Lord and its rider in battle like the good days of old. I'd love to see it for myself. I've only heard my grandpa's tales.'

'It sounds terrifying,' said Issa. Velonorian laughed. 'Look, you don't have to fight, you don't even have to come,' she said, hoping that he would agree to stay.

'My lady Issa, I would not leave your side in battle even if the goddess herself decreed it.' The seriousness in the elf's eyes stilled her tongue. 'I have pledged myself into your service. It would be a great dishonour to me if I did not fulfil that pledge. You saved my people and me, and so I would give my life to protect you. It is only proper and honourable. Besides, you can't do everything alone.'

Issa thought of the shadow knights and the Light Eaters she could not fight. Slowly she nodded. 'Let's hope it never comes to that.'

As Queen Thora finished speaking and turned away from the gathered soldiers, Issa realised Domenon was not amongst her tight pack of bodyguards.

'No Master Wizard?' she said.

'I have not seen Domenon since we arrived at South Reach Lodge,' said Velonorian. 'I have not seen any wizard, so I only assume they are meeting with each other.'

Issa frowned. 'We do not want to go into battle without a wizard from the Circle.' Where was Freydel? She could do with his wise council. Even having Domenon here would reassure her.

'I'm sure they will arrive soon.' He patted her arm, but Issa chewed her lip. There were a hundred things to worry about and so much could go wrong. She hated being a commander, or trying to be. Marakon would know what to do. She should scry for him now; in fact, she should have done it yesterday. The half-elf had seemed so confident last time they spoke, but what if he couldn't open the demon tunnels? What if they were broken after so long? What if he got lost in them and never made it to the battle? He said it would take a day or two to reach her at most but what if the demon tunnels had changed? Her mind rolled over and over and she found herself chewing her fingers.

'Why don't we get a hot cup of chocolate or tea? A walk in the market will take your mind off everything,' said the elf, clearly noticing her fretting.

'That sounds nice,' she said. After, she would try to reach the half-elf commander.

The walk through the busy market and cup of delicious Frayonesse hot chocolate did help alleviate her worries but as soon as she was alone in her room again, they all flooded back to her.

She cradled the raven talisman in her lap.

'Marakon, Marakon, Marakon,' she repeated. In her mind, she kept a clear image of the man holding Velistor. There was a very strong connection between the raven talisman and the spear and it made reaching Marakon much faster and easier. His face formed clearly on the dark flat surface of the talisman. He could not scry for her because he was not a magic wielder but he would feel her searching for him in his mind. As before when she'd scryed for him, she told him to find water, a bowl or a stream. That way even those without magic might be able to see the scryer.

'Issa?' His image wavered as if it were reflected on water.

'Marakon,' she said.

'It's amazing. This time the spear throbbed with light and sound and I felt a pressure in my mind,' said the half-elf sounding excited. 'I found water, like you said, and I can see you a little.'

'If you can hear me, that is good enough. Soon we set sail for Venosia. Find the demon tunnel to Venosia and come with your chosen soldiers and knights,' she said.

'We are ready.' He nodded. 'The west has mostly been secured. The enemy is pinned in three towns but King Navarr's forces can hold them.'

'Do you think you'll reach us before we set sail?' Issa said.

'If my memory and the spear serve me correctly and nothing goes wrong, I can be there in a day.'

'Then Goddess Speed,' said Issa. 'I wish you were here right now. I could do with an experienced commander at my side this minute.'

'Not much fun before battle, is it?' grinned Marakon.

Issa smiled and rubbed her eyes. 'Just don't miss the ships.'

The arched, solid oak doors to the castle were decorated and strengthened with iron studs and stood three times as tall as Asaph. He pushed against one and, to his surprise, it swung open easily without even a creak.

He stood and stared at the immaculate, enormous courtyard. The pale red and blue paving stones were freshly swept and an old sycamore tree stood in the far corner, its leaves full and green as if it were spring and not autumn at all. *Perhaps winter cannot touch here now,* he thought and stepped through the door. The huge courtyard could easily hold three dragons and was bordered by high, pale-red brick walls. On the far side were two more giant oak doorways, much like the first he had entered.

The pages of the Recollection opened in his mind and he saw Ark and Ralan Afisius standing in the courtyard. *Ark's tail was here.* He went to the dragon's tail, seeing it in his mind. Just ahead of him, in the centre of the courtyard, Ralan was stroking Ark's nose.

Asaph laughed. The courtyard was empty now, but the memory remained. The place itself remembered. He walked to another set of the doors and opened them. Nothing was locked, or stiff and rusted with age; everything was clean and working as if it had just been built. None of the shining gold domes looked chipped or worn in any way and they reflected the sunlight, strengthening it so that it was positively warm here.

The next area was enclosed with a high ceiling through which he could see the sky. Though on the outside he had seen it as painted gold, on the inside, looking out, it was see-through, just like the little temple he had rested in on the other side of the lake. This inner area had been made for people as there was a wide stairway flowing up ahead.

The walls were covered in bright, intricately detailed paintings of Ark and Ralan, other dragons and the mountainside—so realistic, clearly a master painter had created them. Asaph went closer to inspect them all; the paint gleamed as if freshly created. He paused by one which depicted the mountains and beyond and frowned.

'Hey, where's the snow?' he said aloud, peering closer. Sure enough, in the painting none of the mountains were covered in snow; instead there were rich, evergreen forests, sparkling lakes and rivers. But even in summer, here in the extreme north, shouldn't there be snow and glaciers?

He focused on the Recollection. What he saw shook him to the core: thousands of years ago there *was* no snow here. Through the eyes of a dragon named Ty, he saw what the picture depicted; tall mountains and endless green valleys fed by gushing rivers. In winter there was snow on the mountain tips but never was the north completely iced over like it was today.

It was like that before Baelthrom came. Baelthrom changed the world and brought the deserts, both the frozen and the dry. The realisation came as a great shock. *How much had changed because of Baelthrom?* He wondered. What would be returned to them when Baelthrom was gone? His imagination began to run wild.

Maioria free. Perhaps, like Issa says, the sickness of death will leave us. Maybe we'll never age and die. He grinned at the thought. He couldn't wait to bring Issa here and show her everything he had discovered. She'd come now it wasn't so cold, he was certain of it.

Wearing a smile, he sat down on the white marble floor and laid back, his arms behind his head as he looked first at the paintings and then up at the clear blue sky. When the dragons returned in a day or two, he'd return to Issa. She would not start the battle alone. He thanked Feygriene for his blessings.

Issa sighed heavily as Marakon's face faded in the talisman. She toyed with the flame ring on her hand: Asaph's mother's ring. She had been a Dragon Lord and had carried his father into battle many times. Would she, too, fly on Asaph's back like the Dragon Riders of old? She smiled at the thought and lay back on the bed. Holding the talisman up, she closed her eyes and reached out to Asaph with her mind as far as she could.

She called for him three times before, suddenly, he was there, a fiery glimmer far away in the Flow. His mind was faint but she could still feel it. He was alive, and that knowledge alone brought unexpected tears to her eyes. She had been worrying deeply about his safety but had been too caught up in her own survival to realise just how much she missed him.

'Asaph,' she whispered, willing his image to form on the talisman, feeling her raven mark tingle as the surface moved. Then she spotted him lying prone with his reddish-blonde hair spread beneath his head and his eyes closed. Immediately she worried but then saw the faint smile upon his face and the colour in his cheeks.

He sleeps. Thank the goddess, he's not dead! But what is he holding? She stared at the huge sword he grasped tightly against his chest; its blood red pommel and bluish blade igniting memory.

'It's the same one,' she said aloud, awestruck. The same blade she had been gifted in the sacred pool by the Guardians of the Portals. It felt like an age ago—so much had happened since. She had held it and lifted it high, though barely survived its rage at being wielded by any other than its rightful owner. Her hand burned now just at the memory.

'You did it,' she whispered in wonder. 'You got the sword and now the dragons will awaken.' She laughed out loud and was certain his smile deepened as he slept. They had already scored a great victory before the battle had even begun. 'Thank you, Zanufey,' she said, feeling faith renewed in her heart.

'Come to me, my love,' she whispered. 'Let us ride into battle as Dragon Lord and Dragon Rider and rekindle the glory days of old.'

For two days Asaph watched the skies, waiting for the dragons to return. He slept in an empty room using his cloak as a mattress and only left the golden castle to find food, mostly in the form of fish caught from a hole he had dug in the ice on the frozen sea to the north. These he brought back, roasted with dragon fire, and ate in the castle.

On the third day, he was fed up with fish and worried sick for Issa. He stared up at the sky where the clouds were turning pink with the setting sun. There was not a glimmer of dragon in it and when he cast his mind out there, he could feel nothing. Had the dragons abandoned him? Had they fallen asleep again? Worse, had they been captured and killed by Baelthrom? No. He'd know if something had happened to them. He'd promised Issa and he'd promised the dragons, so what did he do now? All were relying on him, but if he didn't go to Issa, she could be killed.

It was the thought of her going into battle without him that made up his mind—the dragons were powerful, especially a whole brood of them—and they were late. It was not his fault if they returned and he wasn't here. But if they found him gone would they go their separate ways? He groaned. Why did he know so woefully little about his own kind?

That evening, Asaph sat for hours on a craggy jut of the mountain that overlooked the castle and lake below, deep in thought. Finally, he came to a radical conclusion—one that excited him as much as it chilled him to the bone. Wherever Issa was on her journey to Venosia, he could assist her from afar, effectively, and very soon.

He pulled himself to his feet and turned towards the south where the Blaze of Eight trailed.

Drax lay there, waiting for him. He would approach it at night, cloaked in magic, do as much damage as he could and then flee using Morhork's magic trick to speed him fast away. Such a daring attack would divert Baelthrom's attention away from everywhere else, including what Issa was up to.

Issa was right; they had cowered before Baelthrom for too long, never attacking, always defending. The Dark Rift loomed so close now, they had to risk all or fall forever. They had no other option but to fight. Nothing mattered anymore. The time for battle had come.

CHAPTER 32

Finding the Navadin

MARAKON watched as the blurry image of Issa faded from his water bowl.

The spear in the corner of his tent dimmed and he stood from his crouched position with a sigh. Now the time had come to do something he had been dreading; open a demon tunnel. It was strange knowing he had spent one lifetime desperately trying to close them and now he had to do the opposite in this one.

If only his knights were with him…how he missed them. At least he had Bokaard. The few new recruits to the Knights of the Raven would become friends, in time, but he needed more knights, hundreds more. There just hadn't been enough time to find and train them.

He stepped outside the tent. The heavy darkness was kept back only by a flaming brazier lighting the narrow paths between the soldier's tents.

Avil stood to attention. 'Sir.'

It was comforting to know his loyal soldier stood watch outside his tent again, as if some sense of the old life remained from before the fatal excursion to Haralan that had cost him his whole crew and, very nearly, his sanity.

'Morning, Avil. Please inform my officers that the time has come. I will leave with my unit of one hundred soldiers and knights, as has been decided. Please ready them and tell them to meet me at the southern edge of our camp in half an hour.'

They weren't just any old soldiers and knights; these were the ones he had personally trained. They were the best this current unit had to offer and he'd had to argue at length against the other officers for them to be released. In the end, it took King Navarr's order—a royal decree delivered by courier—for them to finally allow him to take the men he had trained. He couldn't blame the officers though; the soldiers were superb on the battlefield.

'Yes, Sir. You'll be missed. I will await your swift and safe return,' Avil nodded his head respectfully.

'Thank you, Avil. I, also, will miss your impeccable service.'

The man bowed dutifully and disappeared silently amongst the tents of sleeping soldiers.

Marakon went back inside, slipped on his cuirass, strapped on his sword, and tucked knives all about his body. The demon tunnels had not been used in millennia, but he wasn't taking any chances; Issa had made the pact with them, not he. He slung a small sack of food and a water canister over his back, put on his helmet and reached for the spear.

As his hand touched Velistor's cold white surface an ancient memory formed in his mind: a grey slab of rock loomed in a dark forest, its surface illuminated by moonlight; one hundred knights gathered close around him as he stepped forwards gripping the reins of his horse. All was still, no night animals rustled in the bushes, no owl hooted, not even the wind blew as he approached the rock. Pensive fear was a solid thing and the sweat on his palms dampened his gloves, making grasping his sword difficult.

He threw his reins to the nearest knight and took the spear from its holder on his horse's saddle. He held it before him then as he did now— and it looked the same, unaged after thousands of years. He touched the tip of it to the rock. A grey stone door appeared, its magical disguise removed by the power of the spear. Upon it was carved the roaring face of a demon, eyes slitted, fangs bared.

Marakon struck the door with the spear. A great boom and shimmer of magic vibrated outwards, raising every hair on his body. The stone door swung inwards with a great grinding sound and the pitch black entrance yawned before him.

A horse neighed from beyond the tents, breaking the memory. He blinked down at the spear, shaking the vision from his head. Cold sweat clammed his brow and he wiped it away.

'It is different now,' he muttered. *Those demons are gone. Many of them are now our allies, or so they would say.* But no matter how he tried, he couldn't bring himself to trust them fully—but he *could* bring himself to fight alongside them, especially against those Maphraxies who had murdered all his friends and family.

Taking a deep breath, he followed the sparsely lit trail through the mass of tents and came to the edge of the dark forest. During his scouting missions and breaks, he had already discovered two demon tunnels in a one hundred square mile radius. The spear vibrated and hummed whenever he was near, but he had not dared to open them. The closest was a mile away, in a rock much like the one in his memory. They all seemed to need rocks to create the gateway.

'Marakon!' someone called under their breath.

Marakon turned to see Bokaard, in full armour, striding towards him, a smile cracking across his face to reveal white teeth. They slapped each other's shoulders. The big man looked fit and fresh and ready for battle. Thankfully, his confidence was infectious.

'Hail, Marakon,' another voice spoke. They turned to see Justenin, helmet under one arm, with the dwarf, Eiretonne, beside him, leading a marching line of soldiers, pack horses and a handful of war horses—not everyone was a trained knight yet. They moved incredibly silently for one hundred fully armed soldiers, just as he had trained them.

Marakon grasped Justenin's arm. 'Ready to go to hell?'

'As long as you go first, I'll go anywhere,' the blond man grinned, the scar on his cheek becoming even more prominent. Eiretonne simply nodded, a fierce look in his eyes. The dwarf's thick black beard was braided and knotted with runic silver war rings.

Without ceremony, Marakon marched them into the forest.

The Feylint Halanoi had already made many tracks through the forest around the camp. All Marakon had to do was lead his soldiers due south for a mile. They moved as silently as possible, wary of foltoy, Maphraxies and anything else tracking the Feylint Halanoi. Beneath the trees it was very dark, even their torches didn't seem to be able to push back the night.

After half an hour of walking, the spear trembled and gave the faintest glow. Marakon held it up, feeling where it was leading. There, past the ferns, under the bent tree and to the left. He signalled to leave the trail and headed into the undergrowth. The spear glowed brighter and he held it higher for light. The forest became darker and darker; the thorns, vines and canopy were so thick above that he felt like he'd led them into a cave. It was cold too; his breath was visible in the air. He suppressed a shiver.

Always the shadows drew around them, and the warmth of the world fled. He pushed through the gnarly thorns faster, anxious. The others tried to keep up but he didn't care to wait for them. Thorns scraped his breastplate and snagged at his trousers. Abruptly, they gave way and he fell into a clearing where the spear thrummed loudly and vibrated in his hand. He regained his balance and peered into the gloom.

He appeared to be in a bowl in the forest; a sunken patch of earth several yards wide and surrounded by ancient oaks, yews and a tangle of thorn bushes. There, where the light of the spear bathed one edge, was a peculiarly smooth lump of rock, taller than two men and wider than a carriage. It lay in the embrace of thick roots and entwined in ivy. Slowly, he walked towards it. He talked to himself sternly, trying to convince himself to lay his hand upon it, and when he did, all he felt was simply smooth, cold, rock.

He glanced over his shoulder at the soldiers filling the bowl, torches held high to drive back the dark. Their eyes were wide and faces pensive, and the pack horses jittered and stomped. Bokaard nodded at him, followed by Justenin then Eiretonne.

He turned back to the rock, licked his lips, and touched the spear to its surface. A hundred memories came to him of similar moments, yet still, the anxiety never lessened. Undiminished by time or weather, a grey stone door appeared, and upon it, the roaring face of a demon. Marakon let go of his breath and found himself smiling.

'After all this time, can you believe it?' he said to Bokaard who had come to stand beside him. The man shook his head, pursing his lips.

'Well, we've come all this way, I guess I'd better open it,' said Marakon. He thwacked the door with Velistor. A deep boom assaulted their ears and was gone in a moment. Unseen magic, felt as tingling energy, vibrated out from the door, and the demon face flared green then darkened. The stone door groaned inwards.

Marakon stared into the entrance. The blackness within was so deep it looked solid.

Bokaard unsheathed his sword. From behind them, Marakon heard the others do the same. Holding Velistor high, he walked forwards.

Jarlain blinked open her eyes. She was wide-awake and felt as if she hadn't been sleeping at all. The boat rocked gently. Fenn was alert beside her, his ears pricked forwards as they approached a dark shore. Murlonius and Yisufalni sat to attention, their eyes darting left and right. Everything and everyone was silent. The air was pensive though the sea was calm.

Her eyes travelled over the familiar tallen and palm trees, and the humid warmth of her homeland engulfed her. She smiled and hugged her shoulders, an immense feeling of arriving home overcoming her as she blinked back tears. How she'd missed the heat, the smell of the sea and the jungle and, most of all, her people.

She touched the staff by her thigh. Hai was gone, but she carried him with her in the staff of her people. Now she had to gather those who remained and lead them to fight against that which would destroy them all.

She turned to the others and noted the concerned looks on Yisufalni and Murlonius' faces. 'What is it?' she whispered.

'The enemy is near,' said Murlonius quietly. 'The black ships are to the south so I brought us further north whilst you slept.'

'I sense the presence of Life Seekers all around.' Yisufalni shivered. 'The forest could be filled with all manner of Baelthrom's evil.'

A black patch of burnt forest appeared. Many trees were snapped in half and whole areas were blackened.

'Dread Dragons did that,' said Murlonius. 'Maybe this was a town. It's gone now.'

Jarlain swallowed, suddenly wishing she hadn't come. How on earth could she find her people in an endless jungle, and one that was crawling with evil? *The staff. Hai's staff will lead me.*

They passed several blackened patches of land before Murlonius steered the boat towards a suitable beach. Without speaking, to avoid drawing attention, Jarlain jumped out of the boat. A mix of joy and fear spread over her as her feet splashed into warm waters and ground into the soft white sand of her homeland. What would she find here? She had to be strong. Everything that had happened in her life since Marakon had come into it had taught her to be strong. She found her half of the bear stone in her hand and raised it to her lips

Fenn splashed out after her and waded to the shore. She followed him then paused to glance back at Murlonius and Yisufalni. They nodded at her then disappeared into the mist.

Only bright starlight lit the skies, but it was enough to illuminate the white sands and to see by. Jarlain laid a hand on Fenn's neck, very glad to not be here alone. Putting on her helmet and slotting her staff and spear into their hold on her back, she turned towards the forest. A smile spread across her face as she imagined Tarn seeing her dressed like Marakon; a knight in gleaming metal armour. He was going to be very jealous.

A strangled call echoed through the forest, maybe a mile away but no more. Another sounded, but from further away—foltoy calling one to another. Fenn looked at her and with a nod of his great head, she swung her leg over his back. It was time to hunt the enemy.

Fenn's keen smell hunted down the first foltoy in minutes. She spied its black shape slinking through the forest, too big to be a panther. She aimed her spear as it wheeled towards them, fangs bared and drooling. It barely had time to leap before her spear had embedded itself through its throat and back out the base of its skull.

Fenn grunted as if disappointed.

Jarlain shrugged. 'You'll get the next one, I promise.'

Fenn carried her into the dense jungle and she was soon sweating under her armour. It may save her life and look intimidating but it really wasn't suited to this climate. She paused to show him the fallen tallen fruit and, after she'd dismounted, he tucked into several appreciatively.

The smell of undead caught her nose. It wasn't foltoy. A yipping bark was answered by another, then another and two death hounds exploded out of the forest straight at her. Fenn moved so fast he caught one by the throat as the other smacked into his side. From behind, two more pelted through the bushes towards them, howling in glee, fangs bared.

She spread her feet and hunkered down low. Thrusting her spear, she mortally wounded the first in the chest but couldn't pull her weapon free in time as the other hound knocked her to the ground, forcing her to release the spear. It jumped on her back, crushing her with its weight. She had her knife free already and plunged it blindly behind herself, hoping to find its face before it clamped its jaws on her. It howled deafeningly in her ear and black blood sprayed across her face, making her retch.

Suddenly, it was lifted from her back. She heard a snapping sound and the howls stopped abruptly. Jarlain rolled to her feet, wiping the blood from her eyes. Resting her hands on her thighs she panted and stared at Fenn. He, too, was dripping in black blood, but completely unharmed. She laughed and then grinned at him. Five down. Revenge felt good.

They paused at a stream to drink, then washed themselves and her spear, and carried on. There was no sign of the enemy and so she walked rather than ride Fenn. The sky was beginning to brighten and animals and birds were making their presence known. She had a gentle knowing of which way to go, and she knew it came from Hai's staff on her back. Always, they moved at a sloping angle uphill and north.

To The Centre, that's where it led. That's where her people had gone. If any still remained, they would be there.

As the sun rose, it brought with it a sense of safety and confidence she had not felt in the darkness. It was a fake sense of security, however. The undead attacked at any time, just like the Histanatarns, but at least she no longer had to peer into darkness with every shadow making her jump. Sweat trickled down her back and flies annoyed her in a way they had never done before. Now she understood how Marakon must have felt, longing to be cool and left alone by insects; there were definitely less insects in colder climates, she decided.

The jungle they journeyed through was as she remembered it; teeming with life and filled with flora. In places, she could almost pretend nothing had happened and everything was still right with the world. If she turned south, she'd eventually find her home. Everyone would be there waiting for her. Hai and the Elders would welcome her and consider her one of the Elders for surviving all that she had.

Lost in her daydreams, her happy musings were shattered when they came upon acres of burnt jungle where the trees were gone and the land razed. Here, the wind lifted grey and black ash and swirled it in eddies. It felt soft and still warm under her feet; she fancied she could still see the ground smoking. She swallowed hard. There, in the corner under a fallen bough, was what looked like the skull of a poor victim, all blackened with soot. Now she'd seen one, she saw others under fallen trees. She dared not look harder and turned away, thankful that the fire had removed all evidence of who had been slain.

They paused beside a river to eat fruit and nuts and a small portion of her rations, then turned north trying to find a place to ford it. When the sky began to turn pink above the thick canopy, she welcomed the oncoming night and the coolness it would bring.

It was the stillness of the forest that eventually drew her attention and made her pause. Fenn looked at her.

'We're close,' she said.

Within the hour the jungle became less dense and more spread out and she saw what she had been searching for. Ahead of them was a place she had rarely been to: the Centre. The great stone ball stood proudly between the trees, as smooth and perfect as if it had just been made. Jarlain sheathed her spear on her back and took hold of her staff. The Hidden Ones murmured in her mind and she closed her eyes. They gave her a vision.

'What is it?' asked Fenn.

'I see Hai, our leader. He is making this staff, and all the peoples of this land—all who remain—are present. There are so few.'

Tears fell down her cheeks as she watched Hai who was sitting with the staves of all the tribes moulding them into one. Then he was walking to the light. She gasped when she saw great antlers rise, casting long shadows over everything. *Doon, guardian of the forest.* Then Hai and the light were gone.

'He gave his life to tell me,' Jarlain whispered, unable to hold back the tears. She wiped them away and looked at the enormous round stone.

'But where are your people?' asked Fenn.

Jarlain shrugged. Where were they now? She walked towards the stone, aware of its immense height as it towered above her. Holding Hai's staff in one hand, she gently laid a hand on it. The jungle faded into a thick mist that glowed white. The circular stone glowed white too and all around stood the tall, impossibly slender, light beings she called the Hidden Ones. They were guarding this place. As one they nodded at her and then turned to leave, their long legs carrying them gracefully away.

She didn't understand. 'Wait, don't go. Where are my people?'

But the Hidden Ones faded away, the mist dissipated and the glowing stone dimmed as the jungle reformed itself around her. Then people appeared, hundreds of them. Her people and the lighter-skinned tribes of the north. They stood or sat in groups and then all turned to look in her direction. She gasped, seeing Tarn amongst them and then he was running towards her, pushing between the people, and engulfing her in his arms.

'Great Goddess I never thought I'd see you again!' he cried.

Jarlain hugged him back, unable to speak from the emotion that welled within her—that and the fact that her face was pressed into his shoulder. They withdrew. He looked well, if thin and drawn.

'You're dressed like him,' he said, tapping her armour.

'He is well and waiting for us to go to him, as warriors,' Jarlain said.

Tarn's face brightened.

Sharnu hobbled over using a stick to steady herself, a smile spreading over her exhausted features. She had been old before but now she seemed ancient. Without speaking, she embraced Jarlain and both found themselves crying hot tears. Silently, Shufen came to stand beside them, his arm in a sling. One by one, all the people gathered close around her.

'The Hidden Ones, they were protecting you in this place,' Jarlain explained.

'Hai is gone. He made the ultimate sacrifice to save us,' Tarn said, his voice low and filled with emotion. 'We are all that remain. Five thousand, and no more.'

Jarlain didn't know what to say. The numbers were beyond her. 'Hai came to me. If he had not, I would have died. I have so much to tell you.' She shook her head for all she wanted to say.

'My goodness, you have the staff he made?' Tarn's eyes were wide with wonder. 'He drew those symbols, the history of all our peoples in the Elder's sacred tongue.'

She looked at the staff which was now covered in glowing symbols,

symbols that had been invisible before. In wonder, she held it up and stepped back so all the people could see.

'This is the staff of our peoples,' she said loudly. 'Through the grace of Doon, guardian of the forests, Hai found me and saved my life. I return to you now to lead you away from here. Alone, you cannot survive against the might of the Immortal Lord. But together, united with the free peoples across the Great Sea, we have a chance to save our people and our beloved Maioria from being destroyed utterly.'

As she spoke she realised Fenn was not by her side. She turned and saw that he'd slunk into a dark patch between two bushes. She almost laughed knowing he was afraid to frighten the people. She motioned for him to come out. Reluctantly, he crept forwards, paw over paw, his head low and eyes glued to the ground. The people gasped and fell back. They had never seen a bear before but they would recognise the animal's form in their art and ancient carvings.

'Do not be afraid,' Jarlain said and winked at Tarn, who'd turned white. 'Deep within, you remember these magnificent beasts, the bears. Hai showed me our ancestors before he passed. Our ancestors from long, long before now. They were advanced and powerful with their minds, and they were called the Navadin.' Murmurs and frowns of recognition passed across peoples' faces.

'Yes,' Jarlain nodded, smiling. 'You do remember.' Fenn sat on his haunches next to her and she laid a hand upon him. He lifted his head and sniffed the air, pretending to ignore all the people who were looking at him and trembling with fear.

'I call upon all of you gathered here now to return with me to what remains of the Free World where the people are fighting to end this darkness. This land is lost, as well you know. Up and down the coast, the enemy spreads. Were it not for the Hidden Ones protecting you, you would be dead already. That protection is ended and now you are in grave danger. So I ask you to come with me to a land where we can become what we once were; the Navadin of old.

'Through me, mighty Doon has rekindled the gift of bear-speak and I will give this gift to you, should you wish it. The choice is yours but should you want to join me and secure a future for yourselves, then we must leave immediately before the black dragons come.'

Just the thought sent the crowd running to gather their meagre belongings; not one stood idly by. Jarlain laughed, despite the gravity of their situation, and let herself sink down to the ground next to Fenn with a sigh.

'I did it, Hai. I found our people. We are safe and we are saved. The Navadin shall live again.'

CHAPTER 33

Dragon Vengeance

THE lights of Avernayis flickered in the darkness ahead and far below him.

Hidden by magic and flying this high in the sky, Asaph was confident no one would spot him. The birthplace of his father seemed a fitting place to attack.

Coronos Avernayis Dragon Rider, you probably won't approve of what I'm about to do, but I need to do it. Foolish, you'll say, but I know you would have done it yourself once. The time of our greatest trial is before us; either we will fall or we will soar to the skies. I wish you could be here to witness our emancipation and live in a world that is free. I guess you are free now, anyway.

For a moment Asaph closed his eyes, letting the strange human emotions move through him, feeling the wind rush over his enormous body. He allowed his emotions to turn to anger and let it stoke the fire in his belly. He swooped low to get a better look at his enemies.

There were no Dromoorai that he could see but there were many heavily armed Maphraxies patrolling the harbour walls and streets between the ugly grey square buildings. Dark dwarves mingled amongst them and at the end of the pier at the entrance to the port were a gaggle of four or five necromancers. He couldn't see what they were doing but, being magic wielders, they would have to be removed first.

He wheeled upwards in an arc, took a deep breath, and dropped towards them. Their ugly, pasty faces loomed before him fast. Two looked straight at him, their eyes widening a fraction before they were all engulfed in fire and screaming. Three fell into the water, dousing the flames, one started incanting a spell whilst on fire and the other was incinerated on the spot.

His magic cloak gone, Asaph angled his wings and shot into the sky again, drawing the Flow to him. The Maphraxies were roaring and scrambling to defence. He dropped back down fast for another attack before more necromancers could form a magical assault. Two were climbing out of the water using the metal ladders attached to the harbour wall. He doused them in flames again, boiling the one still in the water.

Black fire sizzled harmlessly against his magic shield but blurred his vision, forcing him to dart away. Quickly he returned and grabbed the remaining necromancers in his claws. Their screams were cut short as he crushed them and dropped their bloodied, broken bodies into the sea.

The necromancers now neutralised, Asaph turned to the new threat.

Maphraxies lined the wall and were hastily notching their huge bows. Quickly, he swooped past them spraying fire. He laughed aloud as their bowstrings sizzled to nothing. Some of the Maphraxies ignited in flames and fell into the water in a panic, their heavy army making them sink fast, but most were resistant to his flames, only smouldering at most. He would need blue or even white fire to turn their armour to molten metal—if it was even possible to melt given that it had been forged in the fires of the bowels of Maphrax. Such fire was costly. He'd have to make sure he had enough energy left to escape when the Dread Dragons came.

More bows were gathered and these were swiftly notched with arrows. He came close to give them a target. When they fired he put up his shield and watched the arrows bounce harmlessly off it. With a roar, he descended upon them before they could reload. In each of his four talons, he filled his claws with the enemy and snapped those not fleeing fast enough into his mouth. He came so low his wings glanced off the roofs of buildings, then he was in the sky and heading out to sea. He dropped his load and watched the enemy howl and writhe as they fell hundreds of feet into the ocean to sink to their deaths.

The Under Flow surged, alerting him to necromancers. Magic smacked into him and the wind keeping him airborne simply disappeared. Like a stone, he dropped towards the ocean as if he had just entered a void of nothing. However, his dragon magic was strong and he pulled wind to him, filling his wings and blasting himself upwards towards the clouds. He pinpointed where the offensive magic was coming from and plummeted towards it.

In one of the towers, a pale face appeared, hands moving as it incanted its spell. Asaph didn't pause as he smashed into the tower. Bricks and mortar exploded on impact, crushing anything inside. He circled and hit the tower again, causing it to topple onto fleeing Maphraxies. Again and again he swooped upon the town of Avernayis, breathing blue and white fire on anything and everything, picking up the enemy in his claws and dumping them in the ocean to drown. He let his fury consume him as he rampaged, destroying the port towers, stamping on and crushing entire buildings. Avernayis and his father had been avenged.

The whole place smouldered and not a single building was left whole when he heard the first screech of a Dread Dragon. Panting with exhausted satisfaction, Asaph roared his might, letting them know what he was and who had done this. He could fight a Dromoorai. He turned and scanned the skies. There, just emerging from the thick clouds, was a black speck. It was followed by four more.

Asaph growled—he could fight one Dromoorai, but not five—he'd have to flee. Taking one more satisfied look at the smoking ruin of Avernayis, he bunched his muscles and spread his wings. He tried to leap and nearly wrenched his legs from his feet. His claws were glued to the ground. Looking down he could see nothing wrong. Glimpsing into the Flow he saw thick black chains writhing around his ankles.

A sniggering laugh caught his attention. There, in the rubble, out of reach of his flames, stood the tall thin figure of a necromancer. Gashes of dark red blood smeared its face and it held bloodied hands up commanding the Under Flow.

'All we do is wait for them to take you,' it said in a nasally, snivelling voice. Asaph reached for the Flow but it scattered. He wrenched at his feet and beat his wings furiously, sending debris into a maelstrom around him but nothing released his feet.

Dread Dragons screamed, louder and closer. He looked up at the five fast approaching beasts, not quite able to panic in dragon form, but able to rage at his predicament. He roared and flamed the air uselessly then panted smoke. He would tear the necromancer apart.

The closest Dromoorai came low; he could see the blazing red amulet swinging on its chest. Good, let Baelthrom know he was here. It would complete his mission and divert the Immortal Lord's attention away from Issa and her armies.

The Dromoorai pulled its sword free and whooshed past, striking Asaph on the neck as he, in turn, covered it in flames. Asaph flicked out his tail, smashing into the Dromoorai rider and nearly unseating it. Asaph shook his head, feeling blood trickle just under his ear. It wasn't trying to kill him, just taunting him for fun.

Well, he'd got this far and he didn't intend to be captured by them. Fear of death didn't cross his dragon mind, but he was aware that to the death he would fight. Then again, hadn't all Dragon Lords fought to the death thinking they wouldn't be taken? Asaph snorted black soot in defiance.

The Dromoorai landed behind him some yards away. The rest of them picked their positions around him in the rubble. Asaph racked his brains for a plan, a way out, but nothing came to mind. Slowly the Dread Dragons ambled towards him, their heads lowered and necks snaking, nostrils scenting, eyes alight with the smell of blood and thoughts of food. He snapped at the nearest, reaching further than it expected and catching its muzzle in his jaws. He didn't have a firm grasp and the Dread Dragon wrenched free with a snarl.

The one behind him clamped its jaws on his tail. Pain snaked up his spine and he howled and thrashed. His tail was released by a command from its rider.

'You will be one of us,' rasped the Dromoorai to his right, the sound raking his ears. All their eyes flared red, glowing from the slits of their helmets as they watched him.

Asaph forced his eyes to the ground. He wouldn't look at them; he wouldn't look at Baelthrom. The Under Flow seeped black beneath him, pooling beneath his feet. He tried to lift away from it but his feet remained anchored to the ground. Black smoke billowed around him, thicker and darker. He choked and spat as it filled his lungs and his eyes watered as it rose higher, a slow spinning tornado of black engulfing him.

Things began to dim in his mind; he couldn't see clearly and his senses became confused. He thrashed violently, lifting his head above the blackness as much as he could, seeking breathable air. Was this how he was going to end? He roared and thrashed some more, hunting for the Flow which just wasn't there. He lashed his tail, hoping to catch one unawares, but they were out of reach. He roared again and again, become more rage-filled at his hopeless situation.

A roar answered from far away. It could be another Dromoorai, but his ears were too muffled to determine. Beyond the billowing smoke, all he could see were glowing red eyes and amulets. He gnashed his teeth, only to choke as smoke furled insidiously around his fangs. In a flash of gleaming red, he saw long slender jaws close on a Dread Dragon's throat. An entire sleek body flashed past Asaph's stinging eyes, still anchored to the other dragon's neck, and then a flurry of red wings. Asaph blinked and saw the horrific sight of the Dread Dragon's half exposed throat spraying watery grey blood and gore as it thrashed and threw its rider from its back.

Roaring filled the air and real dragon minds touched his own. Their rage mirrored his. He roared, a pathetic smoke filled rasp. He shuffled helplessly and, amazingly, found his feet to be free. He leapt unsteadily into the air, shaking the Under Flow from his mind, his great wings trembling with the strain. He stared at the long, sleek shape of Garna as she darted past in a blur and attacked the fallen Dromoorai. She lifted it up in her talons and hurled it into the ocean, black claymore striking at air as it tumbled and disappeared with a great splash.

The green dragon with the black horns rolled on top of another Dread Dragon. Rust, the large red male, was locked between two. Asaph went to help him as Garna wheeled around to attack the fifth.

Asaph's teeth clamped onto the Dromoorai rider which had its sword plunged into the green's side, and wrenched it off the Dread Dragon's back whilst remaining airborne. He breathed white fire through his teeth and felt the Dromoorai's armour soften. He crunched and let the crumpled shape fall to the ground.

He wheeled up and then dropped out of the sky, landing all of his weight upon the riderless dragon. It collapsed under him and he clamped his jaws onto the back of its neck. He wrenched and bit madly, letting all his rage consume him until the neck gave a satisfying *snap*. The green finished the other and together they leapt upon Garna's opponent, locking onto the Dread Dragon as she destroyed its rider.

'It's getting away!' roared Rust, leaping into the air as one tried to escape.

The Dromoorai was already a hundred yards high in the sky and heading west.

'Leave it!' said Asaph as the others launched into the air. They paused but were itching to go. 'Let it tell its master what has happened here. It will help deflect attention away from our imminent attack in the south. There is much happening you do not know about, but trust me on this.'

The dragons considered this reluctantly, then one by one settled back down upon the ground and laid their wings neatly against their backs. The green dragon set about licking his deep wound and tending it with magic.

'You left,' said Garna.

'You didn't return,' said Asaph.

'We are late,' nodded Rust. 'It took longer than we thought and we had to eat. We are still weak. We would have been longer but Garna sensed trouble.'

'Where are the others?' asked Asaph.

'Gathering other dragons. There are still many we can't reach,' said Garna, sadness in her voice.

'We cannot stay here. They will return with more,' said Rust.

Rust was right, but Asaph couldn't leave Avernayis in this state. 'Help me cleanse this place. It is…important to me. It was the birthplace of the one who raised me before they murdered him. Destroy everything that is tainted with the black magic,' said Asaph.

The dragons agreed. All dragons were deeply loyal to those who had raised them. Revenge for wrongdoing came as instinct.

Garna breathed fire upon a mostly collapsed tower and the necromancer who had chained Asaph ran out. Asaph leapt and stomped on it, feeling hot mess spurt between his claws. He flicked it off his talons in disgust.

Swiftly, they carried the bodies of the Dread Dragons between them and dumped them into the sea. Tails smashed any standing structure and claws raked blocks of stone into rubble until the whole place was levelled, they even crumbled the new harbour walls into the sea. White fire melted metal and cleansed the ground. Finally, dragon magic dissolved everything to dust and soot. They were done within the hour.

Asaph looked around at the great patch of black ground that had once been Avernayis. Only the remains of the original human houses on edge of the village and the crumbling old pier remained. 'Our fire has cleansed the land so new things can grow. Humans will return and rebuild this place greater than it was before. Thank you, my brethren and sistren, for coming to me. This is our first battle, our first victory. We will not stop until all the world is free of this scourge. Let us rest in the north for a short time and gather the others. Soon a greater battle calls us.'

Asaph leapt into the air with a roar. The other dragons echoed it. Again they roared until the whole coast trembled with their noise.

Issa clenched the rails at the prow of the Atalanph ship she was aboard. She squinted into the morning light, the rushing wind and cold air making her eyes smart. Ehka perched between her hands, balancing himself as the ship swayed in the waves. Velonorian chatted to two other elves in Elvish a few feet away.

Nothing was going to plan and her stomach was in knots. Marakon hadn't arrived and neither had Asaph. Freydel had not been seen for days and neither had Domenon. She felt deserted and alone. Knowing they couldn't wait any longer, she'd boarded a ship and now stood at the front of a long line of vessels. She wanted to feel the glory of it, being on the ocean with an entire fleet around her, but she was fraught with worry.

'They will arrive, they have not deserted you,' said Naksu, laying a pale hand on her arm.

Issa forced a smile at the seer who had silently come to stand beside her. The one good thing that had happened was that the seer along with Orphinius and his new army of elves had arrived by boat yesterday. Issa was very thankful that another Orb Keeper was with her. In a short time, the new elf leader had organised an army of over one thousand elves, and several of them were aboard this ship, along with many Karalanths.

Karalanths and elves respected each other deeply, but the deer-folk had refused to board alongside dwarves. One almost fatal casualty involving a dwarf with a Karalanth knife stuck in him pushed the point home. They were kept far apart after that. It saddened Issa to see their hatred towards the dwarves, but she understood why.

'The Captain says Drumblodd's army is bringing up the rear and King Navarr's soldiers have rendezvoused with the Lans Himay mercenaries. They have just set sail. So you see, there is nothing to worry about.' Naksu smiled.

'Nothing about going to war can make me feel good,' said Issa.

'No true human should ever feel good about war,' said Naksu. 'It is simply what must be done when the balance has swung so far in the enemies' favour.'

'I wish none of this had ever happened. I wish, sometimes, that I had died a long time ago, or had never been born, rather than go through this…pain,' said Issa.

'We are all very glad that you were born and are with us now,' said Naksu, her face serious. 'People might know what it is they have to do but they need a leader to take charge. You are that, whether you like it or not. You know we have no other choice as that black scar in the sky opens up to swallow us. Zanufey is with you and you are with us.'

They didn't say anything for a long time and just stood watching the white horses rise above the deep blue waves. When Naksu turned to go, Issa said, 'Thank you.' Naksu paused and she continued. 'I'm so glad you made it here in time. I need as many friends as I can get. I just wish I had Asaph, Marakon and Freydel with me.'

'I know. They will come.'

The sea was calmer further out into the ocean. A glance behind showed that Davono was a mere sliver of green on the horizon. Soon it would be lost from view. The wind dropped a little and the sea calmed. As the ship swayed less, Issa seated herself cross-legged at the prow and took out her talisman. Ehka hopped down beside her.

'Shall we see where the others are?'

Ehka understood and with a caw launched into the air. She watched him circle above the ship's swaying mast, then closed her eyes and stilled her mind. Entering the Flow, she found Ehka's familiar blue aura and connected with him. Through his eyes, she saw hundreds of ships spreading out behind them on the ocean. Their sails were brilliant white in the sunshine and colourful pennants decorated each of them, flapping taut in the wind. It was a breath-taking sight and one she never thought she would see.

Ehka flew above them all; Davono ships, Atalanph ships, dwarven ships, and now a smattering of elven ships made of beautiful blue oak with spiralling carved designs, unrivalled by the others. Aboard them worked the crews of all those races and nations, including the Karalanths.

Ehka flew further, losing the ships from view and Davono appeared again. He angled to the right to the large port of Teramides. There, streaming out of the harbour were more Davonian ships and aboard each were hundreds more soldiers. *No, not soldiers as such, but mercenaries from Lans Himay,* she thought. They were dressed in greys, browns and animal skins. Most were pale skinned and had brown hair. Men were bearded, and both they and the women were tattooed in blue ink. They looked particularly fearsome with their short swords and their axes. Amongst them were reddish-blond Draxian exiles, similarly dressed and armed.

Issa sighed, thinking of Asaph. She believed Naksu was right. Asaph still had time to reach them. Besides, seeing all these ships and all these soldiers filled her with confidence. Before, she had only imagined how to attack, now she saw them in all their glory, how could they possibly fail?

'Miss! Miss!' a panicked voice hollered, breaking her connection to Ehka.

She blinked and looked behind. Cantering up the deck was Duskar, his black mane streaming out behind him and his coat gleaming magnificently in the sunlight. A stable boy was desperately running after him trying to catch the trailing rope attached to the horse's neck.

Issa stood and laughed as Duskar skidded to a stop and nuzzled her roughly. The stable boy caught up, red faced and panting, and doubled over trying to catch his breath.

'I was moving him to another part of the stable and he leapt the barrier,' he gasped.

Issa grinned. 'I'm sorry, he hates ships. He'll be all right if he sees daylight once a day.' She stroked Duskar's nose and hugged his neck. 'With you by my side, how could I ever doubt?'

With a hand on his back, she stared back out to sea. Far ahead lay Venosia. If she wasn't ready to face the enemy now, she never would be.

Deep within me lies the strength to do the impossible, or at least try. Together, we must all face that which we fear and overcome it. I must, for I am the Raven Queen.

Continued in *War of the Raven*

WAR OF THE RAVEN QUEEN

The Goddess Prophecies

Book 6

Araya Evermore

They had both been chosen: he to save another race; she to save her own from what he had become. Now, both must enter Oblivion and therein decide the fate of all.

The dreaded war has begun and is sweeping across Maioria. Despite gaining victories, Issa is forced to endure terrible loss and face defeat as the Dark Rift descends. For all her powers, she reluctantly realises that nothing can halt the fall into darkness of her world, and that a greater threat is closer than she thinks. A third Raven Queen is rising, and that which she holds most dear will seek to destroy her.

The King has returned, and the sacred pact between man and dragon ignited. As both rally to his side, Asaph, the Dawn Bringer returns to Drax one last time to give his life taking back the land and the throne stolen from him, but the Immortal Lord awaits— and the destruction of the Draxian uprising is already in his grasp.

The dark moon is rising one final time, but when the unthinkable happens and Zanufey falls silent, Issa is forced to look within to find the power and the faith to carry on. Before the darkness consumes her utterly, Issa must give herself fully to the Dark Rift so that all others might live.

In this final book in The Goddess Prophecies Fantasy Epic, Issa must face Zanufey's Fallen and embrace the darkness to save her world and all within it.

"On the edge of Oblivion I stand. I see the light disappearing far above me…the end of all lights.' – Issa

ALSO BY ARAYA EVERMORE

The Goddess Prophecies series:

Goddess Awakening ~ A Prequel

When darkness falls, a heroine will rise.

The Dread Dragons came with the dawn. On dark wings of death they slaughtered every seer and turned their sacred lands to ruin…

Night Goddess ~ Book 1

A world plunging into darkness. An exiled Dragon Lord struggling with his destiny. A young woman terrified of an ancient prophecy she has set in motion.

He came through the Dark Rift hunting for those who had escaped his wrath. Unchecked, his evil spread. Now, the world hangs on a knife-edge and all seems destined to fall. But when the dark moon rises, a goddess awakens, and nothing can stop the prophecy unfolding…

The Fall of Celene ~ Book 2

Impossible Odds, Terrifying Powers

"My name is Issa and I am hunted. I hold a power that I neither understand nor can barely control…"

The battle for Maioria has begun. Issa faces a deadly enemy as the Immortal Lord's attention turns fully in her direction. Nothing will stand in Baelthrom's way—he must destroy this new power that grows with the rising dark moon…

Storm Holt ~ Book 3

Would you sell your soul to save the world?

The Storm Holt... The ultimate Wizard's Reckoning, where all who enter must face their greatest demons. No woman has entered and survived since the Ancients split the magic apart eons ago. Plagued by demons and visions of a strange white spear, Issa must take the Reckoning to find her answers and fight for her soul to prove her worth to the most powerful magic wielders upon Maioria...

Demon Spear ~ Book 4

Demons. Death. Deliverance.

All these Issa must face as darkness strikes into the heart of their last stronghold. Greater demons are rising from the Pit, Carvon is brutally attacked, and a horrifying murder forces Issa and her companions to flee. But despite the devastating loss, she must keep her oath to the Shadow Demons and alone reclaim the spear that can save them all...

Dragons of the Dawn Bringer ~ Book 5

An Exiled King. A Broken Dream. A Sword Forged for Forever.

Issa can trust no one. Her closest allies betray her and nobody is as they seem. When a Dromoorai captures her and a black vortex to another dimension rips into her room, she realises the attacks will never stop and there is far worse than Baelthrom reaching for her out of the Dark Rift...

War of the Raven Queen ~ Book 6

"Be the light unto the darkness...Be the last light in a falling world."

They had both been chosen: he to save another race; she to save her own from what he had become. Now, both must enter Oblivion and therein decide the fate of all...

BOOKS BY JOANNA STARR

Farseeker

Enlightened. Enslaved. Erased.

Earth, 50,000 years ago before the magic vanished. Invaded by aliens posing as gods, advanced civilisations crumbled. Now, these powerful off-worlders war for control of the planet, and the people who remain no longer remember what they once were. Seduced then enslaved, humanity has fallen...

Free Starter Library

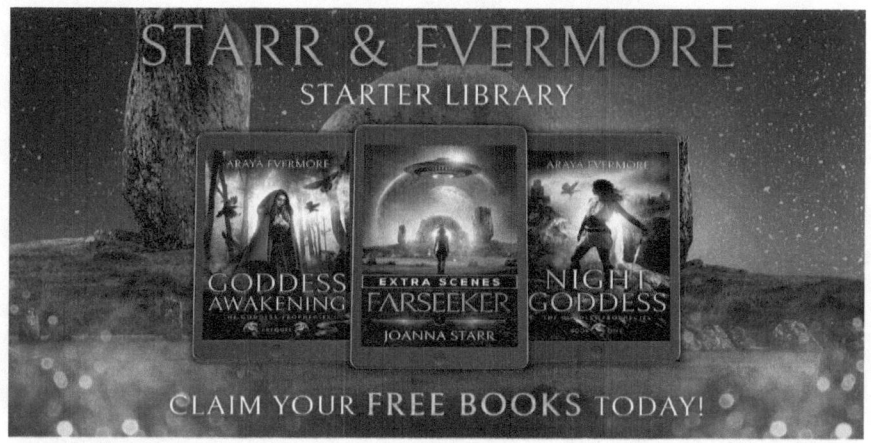

Join the mailing list and get your FREE Starr & Evermore Starter Library available only to subscribers. You'll discover Issa's origin story in my prequel, *Goddess Awakening*, which is not available anywhere else. You'll also get a taster of my latest *Farseeker* series with extra scenes not included in the main story.

To receive this epic free gift, please go to my website below. As a subscriber, you'll also be the first to hear about my latest novels, and lots more exclusive content.

www.joannastarr.com

About the Author

Araya Evermore is the pen name of Joanna Starr - a half-elf and author of the best-selling epic fantasy series, *The Goddess Prophecies*.

Joanna has been exploring other worlds and writing fantasy stories ever since she came to Planet Earth. Finding herself struggling in a world in which she didn't quite fit, escaping into fantasy novels gave her the magic and wonder she craved. Despite majoring in Philosophy & Religion, then Computer Science, she left her career in The City to return to her first love; writing Epic Fantasy.

Originally from the West Country, she's been travelling the world since 2011, and has been on the road so long she no longer comes from any place in particular. So far, she's resided in the Caribbean, United States, Canada, Australia, New Zealand, Spain, Andorra and Malta. Despite loving the mountains, she's actually a sea-based creature and currently resides by the ocean in Ireland.

Aside from writing and working, she spends time talking to trees, swimming with fish, gaming, and playing with swords.

Connect with Joanna online:
www.joannastarr.com
author@joannastarr.com

Enjoyed this book? You can make a big difference...

If you love fantasy books and would like to bring this series to the attention of other fantasy readers, the best thing you can do to reach them is to leave a review.

If you've enjoyed this book I would be very grateful if you could spend just a minute leaving a review, (it can be as long or as short as you like) on the book's Amazon page.

A heartfelt Thank You in advance.